A DEADLY SHADOW

The dark form of the rustler slipped out of sight over the embankment.

"Better go slow an' careful," warned Greaves. "An' only go close enough to call Somers. Mebbe that damn' half-breed Isbel is comin' like some Injun on us."

Jean heard the soft swish of footsteps through wet grass. Then all was still. He lay flat, with his cheek on the sand, and he had to look ahead and upwards to make out the dark figure of Greaves on the bank. One way or another he meant to kill Greaves. If he arose and shot the rustler, that would defeat his plan. Jean wanted to call softly to Greaves—*You're right about the half-breed!*—and then, as he wheeled aghast, to kill him as he moved. But it suited Jean to risk leaping up on the man. Jean did not waste time in trying to understand the strange, deadly instinct that gripped him at the moment, but he realized he had chosen the most perilous plan to get rid of Greaves.

Jean drew a long, deep breath and held it. He let go of his rifle. He rose silently, as a lifting shadow. He drew the Bowie knife....

ZANE GREY™

TONTO BASIN

LEISURE BOOKS NEW YORK CITY

A LEISURE BOOK®

February 2006

Published by special arrangement with Golden West Literary Agency.

Dorchester Publishing Co., Inc.
200 Madison Avenue
New York, NY 10016

ISBN 0-8439-5602-X

Visit us on the web at www.dorchesterpub.com.

FOREWORD
by
Jon Tuska

I grew up in a small town in Wisconsin and for the first ten years of my life lived in a back apartment half a block from the local public library. You had to be ten years of age before you could borrow books from the adult section of the library. When I turned ten and was able to enter the adult stacks, I chose to withdraw two books: *The Bishop Murder Case* (Scribner, 1929) by S. S. Van Dine and *The Lone Star Ranger* (Harper, 1915) by Zane Grey. I recall that I wondered if the story in *The Lone Star Ranger* was anything like *The Lone Ranger* to which I listened on the radio. It wasn't. In fact, it was something of a disappointment because Jennie Lee, the heroine, was of particular interest to me and halfway through the story she vanished, never to return. Decades passed before I found her again.

It was while trying to put together an accurate filmography for Zane Grey, providing the correct literary source for each of the 109 films based on his work, that I was confronted by the problem of *Last of the Duanes*. It had been filmed four times, but there was no such novel. I pursued the matter with Loren Grey, the younger son of Zane Grey and president of Zane Grey, Inc. As far as he knew, there had been such a novel, but it had never been published, somehow having been transformed into *The Lone Star Ranger* upon publication. "Is there a manuscript?" I asked. Loren wasn't certain, but he promised that he would search. Eventually, he did locate his father's handwritten manuscript in the bottom drawer of a file cabinet in the Zane Grey, Inc. room where it had survived for eighty years.

The task, then, was to reconstruct what had happened. In the early years Zane Grey's novels were serialized in pulp magazines, prior to publication by Harper & Bros. Grey had written a long serial titled "The Last of the Duanes" and sent it to editor Bob Davis at *The Argosy*, one of the pulp magazines published by The Frank A. Munsey Company. Davis had previously bought serial rights to a number of Grey's early novels. This time Davis was shocked to find, upon reading this story, that eighteen persons were killed in the course of it. He considered this much too violent to publish. What he agreed to do was to run a drastically abbreviated version that appeared as "The Last of the Duanes" in a single installment in *The Argosy* (9/14).

When it came time to offer the book to Harper & Bros., Grey had lost faith in the original story as he had written it. The book that emerged as *The Lone Star Ranger*, therefore, is for about the first 200 pages the manuscript of "The Last of the Duanes" and is called "Book I: The Outlaw." The remainder of the novel, called "Book II: The Ranger," is actually the second half of the serial "The Lone Star Rangers" from *All-Story Cavalier Weekly* (5/9/14–5/23/14). Apparently Ripley Hitchcock, Grey's editor at Harper & Bros., rewrote the second half of "The Lone Star Rangers," changing it from a first-person narrative into a continuation and conclusion of the hybrid novels titled by him *The Lone Star Ranger*. Since neither story had appeared in anything resembling what Zane Grey had written, it was finally possible to publish each for the first time in book form as the author had intended: *Last of the Duanes* (Leisure Books, 1998) and *Rangers of the Lone Star* (Leisure Books, 1999).

I urged Loren Grey to tell me of any other manuscripts by his father that had met a similar fate. There were, he said, the sections in what became *30,000 on the Hoof* (Harper, 1940) that dealt with Lucinda Huett's rape by a renegade Apache and the decision made by Logan and Lucinda Huett to keep the child and raise him as if he were their own. It is this half-Apache son who alone of the Huetts' sons survives the Great War, returns to the ranch, and proves able to save it. The story was finally published in its entirety as *Woman of the Frontier* (Leisure Books, 2000). Finally, Loren said, he had the complete typescript of his father's major novel set in the back country of Australia that had been cut to a third of its length, ostensibly because of the paper shortage, when it was published as *Wilderness Trek* (Harper, 1944). It was restored to its full length as *The Great Trek* (Five Star Westerns, 1999).

If this sort of thing had happened so often, what, then, of those novels rightly regarded as classics:

Riders of the Purple Sage (Harper, 1912) and its sequel, *The Rainbow Trail* (Harper, 1915)? Zane Grey, Inc. did not have the original holographic manuscripts of these. They had been variously donated by Lina Elise Grey, Zane Grey's widow, to various archives. The holographic manuscript for *The Rainbow Trail* was located in the Special Collections of the Brigham Young University Library. Upon examination, it was found to be significantly different from the published book, especially with regard to the fate of young Fay Larkin, who was forced into a marriage with a Mormon who already had five wives and fifty-five children, and who in time gives birth to a son. The Harper & Bros. edition would have the reader believe Fay Larkin remained a virgin while being held captive in a Mormon town for sealed wives! Critics of Zane Grey, in fact, have singled out this incident as a primary indication that Grey was a hopelessly romantic writer incapable of historical realism. Now to refute them, *The Desert Crucible* (Leisure Books, 2004) has finally been published as the author wrote it. The changes and alterations in *Riders of the Purple Sage* are even more drastic and alter the entire perspective of the story. Retaining its original title, the restored version of this novel will appear as a Leisure Western in 2006.

Zane Grey is not the only American novelist who has had to stand by and watch his work altered, rewritten, changed by the hands of others. William Faulkner's third novel, and the first in his series of novels about the characters and milieu of Yoknapatawpha County, *Sartoris* (Harcourt, Brace, 1929), was rejected by Faulkner's original publisher, Horace Liveright, and after numerous other rejections was only accepted provisionally by Alfred Harcourt if it was mercilessly cut. Irving Howe and other Faulkner critics have always dismissed *Sartoris* as inferior work, but this was singularly due to the fact that the book Faulkner wrote and loved and felt to be his finest to that date was never published in anything like the form he had intended. This had to wait until the appearance of *Flags in the Dust* (Random House, 1973), the restored *Sartoris*, and now a key book for understanding the lives and times of not only the Sartoris family, including Aunt Jenny, but Horace and Narcissa Benbow and local members of the Snopes clan.

The cuts demanded by Alfred Harcourt to *Sartoris* were dictated, according to the underlying correspondence, by a desire to focus the story exclusively on the Sartoris family. The changes made to the novel titled *Tonto Basin* were of a different kind. At the root of the longstanding feud between the Jorths and the Isbels is a woman we never meet, a character dead before the story opens, Ellen Sutton. She was engaged to Gaston Isbel at the time of the outbreak of the War Between the States. While Isbel was away on active duty, Ellen Sutton took up with the disreputable Lee Jorth and they have a child out of wedlock. They never marry; only live together. The child is Ellen Jorth. It is Lee Jorth who tells his daughter how her mother taunted Gaston Isbel when he came back from the war with the sexual relationship she had with Jorth, and how it was this that enraged Isbel and began the feud between the two of them. The burden of having been born of infidelity is one that oppresses Ellen Jorth for most of the novel. The story was serialized as "To the Last Man" in *The Country Gentleman* (5/28/21–7/30/21) and much of this background was excised from the story, leaving a reader baffled as to the source of the passion and hatred in a feud that eventually claims every family member on both sides except for Ellen Jorth and Jean Isbel, the mixed-blood Nez Percé.

Yet, were a reader to believe that censorship in American letters is now something in the distant past, I would disagree. This kind of editorial intervention has only changed its political and moral guise over time; otherwise, it is as powerful and pervasive as ever. When Jane Candia Coleman submitted *I, Pearl Hart* to a major New York publisher in 1997, she was told the novel could not be published as she had written it. Although her story was based on the real Pearl Hart, a woman who committed a daring stage-coach robbery and was sent to Yuma Territorial Prison as a result, the editor wanted several prison scenes added, graphically detailing Pearl's sexual activities with various female inmates. Since nothing of the kind happened to Pearl Hart, the author refused to change history to satisfy any editor. *I, Pearl Hart* (Leisure Books, 2000) was eventually published exactly the way the author intended, true to the character, to her time, and to the land. I believe authors of literary fiction deserve the freedom to tell a story according to their own standard of artistic truth, to listen unhindered to their muse, and to share with us what they have learned. *Tonto Basin* now at last is published as Zane Grey wanted his story to appear.

Chapter One

At the end of a dry, uphill ride over barren country, Jean Isbel unpacked to camp at the edge of the cedars where a little rocky cañon, green with willow and cottonwood, promised water and grass. His animals were tired, especially the pack mules that had carried a heavy load, and with slow heaves of relief they knelt and rolled in the dust. Jean experienced something of relief himself as he threw off his chaps. He had not been used to hot, dusty, glaring days on the barren lands. Stretching his long length beside a tiny rill of clear water that tinkled over the red stones, he drank thirstily. The water was cool, but it had an acrid taste—an alkali bite that he did not like. Not since he had left Oregon had he tasted clear, sweet, cold water, and he missed it just as he longed for the stately shady forests he had loved. This wild endless Arizona land bade fair to earn his hatred.

By the time he had leisurely completed his tasks, twilight had fallen and coyotes had begun their barking. Jean listened to the yelps and to the moan of the cool wind in the cedars with a sense of satisfaction that these lonely sounds were familiar. This cedar wood burned into a pretty fire and the smell of its smoke was newly pleasant.

"Reckon maybe I'll learn to like Arizona," he mused, half aloud. "But I've a hankerin' for waterfalls an' dark green forests. Must be the Indian in me. . . . Anyway, Dad needs me bad, an' I reckon I'm here for keeps."

Jean threw some cedar branches on the fire, in the light of which he opened his father's letter, hoping by repeated

13

reading to grasp more of its strange portent. It had been two months in reaching him, coming by traveler, by stage and train, and then by boat, and finally by stage again. Written in lead pencil on a leaf torn from an old ledger, it would have been hard to read even if the writing had been more legible.

"Dad's writin' was always bad, but I never saw it so shaky," said Jean, thinking aloud.

Grass Valley, Arizona
Son Jean:

Come home. Here's your home and here you're needed. When we left Oregon, we all reckoned you'd not be long behind. But it's four years now. I'm growing old, Son, and you was always my steadiest boy. Not that you ever was so darn steady. Only your wildness seemed more for the woods. You take after Mother, and your brothers Bill and Guy take after me. That's the red and white of it. You're part Indian, Jean, and that Indian I reckon I'm going to need bad.

I'm rich in cattle and horses, and my range here is the best I ever seen. Lately we've been losing stock. But that's not all nor so bad. Sheepmen have moved into the Tonto and are grazing down in Grass Valley. Cattlemen and sheepmen can never bide in this country. We have bad times ahead. Reckon I've more reasons to worry and need you, but you must wait to hear that by word of mouth.

Whatever you're doing, chuck it and rustle for Grass Valley so to make here by spring. I'm asking you to take pains to pack in some guns and a lot of shells. And hide them in your outfit. If you meet

14

anyone when you're coming down into the Tonto, listen more than you talk. And last, Son, don't let anything keep you in Oregon. Reckon you have a sweetheart, and if so fetch her along. With love from your Dad,

Gaston Isbel

Jean pondered over this letter. Judged by memory of his father, who had always been self-sufficient, it had been a surprise and somewhat of a shock. Weeks of travel and reflection had not helped him to grasp the meaning between the lines.

"Yes, Dad's growin' old," mused Jean, feeling a warmth and a sadness stir in him. "He must be 'way over sixty. But he never looked old. . . . So he's rich now an' losin' stock, an' goin' to be sheeped off his range. Dad could stand a lot of rustlin', but not much from sheepmen."

The softness that stirred in Jean merged into a cold, thoughtful earnestness that had followed every perusal of his father's letter. A dark, full current seemed to flow in his veins, and at times he felt it swell and heat. It troubled him, making him conscious of a deeper, stronger self, opposed to his careless, free, and dreamy nature. No ties had bound him in Oregon, except love for the great still forests and the thundering rivers, and this love came from his softer side. It had cost him a wrench to leave. All the way by ship down the coast to San Diego, and across the Sierra Madres by stage, and so on to this last overland travel by horseback, he had felt a retreating of the self that was tranquil and happy, and a domination by this unknown somber self, with its menacing possibilities. Yet, despite a nameless regret and a loyalty to Oregon, when he lay in his blankets, he had to confess a keen interest in his adventurous future, a keen en-

15

joyment of this stark wild Arizona. It appeared to be a different sky stretching in dark, star-spangled dome over him—closer, vaster, bluer. The strong fragrance of sage and cedar floated over him with the campfire smoke, and all seemed drowsily to subdue his thoughts.

At dawn he rolled out of his blankets and, pulling on his boots, began the day with a zest for the work that must bring closer his calling future. White, crackling frost and cold, nipping air were the same keen spurs to action that he had known in the uplands of Oregon, yet they were not wholly the same. He sensed an exhilaration similar to the effect of a strong, sweet wine. His horse and mule had fared well during the night, having been much refreshed by the grass and water of the little cañon. Jean mounted and rode into the cedars with gladness that at last he had put the endless leagues of barren land behind him.

The trail he followed appeared to be seldom traveled. It led, according to the meager information obtainable at the last settlement, directly to what was called the Tonto Rim, and from there Grass Valley could be seen down in the Tonto Basin. The ascent of the ground was so gradual that only in long, open stretches could it be seen. But the nature of the vegetation showed Jean how he was climbing. Scant, low, craggy cedars gave place to more numerous, darker, greener, bushier ones, and then to high, full-foliaged, green-berried trees. Sage and grass in the open flats grew more luxuriously. Then came the piñons, and presently among them the checker-barked junipers. Jean hailed the first pine tree with a hearty slap on the brown, rugged bark. It was a smooth dwarf pine struggling to live. The next one was larger, and after that came several, and beyond them, pines stood up everywhere above the lower trees. The odor of pine needles mingled with the other dry smells that made the wind pleasant to Jean. In an hour from the first line of pines he had ridden beyond the cedars and piñons into a slowly thickening and deepening forest. Underbrush appeared scarce except in ravines, and the ground in open patches held a bleached grass. Jean's eye roved for sight of squirrels, birds, deer, or any moving creature. It appeared to be a dry, uninhabited forest. About midday Jean halted at a pond of surface water, evidently melted snow, and gave his animals a drink. He saw a few old deer tracks in the mud and several huge bird tracks new to him that he concluded must have been made by wild turkeys.

The trail divided at this pond. Jean had no idea which branch he ought to take. "Reckon it doesn't matter," he muttered, as he was about to remount. His horse was standing with ears up, looking back along the trail. Then Jean heard a *clip-clop* of trotting hoofs and presently espied a horseman.

Jean made a pretense of tightening his saddle girths while he peered over his horse at the approaching rider. All men in this country were going to be of exceeding interest to Jean Isbel. This man at a distance rode and looked like all the Arizonians Jean had seen. He had a superb seat in the saddle, and he was long and lean. He wore a huge black sombrero and a soiled red scarf. His vest was open, and he was without a coat.

The rider came trotting up and halted several paces from Jean.

"Hullo, stranger," he said gruffly.

"Howdy yourself," replied Jean. He felt an instinctive importance in the meeting with the man. Never had sharper eyes flashed over Jean and his outfit. The stranger had a dust-colored, sunburned face, long, lean, and hard, a huge sandy mustache that hid his mouth, and eyes of light,

17

piercing intensity. Not very much hard Western experience had passed by this man, yet he was not old, measured by years.

When he dismounted, Jean saw he was tall, even for an Arizonian.

"Seen your tracks back a ways," he said, as he slipped the bit to let his horse drink. "Where bound?"

"Reckon I'm lost all right," replied Jean. "New country for me."

"Shore. I seen that from your tracks an' your last camp. Wal, where was you headin' before you got lost?"

The query was deliberately cool with a dry, crisp ring. Jean felt the lack of friendliness or kindliness in it.

"Grass Valley. My name's Isbel," he replied shortly.

The rider attended to his drinking horse and presently rebridled him, then with long swing of leg he appeared to step into the saddle.

"Shore I knowed you was Jean Isbel," he said. "Everybody in the Tonto has heered old Gass Isbel sent fer his boy."

"Well, then, why did you ask?" inquired Jean bluntly.

"Reckon I wanted to see what you'd say."

"So? All right. But I'm not carin' very much for what *you* say."

Their glances locked steadily then and each measured the other by the intangible conflict of spirit.

"Shore thet's natural," replied the rider. His speech was slow, and the motions of his long, brown hand, as he took a cigarette from his vest, kept time with his words. "But seein' you're one of the Isbels, I'll hev' my say whether you want it or not. My name's Colter, an' I'm one of the sheepmen Gass Isbel's riled with."

"Colter. Glad to meet you," replied Jean. "An' I reckon

18

who riled my father is goin' to rile me."

"Shore. If thet wasn't so, you'd not be an Isbel," returned Colter with a grim little laugh. "It's easy to see you ain't run into any Tonto Basin fellers yet. Wal, I'm goin' to tell you thet your old man gabbed like a woman down at Greaves's store. Bragged about you an' how you could fight an' how you could shoot an' how you could track a hoss or a man! Bragged how you'd chase every sheepherder back up to the Tonto Rim! I'm tellin' you because we want you to git our stand right. We're goin' to run sheep down in Grass Valley."

"A-huh! Well, who's we?" queried Jean curtly.

"Wha-at? . . . we . . . I mean the sheepmen rangin' this rim from Black Butte to the Apache country."

"Colter, I'm a stranger in Arizona," said Jean slowly. "I know little about ranchers or sheepmen. It's true my father sent for me. It's true, I daresay, that he bragged, for he's given to bluster an' blow. An' he's old now. I can't help it if he bragged about me. But if he has, an' if he's justified in his stand against you sheepmen, I'm goin' to do my best to live up to his brag."

"I get your hunch. Shore we understand each other an' that's a powerful help. You take my hunch to your old man," replied Colter, as he turned his horse away toward the left. "That trail leadin' south is yours. When you come to the rim, you'll see a bare spot down in the basin. That'll be Grass Valley."

He rode away out of sight into the woods. Jean leaned against his horse and pondered. It seemed difficult to be just to this Colter, not because of his claims, but because of a subtle hostility that emanated from him. Colter had the hard face, the masked intent, the turn of speech that Jean had come to associate with dishonest men. Even if Jean had

19

not been prejudiced, if he had known nothing of his father's trouble with these sheepmen, and if Colter had met him only to exchange glances and greetings, still Jean would never have had a favorable impression. Colter grated upon him, roused an antagonism seldom felt.

"Heigh-ho," sighed the young man. "Good bye to huntin' an' fishin'. Dad's given me a man's job."

With that, he mounted his horse and started the pack mule into the right-hand trail. Walking and trotting, he traveled all afternoon, toward sunset getting into heavy forests of pine. More than one snowbank showed white through the green, sheltered on the north slopes of shady ravines. It was upon entering this zone of richer, deeper forestland that Jean sloughed off his gloomy forebodings. These stately pines were not the giant firs of Oregon, but any lover of the woods could be happy under them. Higher still he climbed until the forest spread before and around him like a level park, with thicketed ravines here and there on each side. Presently that deceptive level led to a higher bench upon which the pines towered and were matched by beautiful trees he took for spruce. Heavily barked, with regular spreading branches, these conifers rose in symmetrical shape to spear the sky with silver plumes. A graceful, gray-green moss waved like veils from the branches. The air was not so dry and it was colder, with a scent and touch of snow. Jean made camp at the first likely site, taking the precaution to unroll his bed some little distance from his fire. Under the softly moaning pines he felt comfortable, having lost the sense of an immeasurable open space falling away from all around him.

The gobbling of wild turkeys awakened Jean. *Chug-a-lug, chug-a-lug, chug-a-lug-chug.* There was not a great difference between the gobble of a wild turkey and that of a tame one. Jean got up and, taking his rifle, went out into the gray obscurity of dawn to try to locate the turkeys. But it was too dark, and finally, when daylight came, they appeared to be gone. The mule had strayed, and what with finding it and cooking breakfast, and packing, Jean did not make a very early start. On this last lap of his long journey he had slowed down. He was weary of hurrying. The change from weeks in the glaring sun and dust-laden wind to this sweet, cool, darkly green and brown forest was very welcome. He wanted to linger along the shaded trail. This day he made sure would see him reach the Tonto Rim. By and by he lost the trail. It had just worn out from lack of use. But every now and then Jean would cross the old trail again, and, as he penetrated deeper into the forest, every damp or dusty spot showed tracks of turkey, deer, and bear. The amount of bear sign surprised him. Presently his keen nostrils were assailed by a smell of sheep, and soon he rode into a broad sheep trail. From the tracks Jean calculated that the sheep had passed there the day before.

An unreasonable antipathy seemed born in him. To be sure he had been prepared to dislike sheep, and that was why he was unreasonable. But on the other hand this band of sheep had left a broad, bare swath, weedless, grassless, flowerless, in their wake. Where sheep grazed, they destroyed. That was what Jean had against them.

An hour later he rode to the crest of a long, park-like slope where new green grass was sprouting and flowers peeped everywhere. The pines appeared far apart; gnarled oak trees showed rugged and gray against the green wall of woods. A white strip of snow gleamed like a moving stream away down in the woods.

Jean heard the musical tinkle of bells and the baa-baa of sheep and the faint, sweet, bleating of lambs. As he rode to-

21

ward these sounds, a dog ran out from an oak thicket and barked at him. Next Jean smelled a campfire, and soon he caught sight of a curling blue column of smoke, and then a small peaked tent. Beyond the clump of oaks Jean encountered a Mexican lad, carrying a carbine. The boy had a swarthy, pleasant face, and to Jean's greeting he replied: "*Buenas días.*" Jean understood little Spanish and about all he gathered from his simple queries was that the lad was not alone—and that it was lambing time.

This latter circumstance grew noisily manifest. The forest seemed shrilly full of incessant baas and plaintive bleats. All about the camp, on the slope, in the glades, and everywhere, were sheep. A few were grazing; many were lying down; most of them were ewes suckling white, fleecy, little lambs that staggered on their feet. Everywhere Jean saw tiny lambs just born. Their pinpointed bleats pierced the heavier baa-baa of their mothers.

Jean dismounted, and led his horse down toward the camp, where he rather expected to see another and older Mexican from whom he might get information. The lad had walked with him. Down this way the plaintive uproar made by the sheep was not so loud.

"Hello there!" called Jean cheerfully, as he approached the tent. No answer was forthcoming. Dropping his bridle, he went on rather slowly, looking for someone to appear. Then a voice from one side startled him.

" 'Mawnin', stranger."

A girl stepped out from beside a pine. She carried a rifle. Her face flashed richly brown, but she was not Mexican. This fact, and the sudden conviction that she had been watching him, somewhat disconcerted Jean.

"Beg pardon . . . miss," he floundered. "Didn't expect to see a . . . a girl. . . . I'm sort of lost . . . lookin' for the Tonto

Rim . . . an' thought I'd find a sheepherder who'd show me. I can't savvy this boy's lingo."

While he spoke, it seemed to him an intentness of expression, a strain relaxed from her face. A faint suggestion of hostility likewise disappeared. Jean was not even sure that he had caught it, but there had been something that now was gone.

"Shore I'll be glad to show you," she said.

"Thanks, miss. Reckon I can breathe easy now," he replied. "It's a long ride from San Diego. Hot an' dusty! I'm pretty tired. An' maybe this woods isn't good medicine to achin' eyes."

"San Diego! You're from the Coast?"

"Yes."

Jean had doffed his sombrero at sight of her and he still held it, rather deferentially perhaps. It seemed to attract her attention.

"Put on your hat, stranger. Shore I cain't recollect when any man bared his haid to me." She uttered a little laugh in which surprise and frankness mingled with a taint of bitterness.

Jean sat down with his back to a pine, and, laying the sombrero by his side, he looked fully at her, conscious of a singular eagerness, as if he wanted to verify by close scrutiny a first hasty impression. If there had been an instinct in his meeting with Colter, there was more in this. The girl half sat, half leaned against a log, with the shiny little carbine across her knees. She had a level, curious gaze on him, and Jean had never met one just like it. Her eyes were rather a wide oval in shape, clear and steady, with shadows of thought in their amber-brown depths. They seemed to look through Jean, and his gaze dropped first. Then it was he saw her ragged homespun skirt and a few inches of

23

brown bare ankles, strong and round, and crude, worn-out moccasins that failed to hide the shapeliness of her feet. Suddenly she drew back her stockingless ankles and ill-shod little feet. When Jean lifted his gaze again, he found her face half averted and a stain of red in the gold tan of her cheek. That touch of embarrassment somehow removed her from this strong, raw, wild woodland setting. It changed her poise. It detracted from the curious, unabashed, almost bold look that he had encountered in her eyes.

"Reckon you're from Texas," said Jean presently.

"Shore am," she drawled. She had a lazy Southern voice, pleasant to hear. "How'd you-all guess that?"

"Anybody can tell a Texan. Where I came from, there were a good many pioneers an' ranchers from the old Lone Star state. I've worked for several . . . an', come to think of it, I'd rather hear a Texas girl talk than anybody."

"Did you know many Texas girls?" she inquired, turning again to face him.

"Reckon I did . . . quite a good many."

"Did you go with them?"

"Go with them? Reckon you mean keep company. Why, yes, I guess I did . . . a little." Jean laughed. "Sometimes on a Sunday, or a dance once in a blue moon, an' occasionally a ride."

"Shore that accounts," said the girl wistfully.

"For what?" asked Jean.

"Your bein' a gentleman," she replied with force. "Oh, I've not forgotten. I had friends when we lived in Texas . . . three years ago. Shore it seems longer. Three miserable years in this damned country!"

Then she bit her lip, evidently to keep back further unwitting utterance to a total stranger. It was that biting of her lip that drew Jean's attention to her mouth. It held beauty

24

of curve and fullness and color that could not hide a certain sadness and bitterness. Then the whole flashing brown face changed for Jean. He saw that it was young, full of passion and restraint, possessing a power that grew on him. This, with her shame and pathos and familiar utterance of profanity, and the fact that she craved respect, gave a leap to Jean's interest.

"Well, I reckon you flatter me," he said, hoping to put her at her ease again. "I'm only a rough hunter an' fisherman . . . woodchopper an' horse tracker. Never had all the school I needed . . . nor had enough company of nice girls like you."

"Am I nice?" she asked quickly.

"You sure are," he replied, smiling.

"In these rags?" she demanded, with a sudden flash of passion that thrilled him. "Look at the holes." She showed rips and worn-out places in the sleeves of her buckskin blouse, through which gleamed a round brown arm. "I sew when I have anythin' to sew with. . . . Look at my skirt . . . a dirty rag. An' I have only one other to my name . . . look!" Again a color tinged her cheeks, most becoming, and giving the lie to her action. But shame could not check her violence now. A dammed up resentment seemed to have broken out in flood. She lifted the ragged skirt almost to her knees. "No stockings! No shoes! . . . how can a girl be nice when she has no clean decent woman's clothes to wear?"

"How . . . how can . . . a girl . . . ," began Jean, "see here, miss, I'm beggin' your pardon for . . . sort of stirrin' you to forget yourself a little. Reckon I understand. You don't meet many strangers an' I sort of hit you wrong . . . makin' you feel too much . . . an' talk too much. Who an' what you are is none of my business. But we met . . . an' I reckon somethin' has happened . . . perhaps more to me

25

than to you. . . . Now let me put you straight about clothes an' women. Reckon I know most women love nice things to wear, an' think because clothes make them look pretty that they're nicer or better. But they're wrong. You're wrong. Maybe it'd be too much for a girl like you to be happy without clothes. But you can be . . . you are just as nice an' . . . an' fine . . . an', for all you know, a good deal more appealin' to some men."

"Stranger, you shore must excuse my temper an' the show I made of myself," replied the girl with composure. "That, to say the least, was not nice. An' I don't want anyone thinkin' better of me than I deserve. My mother died in Texas, an' I've lived out heah in this wild country . . . a girl alone among rough men. Meetin' you today makes me see what a hard lot they are . . . an' what it's done to me."

Jean smothered his curiosity and tried to put out of his mind a growing sense that he pitied her, liked her.

"Are you a sheepherder?" he asked.

"Shore I am now an' then. My father lives back heah in a cañon. He's a sheepman. Lately there's been herders shot at. Just now we're short, an' I have to fill in. But I like shepherdin' an' I love the woods, the rim rock, an' all the Tonto. If they were all, I'd shore be happy."

"Herders shot at!" exclaimed Jean thoughtfully. "By whom? An' what for?"

"Trouble brewin' between the cattlemen down in the basin an' the sheepmen up on the rim. Dad says there'll shore be hell to pay. I tell him I hope the cattlemen chase him back to Texas."

"Then . . . are you on the ranchers' side?" queried Jean, trying to pretend casual interest.

"No. I'll always be on my father's side," she replied with

26

spirit. "But I'm bound to admit I think the cattlemen have the fair side of the argument."

"How so?"

"Because there's grass everywhere. I see no sense in a sheepman goin' out of his way to surround a cattleman an' sheep off his range. That started the row. Lord knows how it'll end. For 'most all of them heah are from Texas."

"So I was told," replied Jean. "An' I heard most all these Texans got run out of Texas. Any truth in that?"

"Shore I reckon there is," she replied seriously. "But, stranger, it might not be healthy for you to say that anywhere. My dad for one was not run out of Texas. Shore I never can see why he came heah. He's accumulated stock, but he's not rich, nor so well off, as he was back home."

"Are you goin' to stay here always?" queried Jean suddenly.

"If I do, it'll be in my grave," she answered darkly. "But what's the use of thinkin'? People stay places until they drift away. You can never tell. . . . Well, stranger, this talk is keepin' you."

She seemed moody now and a note of detachment crept into her voice. Jean rose at once and went for his horse. If this girl did not desire to talk further, he certainly had no wish to annoy her. His mule had strayed off among the bleating sheep. Jean drove it back, and then led his horse up to where the girl stood. She appeared taller, and although not of robust build she was vigorous and lithe, with something about her that fitted the place. Jean was loathe to bid her good bye.

"Which way is the Tonto Rim?" he asked, turning to his saddle girths.

"South," she replied, pointing. "It's only a mile or so.

I'll walk down with you. Suppose you're on your way to Grass Valley?"

"Yes, I've relatives there," he returned. He dreaded her next question, which he suspected would concern his name. But she did not ask. Taking up her rifle, she turned away. Jean strode ahead to her side. "Reckon if you walk, I won't ride."

So he found himself beside a girl with the free step of a mountaineer. Her bare brown head came up nearly to his shoulder. It was a small, pretty head, graceful, well held, and the thick hair on it was a shiny soft brown. She wore it in a braid, rather untidily and tangled he thought, and it was tied with a string of buckskin. Altogether her apparel proclaimed poverty.

Jean let the conversation languish for a little. He wanted to think what to say presently, and then he felt a rather vague pleasure in stalking beside her. Her profile was straight-cut and exquisite in line. From this side view the soft curve of lips could not be seen.

She made several attempts to start conversation, all of which Jean ignored, manifestly to her growing constraint. Presently Jean, having decided what he wanted to say, suddenly began: "I like this adventure. Do you?"

"Adventure! Meetin' me in the woods?" And she laughed the laugh of youth. "Shore you must be hard up for adventure, stranger."

"Do you like it?" he persisted. And his eyes searched the half-averted face.

"I might like it," she answered frankly, "if . . . if my temper had not made a fool of me. I never meet anyone I care to talk to. Why should it not be . . . be pleasant to run across someone new . . . someone strange in this heah wild country."

28

"We are as we are," said Jean simply. "I didn't think you made a fool of yourself. If I thought so, would I want to see you again?"

"Do you?" The brown face flashed at him with surprise, with a light he took for gladness. Because he wanted to appear calm and friendly, not too eager, he had to deny himself the thrill of meeting those changing eyes.

"Sure I do. Reckon I'm overbold on such short acquaintance. But I might not have another chance to tell you. So please don't hold it against me."

This declaration over, Jean felt relief, and something of exultation. He had been afraid he might not have the courage to make it. She walked on as before, only with her head bowed a little and her eyes downcast. No color but the gold-brown tan and the blue tracery of veins showed in her cheeks. He noticed then a slight swelling quiver of her throat, and he became alive to its graceful contour and to how full and pulsating it was, how nobly it set into the curve of her shoulder. Here in her quivering throat was the weakness of her, the evidence of her sex, the womanliness that belied the mountaineer's stride and the grasp of strong brown hands on a rifle. It had an effect on Jean totally unaccountable to him, both in the strange warmth that stole over him and in the utterance he could not hold back.

"Girl, we're strangers, but what of that? We've met, an' I tell you it means somethin' to me. I've known girls for months an' never felt this way. I don't know who you are an' I don't care. You betrayed a good deal to me. You're not happy. You're lonely. An' if I didn't want to see you again for my own sake, I would for yours. Some things you said I'll not forget soon. I've got a sister, an' I know you have no brother. An' I reckon. . . ."

At this juncture, Jean, in his earnestness and quite

without thought, grabbed her hand. The contact checked the flow of his speech and suddenly made him aghast at his temerity. But the girl did not make any effort to withdraw it. So Jean, inhaling a deep breath and trying to see through his bewilderment, held on bravely. Jean imagined he felt a faint, warm returning pressure. She was young, she was friendless, she was human. By this hand in his, Jean felt more than ever the loneliness of her. Then, just as he was about to speak again, she pulled her hand free.

"Heah's the Tonto Rim," she said in her quaint Southern drawl. "An' there's your Tonto Basin."

Jean had been intent only on the girl. He had kept step beside her without taking note of what was ahead of him. At her words he looked up expectantly, to be struck mute.

He felt a sheer force, a downward drawing of an immense abyss beneath him. As he looked afar, he saw a black basin of timbered country, the darkest, wildest, and ruggedest he had ever gazed upon, a hundred miles of blue distance across to an upflung mountain range, hazy purple against the sky. It seemed to be a stupendous gulf surrounded on three sides by bold, undulating lines of peaks and on his side by a wall so high that he felt lifted aloft on the rim of the sky.

"Southeast you see the Sierra Anchas," said the girl, pointing. "That notch in the range is the pass where sheep are driven to Phoenix and Maricopa. Those big rough mountains to the south are the Mazatzals. 'Round to the west is the Four Peaks Range. An' you're standin' on the Tonto Rim."

Jean could not see at first just what the rim was, but by shifting his gaze westward he grasped this remarkable phenomenon of nature. For leagues and leagues a colossal red and yellow wall, a rampart, a mountain-faced cliff seemed

30

to zigzag westward. Grand and bold were the promontories reaching out over the void. They ran toward the westering sun. Sweeping and impressive were the long lines slanting away from them, sloping darkly spotted down to merge into the black timber. Jean had never seen such a wild and rugged manifestation of nature's depths and upheavals. He was held mute.

"Stranger, look down," said the girl.

Jean's sight was educated to judge heights and depths and distances. This wall on which he stood sheered precipitously down, so far that it made him dizzy to look, and then the craggy, broken cliffs merged into red-sided, cedar-greened slopes running down and down into gorges choked with forests and from which soared up a roar of rushing waters. Slope after slope, ridge beyond ridge, cañon merging into cañon—so the tremendous bowl sank away to its black, deceiving depths, a wilderness across which travel seemed impossible.

"Wonderful!" exclaimed Jean.

"Indeed it is," murmured the girl. "Shore that is Arizona. I reckon I love *this*. The heights an' depths . . . the awfulness of its wildness!"

"An' you want to leave it?"

"Yes an' no. I don't deny the peace that comes to me heah. But not often do I see the basin, an' for that matter one doesn't live on grand scenery."

"Child, even once in a while . . . this sight would cure any misery, if you only see. I'm glad I came. I'm glad *you* showed it to me first!"

She, too, seemed under the spell of a vastness and loneliness and beauty and grandeur that could not but strike the heart.

Jean took her hand again. "Girl, say you will meet me

31

here," he said, his voice ringing deeply in his ears.

"Shore I will," she replied softly, and turned to him. It seemed then that Jean saw her face for the first time. She was beautiful as he had never known beauty. Limned against that scene she gave it life—wild, sweet, young life—the poignant meaning of which haunted yet eluded him. But she belonged there. Her eyes were again searching his, as if for some lost part of herself, unrealized, never known before. Wondering, wistful, hopeful, glad—they were eyes that seemed, surprised, to reveal part of her soul.

When her red lips parted, their tremulous movement was a magnet to Jean. An invisible and mighty force pulled him down to kiss them. Whatever the spell had been, that rude unconscious action broke it.

"Heavens!" He jerked away, as if he expected to be struck. "Girl, I . . . I," he gasped in amazement and sudden, dawning contrition. "I kissed you . . . but I swear it wasn't intentional . . . I never thought. . . ."

The anger that Jean anticipated failed to materialize. He stood, breathing hard, with a hand held out in unconscious appeal. By the same magic, perhaps, that had transfigured her a moment past, she was now invested again by the older character.

"Shore, I reckon my callin' you a gentleman was a little previous," she said with a rather dry brittleness. "But, stranger, you're sudden."

"You're not insulted?" asked Jean hurriedly.

"Oh, I've been kissed before. Shore men are all alike."

"They're not," he replied hotly, with a subtle rush of disillusion, a dulling of enchantment. "Don't you class me with other men who've kissed you. I wasn't myself when I did it . . . an' I'd have gone on my knees to ask your forgiveness . . . but now I wouldn't . . . an' I wouldn't kiss you

32

again, either . . . even if you . . . you wanted it."

Jean read in her strange gaze what seemed to him a vague doubt, as if she was questioning herself.

"Miss, I take that back," added Jean shortly. "I'm sorry. I didn't mean to be rude. It was a mean trick for me to kiss you. A girl alone in the woods who's gone out of her way to be kind to me! I don't know why I forgot my manners. An' I ask your pardon."

She looked away then, and presently pointed far out and down into the Tonto Basin. "There's Grass Valley. That long gray spot in the black. It's about fifteen miles. Ride along the rim that way till you cross a trail. Shore you can't miss it. Then go down."

"I'm much obliged to you," replied Jean, reluctantly accepting what he regarded as his dismissal. Turning his horse, he put his foot in the stirrup, then, hesitating, he looked across the saddle at the girl. Her abstraction, as she gazed away over the purple depths, suggested loneliness and wistfulness. She was not thinking of that scene spread so wondrously before her. It struck Jean she might be pondering a subtle change in his feeling and attitude, something he was conscious of, yet could not define.

"Reckon this is good bye," he said with hesitation.

"*Adiós, señor,*" she replied, facing him again. She lifted the little carbine to the bottom of her elbow and, half turning, appeared ready to depart.

"*Adiós* means good bye?" he queried.

"Yes, good bye till tomorrow or good bye forever. Take it as you like."

"Then you'll meet me here day after tomorrow?" How eagerly he spoke, on impulse, without a consideration of the intangible thing that had changed him.

"Did I say I wouldn't?"

33

"No. But I reckoned you'd not care to . . . after . . . ," he replied, breaking off in some confusion.

"Shore I'll be glad to meet you. Day after tomorrow about mid-afternoon. Right heah. Fetch all the news from Grass Valley."

"All right. Thanks. That'll be . . . fine," replied Jean, and, as he spoke, he experienced a buoyant thrill, a pleasant lightness of enthusiasm, much as always stirred boyishly in him at a prospect of adventure. Before it passed he wondered at it and felt unsure of himself. He needed to think.

"Stranger, shore I'm not recollectin' that you told me who you are," she said.

"No, reckon I didn't tell," he returned. "What difference does that make? I said I didn't care who or what you are. Can't you feel the same about me?"

"Shore . . . I felt that way," she replied, somewhat nonplussed, with the level brown gaze steadily on his face. "But now you make me think."

"Let's meet without knowin' any more about each other than we do now."

"Shore. I'd like that. In this big wild Arizona a girl . . . an' I reckon a man . . . feels so insignificant. What's a name, anyhow? Still, people an' things have to be distinguished. I'll call you 'Stranger' an' be satisfied . . . if you say it's fair for you not to tell me who you are."

"Fair! No, it's not," declared Jean, forced to confession. "My name's Jean . . . Jean Isbel."

"*Isbel!*" she exclaimed with a violent start. "Shore you can't be son of old Gass Isbel. . . . I've seen both his sons."

"He has three," replied Jean with relief, now the secret was out. "I'm the youngest. I'm twenty-four. Never been out of Oregon till now. On my way. . . ."

The brown color slowly faded out of her face, leaving her

34

quite pale, with eyes that began to blaze. The suppleness of her seemed to stiffen.

"My name's Ellen Jorth," she burst out passionately. "Does it mean anythin' to you?"

"Never heard it in my life," protested Jean. "Sure I reckoned you belonged to the sheep raisers who're on the outs with my father. That's why I had to tell you I'm Jean Isbel. But, honest, I never heard of you or anyone by the name of Jorth. . . . Ellen Jorth. It's strange an' pretty. . . . Reckon I can be just as good a . . . a friend to you. . . ."

"No Isbel can ever be a friend to me," she said with bitter coldness. Stripped of her ease and her soft wistfulness, she stood before him one instant entirely another girl, a hostile enemy. Then she wheeled and strode off into the woods.

Jean, in consternation, watched her swiftly draw away with her lithe, free step, wanting to follow her, wanting to call to her, but the resentment roused by her suddenly avowed hostility held him mute in his tracks. He watched her disappear, and, when the brown and green wall of forest swallowed the slender gray form, he fought against the insistent desire to follow her, and fought in vain.

Chapter Two

Ellen Jorth's moccasined feet did not leave a distinguishable trail on the springy pine needle covering of the ground, and Jean could not find any trace of her. A little futile searching to and fro cooled his impulse and called pride to his rescue. Returning to his horse, he mounted, rode out behind the pack mule to start it along, and soon felt the relief of decision and action. Clumps of small pines grew thickly in spots on the Tonto Rim, making it necessary for him to skirt them, at which times he lost sight of the purple basin. Every time he came back to an opening through which he could see the wild ruggedness and colors and distances, his appreciation of their nature grew on him. Arizona from Yuma to the Little Colorado had been to him an endless waste of wind-scoured, sun-blasted barrenness. This black-forested, rock-rimmed land of untrodden ways was a world that in itself would satisfy him. Some instinct in Jean called for a lonely wild land, of fastnesses into which he could roam at will, and be the other strange self that he had always yearned to be but had never been.

Every few moments there intruded into his flowing consciousness the flashing face of Ellen Jorth, the way she had looked at him, the things she had said. "Reckon I was a fool," he soliloquized with an acute sense of humiliation. "She never saw how much in earnest I was." Jean began to remember the circumstances with a vividness that disturbed and perplexed him.

The accident of running across such a girl in that lonely

36

place might be out of the ordinary, but it had happened. Surprise had made him dull. The charm of her appearance, the appeal of her manner, must have drawn him at the very first, but he had not recognized that. Only at her words— "Oh, I've been kissed before."—had his feelings been checked in their heedless progress, and the utterance of them had made a difference he now sought to analyze. Some personality in him, some voice, some idea had begun to defend her even before he was conscious that he had arraigned her before the bar of his judgment. Such defense seemed clamoring in him now and he forced himself to listen. He wanted, in his hurt pride, to justify his amazing surrender to a sweet and sentimental impulse.

He realized now that at first glance he should have recognized in her look, her poise, her voice the quality he called thoroughbred. Ragged and stained apparel did not prove her of a common sort. Jean had known a number of fine and wholesome girls of good family, and he remembered his sister. This Ellen Jorth was that kind of a girl, irrespective of her present environment. Jean championed her loyally, even after he had gratified his selfish pride.

It was then—contending with an intangible and stealing glamour, unreal and fanciful, like the dream of a forbidden enchantment—that Jean arrived at the part in the little woodland drama where he had kissed Ellen Jorth and had been unrebuked. Why had she not resented his action? Dispelled was the illusion he had been dreamily and nobly constructing. *Oh, I've been kissed before!* The shock to him now exceeded his first dismay. Half bitterly she had spoken, and wholly scornful of herself, or of him, or of all men, for she had said all men were alike. Jean chafed under the smart of that, a taunt every decent man hated. Naturally every happy and healthy young man would want to kiss such red sweet lips. But if those lips had been for others—never for him! Jean reflected that not since childish games had he kissed a girl—until this brown-faced Ellen Jorth came his way. He wondered at it. Moreover he wondered at the significance he placed upon it. After all, was it not merely an accident? Why should he remember? Why should he ponder? What was the faint, deep, growing thrill that accompanied some of his thoughts?

Riding along with busy mind, Jean almost crossed a well-beaten trail, leading through a pine thicket and down over the rim. Jean's pack mule led the way without being driven. When Jean reached the edge of the bluff, one look down was enough to fetch him off his horse. That trail was steep, narrow, clogged with stones, and as full of sharp corners as a cross-cut saw. Once on the descent with a packed mule and a spirited horse, Jean had no time for mind-wanderings and very little for occasional glimpses out over the cedar tops to the vast blue hollow, asleep under a westering sun.

The stones rattled, the dust rose, the cedar twigs snapped, the little avalanches of red earth slid down, the iron-shod hoofs rang on the rocks. This slope had been narrow at the apex in the rim where the trail led down a crack, and it widened in fan-shape as Jean descended. He zigzagged down a thousand feet before the slope benched into dividing ridges. Here the cedars and junipers failed and pines once more hid the sun. Deep ravines were black with brush. From somewhere rose a roar of running water, most pleasant to Jean's ears. Fresh deer and bear tracks covered old ones made in the trail.

Those timbered ridges were but billows of that tremendous slope that now sheered above Jean, ending in a magnificent yellow wall of rock, greened in niches, stained by weather rust, carved and cracked and caverned. As Jean descended farther, the hum of bees made melody, the roar of rapid water and the murmur of a rising breeze filled him with the content of the wild. Sheepmen like Colter and wild girls like Ellen Jorth, and all that seemed promising or menacing in his father's letter, could never change the Indian in Jean. So he thought. Hard upon that conclusion rushed another, one which troubled with its stinging revelation—surely these influences he had defied were just the ones to bring out in him the Indian he had sensed but had never known. The eventful day had brought new and bitter food for Jean to reflect upon.

The trail landed him in the boulder-strewn bed of a wide cañon, where the large trees stretched a canopy of foliage that denied the sunlight and where a beautiful brook rushed and foamed. Here, at last, Jean tasted water that rivaled his Oregon springs. "Ah!" he cried, "that sure is good!" Dark and shaded and ferny and mossy was this stream's way, and everywhere were tracks of game, from the giant spread of a grizzly bear to the tiny bird-like imprint of a squirrel. Jean heard familiar sounds of deer cracking the dead twigs, and the chatter of squirrels was incessant. This fragrant cool retreat under the Tonto Rim brought back to him the dim recesses of Oregon forests. After all, Jean felt, he would not miss anything that he had loved in the Oregon Cascades. But what was the vague sense of all not being well with him—the essence of a faint regret—the insistence of a hovering shadow? And then flashed again, etched more vividly by the repetition in memory, a picture of eyes, of lips—of something he had to forget.

Wild and broken as this rolling basin floor had appeared from the rim, the reality of traveling over it made that first impression a deceit of distance. Down here all was in a big, rough, broken scale. Jean did not find even a few rods of level ground. Boulders as large as houses obstructed the streambed; spruce trees eight feet thick tried to lord it over the brawny pines; the ravine was a veritable cañon, from which occasional glimpses through the foliage showed the rim as a lofty red-tipped mountain peak. Jean's pack mule became frightened at scent of a bear or lion, and ran off down the rough trail, imperiling Jean's outfit. It was not an easy task to head him off, nor, when that was accomplished, to keep him to a trot, but his fright and ascending skittishness at least made for fast traveling. Jean calculated that he covered ten miles under the rim before the character of ground and forest began to change.

The trail had turned southeast. Instead of gorge after gorge, red-walled and choked with forest, there began to be rolling ridges, some high, others mere knolls, and a thick cedar growth made up for a falling off of pine. The spruce had long disappeared. Juniper thickets gave way more and more to the beautiful manzanita, and soon on the south slopes appeared cactus and a scrubby live oak. But for the well-broken trail, Jean would have fared ill through this tough brush.

Jean espied several deer, and again a coyote, and what he took to be a small herd of wild horses. No more turkey tracks showed in the dusty patches. He crossed a number of tiny brooklets, and at length came to a place where the trail ended or merged in a rough road that showed evidence of considerable travel. Horses, sheep, and cattle had passed along there that day. This road turned southward, and Jean began to have pleasurable expectations.

The road, like the trail, led down, but no longer at such steep angles and was bordered by cedar and piñon, jack pine and juniper, mescal and manzanita. Quite sharply, going around a ridge, the road led Jean's eye down to a small open plot of marshy, or at least grassy, ground. This green oasis in the wilderness of red and timbered ridges marked another change in the character of the Tonto Basin. Beyond that the country began to spread out and roll gracefully, its dark green forest interspersed with grassy parks, until Jean headed into a long, wide, gray-green valley surrounded by black-fringed hills. His pulses quickened here. He saw cattle dotting the expanse, and here and there along the edge log cabins and corrals.

As a village, Grass Valley could not boast of much apparently in the way of population. Cabins and houses were widely scattered, as if the inhabitants did not care to encroach upon one another, but the one store, built of stone and stamped also with the characteristic isolation, seemed to Jean to be a rather remarkable edifice. It did not strike him exactly like a fort, but, if it had not been designed for defense, it certainly gave that impression, especially from the long low side with its dark eye-like windows about the height of a man's shoulder. Some rather fine horses were tied to a hitching rail. Otherwise, dust and dirt and age and long use stamped this Grass Valley store and its immediate environment.

Jean threw his bridle and, getting down, mounted the low porch and stepped into the wide-open door. A face, gray against the background of gloom inside, passed out of sight just as Jean entered. He knew he had been seen. In the front of the long, rather low-ceilinged store were four men, all absorbed in a game of checkers. Two were playing and two were looking on. One of these, a gaunt-faced man past middle age, casually looked up as Jean came in, but the moment of that casual glance afforded Jean time enough to meet eyes he instinctively distrusted. They masked their penetration. They seemed neither curious nor friendly.

They saw him as if he had been merely thin air.

"Good evenin'," said Jean.

After what appeared to Jean a lapse of time sufficient to impress him with a possible deafness of those men, the gaunt-faced one said: "Howdy, Isbel."

The tone was impersonal, dry, easy, cool, laconic, and yet it could not have been more pregnant with meaning. Jean's sharp sensibilities absorbed much. None of the slouch-sombreroed, long-mustached Texans—for so Jean at once classed them—had ever seen Jean, but they knew him and knew that he was expected in Grass Valley. All but the one who had spoken happened to have their faces in shadow under the wide-brimmed black hats. Motley-garbed, gun-belted, dusty-booted, they gave Jean the same impression of latent force that he had encountered in Colter.

"Will somebody please tell me where to find my father, Gaston Isbel?" inquired Jean with as civil a tongue as he could command.

Nobody paid the slightest attention. It was the same as if Jean had not spoken. Waiting, half amused, half irritated, Jean shot a rapid glance around the store. The place had felt bare, and Jean, peering back through gloomy space, saw that it did not contain much. Dry goods and sacks littered a long rude counter; long rough shelves divided their length into stacks of canned foods and empty sections; a torn shelf back of the counter held a generous burden of cartridge boxes and next to it stood a rack of rifles. On the counter lay open cases of plug tobacco, the odor of which was second in strength only to that of rum.

Jean's swift-roving eye reverted to the men, only three of whom were still absorbed in the greasy checkerboard. The fourth man was the one who had spoken and he now deigned to look at Jean. There was not much flesh stretched over his long, powerful physiognomy. He stroked a lean chin with a big mobile hand that suggested more of holding a bridle than familiarity with a bucksaw or a plow handle. It was a lazy hand. The man looked lazy. If he spoke at all, it would be with lazy speech. Yet Jean had not encountered many men to whom he would have accorded more potency to stir in him the instinct of self-preservation.

"Shore," drawled this gaunt-faced Texan, "old Gass lives aboot a mile down heah." With a slow sweep of the big hand, he indicated a general direction to the south, then, appearing to forget his questioner, he turned his attention back to the game.

Jean muttered his thanks, and, striding out, he mounted again, and drove the pack mule farther down the road. "Reckon I've run into the wrong folks today," he said. "If I remember Dad right, he was a man to make an' keep friends. Somehow I'll bet there's goin' to be hell." Beyond the store were some rather pretty and comfortable houses, little ranch houses back in the coves of the hills. The road turned west and Jean saw his first sunset in the Tonto Basin. It was a pageant of purple clouds with silver edges and a background of deeply rich gold. Presently Jean met a lad driving a cow. "Hello," he said genially and with a double purpose. "My name's Jean Isbel. By Golly, I'm lost in Grass Valley. Will you tell me where my dad lives?"

"Yep. Keep right on, an' you cain't miss him," replied the lad, with a bright smile. "He's lookin' fer you."

"How do you know, boy?" queried Jean, warmed by that smile.

"Aw, I know. It's all over the valley that you'd ride in today. Shore I was the one that tol' yer dad an' he give me a dollar."

"Was he glad to hear it?" asked Jean with a queer sensation in his throat.

"Wal, he plumb was."

"An' who told you I was goin' to ride in today?"

"I heered it at the store," replied the lad with an air of confidence. "Some sheepmen was talkin' to Greaves. He's the storekeeper. I was settin' outside, but I heered. A Mexican come down off the rim terday an' he fetched the news." Here the lad looked furtively around, then whispered: "An' thet greaser was sent by somebody. I never heered no more, but them sheepmen looked pretty sour. An' one of them, comin' out, give me a kick, darn him. It shore is the luckedest day fer us cowmen."

"How's that?"

"Wal, thar's shore a big fight comin' to Grass Valley. My dad says so an' he rides fer your dad. An' if it comes now, you'll be heah."

"A-huh!" Jean laughed. "An' what then, boy?"

The lad turned bright eyes upward. "Aw, now, y'all cain't try thet on me. Ain't you an Injun, Jean Isbel? Ain't you a hoss tracker thet rustlers cain't fool? Ain't you a plumb dead shot? Ain't you wuss'ern a grizzly bear in a rough-an'-tumble? . . . now ain't that fer shore?"

Jean bade the flattering lad a rather sober good day and rode on his way. Manifestly a reputation somewhat difficult to live up to had preceded his entry into the Grass Valley. The first sight of his future home thrilled him through. It was a big, low, rambling log structure standing well out from a wooded knoll at the edge of the valley. Corrals and barns and sheds lay off at the back. To the fore stretched broad pastures where numberless cattle and horses grazed. At sunset the scene was one of rich color. Prosperity and abundance and peace seemed attendant upon that ranch.

44

Lusty voices of burros braying and cows bawling seemed to be welcoming Jean. A hound bayed. The first cool touch of wind fanned Jean's cheek and brought a fragrance of wood smoke and frying ham.

Horses in the pasture romped to the fence and whistled at the newcomers. Jean spied a white-faced black horse that gladdened his sight. "Hello, white face, I'll sure straddle you!" called Jean. Then up the gentle slope he saw the tall figure of his father—the same as he had seen him thousands of times, bare-headed, in shirt sleeves, striding with a long step. Jean waved and called to him.

"Hi, you prodigal!" came the answer. Yes, the voice of his father—and Jean's boyhood memories flashed. He hurried his horse those last few rods. No—Dad was not just the same. His hair shone gray.

"Here I am, Dad!" called Jean, and then he was dismounting. A deep, quiet emotion settled over him, stilling the hurry, the eagerness, the pang in his breast.

"Son, I shore am glad to see you," said his father, and wrung his hand. "Wal, wal! The size of you! Shore you're grown an' how you favor your mother."

Jean felt in the iron clasp of hand, in the uplifting of the handsome head, in the strong, fine light of piercing eyes that there was no difference in the spirit of his father, but the old smile could not hide lines and shades strange to Jean.

"Dad, I'm as glad as you," replied Jean heartily. "It seems long we've been parted, and now I see you. Are you well, Dad, an' all right?"

"Not complainin', Son. I can ride all day same as ever," he said. "Come. Never mind your stock. They'll be looked after. Come, meet the folks . . . wal, wal, you got heah at last."

On the porch of the house a group awaited Jean's coming, rather silently he thought. Wide-eyed children were there, very shy and watchful. The dark face of his sister corresponded with the image of her in his memory. She appeared taller, more womanly, as she embraced him. "Oh, Jean, Jean, I'm glad you've come," she cried, and pressed him to her. Jean felt in her a woman's anxiety for the present as well as affection for the past. He remembered his Aunt Mary, although he had not seen her for years. His half-brothers, Bill and Guy, had changed but a little, except perhaps to grow lean and rangy. Bill resembled his father, although his aspect was jocular rather than serious. Guy was smaller, wiry, and hard as rock, with snapping eyes in a brown still face, and he had the bowlegs of a cattleman. Both had married in Arizona. Bill's wife, Kate, was a stout, comely little woman, mother of three of the children. The other wife was young, a strapping girl, red-headed and freckled, with wonderful lines of pain and strength in her face. Jean remembered as he looked at her that someone had written lines about the tragedy in her life. When she was only a child, the Apaches had murdered all her family. Then, next to greet Jean, were the little children, all shy, yet all manifestly impressed by the occasion. A warmth and intimacy of forgotten family emotions flooded over Jean. Sweet it was to come among these relatives who loved him and welcomed him with quiet gladness. But there seemed more. Jean was quick to see the shadow in the eyes of the women in that household and to sense a strange reliance which his presence brought.

"Son, this heah Tonto is a land of milk an' honey," said his father, as Jean gazed spellbound at the bounteous supper.

Jean certainly performed gastronomic feats on this occasion, to the delight of Aunt Mary and the wonder of the children. "Oh, he's starv-ved to death," whispered one of the little boys to his sister. They had begun to warm to this stranger uncle. Jean had no chance to talk for the mealtime brought a relaxation of restraint and all tried to tell him things at once. In the bright lamplight his father looked easy and happy as he beamed upon Jean.

After supper the men went into an adjoining room that appeared most comfortable and attractive. It was long and the width of the house with a huge stone fireplace, low ceiling of hewn timbers and walls of the same, small windows with inside shutters of wood, and homemade table and chairs and rugs.

"Wal, Jean, do you recollect them shootin' irons?" inquired his father, pointing above the fireplace. Two guns hung on the spreading deer antlers there. One was a musket Jean's father had used in the War Between the States and the other was a long, heavy, muzzleloading flintlock Kentucky rifle with which Jean had learned to shoot.

"Reckon I do, Dad," replied Jean, and, with reverent hands and a rush of memory, he took down the old rifle.

"Jean, you shore handle thet old arm some clumsy," said Guy Isbel dryly. Bill added a remark to the effect that perhaps Jean had been leading a luxurious and tame life back there in Oregon, and then added: "But I reckon he's packin' that six-shooter like a Texan."

"Say, I fetched a gun or two along with me," replied Jean jocularly. "Reckon I near broke my poor mule's back with the load of shells an' guns. Dad, what was the idea askin' me to pack an arsenal?"

"Son, shore all shootin' arms an' such are at a premium in the Tonto," replied his father. "An' I was givin'

47

you a hunch to come loaded."

His cool, drawling voice seemed to put a damper upon the pleasantries. Right there Jean sensed the charged atmosphere. His brothers were bursting with utterance about to break forth, and his father suddenly wore a look that recalled to Jean critical times of days long past, but the entrance of the children and the womenfolks put an end to confidences. Evidently the youngsters were laboring under subdued excitement. They preceded their mother, the smallest boy in the lead. For him this must have been both a dreadful and a wonderful experience, for he seemed to be pushed forward by his sister and brother and mother, and driven by yearnings of his own. "There now, Lee," the boy's mother said. "Ask Uncle Jean . . . what did you fetch us?" The lad hesitated during a shy frightened look at Jean, and then, gaining something from his scrutiny of his uncle, he toddled forward and bravely delivered the question of tremendous importance.

"What did I fetch you, hey?" cried Jean in delight, as he took the lad up on his knee. "Wouldn't you like to know? I didn't forget, Lee. I remembered you all. Oh, the job I had packin' your bundle of presents. . . . Now, Lee, make a guess."

"I dess you fetched a dun," replied Lee.

"A dun! I'll bet you mean a gun." Jean laughed. "Well, you four-year-old Texas gunman! Make another guess."

That appeared too momentous and entrancing for the other two youngsters, and, adding their shrill and joyous voices to Lee's, they besieged Jean.

"Dad, where's my pack?" cried Jean. "These Apaches are after my scalp."

"Reckon the boys fetched it onto the porch," replied the rancher.

Guy Isbel opened the door and went out. "By Golly, heah's three packs," he called. "Which one do you want, Jean?"

"It's a long, heavy bundle all tied up," replied Jean.

Guy came staggering in under a burden that brought a whoop from the youngsters and bright gleams to the eyes of the women. Jean lost none of this. How glad he was that he had tarried in San Francisco because of a mental picture of this very reception in far-off wild Arizona!

When Guy deposited the bundle on the floor, it jarred the room. It gave forth metallic rattling and crackling sounds.

"Everybody stand back an' give me elbow room," ordered Jean majestically. "My good folk, I want you-all to know this is somethin' that doesn't happen often. The bundle you see here weighed about a hundred pounds when I packed it on my shoulder down Market Street in Frisco. It was stolen from me on shipboard. I got it back in San Diego an' licked the thief. It rode on a horse from San Diego to Yuma, an', well, I thought the burro was lost for keeps. I came up by the Colorado River from Yuma to Ehrenberg, an' there went on top of a stage. We got chased by bandits, an' once, when the horses were gallopin' hard, it near rolled off. Then it went on the back of a pack horse, an' helped wear him out. An' I reckon it would be somewheres else now if I hadn't fallen in with a freighter goin' north from Phoenix to the Santa Fé Trail. The last lap, when it sagged the back of a mule, was the riskiest an' full of the narrowest escapes. Twice my mule bucked off his pack an' left my outfit scattered. Worst of all, my precious bundle made the mule top heavy comin' down that place back here where the trail seems to drop off the earth. There I was hard put to keep sight of my pack. Sometimes it was on top an' other

49

times the mule. But it got here at last . . . an' now I'll open it."

After this long and impressive harangue, which at least augmented the suspense of the women and worked the children into a frenzy, Jean leisurely untied the many knots around the bundle and unrolled it. He had packed that bundle for just such travel as it had sustained. Three cloth-bound rifles he laid aside, and with them a long, very heavy package tied between thin wide boards. From this came a metallic clink. "Oh, I know what dem is!" cried Lee, breaking the silence of suspense. Then Jean, tearing open the long, flat parcel, spread before the mute, rapt-eyed youngsters such magnificent things as they had never dreamed of—picture books, mouth harps, dolls, a toy rifle and a toy pistol, a wonderful whistle and a box horn, and last of all a box of candy. Before these treasures on the floor, too magical to be touched at first, the two little boys and their sister simply knelt. That was a sweet full moment for Jean, yet even this was clouded by something that shadowed these innocent children fatefully born in a wild place at a wild time. Next Jean gave to his sister the presents he had brought her—beautiful cloth for a dress, ribbons and a bit of lace, handkerchiefs and buttons and yards of linen, a sewing case, and a whole box of spools of thread, a comb and brush and mirror, and lastly a Spanish brooch inlaid with garnets. "There, Ann," said Jean, "I confess I asked a girl friend in Oregon to tell me some things my sister might like." Manifestly there was not much difference in girls. Ann seemed stunned by this munificence, and, then awakening, she hugged Jean in a way that took his breath. She was not a child any more, that was certain. Aunt Mary turned knowing eyes upon Jean. "Reckon you couldn't have pleased Ann more. She's engaged, Jean, an', when girls are in that state, these things mean a heap. Ann, you'll be married in that!" She pointed to the beautiful folds of material that Ann had spread out.

"What's this?" demanded Jean. His sister's blushes were enough to convict her, and they were mightily becoming, too. "Here, Aunt Mary," went on Jean, "here's yours, an' here's somethin' for each of my new sisters." This distribution left the women as happy and occupied, almost, as the children. It left also another package, the last one in the bundle. Jean laid hold of it, and, lifting it, he was about to speak when he sustained a little shock of memory. Quite distinctly he saw two little feet with bare toes peeping out of worn-out moccasins, and then round, bare, symmetrical ankles that had been scratched by brush. Next he saw Ellen Jorth's passionate face as she looked when she had made the violent action so disconcerting to him. In this happy moment the memory seemed farther off than a few hours. It had crystallized. It amazed while it drew him. As a result he slowly laid this last package aside and did not speak as he had intended to.

"Dad, I reckon I didn't fetch a lot for you an' the boys," continued Jean. "Some knives, some pipes an' tobacco. An', sure, the guns."

"Shore, you're a regular Santa Claus, Jean," replied his father. "Wal, wal, look at the kids. An' look at Mary. An' for the land's sake look at Ann! Wal, wal, I'm gettin' old. I'd forgotten the pretty stuff an' gimcracks that mean so much to women. We're out of the world heah. It's just as well you've lived apart from us, Jean, for comin' back this way, with all that stuff, does us a lot of good. I cain't say, Son, how obliged I am. My mind has been set on the hard side of life. An' it's shore good to forget . . . to see the smiles of the women an' the joy of the kids."

51

At this juncture a tall young man entered the open door. He looked to be a rider. All about him, even his face, except his eyes, seemed old, but his eyes were young, fine, soft, and dark. "How do, y'all," he said evenly.

Ann rose from her knees. Then Jean did not need to be told who this newcomer was. "Jean, this is my . . . my friend, Andrew Colmor." Jean knew that when he met Colmor's grip and the keen flash of his eyes that he was glad Ann had set her heart on one of this kind, and his second impression was something akin to the one given him in the road by the admiring lad. Colmor's estimate of him must have been a monument built of Ann's eulogies. Jean's heart suffered misgivings. Could he live up to the character that somehow had forestalled his advent in Grass Valley? Surely life was measured differently here in the Tonto Basin.

The children, bundling their treasures to their bosoms, were dragged off to bed in some remote part of the house from which their laughter and voices came back with its happy significance. Jean forthwith had an interested audience. How eagerly these lonely pioneer people listened to news of the outside world! Jean talked until he was hoarse. In their turn, his hearers told him much that had never found place in the few and short letters he had received since he had been left in Oregon. His mother, who was part Nez Percé Indian, had pined away in Arizona and found a grave there. That, however, was the only sad note in their reminiscences. Not a word about sheepmen or any hint of rustlers! Jean marked the omission and thought all the more seriously of probabilities because nothing was said. Altogether the evening was a happy reunion of a family at which all the living members were present. Jean grasped that this fact was one of significant satisfaction to his father. "Shore, we're all goin' to live together heah," he declared. "I staked this range. I call most of this valley mine. We'll run up a cabin for Ann soon as she says the word. An' you, Jean, where's your girl? I shore told you to fetch her."

"Dad, I didn't have one," replied Jean.

"Wal, I wish you had," returned the rancher. "You'll go courtin' one of these Tonto hussies that I might object to."

"Why, Father, there's not a girl in the valley Jean would look at," interposed Ann Isbel with spirit.

Jean laughed the matter aside, but he had an uneasy memory. Aunt Mary averred, after the manner of relations, that Jean would play havoc among the women of the settlement. Jean retorted that at least one member of the Isbels should hold out against folly and love and marriage, and fighting the agents that had reduced the family to these few present. "I'll be the last Isbel to go under," he concluded.

"Son, you're talkin' wisdom," said his father. "An' shore that reminds me of the uncle you're named after, Jean Isbel! Wal, he was my youngest brother an' shore a fire-eater. Our mother was a French Creole from Louisiana, an' Jean must have inherited some of his fightin' nature from her. When the War Between the States started, Jean an' I enlisted. I was crippled before we ever got to the front. But Jean went through three years before he was killed. His company had orders to fight to the last man. An' Jean fought an' lived long enough just to be that last man."

At length Jean was finally left alone with his father.

"Reckon you're used to bunkin' outdoors?" grunted the rancher rather abruptly.

"Most of the time," replied Jean.

"Wal, there's room in the house, but I want you to sleep out. Come, get your beddin' an' gun. I'll show you."

They went outside on the porch where Jean shouldered

his roll of tarpaulin and blankets. His rifle, in its saddle sheath, leaned against the door. His father took it up and, half pulling it out, looked at it by the starlight. "Forty-Four, eh? Wal, wal, there's shore no better, if a man can shoot straight." At the moment a big gray dog trotted up to sniff at Jean. "An' heah's your bunkmate, Shepp. He's part loafer, Jean. His mother was a favorite shepherd dog of mine. His father was a big timber wolf that took me two years to kill. Some bad wolf packs runnin' this basin."

The night was cold and still, darkly bright under moon and stars; the smell of hay seemed to mingle with that of cedar. Jean followed his father around the house and up a gentle slope of graze to the edge of the cedar line. Here several trees with low-sweeping, thick branches forming a dense, impenetrable shade.

"Son, your uncle Jean was scout for Liggett, one of the greatest Rebels the South had," said the rancher. "An' you're goin' to be scout for the Isbels of Tonto. Reckon you'll find it 'most as hot as your uncle did. Spread your bed inside. You can see out, but no one can see you. Reckon there's been some queer happenin's 'round heah lately. If Shepp could talk, he'd shore have lots to tell us. Bill an' Guy have been sleepin' out, trailin' strange lion tracks, an' all that. But shore whoever's been prowlin' around heah was too sharp for them. Some bad, crafty, light-steppin' woodsmen 'round heah, Jean. Three mawnin's ago, just after daylight, I stepped out the back door. An' some one of those sneaks I'm talkin' aboot took a shot at me. Missed my head by a quarter of an inch! To-morrow I'll show you the bullet hole in the door post an' some of my gray hairs that're stickin' in it!"

"Dad!" ejaculated Jean with a hand outstretched. "That's awful. You frighten me."

"No time to be scared," replied his father calmly. "They're shore goin' to kill me. That's why I wanted you home. . . . In there with you now. Go to sleep. You shore can trust Shepp to wake you if he gets scent or sound. An' good night, my son. I'm sayin' that I'll rest easy tonight."

Jean mumbled a good night and stood watching his father's shining white head move away under the starlight. Then the tall dark form vanished, a door closed, and all was still. The dog Shepp licked Jean's hand. Jean felt grateful for that warm touch. For a moment he sat on his roll of bedding, his thought still locked on the shuddering revelation of his father's words: *They're shore goin' to kill me*. The shock of inaction passed. Jean pushed his pack in the dark opening, and, crawling inside, he unrolled it and made his bed.

When at length he was comfortably settled for the night, he breathed a long sigh of relief. What bliss to relax! A throbbing and burning of his muscles seemed to begin with his rest. The cool starlit night, the smell of cedar, the moan of wind, the silence all were real to his senses. After long weeks of arduous travel he was home. The warmth of the welcome still lingered, but it seemed to have been pierced by an icy thrust. What lay before him? The shadow in the eyes of his aunt, in the younger fresher eyes of his sister—Jean connected that with the meaning of his father's tragic words. Far past was the morning that had been so keen—the breaking of camp in the sunlit forest—the riding down the brown aisles under the pines—the music of bleating lambs that had called him not to pass by. Thought of Ellen Jorth recurred. Had he met her only that morning? She was up there in the forest, asleep under the starlit pines. Who was she? What was her story? That savage fling of her skirt, her little speech, and passionate, flaming face—they

55

haunted Jean. They were crystallizing into simpler memories, growing away from his bewilderment, and therefore at once sweeter and more doubtful. "Maybe she meant differently from what I thought," Jean soliloquized. "Anyway, she was honest." Both shame and thrill possessed him at the recall of an insidious idea—dare he go back and find her and give her the last package of gifts he had brought from the city? What might they mean to poor ragged untidy beautiful Ellen Jorth? The idea grew on Jean. It could not be dispelled. He resisted stubbornly. It was bound to go to its fruition. Deeply into his mind had sunk an impression of her need—a material need that brought spirit and pride to abasement. From one picture to another his memory wandered, from one speech and act of hers to another, choosing, selecting, casting aside, until clear and sharp as the stars shone the words—*Oh, I've been kissed before!*—that stung him now. By whom? Not by one man, but by several, by many, she had meant. Pshaw! He had only been sympathetic and drawn by a strange girl in the woods. Tomorrow he would forget. Work there was for him in Grass Valley. He reverted uneasily to the remark of his father until at last sleep claimed him.

A cold nose against his chest, a low whine awakened Jean. Shepp was beside him, keen, wary, intense. The night appeared well advanced toward dawn. Far away a cock crowed, then near at hand one answered in clarion voice. "What is it, Shepp?" whispered Jean, and he sat up. The dog smelled or heard something suspicious to his nature, but whether man or animal Jean could not tell.

56

Chapter Three

The morning star, large, intensely blue-white, magnificent
in its dominance of the clear night sky, hung over the dim,
dark valley ramparts. The moon had gone down, and all the
other stars were wan pale ghosts. Presently the strained
vacuum of Jean's ears vibrated to a low roar of many hoofs.
It came from the open valley, along the slope to the south.
Shepp acted as if he wanted the word to run. Jean laid a
hand on the dog. "Hold on, Shepp," he whispered. Then,
hauling on his boots and slipping into his coat, Jean took his
rifle, and stole out into the open. Shepp appeared to be well
trained, for it was evident that he had a strong natural tendency to run off and hunt for whatever had roused him.
Jean thought it more than likely that the dog scented an animal of some kind. If there were men prowling around the
ranch, Shepp might have been just as vigilant, but it seemed
to Jean that the dog would have shown less eagerness to
leave him, or none at all.

In the stillness of the morning it took Jean a moment to
locate the direction of the wind, which was very light and
coming from the south. In fact, that little breeze had borne
the low roar of tramping hoofs. Jean circled the ranch house
to the right, and kept along the slope at the edge of the cedars. It struck him suddenly how well fitted he was for work
of this sort. All he had ever done, except for his few years in
school, had been done in the open. All the leisure he had
ever been able to maintain had been given to his ruling passion for hunting and fishing. Love of the wild had been

born in Jean. At this moment he experienced a grim assurance of what his instinct and his training might accomplish, if directed to a stern and daring end. Perhaps his father understood this, perhaps the old Texan had some little reason for his confidence.

Every few paces Jean halted to listen. All objects, of course, were indistinguishable in the dark gray obscurity, except when he came close upon them. Shepp showed an increasing eagerness to bolt out into the void. When Jean had traveled half a mile from the house, he heard a scattered trampling of cattle on the run, and farther out a low strangled bawl of a calf. "A-huh," muttered Jean. "Cougar or some varmint pulled down that calf." Then he discharged his rifle in the air and yelled with all his might. It was necessary then to yell again to hold Shepp back.

Thereupon Jean set forth down the valley, and tramped out and across and around, as much to scare away whatever had been after the stock as to look for the wounded calf. More than once he heard cattle moving away ahead of him, but he could not see them. Jean let Shepp go, hoping the dog would strike a trail, but Shepp neither gave tongue nor came back. Dawn began to break, and in the growing light Jean searched around until at last he stumbled over a dead calf, lying in a little bare wash where water ran in wet seasons. Big wolf tracks showed in the soft earth. "Loafers," said Jean, as he knelt and just covered one track with his spread hand. "We had wolves in Oregon, but not as big as these. Wonder where that wolf-dog, Shepp, went. Wonder if he can be trusted where wolves are concerned. I'll bet not, if there's a she-wolf runnin' around."

Jean found tracks of two wolves, and he trailed them out of the wash, then lost them in the grass. But guided by their direction, he went on, and climbed a slope to the cedar line, where in the dusty patches he found the tracks again. "Not scared much," he muttered, as he noted the slow-trotting tracks. "Well, you old gray loafers, we're goin' to clash." Jean knew from many a futile hunt that wolves were the wariest and most intelligent of wild animals in the West. From the top of a low foothill he watched the sun rise, and then no longer wondered why his father waxed eloquent over the beauty and location and luxuriance of this grassy valley. It was large enough to make rich a good many ranchers. Jean tried to restrain any curiosity as to his father's dealings in Grass Valley until the situation had been made clear.

Moreover, Jean wanted to love this wonderful country. He wanted to be free to ride and hunt and roam to his heart's content, and, therefore, he dreaded hearing his father's claims. Jean threw off forebodings. Nothing ever turned out as badly as it presaged. He would think the best until certain of the worst. The morning was gloriously bright, and already the frost was glisteningly wet on the stones. Grass Valley shone like burnished silver dotted with innumerable black spots. Burros were braying their discordant messages to one another; the colts were romping in the fields; stallions were whistling; cows were bawling. A cloud of blue smoke hung low over the ranch house, slowly wafting away in the wind. Far out in the valley a dark group of horsemen were riding toward the village. Jean glanced thoughtfully at them and reflected that he seemed destined to harbor suspicion of all men new and strange to him. Above the distant village stood the darkly green foothills leading up to the craggy slopes and then ending in the Tonto Rim, a red, black-fringed mountain front, beautiful in the morning sunlight, lonely, serene, and mysterious against the level skyline. Mountains, ranges, distances unknown to Jean always called to him—to come, to seek, to explore, to find, but no wild horizon ever before beckoned to him as this one. The subtly vague emotion that had gone to sleep with him last night awoke now hauntingly. It took effort to dispel the desire to think, to wonder.

Upon his return to the house, he went around on the valley side, so as to see the place by light of day. His father had built for permanence. Evidently there had been three constructive periods in the history of that long, substantial, picturesque log house. Few nails and little sawed lumber and no glass had been used. Strong and skillful hands, axes and a crosscut saw had been the prime factors in erecting this habitation of the Isbels.

"Good mawnin', Son!" called his father's cheery voice from the porch. "Shore we-all heard you shoot an' the crack of that Forty-Four was as welcome as May flowers."

Bill Isbel looked up from a task over a saddle girth and inquired pleasantly if Jean ever slept of nights.

Guy Isbel laughed and there was warm regard in the gaze he bent on Jean. "You ole Indian," he drawled slowly. "Did you get a bead on anythin'?"

"No. I shot to scare away what I found to be some of your loafers," replied Jean. "I heard them pullin' down a calf. An' I found tracks of two whoppin' big wolves. I found the dead calf, too. Reckon the meat can be saved. Dad, you must lose a lot of stock here."

"Wal, Son, you shore hit the nail on the haid," replied the rancher. "What with lions an' bears an' loafers . . . an' two-footed loafers of another breed . . . I've lost five thousand dollars in stock this last year."

"Dad! You don't mean it!" exclaimed Jean in astonishment. To him that sum represented a small fortune.

"I shore do," answered his father.

Jean shook his head as if he could not understand such an enormous loss where there were keen, able-bodied men about. "But that's awful, Dad. How could it happen? Where were your herders an' cowboys? An' Bill an' Guy?"

Bill Isbel shook a vehement fist at Jean and retorted in earnest, having manifestly been hit in a sore spot. "Where was me an' Guy, huh? Wal, my Oregon brother, we was heah, all year, sleepin' more or less about three hours out of every twenty-four . . . ridin' our boots off . . . an' we couldn't keep down that loss."

"Jean, you-all have a mighty tumble comin' to you out heah," said Guy complacently.

"Listen, Son," spoke up the rancher. "You want to have some hunches before you figure on our troubles. There's two or three packs of loafers, an' in wintertime they are hell to deal with. Lions thick as bees, an' shore bad when the snow's on. Bears will kill a cow now an' then. An' whenever an' old silvertip comes moseyin' across from the Mazatzals, he kills stock. I'm in with half a dozen cattlemen. We all work together, an' the whole outfit cain't keep these varmints down. Then two years ago the Hash Knife Gang come into the Tonto."

"Hash Knife Gang? What a pretty name!" replied Jean. "Who're they?"

"Rustlers, Son. An' shore the real old Texas brand. The old Lone Star state got too hot for them, an' they followed the trail of a lot of other Texans who needed a healthier climate. Some two hundred Texans around heah, Jean, an' maybe a matter of three hundred inhabitants in the Tonto, all told, good an' bad. Reckon it's aboot half an' half."

A cheery call from the kitchen interrupted the conversation of the men.

"You-all come to breakfast!"

61

During the meal, the old rancher talked to Bill and Guy about the day's order of work and from this Jean gathered an idea of what a big cattle business his father conducted. After breakfast Jean's brothers manifested keen interest in the new rifles. These were unwrapped and cleaned, and taken out for testing. The three rifles were .44-caliber Winchesters, the kind of rifle Jean had found most effective. He tried them out first, and the shots he made were satisfactory to him, and amazing to the others. Bill had used an old Henry rifle. Guy did not favor any particular rifle. The rancher pinned his faith on the famous old .50-caliber single-shot buffalo gun, mostly called a needle gun. "Wal, reckon I'd better stick to mine. Shore you cain't teach an old dog new tricks. But you boys may do well with the Forty-Fours. Pack 'em on your saddles an' practice when you see a coyote."

Jean found it difficult to convince himself that this interest in rifles and marksmanship had any sinister compulsion back of it. His father and brothers had always been this way. Rifles were as important to pioneers as plows, and their skillful use was an achievement every frontiersman tried to attain. Friendly rivalry had always existed among the members of the Isbel family—even Ann Isbel was a good shot. But such proficiency in the use of firearms and life in the open that was correlative with it had not dominated them as it had Jean. Bill and Guy Isbel were born cattlemen—chips off the old block. Jean began to hope that his father's letter was an exaggeration and particularly that the fatalistic speech of last night—"They are goin' to kill me."—was just a moody inclination to see the worst side. Still, even as Jean tried to persuade himself of this more hopeful view, he recalled many references to the peculiar reputation of Texans for gun-throwing, for feuds, for never-ending hatreds. In Oregon the Isbels had lived among industrious and peaceful pioneers from all over the States. To be sure the life had been rough and primitive, and there had been fights on occasions, although no Isbel had ever killed a man. But now they had become fixed in a wilder and sparsely settled country, among men of their own breed. Jean was afraid his hopes had only sentiment to foster them. Nevertheless he forced back a strange brooding mental state and resolutely held up the brighter side. Whatever the evil conditions existing in Grass Valley, they could be met with intelligence and courage, with an absolute certainty that it was inevitable they must pass away. Jean refused to consider the old fatal law that at certain wild times and wild places in the West certain men had to pass away to change evil conditions.

"Wal, Jean, ride around the range with the boys," said the rancher. "Meet some of my neighbors, Jim Blaisdell in particular. Take a look at the cattle. An' pick out some hosses for yourself."

"I've seen one already," declared Jean quietly. "A black with white face. I'll take him."

"Shore you know a hoss. To my eye, he's my pick. But the boys don't agree. Bill 'specially has degenerated into a fancier of pitchin' hosses. Ann can ride that black. You try him this mawnin' . . . an', Son, enjoy yourself."

True to his first impression, Jean named the black horse Whiteface and fell in love with him before ever he swung a leg over him. Whiteface appeared spirited yet gentle. He had been trained instead of being broken. Of hard bits and quirts and spurs he had no experience. He liked to do what his rider wanted him to do. A hundred or more horses grazed in the grassy meadows, and, as Jean rode in among them, it was a pleasure to see stallions throw heads and ears up, and whistle or snort. Whole troops of colts and two-year-olds raced with flying tails and manes.

Beyond these pastures stretched the ranges and Jean saw the gray-green expanse speckled by thousands of cattle. The scene was inspiring. Jean's brothers led him all around, meeting some of the herders and riders employed on the ranch, one of whom was a burly, grizzled man with eyes reddened and narrowed by much riding in wind and sun and dust. His name was Evarts and he was father of the lad who Jean had met near the village. Evarts was busily skinning the calf that had been killed by the wolves. "See heah, you Jean Isbel," said Evarts. "It shore was about time you come home. We-all hears you hev' an eye fer tracks. Wal, mebbe you can kill Old Gray, the loafer that did this job. He's pulled down nine calves an' yearlin's this last two months that I know of. An' we've not had the spring roundup."

Grass Valley widened to the southeast. Jean would have been perplexed by having to estimate the square miles in it. Yet it was not vast acreage so much as rich pasture that made it such a wonderful range. Several ranches lay along the western slope of this section. Jean was informed that open parks and swales, and little valleys nestling among the foothills, wherever there was water and grass, had been settled by ranchers. Every summer a few more families ventured in.

Blaisdell struck Jean as being a lion-like type of Texan, both in his broad bold face, his huge head with its upstanding tawny hair like a mane, and in the speech and force that betokened the nature of his heart. He was not as old as Jean's father. He had a rolling voice, with the same drawling intonation characteristic of all Texans, and blue eyes that still held the fire of youth. Quite a marked contrast he presented to the lean, rangy, hard-jawed, intent-eyed men Jean had begun to accept as Texans.

Blaisdell took time for a curious scrutiny and study of Jean that, frank and kindly as it was and evidently adjusting the impressions gotten from hearsay, still bespoke the attention of one used to judging men for himself, and in this particular case having reasons of his own for so doing.

"Wal, you're like your sister Ann," said Blaisdell. "Which you may take as a compliment, young man. Both of you favor your mother. But you're an Isbel. Back in Texas there are men who never wear a glove on their right hands, an' shore I reckon, if one of them met up with you sudden, he'd think some graves had opened an' he'd go for his gun."

Blaisdell's laugh pealed out with a deep pleasant roll. Thus he planted in Jean's sensitive mind a significant thought-provoking idea about the Isbels past and gone. His further remarks, likewise, were exceedingly interesting to Jean. The settling of the Tonto Basin by Texans was a subject often in dispute. His own father had been in the first party of adventurous pioneers who had traveled up from the south to cross over the Reno Pass of the Mazatzals, into the basin. "Newcomers from outside get impressions of the Tonto accordin' to the first settlers they meet," declared Blaisdell. "An' shore it's my belief these first impressions never change. Just so strong they are! Wal, I've heard my father say there were men in his wagon train that got run out of Texas, but he swore he wasn't one of them. So I reckon that sort of talk held good for twenty years, an' for all the Texans who emigrated, except, of course, such notorious rustlers as Daggs, an' men of his ilk. Shore we've got some badmen heah. There's no law. Possession used to mean more than it does now. Daggs an' his Hash Knife Gang have begun to hold forth with a high hand. No small rancher can keep enough stock to pay for his labor."

At the time of which Blaisdell was speaking—1887— there were not many sheepmen and cattlemen in the Tonto, considering its vast area, but these, on account of the extreme wildness of the broken country, were limited to the comparatively open Grass Valley and its adjacent environs. Naturally as the inhabitants increased and stock raising grew in proportion, grazing and water rights had become matters of extreme importance. Sheepmen ran their flocks up on the Tonto Rim in summertime and down in the Tonto Basin in wintertime. A sheepman could throw a few thousand sheep around a cattleman's ranch and ruin him. The range was free. It was as fair for sheepmen to graze their herds anywhere as it was for cattlemen. This, of course, did not apply to the few acres of cultivated ground that a rancher could call his own, but very few cattle could have been raised on such limited areas. Blaisdell said that the sheepmen were unfair because they could have done just as well, although perhaps at more labor, by keeping to the ridges and leaving the open valley and little flats to the ranchers. Formerly there had been room enough for all. Now the grazing ranges were being encroached upon by sheepmen newly come to the Tonto. To Blaisdell's way of thinking this rustler menace was more serious than the sheeping-off of the range for the simple reason that no cattleman knew exactly who the rustlers were and the more complex and significant reason that the rustlers did not steal sheep.

"Texas was over-stocked with badmen an' fine steers," concluded Blaisdell. "Most of the first an' some of the last have struck the Tonto. The sheepmen have now got distributin' points for wool an' sheep at Maricopa an'

Phoenix. They've shore waxed strong an' bold."

"A-huh . . . an' what's likely to come of these men?" queried Jean.

"Ask your dad," replied Blaisdell.

"I will. But I reckon I'd be obliged for your opinion."

"Wal, short an' sweet it's this . . . Texas cattlemen will never allow the range they stocked to be overrun by sheepmen."

"Who's this man, Greaves?" went on Jean. "Never run into anyone like him."

"Greaves is hard to figure. He's a snaky customer in deals. But he seems to be good to the poor people 'round heah. Says he's from Missouri. Ha! Ha! He's as much Texan as I am. He rode into the Tonto without even a pack to his name. An' presently he builds his stone house an' freights supplies in from Phoenix. Appears to buy an' sell a good deal of stock. For a while it looked like he was steerin' a middle course between cattlemen an' sheepmen. Both sides made a rendezvous of his store, where he heard the grievances of each. Lately he's leanin' to the sheepmen. No-body has accused him of that yet. But it's time some cat-tleman called his bluff."

"Of course, there are honest and square sheepmen in the basin?" queried Jean.

"Yes, an' some of them are not unreasonable. But the new fellows that dropped in on us the last few years . . . they're the ones we're goin' to clash with."

"This . . . sheepman . . . Jorth?" went on Jean, in slow hesitation, as if compelled to ask what he would rather not learn.

"Jorth must be the leader of this sheep faction that's harryin' us ranchers. He doesn't make threats or roar around like some of them. But he goes on raisin' an' buyin'

67

more an' more sheep. An' his herders have been grazin' down all around us this winter. Jorth's got to be reckoned with."

"Who is he?"

"Wal, I don't know enough to talk about. Your dad never said so, but I think he an' Jorth knew each other in Texas years ago. I never saw Jorth but once. That was in Greaves's barroom. Your dad an' Jorth met that day, for the first time in this country. Wal, I've not known men for nothin'. They just stood stiff an' looked at each other. Your dad was aboot to draw. But Jorth made no sign to throw a gun."

Jean saw the growing and weaving and thickening threads of a tangle that had already involved him, and the sudden pang of regret he sustained was not wholly because of sympathies with his own people. "The other day, back up in the woods on the rim, I ran into a sheepman who said his name was Colter. Who is he?"

"Colter? Shore, he's a new one. What'd he look like?"

Jean described Colter with a readiness that spoke volumes for the vividness of his impressions.

"I don't know him," replied Blaisdell. "But that only goes to prove my contention that any fellow runnin' wild in the woods can say he's a sheepman."

"Colter surprised me by callin' me by my name," continued Jean. "Our little talk wasn't exactly friendly. He said a lot about my bein' sent for to run sheepherders out of the country."

"Shore that's all over," replied Blaisdell seriously. "You're a marked man already."

"What started such rumor?"

"Shore you cain't prove it by me. But it's not taken as rumor. It's got to the sheepmen as hard as bullets."

68

"A-huh, that accounts for Colter's seemin' a little sore under the collar. Well, he said they were goin' to run sheep over Grass Valley, an' for me to take that hunch to my dad."

Blaisdell had his chair tilted back and his heavy boots against a post of the porch. Down he thumped. His neck corded with a sudden rush of blood and his eyes changed to blue fire. "The hell he did!" he ejaculated in furious amazement.

Jean gauged the brooding, rankling hurt of this old cattleman by his sudden break from the cool, lazy Texan manner. Blaisdell cursed under his breath, swung his arms violently, as if to throw a last doubt or hope aside, and then relapsed to his former state. He laid a brown hand on Jean's knee.

"Two years ago I called the cards," he said quietly. "It means a Grass Valley war."

Not until late that afternoon did Jean's father broach the subject uppermost in his mind. Then at an opportune moment he drew Jean away into the cedars out of sight.

"Son, I shore hate to make your homecomin' unhappy," he said with evidence of agitation, "but so help me God I have to do it!"

"Dad, you called me prodigal, an' I reckon you was right. I've shirked my duty to you. I'm ready now to make up for it," replied Jean feelingly.

"Wal, wal, shore that's fine-spoken, my boy. . . . Let's set down heah an' have a long talk. First off, what did Jim Blaisdell tell you?"

Briefly Jean outlined the neighbor rancher's conversation. Then Jean recounted his experience with Colter and concluded with Blaisdell's reception of the sheepmen's threat. If Jean expected to see his father rise up like a lion in his wrath, he made a huge mistake. This news of Colter and his talk never struck even a spark from Gaston Isbel.

"Wal," he began thoughtfully, "reckon there are only two points in Jim's talk I need touch on. There's shore goin' to be a Grass Valley war. An' Jim's idea of the cause of it seems to be pretty much the same as that of all the other cattlemen. It'll go down a black blot on the history page of the Tonto Basin as a war between rival sheepmen an' cattlemen. Same old fight over water an' grass! Jean, my son, that is wrong. It'll not be a war between sheepmen an' cattlemen, but a war of honest ranchers against rustlers maskin' as sheep raisers. Mind you, I don't belittle the trouble between sheepmen an' cattlemen in Arizona. It's real an' it's vital an' it's serious. It'll take law an' order to straighten out the grazin' question. Someday the government will keep sheep off of cattle ranges. So get things right in your mind, my son. You can trust your dad to tell the absolute truth. In this fight that'll wipe out some of the Isbels . . . maybe all of them . . . you're on our side of justice an' right. Knowin' that, a man can fight a hundred times harder than he who knows he is a liar an' a thief."

The old rancher wiped his perspiring face and breathed slowly and deeply. Jean sensed in him the rise of a tremendous emotional strain. Wonderingly he watched the keen-lined face. More than material worries were at the root of brooding, mounting thoughts in his father's eyes.

"Now next, take what Jim said about your comin' to chase these sheepherders out of the valley. Jean, I started that talk. I had my tricky reasons. I know these greaser sheepherders an' I know the respect Texans have for a gunman. Some say I bragged. Some say I'm an old fool in his dotage, ravin' aboot a favorite son. But they are people who hate me an' are afraid. True, Son, I talked with a purpose, but shore I was mighty cold an' steady when I did it. My feelin' was that you'd do what I'd do if I were thirty years younger. No, I reckoned you'd do more, for I figured on your blood. Jean, you're Indian an' Texan an' French, an' you've trained yourself in the Oregon woods. When you were only a boy of twenty, few marksmen I ever knew could beat you, an' I never saw your equal for eye an' ear, for trackin' a hoss, for all the gifts that make a woodsman. Wal, rememberin' this an' seein' the trouble ahead for the Isbels, I just broke out whenever I had a chance. I bragged before men I'd reason to believe would take my words deep. For instance not long ago I missed some stock, an' happenin' into Greaves's place one Saturday night I shore talked loud. His barroom was full of men an' some of them were in my black book. Greaves took my talk a little testy. He said . . . 'Wal, Gass, mebbe you're right aboot some of these cattle thieves livin' among us, but ain't they jest as liable to be some of your friends or relatives as Ted Meeker's or mine or anyone around heah?' That was where Greaves an' me fell out. I yelled at him . . . 'No, by God, they're not. My record heah an' that of my people is open. The least I can say for you, Greaves, an' your crowd is that your records fade away on dim trails.' Then he said nasty-like . . . 'Wal, if you could work out all the dim trails in the Tonto, you'd shore be surprised!' Then I roared. Shore that was the chance I was lookin' for. I swore the trails he hinted at would be tracked to the holes of the rustlers who made them. I told him I had sent for you an', when you got heah, these slippery mysterious thieves, whoever they were, would shore have hell to pay. Greaves said he hoped so, but he was afraid I was partial to my Indian son. Then we had hot words. Blaisdell got between us. When I was leavin', I took a partin' fling at him. 'Greaves, you ought to know the Isbels, considerin' you're from Texas. Maybe you've got reasons for throwin' taunts at my claims for my son Jean. Yes, he's got Indian in him an' that'll be the worse for the men who will have to meet him. I'm tellin' you, Greaves, Jean Isbel is the black sheep of the family. If you ride down his record, you'll find he's shore in line to be another Poggin, or Reddy Kingfisher, or Hardin or any of the Texas gunmen you ought to remember. Greaves, there are men rubbin' elbows with you right heah that my Indian son is goin' to track down!' "

Jean bent his head in stunned cognizance of the notoriety with which his father had chosen to affront any and all Tonto Basin men who were under the ban of his suspicion. What a terrible reputation and trust to have saddled upon him! Thrills and strange heated sensations seemed to rush together inside Jean, forming a hot ball of fire that threatened to explode. A retreating self made full protests. He felt his now pale face giving away before this older, grimmer man.

"Son, if I could have looked forward to anythin' but blood spillin', I'd never have given you such a reputation to uphold," continued the rancher. "What I'm goin' to tell you now is my secret. My other sons an' Ann have never heard it. Jim Blaisdell suspects there's somethin' strange, but he doesn't know. I'll shore never tell anyone else but you. An' you must promise to keep my secret now an' after I am gone."

"I promise," said Jean.

"Wal, now to get it out," began his father, breathing hard. His face twitched and his hands clenched. "The sheepman heah I have to reckon with is Lee Jorth, a lifelong enemy of mine. We were born in the same town, played to-

72

gether as children, an' fought with one another as boys. We never got along together. An' we both fell in love with the same girl. It was nip and tuck for a while. Ellen Sutton belonged to one of the old families of the South. She was a beauty, rich an' courted, an' I reckon it was hard for her to choose. But I won her an' we became engaged. Then the war broke out. I enlisted with my brother Jean. He advised me to marry Ellen before I left. But I would not. That was the blunder of my life. Soon after our partin', her letters ceased to come. But I didn't distrust her. That was a terrible time an' all was confusion. Then I got crippled an' put in a hospital. An' in aboot a year I was sent back home."

At this juncture Jean refrained from further gaze at his father's face.

"Lee Jorth had gotten out of goin' to war," went on the rancher in a lower, thicker voice. "He'd taken my sweetheart, Ellen. I knew the story long before I got well. He had run after her like a hound after a hare. An' Ellen let him. Wal, when I was able to get aboot, I went to see Jorth an' Ellen. I confronted them. I had to know why she had gone back on me. Lee Jorth hadn't changed any with all his good fortune. He was a liar an' a cheat even in this. He'd made Ellen believe in my dishonor. But I reckon, lies or no lies, Ellen Sutton was faithless. In my absence he had won her away from me. An' I saw that she loved him as she had never loved me. I reckon that killed all generosity in me. If she'd been imposed upon an' weaned away by his lies, an' had regretted me a little, I'd have forgiven, perhaps. But she worshipped him. She was his slave. An' I, wal, I learned what hate was.

"The war ruined the Suttons, same as so many Southerners. Lee Jorth went in for raisin' cattle. He'd gotten the Sutton range, an' after a few years he began to accumulate

73

stock. In those days every cattleman was a little bit of a thief. Every cattleman drove in an' branded calves he couldn't swear was his. Wal, the Isbels were the strongest cattle raisers in that country. An' I laid a trap for Lee Jorth, caught him in the act of brandin' calves of mine I'd marked, an' I proved him a thief. I made him a rustler. I ruined him. We met once. But Jorth was one Texan not strong on the draw, at least against an Isbel. He left the country. He had friends an' relatives, an' they started him at stock raisin' again. But he began to gamble an' he got in with a shady crowd. He went from bad to worse, an' then he came back home. When I saw the change in proud, beautiful Ellen Sutton an' how she still worshipped Jorth, it shore drove me near mad between pity an' hate. Wal, I reckon in a Texan hate outlives any other feelin'. There came a strange turn of the wheel an' my fortunes changed. Like most young bloods of the day I drank an' gambled. An' one night I run across Jorth an' some of his friends. We began to gamble. One of his crowd was a cardsharp an' he fleeced me. We quarreled. Guns were thrown. I killed my man. Aboot that period the Texas Rangers had come into existence. An', Son, when I said I never was run out of Texas, I wasn't holdin' to strict truth. I rode out on a hoss.

"I went to Oregon. There I married soon, an' there Bill an' Guy were born. Their mother did not live long. An' next I married your mother, Jean. She had some Indian blood, which for all I could see made her only the finer. She was a wonderful woman an' gave me the only happiness I ever knew. You remember her, of course, an' those home days in Oregon. I reckon I made another great blunder when I moved to Arizona. But the cattle country had always called me. I had heard of this wild Tonto Basin an' how Texans were settlin' here. An' Jim Blaisdell sent me word to come . . . that this shore was a garden spot of the West. Wal, it is. But I lost your mother heah.

"Three years ago Lee Jorth drifted into the Tonto. An' strange to me, along aboot a year or so after his comin', the Hash Knife Gang rode up from Texas. Jorth went in for raisin' sheep. Along with some other sheepmen he lives up in the rim cañons. Somewhere back in the wild brakes is the hidin' place of the Hash Knife Gang. Nobody but me I reckon associates Colonel Jorth, as he's called, with Daggs an' his gang. Maybe Blaisdell an' a few others have a hunch. But that's no matter. As a sheepman Jorth has a legitimate grievance with the cattlemen. But what could be settled by a square consideration for the good of all an' the future, Jorth will never settle. He'll never settle because he is now no longer an honest man. He's in with Daggs. I cain't prove this, Son, but I know it. I saw it in Jorth's face when I met him that day with Greaves. I saw more. I shore saw what he is up to. He'd never meet me at an even break. He's dead set on usin' this sheep an' cattle feud to ruin my family an' me, even as I ruined him. But he means more, Jean. This will be war between Texans, an' a bloody war. There are bad men in this Tonto . . . some of the worst that didn't get shot in Texas. Jorth will have some of these fellows. Now, are we goin' to wait to be sheeped off our range an' to be murdered from ambush?"

"No, we are not," replied Jean quietly.

"Wal, come down to the house," replied the rancher, and led the way without speaking until he halted by the door. There he placed his finger on a small hole in the wood at about the height of a man's head. Jean saw it was a bullet hole and that a few gray hairs stuck to its edges. The rancher stepped closer to the door post, so that his head was within an inch of the wood. Then he looked at Jean with eyes in which there glinted dancing specks of fire, like wild sparks.

"Son, this sneakin' shot at me was made three mawnin's ago. I recollect movin' my haid just when I heard the crack of a rifle. Shore was surprised. But I got inside quick."

Jean scarcely heard the latter part of this speech. He seemed doubled up inwardly, in hot and cold convulsions of changing emotion. A terrible hold upon his consciousness was about to break and let go. The first shot had been fired and he was an Isbel. Indeed, his father had made him ten times an Isbel. Blood was thick. His father did not speak to dull ears. This strife of rising tumult in him seemed the affect of years of calm, of peace in the words, of dreamy waiting for he knew not what. It was the passionate, primitive life in him that had awakened to the call of blood ties.

"That's aboot all, Son," concluded the rancher. "You understand now why I feel they're goin' to kill me. I feel it heah." With a solemn gesture he placed his broad hand over his heart. "An', Jean, strange whispers come to me at night. It seems like your mother was callin' or tryin' to warn me. I cain't explain these queer whispers. But I know what I know."

"Jorth has his followers. You must have yours," replied Jean tensely.

"Shore, Son, an' I can take my choice of the best men heah," replied the rancher with pride. "But I'll not do that. I'll lay the deal before them an' let them choose. I reckon it'll not be a long-winded fight. It'll be short an' bloody, after the way of Texans. I'm lookin' to you, Jean, to see that an Isbel is the last man!"

"My God . . . Dad! Is there no other way?" asked Jean hoarsely, and his hand went out.

"Son, you'd not ask that if you'd been heah long."

"Think of my sister Ann . . . of my brothers' wives . . . of . . . of other women! Dad, these damned Texas feuds are cruel, horrible!" burst out Jean in a passionate protest.

"Jean, would it be any easier for our women if we let those men shoot us down in cold blood?"

"Oh, no . . . no, I see, there's no hope of . . . of. . . . But, Dad, I wasn't thinkin' about myself. I don't care. Once started, I'll . . . I'll be what you bragged I was. Only it's so hard to . . . to give in. . . ."

Jean leaned an arm against the side of the cabin, and, bowing his face over it, he surrendered to the irresistible contention within his breast. As if with a wrench that strange inward hold broke. He let down. He went back. Something young, fine, and sweet died—something that was boyish and hopeful—and in its place slowly rose the dark tide of his inheritance—the savage instinct of self-preservation bequeathed by his Indian mother and the fierce feudal blood-lust of his Texan father.

Then, as he raised himself, gripped by a sickening coldness in his breast, he remembered Ellen Jorth's face as she had gazed dreamily down off the Tonto Rim—so soft, so different, with tremulous lips, sad, musing, with a far-seeing stare of dark eyes, peering into the unknown, the instinct of life still unlived. With confused vision and nameless pain Jean thought of her.

"Dad, it's hard on . . . the . . . the young folks," he said bitterly. "The sins of the fathers, you know . . . ? An' the other side. How about Jorth? Has he any children?"

What a curious gleam of surprise and conjecture Jean encountered in his father's gaze!

"He has a daughter. Ellen Jorth. Named after her mother. The first time I saw Ellen Jorth I thought she was a

77

ghost of the girl I had loved an' lost. Sight of her was like a blade in my side. But the looks of her an' what she is . . . they don't gibe. Old as I am, my heart . . . bah! Ellen Jorth is a damned hussy."

Jean Isbel went off alone into the cedars. Surrender and resignation to his father's creed should have ended his perplexity and worry. His instant and burning resolve to be as his father had represented him should have opened his mind to slow cunning, to the craft of the Indian, to the development of hate. But there seemed to be an obstacle. A cloud in the way of vision! A face limned on his memory!

Those damning words of his father's had been a shock—how little or great he could not tell. Was it only a day since he had met Ellen Jorth? What had made all the difference? Suddenly like a breath the fragrance of her hair came back to him. Then the sweet coolness of her lips! Jean trembled. He looked around him as if he were pursued or surrounded by eyes, by instincts, by fears, by incomprehensible things.

"A-huh, that must be what ails me," he muttered. "The look of her . . . an' that kiss . . . they've gone hard with me. I should never have stopped to talk . . . an' now I'm goin' to kill her father an' leave her to God knows what."

Something was wrong somewhere. Jean absolutely forgot that within the hour he had pledged his manhood, his future, and his life to a feud that could be blotted out only in blood. If he had understood himself, he would have realized that the pledge was no more thrilling and unintelligible in its possibilities than this instinct that drew him irresistibly.

"But Ellen Jorth! So . . . that explains the . . . the way she acted. Why she never hit me when I kissed her . . . an' her words, so easy an' cool-like. Hussy? That means she's bad . . . bad! Scornful of me . . . maybe disappointed be-

78

cause my kiss was innocent. It was, I swear. An' all she said . . . 'Oh, I've been kissed before.' "

Jean grew furious with himself for the spreading of a new sensation in his breast that seemed now to ache. Had he become infatuated, all in a day, with this Ellen Jorth? Was he jealous of the men who had the privilege of her kisses? No! But his reply was hot with shame, with uncertainty. The thing that was wrong seemed outside of himself. A blunder was no crime. To be attracted by a pretty girl in the woods—to yield to an impulse was no disgrace, nor wrong. He had been foolish over a girl before, although not to such a rash extent. Ellen Jorth had stuck in his consciousness and with her a sense of regret. Then swiftly he recalled his father's bitter words, the revealing—"But the looks of her an' what she is . . . they don't gibe!" In the import of these words hid the meaning of the wrong that troubled him. Broodingly he pondered over them.

"The looks of her. Yes, she was pretty. But it didn't dawn on me at first. I . . . I was sort of excited. I liked to look at her, but didn't think." And now consciously her face was called up, infinitely sweeter and more impelling for the deliberate memory. Flash of brown skin, smooth and clear—lone gaze of dark, wide eyes, steady, bold, unseeing—red, curved lips, sad and sweet—her strong clean fine face rose before Jean, eager and wistful one moment, softened by dreamy musing thought, and the next stormily passionate, full of hate, full of longing, but the more mysterious and beautiful.

"She looks like that, but she's bad," concluded Jean with bitter finality. "I might have fallen in love with Ellen Jorth if . . . if she'd been different."

But the conviction forced upon Jean did not dispel the haunting memory of her face, nor did it wholly silence the

79

deep and stubborn voice of his consciousness. Later that afternoon he sought a moment with his sister.

"Ann, did you ever meet Ellen Jorth?" he asked.

"Yes, quite often, but not lately," replied Ann.

"Well, I met her as I was ridin' along yesterday. She was herdin' sheep," went on Jean rapidly. "I asked her to show me the way to the rim. An' she walked with me a mile or so. I can't say the meetin' was not interestin', at least to me. . . . Will you tell me what you know about her?"

"Sure, Jean," replied his sister with her dark eyes fixed wonderingly and kindly on his troubled face. "I've heard a great deal, but in this Tonto Basin I don't believe all I hear. What I know I'll tell you. I first met Ellen Jorth two years ago. We didn't know each other's names then. She was the prettiest girl I ever saw. I liked her. She liked me. She seemed unhappy. The next time we met was at a roundup. There were other girls with me and they snubbed her! But I left them and went around with her. That snub cut her to the heart. She was lonely, she had no friends. She talked about herself . . . how she hated the people but loved Arizona. She had nothin' fit to wear. Her father had seen better days. I didn't need to be told that she'd once been used to riches. I never knew as well-educated and nice a girl as Ellen Jorth. Just when it looked as if we were goin' to be friends, she told me who she was and asked me my name. I told her. Jean, I couldn't have hurt her more if I'd slapped her face. She turned white. She gasped. And then she ran off. The last time I saw her was about a year ago. I was ridin' a short-cut trail to the ranch where a friend lived. And I met Ellen Jorth ridin' with a man I'd never seen. The trail was evergreen and shady. They were ridin' close and didn't see me right off. The man had his arm around her. She pushed him away. I saw her laugh. Then he got hold of her again and was kissin' her when his horse shied at sight of mine. They rode by me then. Ellen Jorth held her head high and never looked at me."

"Ann, do you think she's a bad girl?" demanded Jean bluntly.

"Bad? Oh, Jean!" exclaimed Ann in surprise and embarrassment.

"Dad said she's a damned hussy."

"Jean, Dad hates the Jorths!"

"Sister, I'm askin' you what you think of Ellen Jorth. Would you be friends with her if you could?"

"Yes."

"Then you don't believe she's bad?"

"No. Ellen Jorth is lonely, empty. She has no mother. She lives alone among rough men. Such a girl cain't keep men from handlin' her and kissin' her. Maybe she's too free. Maybe she's wild. But she's honest, Jean. You can trust a woman to tell. When she rode past me that day, her face was white and proud. She was a Jorth and I was an Isbel. She hated herself . . . she hated me. But no bad girl could look like that. She knows what's said of her all around the valley. But she doesn't care. She'd encourage gossip."

"Thank you, Ann," replied Jean huskily. "Please keep this . . . this meetin' of mine with her all to yourself, won't you?"

"Why, Jean, of course, I will."

Jean wandered away again, peculiarly grateful to Ann for reminiscing and upholding something in him that seemed a wavering part of the best of him—a chivalry that had demanded to be killed by judgment of a righteous woman. He was conscious of an uplift, a gladdening of his spirit. Yet the ache remained. More than that he found himself plunged deeper into conjecture, doubt. Had not the Ellen

Jorth incident ended? He denied his father's indictment of her and accepted the faith of his sister. "Reckon that's about all, as Dad says," he soliloquized. Yet was that all? He paced under the cedars. He watched the sun set. He listened to the coyotes. He lingered there after the call for supper, and out of the tumult of his conflicting emotions and ponderings there evolved the staggering consciousness that he must see Ellen Jorth again.

Chapter Four

Ellen Jorth hurried back into the forest, hotly resentful of the accident that had thrown her in contact with an Isbel. Disgust filled her—disgust that she had been amiable to a member of the hated family that had ruined her father. The surprise of this meeting did not come to her while she was under the spell of stronger feeling. She walked under the trees swiftly, with head erect, looking straight before her, and every step seemed a relief.

Upon reaching camp, her attention was distracted from herself. Pepe, the Mexican boy, with his shepherd dogs was trying to drive the sheep into a closer bunch to save the lambs from coyotes. Ellen loved the fleecy, tottering little lambs and at this season she hated all the prowling beasts of the forest. From this time on for weeks the flock would be besieged by wolves, lions, bears, the last of which was often bold and dangerous. The old grizzlies that killed the ewes to eat only the milk bags were particularly dreaded by Ellen. She was a good shot with a rifle but had orders from her father to let the bears alone. Fortunately such sheep-killing bears were but few and were left to be hunted by men from the ranch. Mexican sheepherders could not be depended on to protect their flocks from bears. Ellen helped Pepe drive in the stragglers, and she took several shots at coyotes skulking along the edge of the brush. The open glade in the forest was favorable for herding the sheep at night and the dogs could be depended upon to guard the flock and, in most cases, to drive predatory beasts away.

After this task, which brought the time to sunset, Ellen had supper to cook and eat. Darkness came, and a cool night wind set in. Here and there a lamb bleated plaintively. With her work done for the day, Ellen sat before a ruddy campfire and found her thoughts again centering around the singular adventure that had befallen her. Disdainfully she strove to think of something else, but there was nothing that could dispel the interest of her meeting with Jean Isbel. Thereupon she impatiently surrendered to it and recalled every word and action that she could remember. In the process of this meditation she came to an action of hers, recollection of which brought the blood tingling to her neck and cheeks, so imminently and burningly that she covered them with her hands. *What did he think of me?* she mused doubtfully. It did not matter what he thought, but she could not help wondering. When she came to the memory of his kiss, she suffered more than the sensation of throbbing, scarlet cheeks. Scornfully and bitterly she burst out: "Shore he couldn't have thought much good of me."

The half hour following this reminiscence was far from being pleasant. Proud, passionate, strong-willed Ellen Jorth found herself being a victim of conflicting emotions. The events of the day were too close. She could not understand them. Disgust and disdain and scorn could not make this meeting with Jean Isbel as if it had never been. Pride could not efface it from her mind. The more she reflected, the harder she tried to forget, the stronger grew a significance of interest. When a hint of this dawned upon her consciousness, she resented it so forcibly that she lost her temper, scattered the campfire, and went into the little teepee tent to roll in her blankets.

Thus settled, snug and warm for the night, with a shepherd dog curled at the opening of her tent, she shut her eyes and confidently bade sleep end her perplexities. But sleep did not come at her invitation. She found herself wide awake, keenly sensitive to the sputtering of the campfire, the tinkling of bells on the rams, the bleating of lambs, the sough of wind in the pines, and the hungry, sharp bark of coyotes off in the distance. Darkness had no respect for her pride. The lonesome night with its emptiness of solitude seemed to induce clamoring and strange thoughts, a confusing ensemble of all those that had annoyed her during the daytime. Only after long hours did sheer weariness bring her to slumber.

Ellen awakened late and failed of her usual alacrity. Both Pepe and the shepherd dog appeared to regard her with surprise and solicitude. Ellen's spirit was low this morning; her blood ran sluggishly. She had to fight a mournful tendency to feel sorry for herself and at first she was not very successful. There seemed to be some kind of pleasure in reveling in melancholy that her common sense told her had no reason for existence. This state of mind persisted in spite of common sense.

"Pepe, when is Antonio comin' back?" she asked.

The boy could not give her a satisfactory answer. Ellen had willingly taken the sheepherder's place for a few days, but now she was impatient to go home. She looked down the green and brown aisles of the forest until she was tired. Antonio did not return. Ellen spent the day with the sheep, and in the manifold task of caring for a thousand newborn lambs she forgot herself. This day saw the end of lambing time for that season. The forest resounded to a babble of baas and bleats. When night came, she was glad to go to bed, for what with loss of sleep and weariness she could scarcely keep her eyes open.

The following morning she awakened early, bright,

eager, expectant, full of bounding life, strangely aware of the beauty and sweetness of the scented forest, strangely conscious of some nameless stimulus to her feelings. Not long was Ellen in associating this new and delightful variety of sensations with the fact that Jean Isbel had set today for his ride up to the Tonto Rim to see her. Ellen's joyousness fled; her smile faded. The spring morning lost its magic radiance.

"Shore there's no sense in me lyin' to myself," she soliloquized thoughtfully. "It's queer of me . . . feelin' glad about him without knowin'? Lord, I must be lonesome! To be glad of seein' an Isbel, even if he is different!"

Soberly she accepted the astounding reality. Her confidence died with her gaiety; her vanity began to suffer. She caught at her admission that Jean Isbel was different; she resented it in amazement; she ridiculed it; she laughed at her naïve confession. She could arrive at no conclusion other than that she was a weak-minded, fluctuating, inexplicable little fool.

But for all that she found her mind had been made up for her, without her consent or desire, before her will had been consulted, and that inevitably and unalterably she meant to see Jean Isbel again. Long she battled with this strange decree. One moment she won a victory over this new curious self, only to lose it the next. At last out of her conflict there emerged a few convictions that left her with some shreds of pride. She hated all Isbels, and particularly she hated Jean Isbel. She was only curious—intensely curious to see if he would come back, and, if he did come, what he would do. She wanted only to watch him from some covert. She would not go near him, not let him see her or guess of her presence. Thus she assuaged her hurt vanity—thus she stifled her miserable doubts.

Long before the sun had begun to slant westward toward the mid-afternoon Jean Isbel had set as a meeting time, Ellen directed her steps through the forest to the Tonto Rim. She felt ashamed of her eagerness. She had a guilty conscience that no strange thrills could silence. It would be fun to see him, to watch him, to let him wait for her, to fool him. Like an Indian she chose the soft pine-needle mats to tread upon, and her light moccasined feet left no trace. Like an Indian, also, she made a wide detour and reached the rim a quarter of a mile west of the spot where she had talked with Jean Isbel. Here, turning east, she took care to step on the bare stones. This was an adventure, seemingly the first she had ever had in her life. Assuredly she had never before come directly to the rim without halting to look, to wonder, to worship. This time she scarcely glanced into the blue abyss. All absorbed was she in hiding her tracks. Not one chance in a thousand would she risk. The Jorth pride burned even while the feminine side of her dominated her actions. She had some difficult, rocky points to cross, then windfalls to round, and at length reached the covert she desired. A rugged, yellow point of the rim stood somewhat higher than the spot Ellen wanted to watch. A dense thicket of jack pines grew to the very edge. It afforded an ambush that even the Indian eye that Jean Isbel was credited with could never penetrate. Moreover, if by accident she made a noise and excited suspicion, she could retreat unobserved and hide in the huge rocks below the rim where a ferret could not locate her.

With her plan decided upon, Ellen had nothing to do but wait. So she repaired to the other side of the pine thicket to the edge of the rim where she could watch and listen. She knew that long before she saw Isbel, she would hear his horse. It was altogether unlikely that he would come on foot.

Shore, Ellen Jorth, you're a queer girl, she mused. *I reckon I wasn't well acquainted with you.*

Beneath her yawned a wonderful deep cañon, rugged and rocky with but few pines on the north slope, thick with dark green timber on the south slope. Yellow and gray crags, like turreted castles, stood up out of the sloping forest on the side opposite her. The trees were all sharp, spear-pointed. Patches of light green aspens showed strikingly against the dense black. The great slope beneath Ellen was serrated with narrow deep gorges, almost cañons in themselves. Shadows alternated with clear bright spaces. The mile-wide mouth of the cañon opened upon the basin down into a world of wild, timbered ranges and ravines, valleys and hills that rolled and tumbled in dark green waves to the Sierra Anchas Mountains. But for once Ellen seemed singularly unresponsive to this panorama of wildness and grandeur. Her ears were like those of a listening deer, and her eyes continually reverted to the open places along the rim.

At first, in her excitement, time flew by. Gradually, however, as the sun moved westward, she began to be restless. The soft thud of dropping pine cones, the rustling of squirrels up and down the shaggy-barked spruces, the cracking of weathered bits of rock—these caught her keen ears many times and brought her up erect and thrilling. Finally she heard a sound suggesting an unshod hoof on stone. Stealthily, then, she took her rifle and slipped back through the pine thicket to the spot she had chosen. The little pines were so close together that she had to crawl between their trunks. The ground was covered with a soft bed of pine needles, brown and fragrant. In her hurry she pricked her ungloved hand on a sharp pine cone and drew blood. She sucked the tiny wound. *Shore I'm wonderin' if that's a bad omen,* she mused, darkly thoughtful. Then she resumed her sinuous approach to the edge of the thicket, and presently reached it.

Ellen lay flat a moment to recover her breath, then raised herself on her elbows. Through an opening in the fringe of buck brush she could plainly see the promontory where she had stood with Jean Isbel and also the approaches by which he might come. Rather nervously she realized that her covert was hardly more than a hundred feet from the promontory. It was imperative that she be absolutely silent. Her eyes searched the openings along the rim. The gray form of a deer crossed one of these, and she concluded it had made the sound she had heard. Then she lay down more comfortably and waited. Resolutely she held, as much as possible, to her sensitive perceptions. The meaning of Ellen Jorth, lying in ambush just to see an Isbel, was a conundrum she refused to ponder in the present. She was doing it, and the physical act had its fascination. Her ears, tuned to all the sounds of the lonely forest, caught them and arranged them according to her knowledge of woodcraft.

A long hour passed by. The sun had slanted to a point halfway between the zenith and the horizon. Suddenly a thought confronted Ellen Jorth. "He's not comin'," she whispered. The instant that idea presented itself, she felt a blank sense of loss, a vague regret—something that must have been disappointment. Unprepared for this, she was held by surprise for a moment, and then she was stunned. Her spirit, swift and rebellious, had no time to rise in her defense. She was a lonely, guilty, miserable girl, too weak for pride to uphold, too fluctuating to know her real self. She stretched there, burying her face in the pine needles, digging her fingers into them, wanting nothing so much as that they might hide her. The moment was incomprehensible to Ellen and utterly intolerable. The sharp pine needles, piercing her wrists and cheeks, and her hot heaving breast seemed to give her exquisite relief.

The shrill snort of a horse sounded near at hand. With a shock Ellen's body stiffened. Then she quivered a little and her feelings underwent swift change. Cautiously and noiselessly she raised herself upon her elbows and peeped through the opening in the brush. She saw a man tying a horse to a bush somewhat back from the rim. Drawing a rifle from its saddle sheath, he threw it over his arm, and walked to the edge of the precipice. He gazed across the basin and appeared lost in contemplation or thought. Then he turned to look back into the forest, as if he expected someone.

Ellen recognized the lithe figure, the dark face so like an Indian's. It was Isbel. He had come. Somehow his coming seemed wonderful and terrible. Ellen shook as she leaned on her elbows. Jean Isbel, true to his word, in spite of her scorn, had come back to see her. The fact seemed monstrous. He was an enemy of her father. Long had range rumor been bandied from lip to lip—old Gass Isbel had sent for his Indian son to fight the Jorths. Jean Isbel—son of a Texan—unerring shot—peerless tracker—a bad and dangerous man! Then there flashed over Ellen a burning thought—if it were true, if he was an enemy of her father's, if a fight between Jorth and Isbel was inevitable, she ought to kill this Jean Isbel right there in his tracks as he boldly and confidently waited for her. Fool he was to think she would come. Ellen sank down and dropped her head until the strong tremor of her arms eased. That dark and grim flash of thought retreated. She had not come to murder a man from ambush, but only to watch him, to try to see what he meant, what he thought, to allay a strange curiosity.

90

After a while she looked again. Isbel was sitting in an upheaved section of the rim, in a comfortable position from which he could watch the openings in the forest and gaze as well across the west curve of the basin to the Mazatzals. He had composed himself to wait. He was clad in a buckskin suit, rather new, and it certainly showed off to advantage, compared with the ragged and soiled apparel Ellen remembered. He did not look so large. Ellen was used to the long lean rangy Arizonians and Texans. This man was built differently. He had the widest shoulders of any man she had ever seen and they made him appear rather short. But his lithe, powerful limbs proved he was not short. Whenever he moved, the muscles rippled. His hands were clasped around a knee—brown, sinewy hands, very broad, and fitting the thick muscular wrists. His collar was open, and he did not wear a scarf as did all the men Ellen knew. Then her intense curiosity at last brought her steady gaze to Jean Isbel's head and face. He wore a cap, evidently of some thin fur. His hair was straight and short and in color a dead raven-black. His complexion was dark, clear, tan, with no trace of red. He did not have the prominent cheek bones or the high-bridged nose usual with white men who were part Indian. Still he had the Indian look. Ellen caught that in the dark, intent, piercing eyes, in the wide, level, thoughtful brows, in the stern impassiveness of his smooth face. He had a straight sharp-cut profile.

Ellen thought to herself: *I saw him right the other day. Only I'd not admit it. The finest-looking man I ever saw in my life is a damned Isbel! Was that what I came out heah for?*

She lowered herself once more, and, folding her arms under her breasts, she reclined comfortably on them and searched out a smaller peep hole from which she could spy upon Isbel. As she watched him, the new and perplexing side of her mind waxed busier. Why had he come back? What did he want of her? Acquaintance, friendship, was impossible for them. He had been respectful, deferential toward her in a way that had strangely pleased until the surprising moment when he had kissed her. That had only disrupted her rather dreamy pleasure in a situation she had not experienced before. All the men she had met in this wild country were rough and bold, most of them wanted to marry her, and, failing that, they had persisted in amorous attentions not particularly flattering or honorable. They were a bad lot, and contact with them had dulled some of her sensibilities. But this Jean Isbel had seemed a gentleman. She struggled to be fair, trying to forget her antipathy, as much to understand herself as to give him due credit. True, he had kissed her, crudely and forcibly. But that kiss had not been an insult. Ellen's finer feeling forced her to believe this. She remembered the honest amazement and shame and contrition with which he had faced her, trying awkwardly to explain his bold act. Likewise, she recalled the subtle swift change in him at her words: "Oh, I've been kissed before!" She was glad she had said that. Still— was she glad, after all?

She watched him. Every little while he shifted his gaze from the blue gulf beneath him to the forest. When he turned thus, the sun shone on his face, and she caught the piercing gleam of his dark eyes. She saw, too, that he was listening. Watching and listening for her! Ellen had to still a tumult within her. It made her feel very young, very shy, very strange. All the while she hated him because he manifestly expected her to come. Several times he rose and walked a little way into the woods. The last time he looked at the westering sun and shook his head. His confidence had gone. Then he sat and gazed down into the void. But

Ellen knew he did not see anything there. He seemed an image carved in the stone of the rim, and he gave Ellen a singular impression of loneliness and sadness. Was he thinking of the miserable battle his father had summoned him to lead—of what it would cost—of its useless pain and hatred? Ellen seemed to divine his thoughts. In that moment she softened toward him, and in her soul quivered and stirred an intangible something that was like pain, that was too deep for her understanding. She felt sorry for an Isbel until the old pride resurged. What if he had admired her? She remembered his interest, the wonder and admiration, the growing light in his eyes. It had not been repugnant to her until he disclosed his name. *What's in a name?* she mused, recalling poetry learned in her girlhood. *"A rose by any other name would smell as sweet!" He's an Isbel . . . yet he might be splendid . . . noble. . . . Bah! He's not . . . and I would hate him anyhow.*

All at once Ellen felt cold shivers steal over her. Isbel's piercing gaze was directed straight at her hiding place. Her heart stopped beating. If he discovered her there, she felt that she would die of shame. Then she became aware that a blue jay was screeching in a pine above her, and a red squirrel somewhere near was chattering his shrill annoyance. These two denizens of the woods could be depended upon to espy the wariest hunter and make known his presence to their kind. Ellen had a moment of more than dread. This keen-eyed, keen-eared Indian might see right through her brushy covert, might hear the throbbing of her heart. It relieved her immeasurably to see him turn away and take to pacing the promontory, with his head bowed and his hands behind his back. He had stopped looking off into the forest. Presently he wheeled to the west, and by the light upon his face Ellen saw that the time was near sunset. Turkeys were beginning to gobble back on the ridge.

Isbel walked to his horse, and appeared to be untying something from the back of his saddle. When he came back, Ellen saw that he carried a small package apparently wrapped in paper. With this under his arm, he strode off in the direction of Ellen's camp and soon disappeared in the forest.

For a little while Ellen lay there in bewilderment. If she had made conjectures before, they were now multiplied. Where was Jean Isbel going? Ellen sat up suddenly. *Well, shore this heah beats me,* she thought. *What did he have in that package? What was he goin' to do with it?* It took no little will power to hold her there when she wanted to steal after him through the woods and find out what he meant. But his reputation influenced her and she refused to pit her cunning in the forest against his. It would be better to wait until he returned to his horse. Thus decided, she lay back again in her covet and gave her mind over to pondering curiosity. Sooner than she expected, she espied Isbel approaching through the forest empty-handed. He had not taken his rifle. Ellen averted her glance a moment and thrilled to see the rifle leaning against a rock. Verily Jean Isbel had been far removed from hostile intent that day. She watched him stride swiftly up to his horse, untie the halter, and mount. Ellen had an impression of his arrow-like straight figure and sinuous grace and ease. Then he looked back at the promontory, as if to fix a picture of it in his mind, and rode away along the Tonto Rim. She watched him out of sight. What ailed her? Something was wrong with her, but she recognized only relief.

When Isbel had been gone long enough to assure Ellen that she might safely venture forth, she crawled through the pine thicket to the rim on the other side of the point. The sun was setting behind the Black Range, shedding a golden glory over the basin. Westward the zigzag rim reached like a streamer of fire into the sun. The vast promontory jutted out with blazing beacon lights upon their stone-walled faces. Deep down the basin was turning shadowy dark blue, going to sleep for the night.

Ellen bent swift steps toward her camp. Long shafts of gold preceded her through the forest. Then they paled and vanished. The tips of pines and spruces turned gold. A hoarse-voiced old turkey gobbler was booming his *chug-a-lug* from the highest ground, and the softer cluck of hen-turkeys answered him. Ellen was almost breathless when she arrived. Two packs and a couple of lop-eared burros attested to the fact of Antonio's return. This was good news for Ellen. She heard the bleat of lambs and tinkle of bells coming nearer and nearer, and she was glad to feel that, if Isbel had visited her camp, most probably it was during the absence of the herders.

The instant she glanced into her tent she saw the package Isbel had carried. It lay on her bed. Ellen stared blankly. "The . . . the impudence of him!" she ejaculated. Then she kicked the package out of the tent. Words and action seemed to liberate a dammed-up hot fury. She kicked the package again, and thought she would kick it into the smoldering campfire, but somehow she stopped short of that. She left the thing there on the ground.

Pepe and Antonio hove in sight, driving in the tumbling woolly flock. Ellen did not want them to see the package, so with contempt for herself, and somewhat lessening anger, she kicked it back into the tent. What was in it? She peeped inside the tent, devoured by curiosity. Neat, well-wrapped, and tied packages like that were not often seen in the Tonto Basin. Ellen decided she would wait until after supper and at a favorable moment lay it unopened on the fire. What did she care what it contained? Manifestly it was a gift. She argued that she was highly incensed with this insolent Isbel who had the effrontery to approach her with some sort of present.

It developed that the usually cheerful Antonio had returned taciturn and gloomy. All Ellen could get out of him was that the job of sheepherder had taken on hazards inimical to peace-loving Mexicans. He had heard something he would not tell. Ellen helped prepare the supper, and she ate in silence. She had her own brooding troubles. Antonio presently told her that her father had said she was not to start back home after dark. After supper the herders repaired to their own tents, leaving Ellen the freedom of her campfire. Wherewith she secured the package and brought it forth to burn. Feminine curiosity rankled strong in her breast. Yielding, so far as to shake the parcel and press it, and finally tear a corner off the paper, she saw some words written in lead pencil. Bending nearer the blaze, she read: **For my sister Ann.** Ellen gazed at the big, bold handwriting, quite legible and fairly well done. Suddenly she tore the outside wrapper off completely. From printed words on the inside she gathered that the package had come from a store in San Francisco. "Reckon he fetched home a lot of presents for his folks . . . the kids . . . and his sister," muttered Ellen. "That was nice of him. Whatever this is, he shore meant it for sister Ann. Ann Isbel. Why she must be that black-eyed girl I met and liked so well before I knew she was an Isbel. His sister!"

Whereupon for the second time Ellen deposited the fascinating package in her tent. She could not burn it up just then. She had other emotions besides scorn and hate, and memory of that soft-voiced, kind-hearted, beautiful Isbel

96

girl checked her resentment. "I wonder if he is like his sister?" she said thoughtfully. It appeared to be an unfortunate thought. Jean Isbel certainly resembled his sister. "In fact, they belong to the family that ruined Dad."

Ellen went to bed without opening the package or without burning it, and to her annoyance, whatever way she laid, she appeared to touch this strange package. There was not much room in the little tent. First she put it at her head beside her rifle, but when she turned over, her cheek came in contact with it. Then she felt as if she had been stung. She moved it again, only to touch it presently with her hand. Next she flung it to the bottom of her bed where it fell upon her feet, and, whatever way she moved them, she could not escape the pressure of this undesirable and mysterious gift.

By and by she fell asleep, only to dream that the package was a caressing hand, stealing about her, feeling for hers and holding it with soft strong clasp. When she awoke, she had the strangest sensation in her right palm. It was moist, throbbing, hot, and the feel of it on her cheek was strangely thrilling and comforting. She lay awake then. The night was dark and still. Only a low moan of wind in the pines and the faint tinkle of a sheep bell broke the serenity. She felt very small and lonely, lying there in the deep forest, and try how she would it was impossible to think the same then as she did in the clear light of day. Resentment, pride, anger—they seemed abated now. If the events of the day had not changed her, they had at least brought up softer and kinder memories and emotions than she had known for long. Nothing hurt and saddened her so much as to remember the gay, happy days of her childhood, her sweet mother, her old home. Then her thought returned to Isbel and his gift. It had been years since anyone had made her a gift. What could this one be? It did not matter. The wonder was that Jean Isbel should bring it to her and that she could be perturbed by its presence. "He meant it for his sister and so he thought well of me," she said in finality.

Morning brought Ellen further vacillation. At length she rolled the obnoxious package inside her blankets, saying that she would wait until she got home and then consign it cheerfully to the flames. Antonio tied her pack on a burro. She didn't have a horse and, therefore, had to walk the several miles to her father's ranch.

She set off at a brisk pace, leading the burro and carrying her rifle. Soon she was deep in the fragrant forest. The morning was clear and cool, with just enough frost to make the sunlit grass sparkle like diamonds. Ellen felt fresh, buoyant, singularly full of life. Her youth would not be denied. It was pulsing, yearning. She hummed an old Southern tune and every step seemed one of pleasure in action, of advance toward some intangible future happiness. All that was unknown of life called to her. Her heart beat high in her breast and she walked as one in a dream. Her thoughts were swift-changing, intimate, deep, and vague, not of yesterday or today, nor of reality.

The big, gray, white-tailed squirrels crossed ahead of her on the trail, scampered over the piney ground to hop on tree trunks, and there they paused to watch her pass. The vociferous little red squirrels barked and battered at her. From every thicket sounded the gobble of turkeys. The blue jays squatted in the tree tops. A deer lifted its head from browsing and stood motionless, with long ears erect, watching her go by.

Thus happily and dreamily absorbed, Ellen covered the forest miles, and soon reached the trail that led down into the wild brakes of Chevelon Cañon. It was rough going and less conducive to sweet wanderings of mind. Ellen slowly lost them, and then a familiar feeling assailed her, one she never failed to have upon returning to her father's ranch—a reluctance, a bitter dissatisfaction with her home, a loyal struggle against the vague sense that all was not as it should be.

At the head of this cañon in a little, level, grassy meadow stood a rude one-room log shack with a leaning red stone chimney on the outside. This was the abode of a strange old man who had long lived there. His name was John Sprague and his occupation was raising burros. No sheep or cattle or horses did he own, not even a dog. Rumor had said Sprague was a prospector, one of the many who had searched that country for the Lost Dutchman gold mine. Sprague knew more about the Tonto Basin and Tonto Rim than any sheepman or rancher. From Black Butte to the Cibique, and from Chevelon Butte to Reno Pass he knew every trail, cañon, ridge, and spring, and could find his way to them in the darkest night. His fame, however, depended mostly upon the fact that he did nothing but raise burros and would raise none but black burros with white faces. These burros were the finest bred in all the basin and were in great demand. Sprague sold a few every year. He had made a present of one to Ellen although he hated to part with them. This old man was Ellen's one and only friend.

Upon her trip out to the rim with the sheep, Uncle John, as Ellen called him, had been away on one of his infrequent visits to Grass Valley. It pleased her now to see a blue column of smoke lazily lifting from the old chimney and to hear the discordant bray of burros. As she entered the clearing, Sprague saw her from the door of his shack.

"Hello, Uncle John!" she called.

"Wal, if it ain't Ellen," he replied heartily. "When I seen

thet white-faced jinny, I knowed who was leadin' her. Where you been, girl?"

Sprague was a little stoop-shouldered old man, with grizzled head and face, and shrewd gray eyes that beamed kindly on her over his ruddy cheeks. Ellen did not like the tobacco stain on his grizzled beard or the dirty, motley, ragged, ill-smelling garb he wore, but she had ceased her useless attempts to make him more cleanly.

"I've been herdin' sheep," replied Ellen. "And where have you been, Uncle? I missed you on the way over."

"Been packin' in some grub, an' I reckon I stayed longer in Grass Valley than I recollect. But thet was only natural, considerin'. . . ."

"What?" asked Ellen bluntly, as the old man paused.

Sprague took a black pipe out of his vest pocket and began rimming the bowl with his fingers. The glance he bent on Ellen was thoughtful and earnest and so kind that she feared it was pity. Ellen suddenly burned for news from the village.

"Wal, come in an' set down, won't you?" he asked.

"No, thanks," replied Ellen, and she took a seat on the chopping block. "Tell me, Uncle, what's goin' on down in the valley?"

"Nothin' much yet . . . except talk. An' thar's a heap of thet."

"*Humph!* There always was talk," declared Ellen contemptuously. "A nasty gossipy catty hole, that Grass Valley!"

"Ellen, thar's goin' to be war . . . a bloody war in the ole Tonto Basin," went on Sprague seriously.

"War? Between whom?"

"Wal, the ranchers on one side," he replied slowly.

"What ranchers?"

"The Isbels an' whatever men they pick. I reckon most people from thar, an' all the cattlemen, air on old Gass's side. Blaisdell, Gordon, Fredericks, Blue . . . they'll all be in it."

"Who are they goin' to fight?" queried Ellen sharply.

"Wal, the open talk is thet the sheepmen are forcin' this war. But thar's talk not so open an', I reckon, not very healthy for any man to whisper hyarabouts."

"Uncle John, you needn't be afraid to tell me anythin'," said Ellen. "I'd never give you away. You've been a good friend to me."

"Reckon I want to be, Ellen," he returned, nodding his shaggy head. "It ain't easy to be fond of you as I am an' keep my mouth shet. . . . I'd like to know somethin'. Have you any relatives away from hyar thet you could go to till this fight's over?"

"No. All I have so far as I know are right heah."

"How about friends?"

"Uncle John, I have none," she said sadly, with bowed head.

"Wal, wal, I'm sorry. I was hopin' you might git away."

She lifted her face. "Shore you don't think I'd run off if my dad got in a fight?" she flashed.

"I hope you will."

"I'm a Jorth," she said darkly, and dropped her head again.

Sprague nodded gloomily. Evidently he was perplexed and worried, and strangely swayed by affection for her.

"Would you go away with me?" he asked. "We could pack over to the Mazatzals and live thar till this blows over."

"Thank you, Uncle John. You're kind and good. But I'll stay with my father. His troubles are mine."

101

"A-huh! Wal, I might have reckoned so. Ellen, how do you stand on this hyar sheep an' cattle question?"

"I think what's fair for one is fair for another. I don't like sheep as much as I like cattle. But thet's not the point. The range is free. Suppose you had cattle and I had sheep. I'd feel as free to run my sheep anywhere as you were to run your cattle."

"Right. But what if you throwed your sheep 'round my range an' sheeped off the grass, so my cattle would hev' to move or starve?"

"Shore I wouldn't throw my sheep 'round your range," she declared stoutly.

"Wal, you've answered half of the question. An', now, supposin' a lot of my cattle was stolen by rustlers, but not a single one of your sheep. What'd you think then?"

"I'd shore think rustlers chose to steal cattle because there was no profit in stealin' sheep."

"Egzactly. But wouldn't you have a queer idee about it?"

"I don't know. Why queer? What're you drivin' at, Uncle John?"

"Wal, wouldn't you git kind of a hunch thet the rustlers was . . . say, a leetle friendly toward the sheepmen?"

Ellen felt a sudden vibrating shock. The blood rushed to her temple. Trembling all over, she rose. "Uncle John!" she cried.

"Now, girl, you needn't fire up thet way. Set down an' don't. . . ."

"Dare you insinuate my father has . . . ?"

"Ellen, I ain't insinuatin' nothin'," interrupted the old man. "I'm just askin' you to think. Thet's all. You're 'most grown into a young woman now. An' you've got sense. There's bad times ahead, Ellen. An' I hate to see you mix in them."

"Oh, you do make one think," replied Ellen with smarting tears in her eyes. "You make me unhappy. Oh, I know my dad is not liked in this cattle country. But it's unjust. He happened to go in for sheep raising. I wish he hadn't. It was a mistake. Dad always was a cattleman till we came heah. He made enemies . . . who . . . who ruined him. And everywhere misfortune crosses his trail. . . . But, oh, Uncle John, my dad is an honest man."

"Wal, child, I didn't mean to . . . to make you cry," said the old man feelingly, and he averted his troubled gaze. "Never mind what I said. I'm an old meddler. I reckon nothin' I could do or say would ever change what's goin' to happen. If only you wasn't a girl! Thar I go ag'in . . . Ellen, face your future an' fight your way, all youngsters hev' to do thet. An' it's the right kind of fight thet makes the right kind of man or woman. Only you must be sure to find yourself. An' by thet I mean to find the real true honest-to-God best in you an' stick to it an' die fightin' for it. You're a young woman, almost, an' a blamed handsome one. Which means you'll hev' man trouble an' a harder fight. This country ain't easy on a woman when once slander has marked her."

"What do I care for the talk down in that basin," returned Ellen. "I know they think I'm a hussy. I've let them think it. I've helped them to."

"You're wrong, child," said Sprague earnestly. "Pride an' temper! You must never let anyone think bad of you, much less help them to."

"That's everybody down there," cried Ellen passionately. "I hate them so, I'd glory in their thinkin' me bad. My mother belonged to the bad blood in Texas. I am her daughter. I know *who and what I am!* That uplifts me wherever I meet the sneaky sly suspicions of them basin people.

It shows me the difference between them and me. That's what I glory in."

"Ellen, you're a wild, headstrong child," rejoined the old man in severe tones. "Word has been passed against your good name . . . your honor . . . an' haven't you given cause fer thet?"

Ellen felt her face blanch and all her blood rush back to her heart in sickening force. The shock of his words was like a stab from a cold blade. If their meaning, and the stern just light of the old man's glance, did not kill her pride and vanity, they surely killed her girlishness. She stood mute, staring at him, with her brown trembling hands stealing up toward her bosom, as if to ward off another and a mortal blow.

"Ellen!" burst out Sprague hoarsely. "You mistook me. Aw, I didn't mean . . . what you think. I swear . . . Ellen, I'm old an' blunt. I ain't used to wimmen. But I've love for you, child, an' respect, jest the same as if you was my own . . . an' I *know* you're good. Forgive me . . . I meant only . . . hev'n't you been, say, sort of careless . . . ?"

"Careless?" queried Ellen bitterly and low.

"An' powerful thoughtless an' . . . an' blind . . . lettin' men kiss you an' fondle you . . . when you're really a growed-up woman now?"

"Yes . . . I have," whispered Ellen.

"Wal, then why did you let them?"

"I . . . I don't know. I didn't think. The men never let me alone . . . never . . . never. I got tired of everlastingly pushin' them away and sometimes . . . when they were kind . . . and I was lonely for something, I . . . I didn't mind if one or another fooled 'round me. I never thought. It never looked as you have made it look. Then . . . those few times ridin' the trail to Grass Valley . . . when people saw me . . .

then I guess I encouraged such attentions. Oh, I must be . . . I am a shameless little hussy!"

"Hush thet kind of talk," said the old man as he took her hand. "Ellen, you're only young an' lonely an' bitter. No mother . . . no friends . . . no one but a lot of rough men! It's a wonder you hev' kept yourself good. But now your eyes are open, Ellen. They're brave an' beautiful eyes, girl, an', if you stand by the light in them, you will come through any trouble. An' you'll be happy. Don't ever forgit thet. Life is bad enough, God knows, but it's unfailin' true in the end to the man or woman who picks the best in them an' stands by it."

"Uncle John, you talk so . . . so kindly. You make me have hope. There seemed really so little for me to live for . . . hope for. But I'll never be a coward again . . . nor a thoughtless fool. I'll find some good in me . . . or make some . . . and never fail it, come what will. I'll remember your words. I'll believe the future holds wonderful things for me. I'm only eighteen. Shore, all my life won't be lived heah. Perhaps this threatened fight over sheep and cattle will blow over. Somewhere there must be some nice girl to be a friend . . . a sister to me . . . and maybe some man who'd believe in spite of all they say . . . that I'm not a hussy."

"Wal, Ellen, you remind me of what I was wantin' to tell you when you first got here. Yesterday I heard you called thet name in a barroom an' thar was a feller thar who raised hell. He near killed one man an' made anther plumb eat his words. An' he scared that crowd stiff."

Old John Sprague shook his grizzled head and laughed, leaning upon Ellen as if the memory of what he had seen had warmed his heart.

"Was it . . . you?" asked Ellen tremulously.

"Me. Aw, I wasn't nowhere. Ellen, this feller was quick as a cat in his actions an' his words was like lightnin'."

"Who?" she whispered.

"Wal, no one else but a stranger jest come to these parts . . . an Isbel, too. Jean Isbel."

"Oh," murmured Ellen faintly.

"In a barroom full of men almost all of them in sympathy with the sheep crowd . . . most of them on the Jorth side . . . this Jean Isbel resented an insult to Ellen Jorth."

"No!" cried Ellen. Something terrible was happening to her mind or her heart.

"Wal, he sure did," replied the old man, "an' it's goin' to be good for you to hear all about it."

Chapter Five

Old John Sprague launched into his narration with evident zest. "I hung 'round Greaves's store most of two days. An' I heered a heap. Some of it was jest plain ole men's gab, but I reckon I got the drift of things concernin' Grass Valley. Yestiddy mornin' I was packin' my burros in Greaves's back yard, takin' my time carryin' out supplies from the store. An' at last, when I went in, I seen a strange feller was thar. Strappin' young man . . . not so young, either . . . an' he had on buckskin. Hair black as my burros, dark face, sharp eyes . . . you'd've took him fer an Injun. He carried a rifle . . . one of them new Forty-Fours . . . an' also somethin' wrapped in paper thet he seemed particular careful about. He wore a belt 'round his middle an' thar was a Bowie knife in it, carried like I've seen scouts an' Injun fighters hev' on the frontier in the 'Seventies. Thet looked queer to me, an' I reckon to the rest of the crowd thar. No one overlooked the big six-shooter he packed Texas fashion. Wal, I didn't hev' no idee this feller was an Isbel until I heered Greaves call him thet.

" 'Isbel,' said Greaves, 'reckon your money's counterfeit hyar. I cain't sell you anythin'!'

" 'Counterfeit? . . . not much,' spoke up the young feller, an' he flipped some gold twenties on the bar, where they rung like bells. 'Why not? Ain't this a store? I want a cinch strap.'

"Greaves looked particular sore thet mornin'. I'd been watchin' him fer two days. He didn't hev' much sleep, fer I

107

had my bed back of the store an' I heered men come in the night an' hev' long confabs with him. Whatever was in the wind hadn't pleased him none. An' I calkilated thet young Isbel wasn't a sight good fer Greaves's sore eyes, anyway. But he paid no more attention to Isbel. Acted jest as if he hedn't heered Isbel say he wanted a cinch strap.

"I stayed inside the store then. Thar was a lot of fellers I'd seen, an' some I knowed. Couple of card games goin' an' drinkin', of course. I soon gathered thet the general atmosphere wasn't friendly to Jean Isbel. He seen thet quick enough, but he didn't leave. Between you an' me, I sort of took a likin' to him. An' I sure watched him as close as I could, not seemin' to, you know. Reckon they all did the same, only you couldn't see it. It got jest about the same as if Isbel hadn't been in thar, only you knowed it wasn't really the same. Thet was how I got the hunch the crowd was all sheepmen or their friends. The day before I'd heered a lot of talk about this young Isbel, an' what he'd come to Grass Valley fer, an' what a bad *hombre* he was. An' when I seen him, I was bound to admit he looked his reputation.

"Wal, pretty soon in comes two more fellers, an' I knowed both of them. You know them, I'm sorry to say. Fer I'm comin' to facts now thet will shake you. The first feller was your father's Mexican foreman, Lorenzo, an' the other was Simm Bruce. I reckon Bruce wasn't drunk, but he'd sure been lookin' on red licker. When he seen Isbel, darn me if he didn't swell an' bristle all up like a mad ole turkey gobbler.

" 'Greaves,' he said, 'if thet feller's Jean Isbel, I ain't hankerin' fer the company you-all keep.' An' he made no bones of pointin' right at Isbel. Greaves looked up, dry an' sour, an' he bit out spiteful-like . . . 'Wal, Simm, we ain't got a hell of a lot of choice in this heah matter. Thet's Jean

Isbel, shore enough. Mebbe you can persuade him thet his company an' his custom ain't wanted 'round heah.'

"Jean Isbel set on the counter an' took it all in, but he didn't say nothin'. The way he looked at Bruce was sure enough for me to see thet thar might be a surprise any minnit. I've looked at a lot of men in my day, an' can sure feel events comin'. Bruce got himself a stiff drink an' then he straddles over the floor in front of Isbel.

" 'Air you Jean Isbel, son of ole Gass Isbel?' asked Bruce, sort of lolling back an' givin' a hitch to his belt.

" 'Yes, sir, you've identified me,' said Isbel, nice an' polite.

" 'My name's Bruce. I'm rangin' sheep heahaboots, an' I hev' interest in Kurnel Lee Jorth's bizness.'

" 'How do, Mister Bruce,' replied Isbel, very civil an' cool as you please. Bruce had a dry eye fer the crowd thet was now listenin' an' watchin'.' He swaggered closer to Isbel.

" 'We heered you-all come into the Tonto Basin to run us sheepmen off the range. How aboot thet?'

" 'Wal, you heered wrong,' said Isbel quietly. 'I came to work fer my father. Thet work depends on what happens.'

"Bruce began to get redder of face an' he shook a husky hand in front of Isbel. 'I'll tell you this heah, my Nez Percé Isbel,' an', when he sort of choked fer more wind, Greaves spoke up . . . 'Simm, I shore reckon thet Nez Percé handle will stick!' An' the crowd haw-hawed. Then Bruce got goin' ag'in. 'I'll tell you this heah, Nez Percé, there's been enough happen' already to run you out of Arizona.'

" 'Wal, you don't say! What, for instance?' asked Isbel, quick an' sarcastic.

"Thet made Bruce bust out puffin' an' spittin'. 'Wha-ttt, fer instance? Hah! Why, you damn' half-breed, you'll git run out fer makin' up to Ellen Jorth. Thet won't go in this heah country. Not for any Isbel.'

" 'You're a liar!' called Isbel, an' like a big cat he dropped off the counter. I heered his moccasins pat soft on the floor, an' I bet to myself thet he was as dangerous as he was quick. But his voice an' his looks didn't change even a leetle.

" 'I'm not a liar!' yelled Bruce. 'I'll make you eat thet. I can prove what I say . . . you was seen with Ellen Jorth . . . up on the rim . . . day before yestiddy. You was watched. You was with her. You made up to her. You grabbed her an' kissed her! An' I'm heah to say, Nez Percé, thet you're a marked man on this range.'

" 'Who saw me?' asked Isbel, quiet and cold. I saw then thet he had turned white in the face.

" 'You cain't lie out of it!' hollered Bruce, wavin' his hands. 'We got you daid to rights. Lorenzo saw you . . . followed you . . . watched you.' Bruce pointed at the grinnin' greaser. 'Lorenzo is Kurnill Jorth's foreman. He seen you maulin' Ellen Jorth. An' when he tells the Kurnel an' Tad Jorth an' Jackson Jorth . . . haw, haw, haw! . . . why, hell'd be a cooler place fer you than this heah Tonto.'

"Greaves an' his gang had come 'round, sure tickled to their gizzards at this mess. I noticed howsomever thet they was Texans enough to keep back to one side in case this Isbel started any action. Wal, Isbel took a look at Lorenzo. Then with one swift grab he jerked the little greaser off his feet an' pulled him close. Lorenzo stopped grinnin'. He began to look a leetle sick. But it was plain he had right on his side.

" 'You say you saw me?' demanded Isbel.

" '*Sí, señor,*' replied Lorenzo.

" 'What did you see?'

110

" 'I see *señor* an' *señorita*. I hide by manzanita. I see *señorita* like *grande señor* ver mooch. She like *señor*'s keese. She. . . .'

"Then Isbel hit the leetle greaser a back-handed crack in the mouth. Sure it was a crack. Lorenzo went over the counter backwards an' landed like a pack load of wood. An' he didn't get up.

" 'Mister Bruce,' said Isbel, 'an' you fellers who heered thet lyin' greaser . . . I did meet Ellen Jorth. An' I lost my head. I . . . I kissed her. But it was an accident. I meant no insult. I apologized . . . I tried to explain my crazy action. Thet was all. The greaser lied. Ellen Jorth was kind enough to show me the trail. We talked a little. Then . . . I suppose . . . because she was young an' pretty an' sweet . . . I lost my head. She was absolutely innocent. Thet damned greaser told a bare-faced lie when he said she liked me. The fact was she despised me. She said so. An', when she learned I was Jean Isbel, she turned her back on me an' walked away.' "

At this point of his narrative the old man halted as if to impress Ellen not only with what had just been told but particularly what was to follow. The reciting of this tale had evidently given Sprague an unconscious pleasure. He glowed. He seemed to carry the burden of a secret that he yearned to divulge. As for Ellen she was deadlocked in breathless suspense. All her emotions waited for the end. She begged Sprague to hurry.

"Wal, I wish I could skip the next chapter an' hev' only the last to tell," rejoined the old man, and he put a heavy but solicitous hand upon hers. "Simm Bruce haw-hawed loud. 'Say, Nez Percé,' he calls out, most insolent-like, 'we-all air too good sheepmen to hev' the wool pulled over our eyes. We shore know what you meant by Ellen Jorth. But

you wasn't smart when you told her you was Jean Isbel!
Haw, haw!'

"Isbel flashed a strange, surprised look from the red-faced Bruce to Greaves, and to the other men. I take it he was wonderin' if he'd heered right or if they'd got the same hunch thet'd come to him. An' I reckon he determined to make sure.

" 'Why wasn't I smart?' he asked.

" 'Shore you wasn't smart if you was aimin' to be one of Ellen Jorth's lovers,' said Bruce with a leer. 'Fer, if you hadn't given yourself away, you could hev' had her easy enough.'

"There was no mistakin' Bruce's meanin', an', when he got it out, some of the men thar laughed. Isbel kept lookin' from one to another of them. Then facin' Greaves, he said deliberately . . . 'Greaves, this drunken Bruce is excuse enough fer a showdown. I take it thet you an' he an' all these fellers are sheepmen, an' you're goin' on Jorth's side of the fence in the matter of this sheep rangin'.'

" 'Wal, Nez Percé, I reckon you hit plumb center,' said Greaves dryly. He spread wide his big hands to the other men, as if to say they'd might as well own the gig was up.

" 'All right. You're Jorth's backers. Have any of you a word to say in Ellen Jorth's defense? I tell you the Mexican lied. Believin' me or not doesn't matter. But this vile-mouthed Bruce hinted against thet girl's honor.'

"Ag'in some of the men laughed, but not so noisy, an' there was a nervous shufflin' of feet. Isbel looked sort of queer. His neck had a bulge 'round his collar. An' his eyes was like black coals of fire.

"Greaves spread his big hands again, as if to wash them of this part of the dirty argument. 'When it comes to any wimmen, I pass . . . much less play a hand fer a wildcat like

Jorth's gurl,' said Greaves, sort of cold an' thick. 'Bruce shore ought to know her. Accordin' to talk heahabouts an' what he says, Ellen Jorth has been his gurl fer two years?'

"Then Isbel turned his attention to Bruce an' I fer one begun to shake in my boots.

" 'Say thet to me!' he called.

" 'Shore she's my gurl, an' thet's why I'm a-goin' to hev' you run off this range.'

"Isbel jumped at Bruce. 'You damned drunken cur! You vile-mouthed liar! I may be an Isbel, but, by God, you can't slander thet girl to my face!' Then he moved so quick I couldn't see what he did, but I heered his fist hit Bruce. It sounded like an axe ag'in' a beef. Bruce fell clear across the room. An' by Jiminy, when he landed, Isbel was thar. As Bruce staggered up all bloody-faced, bellowin' an' spittin' out teeth, Isbel eyed Greaves's crowd an' said . . . 'If any of you make a move, it'll mean gun play!' Nobody moved, thet's sure. In fact none of Greaves's outfit was packin' guns, at least in sight. When Bruce got all the way up . . . he's a tall fellar . . . why Isbel took a full swing at him, an' knocked him back across the room ag'in' the counter. You know when a fellar's hurt by the way he yells. Bruce got thet second smash right on his big red nose. I never seen anyone so quick as Isbel. He vaulted over thet counter jest the second Bruce fell back on it, an' then with Greaves's gang in front, so he could catch any moves of theirs, he jest slugged Bruce right an' left, an' banged his head on the counter. Then, as Bruce sunk limp an' slipped down, lookin' like a bloody sack, Isbel let him fall to the floor. Then he vaulted back over the counter. Wipin' the blood off his hands, he throwed his kerchief down in Bruce's face. Bruce wasn't dead or bad hurt. He'd jest been beaten bad. He was moanin' an' slobberin'. Isbel kicked him, not hard,

113

but jest sort of disgustful. Then he faced thet crowd. 'Greaves, thet's what I think of your Simm Bruce. Tell him next time he sees me to run or pull a gun.' An' then Isbel grabbed his rifle an' package off the counter an' went out. He didn't even look back. I seen him mount his horse an' ride away. Now, girl, what hev' you to say?"

Ellen could only say good bye and the word was so low as to be almost inaudible. She ran to her burro. She could not see very clearly through tear-blurred eyes and her shaking fingers were all thumbs. It seemed she had to rush away . . . somehow . . . anywhere, not to get away from kind old John Sprague but from herself . . . this palpitating, bursting self whose feet stumbled down the trail. All . . . all seemed ended for her. That interminable story! It had taken hours. And every minute of it she had been helplessly torn asunder by feelings she had never known she possessed. This Ellen Jorth was an unknown creature. She sobbed now as she dragged the burro down the cañon trail. She sat down only to rise. She hurried only to stop. Driven, pursued, barred, she had no way to escape the flaying thoughts, no time or will to repudiate them. The death of her girlhood, the rending aside of a veil of maiden mystery only vaguely, instinctively guessed, the barren sordid truth of her life as seen by her enlightened eyes, the bitter realization of the vileness of the men of her clan in contrast to the manliness and chivalry of an enemy, the hard facts of unalterable repute as created by slander and fostered by low minds—all these were forces in a cataclysm that had suddenly caught her heart and whirled her through changes, immense and agonizing, to bring her face to face with reality, to force upon her suspicion and doubt of all she had trusted, to warn her of the dark, impending horror of a tragic, bloody feud, and lastly to teach her the supreme truth at once so

114

glorious and so terrible—that she could not escape the doom of womanhood.

About noon that day Ellen Jorth arrived at The Knoll, which was the location of her father's ranch. Three cañons met there to form a larger one. The Knoll was a symmetrical hill situated at the mouth of the three cañons. It was covered with brush and cedars, with here and there lichened rocks showing above the bleached grass. Below The Knoll was a wide grassy flat, or meadow, through which a willow-bordered stream cut its rugged, boulder-strewn bed. Water flowed abundantly at this season, and the deep washes leading down from the slopes attested to the fact of cloudbursts and heavy storms. This meadow valley was dotted with horses and cattle, and meandered away between the timbered slopes to lose itself in a green curve. A singular feature of this cañon was that a heavy growth of spruce trees covered the slope facing northwest, and the opposite slope, exposed to the sun and therefore less snow-bound in winter, held a sparse growth of yellow pines. The ranch house of Colonel Jorth stood around the rough corner of the largest of the three cañons. Rather well hidden, it did not obtrude its rude and broken-down log cabins, its squalid surroundings, its black mud holes of corrals upon the beautiful and serene meadow valley.

Ellen Jorth approached her home slowly with dragging, reluctant steps, and never before in the three unhappy years of her existence there had the ranch seemed so bare, so uncared for, so repugnant to her. As she had seen herself with clarified eyes, so now she saw her home. The cabin that Ellen lived in with her father was a single-room structure with one door and no windows. It was about twenty feet square. The huge, rugged, stone chimney had been built on the outside with the wide-open fireplace set inside the logs. Smoke was rising from the chimney. As Ellen halted at the door and began unpacking her burro, she heard the loud, lazy laughter of men. An adjoining log cabin had been built in the section with a wide-roofed hall or space between them. The door in each cabin faced the other, and there was a tall man standing in one. Ellen recognized Daggs, a neighbor sheepman, who evidently spent more time with her father than at his own home, wherever that was. Ellen had never seen it. She heard this man drawl: "Jorth, heah's your kid come home."

Ellen carried her bed inside the cabin, and unrolled it upon a couch built of boughs in the far corner. She had forgotten Jean Isbel's package, and now it fell out under her sight. Quickly she covered it. A Mexican woman, a relative of Antonio's and the only servant about the place, was squatting Indian-fashion before the fireplace, stirring a pot of beans. She and Ellen did not get along well together, and few words ever passed between them. Ellen had a canvas curtain stretched upon a wire across the small triangular corner, and that afforded her a little privacy. Her possessions were limited in number. The crude square table she had constructed herself. Upon it was a little, old-fashioned, walnut-framed mirror, a brush and comb, and a dilapidated ebony cabinet that contained odds and ends the sight of which always brought a smile of derisive self-pity to her lips. Under the table stood an old leather trunk. It had come with her from Texas and contained clothing and belongings of her mother's. Above the couch on pegs hung her scant wardrobe. A tiny shelf held several worn-out books.

When her father slept indoors, which was seldom except in winter, he occupied a couch in the opposite corner. A rude cupboard had been built against the logs next to the fireplace. It contained supplies and utensils. In the last corner, somewhat closer to the door, stood a crude table and two benches. The cabin was dark and smelled of smoke, of the stale odor of past cooked meals, of the mustiness of dry-rotting timber. Streaks of light showed through the roof where the rough-hewn shingles had split or weathered. A strip of bacon hung upon one side of the cupboard and upon the other a haunch of venison. Ellen detested the Mexican woman because she was dirty. The inside of the cabin presented the same unkempt appearance usual to it after Ellen had been away for a few days. Whatever Ellen had lost during the retrogression of the Jorths, she had kept her habits of cleanliness, and, straightening upon her return, she set to work.

The Mexican woman sullenly slouched away to her own quarters outside and Ellen was left to the satisfaction of labor. Her mind was as busy as her hands. As she cleaned and swept and dusted, she heard from time to time the voices of men, the *clip-clop* of shod horses, the bellow of cattle. A considerable time elapsed before she was disturbed.

A tall shadow darkened the doorway.

"Howdy, little one," said a lazy, drawling voice. "So you-all got home?"

Ellen looked up. A superbly built man leaned against the doorpost. Like most Texans he was light-haired and light-eyed. His face was lined and hard. His long sandy mustache hid his mouth and drooped with a curl. Spurred, booted, belted, packing a heavy gun low down on his hip, he gave Ellen an entirely new impression. Indeed, she was seeing everything strangely.

"Hello, Daggs," replied Ellen. "Where's my dad?"

"He's playin' cairds with Jackson an' Colter. Shore's

117

playin' bad, too, an' it's gone to his haid."

"Gamblin'?" queried Ellen.

"Mah child, when'd Kurnel Jorth ever play for fun?" said Daggs with a lazy laugh. "There's a stack of gold on the table. Reckon your Uncle Jackson will win it. Colter's shore out of luck."

Daggs stepped inside. He was graceful and slow. His long spurs clinked. He laid a rather compelling hand on Ellen's shoulder.

"Heah, mah gal, give us a kiss," he said.

"Daggs, I'm not your girl," replied Ellen as she slipped out from under his hand.

Then Daggs put his arm around her, not with violence or rudeness, but with an indolent, affectionate assurance, at once bold and self-contained. Ellen, however, had to exert herself to get free of him, and, when she had placed the table between them, she looked him squarely in the eyes.

"Daggs, you keep your paws off me," she said.

"Aw, now, Ellen, I ain't no bear," he remonstrated. "What's the matter, kid?"

"I'm not a kid. And there's nothin' the matter. You're to keep your hands to yourself, that's all."

He tried to reach her across the table, and his movements were lazy and slow, like his smile. His tone was coaxing. "Mah dear, shore you set on my knee just the other day, now, didn't you?"

Ellen felt the blood sting her cheeks. "I was a child," she returned.

"Wal, listen to this heah grown-up young woman. All in a few days! Don't be in a temper, Ellen. Come, give us a kiss."

She deliberately gazed into his eyes. Like the eyes of an eagle, they were clear and hard, just now warmed by the dalliance of the moment, but there was no light, no intelligence in them to prove he understood her. The instant separated Ellen immeasurably from him and from all of his ilk.

"Daggs, I was a child," she said. "I was lonely . . . hungry for affection. I was innocent. Then I was careless, too, and thoughtless when I should have known better. But I hardly understood you men. I put such thoughts out of my mind. I know now . . . know what you mean . . . what you have made people believe I am."

"A-huh! Shore I get your hunch," he returned with a change of tone. "But I asked you to marry me."

"Yes, you did. The first day you got back to my dad's house. You asked me to marry you after you found you couldn't have your way with me. To you the one didn't mean any more than the other."

"Shore I did more than Simm Bruce an' Colter," he retorted. "They never asked you to marry."

"No, they didn't. And if I could respect them at all, I'd do it because they didn't ask me."

"Wal, I'll be dog-goned!" ejaculated Daggs thoughtfully as he stroked his long mustache.

"I'll say to them what I've said to you," went on Ellen. "I'll tell Dad to make you let me alone. I wouldn't marry one of you . . . you loafers to save my life. I'm very suspicious about you. You're a bad lot."

Daggs changed subtly. The whole indolent nonchalance of the man vanished in an instant. "Wal, Miss Jorth, I reckon you mean we're a bad lot of sheepmen?" he queried in the cool easy speech of a Texan.

"No," flashed Ellen. "Shore I don't say sheepmen. I say you're a *bad lot*."

"Oh, the hell you say!" Daggs spoke as he might have spoken to a man, then, tuning swiftly on his heel, he left

119

her. Outside, he encountered Ellen's father. She heard Daggs speak: "Lee, your little wildcat is shore heah. An' take mah hunch. Somebody has been talkin' to her."

"Who has?" asked her father in his husky voice. Ellen knew at once that he had been drinking.

"Lord only knows," replied Daggs. "But shore it wasn't any friends of ours."

"We cain't stop people's tongues," said Jorth resignedly.

"Wal, I ain't so shore," continued Daggs with his slow, cool laugh. "Reckon I never yet heered any daid men's tongues wag."

Then the musical tinkle of his spurs sounded more faintly. A moment later Ellen's father entered the cabin. His dark, moody face brightened at sight of her. Ellen knew she was the only person in the world left for him to love, and she was sure of his love. Her very presence always made him different. Through the years, the darker their misfortunes, the further he slipped away from better days, the more she loved him.

"Hello, my Ellen," he said, and he embraced her. When he had been drinking, he never kissed her. "Shore I'm glad you're home. This heah hole is bad enough any time, but when you're gone, it's black. I'm hungry."

Ellen laid food and drink on the table, and for a little while she did not look directly at him. She was concerned about this new, searching power of her eyes. In relation to him she vaguely dreaded it.

Lee Jorth had once been a singularly handsome man. He was tall, but did not have the figure of a horseman. His dark hair was streaked with gray and was white over his ears. His face was sallow and thin, with deep lines. Under his round, prominent, brown eyes, like deadened furnaces, were blue swollen welts. He had a bitter mouth and weak chin, not wholly concealed by dark gray mustache and pointed beard. He wore a long frock coat and a wide-brimmed sombrero, both black in color, and so old and stained and frayed that along with the fashion of them they betrayed that they had come from Texas with him. Jorth always persisted in wearing a white linen shirt, likewise a relic of his Southern prosperity, and today it was as ragged and soiled as usual.

Ellen watched her father eat and waited for him to speak. It occurred to her strangely that he never asked about the sheep or the newborn lambs. She divined with a subtle new woman's intuition that he cared nothing for his sheep.

"Ellen, what riled Daggs?" inquired her father presently. "He shore had fire in his eye."

Long ago, Ellen had betrayed an indignity she had suffered at the hands of a man. Her father had nearly killed him. Since then she had taken care to keep her troubles to herself. If her father had not been blind and absorbed in his own brooding, he would have seen a thousand things sufficient to inflame his Southern pride and temper.

"Daggs asked me to marry him again and I said he belonged to a bad lot," she replied.

Jorth laughed in scorn. "Fool! My God, Ellen, I must have dragged you low . . . that every damned rus . . . er . . . sheepman who comes along thinks he can marry you."

At the break in his words, the incompleted meaning, Ellen dropped her eyes. Little things once not noted by her had come now to have a fascinating significance.

"Never mind, Dad," she replied. "They cain't marry me."

"Daggs said somebody had been talkin' to you. How aboot that?"

"Old John Sprague had just gotten back from Grass Valley," said Ellen. "I stopped in to see him. Shore, he told me all the village gossip."

121

"Anythin' to interest me?" he queried darkly.

"Yes, Dad, I'm afraid a good deal," she said hesitatingly. Then in accordance with a decision Ellen had made, she told him of the rumored war between sheepmen and cattlemen; that old Isbel had Blaisdell, Gordon, Fredericks, Blue, and other well-known ranchers on his side; that Isbel's son Jean had come from Oregon with a wonderful reputation as fighter and scout and tracker; that it was no secret how Colonel Lee Jorth was at the head of the sheepmen; that a bloody war was sure to come.

"Hah!" exclaimed Jorth with a stain of red in his sallow cheek. "Reckon none of that is news to me. I knew all that."

Ellen wondered if he had heard of her meeting with Jean Isbel. If not, he would hear as soon as Simm Bruce and Lorenzo came back. She decided to forestall them.

"Dad, I met Jean Isbel. He came into my camp. Asked the way to the rim. I showed him. We . . . we talked a little and shore were gettin' acquainted when . . . when he told me who he was. Then I left him . . . hurried back to camp."

"Colter met Isbel down in the woods," replied Jorth ponderingly. "Said he looked like an Indian . . . a hard an' slippery customer to reckon with."

"Shore I guess I can endorse what Colter said," returned Ellen dryly. She could have laughed aloud at her deceit. Still she had not lied.

"How'd this heah young Isbel strike you?" queried her father, suddenly glancing up at her.

Ellen felt the slow, sickening, guilty steal of blood rise in her face. She was helpless to stop it. But her father evidently never saw it. He was looking at her without seeing her.

"He . . . he struck me as different from men heah," she stammered.

"Did Sprague tell you aboot this half-Indian Isbel . . . aboot his reputation?"

"Yes."

"Did he look to you like a real woodsman?"

"Indeed, he did. He wore buckskin. He stepped quiet and soft. He acted at home in the woods. He had eyes black as night and sharp as lightnin'. They shore saw aboot all there was to see."

Jorth chewed at his mustache and lost himself in brooding thought.

"Dad, tell me, is there goin' to be a war?" asked Ellen.

What a strange rolling flash blazed in his eyes! His body jerked. "Shore. You might as well know."

"Between sheepmen and cattlemen?"

"Yes."

"With you, Dad, at the haid of one faction, and Gaston Isbel the other?"

"Daughter, you have it correct, so far as you go."

"Oh! Dad, cain't this fight be avoided?"

"You forget you're from Texas," he replied.

"Cain't it be helped?" she repeated stubbornly.

"No!" he declared with deep, hoarse passion.

"Why not?"

"Wal, we sheepmen are goin' to run sheep anywhere we like on the range. An' cattlemen won't stand for that."

"But Dad, it's so foolish," declared Ellen earnestly. "You sheepmen do not have to run sheep over the cattle range."

"I reckon we do!"

"Dad, that argument doesn't go with me. I know the country. For years to come there will be room for both sheep and cattle without over-runnin'. If some of the range is better in water and grass, then whoever got there first

123

should have it. That shore is only fair. It's common sense, too."

"Ellen, I reckon some cattle people have been prejudicin' you," said Jorth bitterly.

"Dad!" she cried hotly.

This had grown to be an ordeal for Jorth. He seemed a victim of contending tides of feeling. Some will or struggle broke within him and the change was manifest. Haggard, shifty-eyed, with wobbling chin, he burst into speech.

"See heah, girl. You listen. There's a clique of ranchers down in the basin, all those you named, with Isbel at their haid. They have resented sheepmen comin' down into the valley. They want it all to themselves. That's one reason. Shore there's another. All the Isbels are crooked. They're cattle and horse thieves . . . have been for years. Gaston Isbel always was a maverick rustler. He's gettin' old now an' rich, so he wants to cover his tracks. He aims to blame this cattle rustlin' an' horse stealin' on to us sheepmen an' run us out of the country."

Gravely Ellen Jorth studied her father's face, and the newly found truth-seeing power of her eyes did not fail her. In part, perhaps in all, he was telling lies. She shuddered a little, loyally battling against the insidious convictions being brought to fruition. Perhaps in his brooding over his failures and troubles he had leaned toward false judgments. Ellen could not attach dishonor to her father's motives or speeches. For long, however, something about him had troubled her, perplexed her, baffled her. Fearfully she believed she was coming to some revelation, and despite her keen determination to know she found herself shrinking.

"Dad, Mother told me before she died that the Isbels had ruined you," said Ellen, very low. It hurt her so to see her father cover his face that she could hardly go on. "If

124

they ruined you, they ruined all of us. I know what we had once . . . what we lost again and again . . . and I see what we are come to now. Mother hated the Isbels. She taught me to hate the very name. But I never knew how they ruined you . . . or why . . . or when. And I want to know now."

Then it was not the face of a liar that Jorth disclosed. The present was forgotten. He lived in the past. He even seemed younger in the revivifying flash of hate that made his face radiant. The lines burned out. Hate gave him back the spirit of his youth.

"Gaston Isbel an' I were boys together in Weston, Texas," began Jorth in swift passionate voice. "We went to school together. We loved the same girl . . . your mother. When the war broke out, she was engaged to Isbel. His family was rich. They influenced her people. But she loved me. He came back an' faced us. God! I'll never forget that. Your mother confessed her unfaithfulness . . . by heaven! She taunted him with it. Isbel accused me of winnin' her by lies. But she took the sting out of that. Isbel never forgave her an' he hounded me to ruin. He made me out a cardsharp, cheatin' my best friends. I was disgraced. Later he tangled me in the courts . . . he beat me out of property . . . an' last, by convictin' me of rustlin' cattle, he run me out of Texas."

Black and distorted now, Jorth's face was a spectacle to make Ellen sick with a terrible passion of despair and hate. The truth of her father's ruin and her own were enough. What mattered all else? Jorth beat the table with fluttering, nerveless hands that seemed all the more significant for the lack of physical force.

"An' so help me God it's got to be wiped out in blood!" he hissed.

That was his answer to the wavering remonstrance and

125

nobility of Ellen. She, in her turn, had no answer to make. She crept away into the corner behind the curtain, and there on her couch in the semidarkness she lay with strained heart and a resurging, unconquerable tumult in her mind. She lay there from the middle of that afternoon until the next morning.

When she awakened, she expected to be unable to rise— she hoped she could not—but life seemed multiplied in her and inaction was impossible. Something young and sweet and hopeful that had been in her did not greet the sun this morning. In their place was a woman's passion to learn for herself, to watch events, to meet what must come, to survive.

After breakfast, at which she sat alone, she decided to put Isbel's package out of the way, so that it would not be subjecting her to continued annoyance. The moment she picked it up, the old curiosity assailed her.

"Shore I'll see what it is, anyway," she muttered, and with swift hands she opened it, the fear gone. The action disclosed two pairs of fine soft shoes, of a style she had never seen, and four pairs of stockings, two of strong serviceable wool, and the other two of a finer texture. Ellen looked at them in amazement. Of all things in the world, these would have been the last she expected to see, and, strangely, they were what she wanted and needed most. Naturally, then, Ellen made the mistake of taking them in her hands to feel their softness and warmth.

"Shore! He saw my bare legs! And he brought me these presents he'd intended for his sister. He was ashamed for me . . . sorry for me. And I thought he looked at me bold-like, as I'm used to being looked at heah! Isbel or not, he's shore. . . ."

But Ellen Jorth could not utter aloud the conviction her

intelligence tried to force upon her.

It'd be a pity to burn them, she mused. *I can't do it. Sometime I might send them to Ann Isbel.*

Whereupon she wrapped them up again and hid them in the bottom of the old trunk, and slowly, as she lowered the lid, looking darkly, blankly at the wall, she whispered: "Jean Isbel! I hate him!"

Later, when Ellen went outdoors, she carried her rifle, which was unusual for her unless she intended to go into the woods. The morning was sunny and warm. A group of shirt-sleeved men lounged in the hall and before the porch of the double cabin. Her father was pacing up and down, talking forcibly. Ellen heard his hoarse voice. As she approached, he ceased talking and his listeners relaxed their attention. Ellen's glance ran over them swiftly—Daggs, with his superb head, like that of a hawk, uncovered to the sun; Colter with his lowered, secretive look, his sand-gray, lean face; Jackson Jorth, her uncle, huge, gaunt, hulking, with white in his black beard and hair, and the fire of a ghoul in his hollow eyes; Tad Jorth, another brother of her father's, younger, red of eye and nose, a weak-chinned drinker of rum. Three other limber-legged Texans lounged there, partners of Daggs, and they were sun-browned, light-haired, blue-eyed men singularly alike in appearance from their dusty high-heeled boots to their broad black sombreros. They claimed to be sheepmen. All Ellen could be sure of was that Rock Wells spent most of his time there, doing nothing but look for a chance to waylay her, Springer was a gambler, and the third, who answered to the strange name of Queen, was a silent, lazy, watchful-eyed man who never wore a glove on his right hand and who never was seen without a gun within easy reach of that hand.

127

"Howdy, Ellen. Shore you ain't goin' to say good mornin' to this heah bad lot?" drawled Daggs with good-natured sarcasm.

"Why, shore. Good morning, you hard-working, industrious, *mañana* sheep raisers," replied Ellen coolly.

Daggs stared. The others appeared taken aback by a greeting so foreign from any they were accustomed to from her. Jackson Jorth let out a gruff: "Haw, haw." Some of them doffed their sombreros, and Rock Wells managed a lazy, polite good morning. Ellen's father seemed most significantly struck by her greeting and the least amused.

"Ellen, I'm not likin' your talk," he said with a frown.

"Dad, when you play cards, don't you call a spade a spade?"

"Why, shore I do."

"Well, I'm calling spades, spades."

"A-huh," grunted Jorth, furtively dropping his eyes. "Where you goin' with your gun? I'd rather you hung 'round heah now."

"Reckon I might as well get used to packing my gun all the time," replied Ellen. "Reckon I'll be treated more like a man."

Then the event Ellen had been expecting all morning took place. Simm Bruce and Lorenzo rode around the slope of The Knoll and trotted toward the cabin. Interest in Ellen was relegated to the background.

"Shore they're bustin' with news," declared Daggs.

"They been ridin' some, you bet," remarked another.

"Huh!" exclaimed Jorth. "Bruce shore looks queer to me."

"Red liquor," said Tad Jorth sententiously. "You-all know the brand Greaves hands out."

"Naw, Simm ain't drunk," said Jackson Jorth. "Look at his bloody shirt."

The cool, indolent interest of the crowd vanished at the red color pointed out by Jackson Jorth. Daggs rose in a single, springy motion to his lofty height. The face he turned to Jorth was alight, sinister and magnetic.

"Jorth, you remember my hunch. I called the trick," he said with a ring in his voice. "It's first blood for the Isbels!"

Jorth dropped back in his chair. None of them spoke or stirred. Bruce rode in ahead of Lorenzo, threw his bridle, swung a long leg, and dismounted.

"Hullo, boys. I'm back an' not so damn' glad to see you-all," he said. His open vest showed a soiled, collarless shirt splotched with blood all around his breast and neck. His face was swollen and bruised with unhealed cuts. Where his right eye should have been, there was a puffed, dark purple bulge. His other eye, however, gleamed with hard and sullen light. He stretched a big shaking hand toward Jorth.

"Thet Nez Percé Isbel beat me half to death," he bellowed.

Jorth stared hard at the tragic, almost grotesque figure, at the battered face, but speech failed him. It was Daggs who answered Bruce.

"Wal, Simm, I'll be damned if you don't look it."

"Beat you! What with?" burst out Jorth explosively.

"I thought he was swingin' an axe, but Greaves swore it was his fists," bawled Bruce in misery and fury.

"Where was your gun?" queried Jorth sharply.

"Gun? Hell!" exclaimed Bruce, flinging with his arms. "Ask Lorenzo. He had a gun. An' he got a biff in the jaw before my turn come. Ask him?"

Attention thus directed to the Mexican showed a heavily discolored swelling upon the side of his olive-skinned face.

129

Lorenzo looked only serious.

"Hah! Speak up!" shouted Jorth impatiently.

"*Señor* Isbel heet me ver' quick," replied Lorenzo with expressive gesture. "I see thousand stars . . . then moocho black . . . all like night."

At that some of Daggs's men lolled back with dry, crisp laughter. Daggs's hard face rippled with a smile. But there was no humor in anything for Colonel Jorth.

"Tell us what come off. Quick!" he ordered. "Where did it happen? Why? Who saw it? What did you do?"

Bruce lapsed into a sullen impressiveness. "Wal, I happened in Greaves's store an' run into Jean Isbel. Shore was lookin' fer him. I had my mind made up what to do, but I got to shootin' off my gab instead of my gun. I called him Nez Percé . . . an' I throwed all thet talk in his face about old Gass Isbel sendin' fer him . . . an' I told him he'd git run out of the Tonto. Reckon I was jest warmin' up . . . but then it all happened. He slugged Lorenzo jest once, an' Lorenzo slid peaceful-like to bed behind the counter. I hadn't time to think of throwin' a gun before he whaled into me. He knocked out two of my teeth. An' I swallowed one of them."

Ellen stood in the background behind three of the men and in the shadow. She did not join in the laugh that followed Bruce's remarks. She had known that he would lie. Uncertain yet of her reaction to this, but more bitter and furious as he revealed his utter baseness, she waited for more to be said.

"Wal, I'll be dog-goned," drawled Daggs.

"What do you make of this kind of fightin'?" queried Jorth.

"Darn' if I know," replied Daggs in perplexity. "Shore an' sartin it's not the way of a Texan. Mebbe this young

130

Isbel really is what old Gass swears he is. Shore, Bruce ain't nothin' to give an edge with a real gunfighter. Looks to me like Isbel bluffed Greaves an' his gang, an' licked your men without throwin' a gun."

"Maybe Isbel doesn't want the name of drawin' first blood," suggested Jorth.

"Thet'd be like Gass," spoke up Rock Wells quietly. "I oncet rode fer Gass in Texas."

"Say, Bruce," said Daggs, "was this heah palaverin' of yours an' Jean Isbel's aboot the old stock dispute? Aboot his father's range an' water? An' partikler aboot sheep?"

"Wal . . . I . . . I yelled a heap," declared Bruce haltingly, "but I don't recollect all I said. I was riled . . . shore, though . . . it was the same old argyment thet's been fetchin' us closer an' closer to trouble."

Daggs removed his keen, hawk-like gaze from Bruce. "Wal, Jorth, all I'll say is this . . . if Bruce is tellin' the truth, we ain't got a hell of a lot to fear from this young Isbel. I've known a heap of gunfighters in my day an' Jean Isbel don't run true to class. Shore there never was a gunman who'd risk cripplin' his right hand by sluggin' anybody."

"Wal," broke in Bruce sullenly, "you-all can take it daid straight or not. I don't give a damn. But you've shore got my hunch thet Nez Percé Isbel is liable to handle any of you fellars jest as he did me, an' jest as easy. What's more, he's got Greaves figgered. An' you-all know that Greaves is as deep in. . . ."

"Shut up that kind of gab," demanded Jorth stridently, "an' answer me. Was the row in Greaves's barroom aboot sheep?"

"Aw, hell! I said so, didn't I?" shouted Bruce with a fierce uplift of his distorted face.

Ellen strode out from the shadow of the tall man who had obscured her.

"Bruce, you're a liar!" she said bitingly.

The surprise of her sudden appearance seemed to root Bruce to the spot. All but the discolored places in his face turned white. He held his breath a moment, then expelled it hard. His effort to recover from the shock was painfully obvious. He stammered incoherently.

"Shore you're more than a liar, too," cried Ellen, facing him with blazing eyes. The rifle, gripped in both hands, seemed to declare her intent of menace. "That row was not aboot sheep. Jean Isbel didn't beat you for anythin' aboot sheep. Old John Sprague was in Greaves's store. He heard you. He saw Jean Isbel beat you as you deserved. An' he told *me!*"

Ellen saw Bruce shrink in fear of his life, and despite her fury she was filled with disgust that he could imagine she would have his blood on her hands. Then she divined that Bruce saw more in the gathering storm in her father's eyes than he had to fear from her.

"Girl, what the hell are you sayin'?" hoarsely called Jorth in dark amazement.

"Dad, you leave this to me," she retorted.

Daggs stepped beside Jorth, significantly on his right side. "Let her alone, Lee," he advised coolly. "She's shore got a hunch on Bruce."

"Simm Bruce, you cast a dirty slur on my name," cried Ellen passionately.

It was then that Daggs grasped Jorth's right arm and held it tightly. "Jest what I thought," he said. "Stand still, Lee. Let's see the kid make him slow down."

"That's what Jean Isbel beat you for," went on Ellen. "For slandering a girl who wasn't there . . . me! You rotten liar!"

"But, Ellen, it wasn't all lies," said Bruce huskily. "I was half drunk . . . an' horrible jealous. You know Lorenzo seen Isbel kissin' you. I can prove that."

Ellen threw up her hand and a scarlet wave of shame and anger flooded her face. "Yes," she cried ringingly, "he saw Jean Isbel kiss me. Once! An' it was the only decent kiss I've had in years. He meant no insult. I didn't know who he was. An' through his kiss I learned the difference between men. You made Lorenzo lie. An' if I had a shred of good name left in Grass Valley, you dishonored it. You made *him* think I was your girl! Damn you! I ought to kill you. Eat your words now . . . take them back . . . or I'll cripple you for life!"

Ellen lowered the cocked rifle toward his feet.

"Shore, Ellen, I take back . . . all I said," gulped Bruce. He gazed at the quivering rifle barrel and then into the face of Ellen's father. Instinct told him where his real peril lay.

Here the cool and tactful Daggs showed himself master of the situation.

"Heah, listen!" he called. "Ellen, I reckon Bruce was drunk an' out of his haid. He's shore ate his words. Now we don't want any cripples in this camp. Let him alone. Your dad got me heah to lead the Jorths, an' that's my say to you. Simm, you're shore a low-down, lyin' rascal. Keep away from Ellen after this or I'll bore you myself. Jorth, it won't be a bad idee for you to forget you're a Texan till you cool off. Let Bruce stop some Isbel lead. Shore the Jorth-Isbel war is aboot on, an' I reckon we'd be smart to believe old Gass's talk aboot his Nez Percé son."

Chapter Six

From this hour Ellen Jorth bent all of her lately awakened intelligence and will to the only end that seemed to hold possible salvation for her. In the crisis sure to come she did not want to be blind or weak. Dreaming and indolence, habits born in her which were often a comfort to one as lonely as she, would ill fit her for the hard test she divined and dreaded. In the matter of her father's fights, she must stand by him whatever the issue or the outcome; in what pertained to her own principles, her womanhood, and her soul, she stood absolutely alone. Therefore, Ellen put dreams aside, and indolence of mind and body behind her. Many tasks she found, and, when these were done for a day, she kept active in other ways, thus earning the poise and peace of labor.

Jorth rode off every day, sometimes with one or two of the men, often with a larger number. If he spoke of such trips to Ellen, it was to give an impression of visiting the ranches of his neighbors or the various sheep camps. Often he did not return the day he left. When he did get back, he smelled of rum and appeared heavy from need of sleep. His horses were always dust- and sweat-covered. During his absence Ellen fell victim to anxious dread until he returned. Daily he grew darker and more haggard of face, more obsessed by some impending fate. Often he stayed up late, haranguing with the men in the dim-lit cabin, where they drank and smoked but seldom gambled any more. When the men did not gamble, something immediate and perturbing was on their minds. Ellen had not yet lowered herself to the deceit and suspicion of eavesdropping but she realized that there was a climax approaching in which she would deliberately do so.

In those closing days of May, Ellen learned the significance of many things that previously she had taken as a matter of course. Her father did not run a ranch. There was absolutely no ranching done, and little work. Often Ellen had to chop wood herself. Jorth did not possess a plow. Ellen was bound to confess that the evidence of this lack dumbfounded her. Even old John Sprague raised some hay, beets, turnips. Jorth's cattle and horses fared ill during the winter. Ellen remembered how they used to chew up four-inch oak saplings and aspens. Many of them died in the snow. The flocks of sheep, however, were driven down into the basin in the fall and across the Reno Pass to Phoenix and Maricopa.

Ellen could not discover a fence post on the ranch or a piece of salt for the horses and cattle, or a wagon, or any sign of a sheep-shearing outfit. She had never seen any sheep sheared. Ellen could never keep track of the many and different horses running loose and hobbled around the ranch. There were droves of horses in the woods, and some of them wild as deer. According to her long-established understanding, her father and her uncles were keen on horse trading and buying. Then the many trails leading away from the Jorth Ranch—these grew to have a fascination for Ellen and the time came when she rode out on them to see for herself where they led. The sheep ranch of Daggs, supposed to be only a few miles across the ridges down in Bear Cañon, never materialized at all for Ellen. This circumstance so interested her that she went up to see her friend Sprague and get him to direct her to Bear Cañon so that she

135

would be sure not to miss it and she rode from the narrow, maple-thicketed head of it near the Tonto Rim down all its length. She found no ranch, no cabin, not even a corral in Bear Cañon. Sprague said there was only one cañon by that name. Daggs had assured her of the exact location of his place, and so had her father. Had they lied? Were they mistaken in the cañon? There were many cañons, all heading up near the rim, all running and widening down for miles through the wooded mountain, and vastly different from the deep, short, yellow-walled gorges that cut into the rim from the basin side. Ellen investigated the cañons within six or eight miles of her home, both to east and west. All she discovered were a couple of old log cabins, long deserted. Still she did not follow out all the trails to their ends. Several of them led far into the deepest, roughest, wildest brakes of gorge and thicket that she had seen. No cattle or sheep had ever been driven over these trails.

This riding around of Ellen's at length got to her father's ears. Ellen expected that a bitter quarrel would ensue, for she certainly would refuse to be confined to the camp, but her father only asked her to limit her riding to the meadow valley, and straightway forgot all about it. In fact, his abstraction one moment, his intense nervousness the next, his harder drinking and fiercer harangues with the men, grew to be distressing for Ellen. They presaged his further deterioration and the ever-present evil of the growing feud.

One day Jorth rode home in the early morning, after an absence of two nights. Ellen heard the *clip-clop* of horses long before she saw them.

"Hey, Ellen, come out heah!" called her father.

Ellen left her work and went outside. A stranger had ridden in with her father, a young giant whose sharp-featured face appeared marked by ferret-like eyes and a

136

fine, light, frizzy beard. He was long, loose-jointed, not heavy of build, and he had the largest hands and feet Ellen had even seen. Next Ellen espied a black horse they had evidently brought with them. Her father was holding a rope halter. At once the black horse struck Ellen as being a beauty and a Thoroughbred.

"Ellen, heah's a horse for you," said Jorth with something of pride. "I made a trade. Reckon I wanted him myself, but he's too gentle for me. An' maybe a little small for my weight."

Delight visited Ellen for the first time in many days. Seldom had she owned a good horse, and never one like this.

"Oh, Dad!" she exclaimed in her gratitude.

"Shore he's yours on one condition," said her father.

"What's that?" asked Ellen as she laid caressing hands on the restless horse.

"You're not going to ride him out of the cañon?"

"Agreed. All daid black, isn't he, except that white face? What's his name, Dad?"

"I forgot to ask," replied Jorth, as he began unsaddling his own horse. "Slater, what this heah black's name?"

The lanky giant grinned: "I reckon it was Spades."

"Spades?" ejaculated Ellen blankly. "What a name! Well, I guess it's as good as any. He's shore black."

"Ellen, keep him hobbled when you're not ridin' him," was her father's parting advice, as he walked off with the stranger.

Spades was wet and dusty and his satiny skin quivered. He had fine, dark, intelligent eyes that watched Ellen's every move. She knew how her father and his friends dragged and jammed horses through the woods and over the rough trails. It did not take her long to discover that this

137

horse had been a pet. Ellen cleaned his coat and brushed him and fed him. Then she fitted her bridle to suit his head and saddled him. His evident response to her kindness assured her that he was gentle, so she mounted and rode him, to discover he had the easiest gait she had ever experienced. He walked and trotted to suit her will, but when left to choose his own gait, he fell into a graceful little pace that was very easy for her. He appeared quite ready to break into a run at her slightest bidding, but Ellen satisfied herself on the first ride with his slower gaits.

"Spades, you've shore cut out my burro Jinny," said Ellen regretfully. "Well, I reckon women are fickle."

Next day she rode up the cañon to show Spades to her friend John Sprague. The old burro breeder was not at home. As his door was open, however, and a fire smoldering, Ellen concluded he would soon return. So she waited. Dismounting, she left Spades free to graze on the new green grass that carpeted the ground. The cabin and little level clearing accentuated the loneliness and wildness of the forest. Ellen always liked it here and had once been in the habit of visiting the old man often, but of late she had stayed away, for the reason that Sprague's talk and his news and his poorly hidden pity depressed her.

Presently she heard hoof beats on the hard-packed trail leading down the cañon in the direction from which she had come. Scarcely likely was it that Sprague should return from this direction. Ellen thought her father had sent one of the herders for her. But when she got a glimpse of the approaching horseman, down in the aspens, she failed to recognize him. After he had passed one of the openings, she heard his horse stop. Probably the man had seen her; at least, she could not otherwise account for his stopping. The glimpse she had of him had given her the impression that he was

138

bending over, peering ahead in the trail, looking for tracks. Then she heard the rider come on again, more slowly this time. At length the horse trotted out into the opening, to be hauled up short. Ellen recognized the buckskin-clad figure, the broad shoulders, the dark face of Jean Isbel.

Ellen fell prey to the strangest quaking sensation she had ever suffered. It took violence of her newborn spirit to subdue that feeling. Isbel rode slowly across the clearing toward her. For Ellen his approach seemed singularly swift— so swift that her surprise, dismay, conjecture, and anger obstructed her will. The outwardly calm and cold Ellen Jorth was a travesty that mocked her—that she felt he would discern.

The moment Isbel drew close enough for Ellen to see his face, she experienced a strong shuddering repetition of her first shock of recognition. He was not the same. The light, the youth was gone. This, however, did not cause her emotion. Was it not a sudden transition of her nature to the dominance of hate? Ellen seemed to feel the shadow of her unknown self standing with her.

Isbel halted his horse. Ellen had been near the trunk of a fallen pine, and she instinctively backed against it. How her legs trembled! Isbel took off his cap and crushed it nervously in his bare brown hand.

"Good mornin', Miss Ellen," he said.

Ellen did not return his greeting, but queried almost breathlessly: "Did you come by our ranch?"

"No, I circled," he replied.

"Jean Isbel! What do you want heah?" she demanded.

"Don't you know?" he returned. His eyes were intensely black and piercing. They seemed to search Ellen's very soul. To meet their gaze was an ordeal that only her rousing fury sustained.

Ellen felt on her lips a scornful allusion to his half-breed Indian traits and the reputation that had preceded him, but she could not utter it.

"No," she replied.

"It's hard to call a woman a liar," he returned bitterly. "But you must be . . . seein' you're a Jorth."

"Liar! Not to you, Jean Isbel," she retorted. "I'd not lie to you to save my life."

He studied her with keen, sober, moody intent. The dark fire of his eyes thrilled her.

"If that's true, I'm glad," he said.

"Shore it's true. I've no idea why you came heah!"

Ellen did have a dawning idea that she could not force into oblivion. But if she ever admitted it to her consciousness, she must fail in the contempt and scorn and fearlessness she chose to throw in this man's face.

"Does old Sprague live here?" asked Isbel.

"Yes. I expect him back soon. Did you come to see him?"

"No. Did Sprague tell you anythin' about the row he saw me in?"

"He did not," replied Ellen, lying with stiff lips. She—who had sworn she could not lie!—felt the hot blood leaving her heart, mounting in a wave. All her conscious will seemed impelled to deceive. What had she to hide from Jean Isbel? And a quiet, small voice replied that she had to hide the Ellen Jorth who had waited for him that day, who had spied upon him, who had treasured a gift she could not destroy, who had hugged to her unstable heart the fact that he had fought for her name.

"I'm glad of that," Isbel was saying thoughtfully.

"Did you come heah to see me?" interrupted Ellen. She felt that she could not endure this reiterated suggestion of fineness, of consideration in him. She would betray herself—betray what she did not even realize herself. She must force other footing—and that should be the one of strife between the Jorths and Isbels.

"No . . . honest I didn't, Miss Ellen," he rejoined humbly. "I'll tell you presently why I came. But it wasn't to see you. I don't deny I waited . . . but that's no matter. You didn't meet me that day on the Tonto Rim."

"Meet you?" she echoed coldly. "Shore you never expected me?"

"Somehow I did," he replied with those penetrating eyes on her. "I put somethin' in your tent that day. Did you find it?"

"Yes," she replied with the same casual coldness.

"What did you do with it?"

"I kicked it out, of course," she replied.

She saw him flinch.

"And you never opened it?"

"Certainly not," she retorted, as if proud. "Don't you know anythin' about . . . about people? Shore, even if you are an Isbel, you never were born in Texas."

"Thank God I wasn't," he replied. "I was born in a beautiful country of green meadows and deep forests and white rivers, not in a barren desert where men live dry and hard as the cactus. Where I came from, men don't live on hate. They can forgive."

"Forgive! Could you forgive a Jorth?"

"Yes, I could."

"Shore that's easy to say . . . with the wrongs all on your side," she declared bitterly.

"Ellen Jorth, the first wrong was on your side," returned Jean, his voice full. "Your father stole my father's sweetheart . . . by lies, by slander, by dishonor, by makin' terrible love to her in his absence."

"It is a lie!" cried Ellen passionately.

"It's *not!*" he declared solemnly.

"Jean Isbel, I say you lie!"

"No! *I* say you've been lied to," he thundered.

The tremendous force of his spirit seemed to fling truth at Ellen. It weakened her.

"But . . . Mother loved Dad . . . best."

"Yes, afterwards. No wonder, poor woman . . . but it was the action of your father and your mother that ruined all their lives. You've got to know the truth, Ellen Jorth. All the years of hate have borne their fruit. God Almighty can never save us now. Blood must be spilled. The Jorths and the Isbels can't live on the same earth, and you've got to know the truth because the worst of this hell falls on you and me."

The hate that he spoke of alone upheld her. "Never, Jean Isbel," she cried. "I'll never know truth from you. I'll never share anythin' with you . . . not even hell."

Isbel dismounted, and stood before her, still holding his bridle reins. The bay horse champed his bit and tossed his head.

"Why do you hate me so?" he asked. "I just happen to be my father's son. I never harmed you or any of your people. I met you . . . fell in love with you in a flash . . . though I never knew it till after. Why do you hate me so terribly?"

Ellen felt a heavy, stifling pressure within her breast. "You're an Isbel. Don't speak of love to me."

"I didn't intend to. But your . . . your hate seems unnatural. And we'll probably never meet again. I can't help it. I love you. Love at first sight! Jean Isbel and Ellen Jorth! Strange, isn't it? It was all so strange. My meetin' you so lonely and unhappy . . . my seein' you so sweet and beautiful . . . my thinking you so good in spite of. . . ."

"Shore it was strange," interrupted Ellen with a scornful laugh. She had found her defense. In hurting him she could hide her own hurt. "Thinkin' me so good in spite of . . . ha! ha! . . . and I said I'd been kissed before!"

"Yes, in spite of everything," he said.

Ellen could not look at him as he loomed over her. She felt a wild tumult in her heart. All that crowded to her lips for utterance was false. "Yes . . . I kissed before I met you . . . and since," she said mockingly. "And I laugh at what you call love, Jean Isbel."

"Laugh if you want . . . but believe it was sweet, honorable . . . the best in me," he replied in deep earnestness.

"Bah!" cried Ellen with all the force of her pain and shame and hate.

"By heaven, you must be different from what I thought!" exclaimed Isbel huskily.

"Shore if I wasn't, I'd make myself. . . . Now, Mister Jean Isbel, get on your horse an' go."

Something of composure came to Ellen with these words of dismissal, and she glanced up at him with half-veiled eyes. His changed aspect prepared her for some stunning blow.

"That's a pretty black horse."

"Yes," replied Ellen blankly.

"Do you like him?"

"I . . . I love him."

"All right, I'll give him to you, then. He'll have less work and kinder treatment than if I used him. I've got some pretty hard rides ahead of me."

"You . . . you give . . . ?" whispered Ellen slowly stiffening.

"Yes. He's mine," replied Isbel. With that he turned to

whistle. Spades threw up his head, snorted, and started forward at a trot. He came faster the closer he got, and, if ever Ellen saw the joy of a horse at sight of a beloved master, she saw it then. Isbel laid a hand on the animal's neck and caressed him. Then, turning back to Ellen, he went on speaking: "I picked him from a lot of fine horses of my father's. We got along well. My sister Ann rode him a good deal. He was stolen from our pasture day before yesterday. I took his trail and tracked him up here. Never lost his trail till I got to your ranch where I had to circle till I picked it up again."

"Stolen . . . pasture . . . tracked him up heah?" echoed Ellen without any evidence of emotion whatever. Indeed, she seemed to have been turned to stone.

"Trackin' him was easy. I wish for your sake it'd been impossible," he said bluntly.

"For my sake?" she echoed in precisely the same tone.

Manifestly that tone irritated Isbel beyond control. He misunderstood it. With a hand far from gentle he pushed her bent head back so he could look into her face.

"Yes, for your sake," he declared harshly. "Haven't you sense enough to see that? What kind of a game do you think you can play with me?"

"Game? Game of what?" she asked.

"Why a . . . a game of ignorance . . . innocence . . . any old game to fool a man who's tryin' to be decent."

This time Ellen mutely looked her dull, blank questioning, and it inflamed Isbel.

"You know your father's a horse thief!" he thundered.

Outwardly Ellen remained the same. She had been prepared for an unknown and a terrible blow. It had fallen. Her face, her body, her hands, locked with the supreme fortitude of pride and sustained by hate, gave no betrayal of the crashing, thundering ruin within her mind and soul. Motionless she leaned there, meeting the piercing fire of Isbel's eyes, seeing in them a righteous and terrible scorn. In one flash the naked truth seemed to blaze at her. The faith she had fostered died a sudden death. A thousand perplexing problems were solved in a second of swirling, revealing thought.

"Ellen Jorth, you know your father's in with this Hash Knife Gang of rustlers!" thundered Isbel.

"Shore," she replied with the cool, easy, careless defiance of a Texan.

"You know he's got this Daggs to lead his faction against the Isbels."

"Shore."

"You know this talk of sheepmen buckin' the cattlemen is all a blind?"

"Shore," reiterated Ellen.

Isbel gazed darkly down upon her. With his anger spent for the moment, he appeared ready to end the interview, but he seemed fascinated by the strange look of her, by the incomprehensible something she emanated. Havoc gleamed in her pale set face. He shook his dark head and his broad hand went to his breast.

"To think I fell in love with such as you!" he exclaimed, and his other hand swept out in a tragic gesture of helpless pathos and impotence.

The hell Isbel had hinted at now possessed Ellen, body, mind, and soul. Disgraced, scorned by an Isbel, yet loved by him? In that divination there flamed up a wild, fierce passion to hurt, to rend, to flay, to fling back upon him a stinging agony. Her thoughts flew upon her like whips. Pride of the Jorths! Pride of the old Texan blue blood! It lay dead at her feet, killed by the scornful words of the last of that family to which she owed her degradation. Daughter of a horse thief and rustler! Dark and evil and grim set the forces within her, accepting her fate, damning her enemies, true to the blood of the Jorths. The sins of the father must be visited upon the daughter.

"Shore you might have had me . . . that day on the rim . . . if you hadn't told your name," she said mockingly, and she gazed into his eyes with all the mystery of a woman's nature.

Isbel's powerful frame shook as with an ague. "Girl, what do you mean?"

"Shore, I'd have been plumb fond of havin' you make up to me," she drawled. It possessed her now with irresistible power, this fact of the love he could not help. Some fiendish woman's satisfaction dwelt in her consciousness, of her power to kill the noble, the faithful, the good in him.

"Ellen Jorth, you lie!" he burst out hoarsely.

"Jean, shore I'd been a toy and a rag for these rustlers long enough. I was tired of them . . . I wanted a new lover . . . and, if you hadn't give yourself away. . . ."

Isbel moved so swiftly that she did not realize his intention until his hard hand smote her mouth. Instantly she tasted the hot salty blood from a cut lip.

"Shut up, you hussy," he ordered roughly. "Have you no shame? My sister Ann spoke well of you. She made excuses . . . she pitied you."

That for Ellen seemed the culminating blow under which she almost sank. But one moment longer could she maintain this unnatural and terrible poise. "Jean Isbel . . . go along with you," she said impatiently. "I'm waiting heah for Simm Bruce!"

At last it was as if she had struck his heart. Because of doubt of himself and a stubborn faith in her, his passion and jealousy were not proof against this last stab. Instinctive subtlety inherent in Ellen had prompted the speech that tortured Isbel. How the shock to him rebounded on her! She gasped as he lunged for her, too swift for her to move a hand. One arm crushed around her like a steel band, the other, hard across her breast and neck, forced her head back. Then she tried to wrestle away, but she was utterly powerless. His dark face bent down closer and closer. Suddenly Ellen ceased trying to struggle. She was like a stricken creature paralyzed by the piercing hypnotic eyes of a snake. Yet, in spite of her terror, if he meant death by her, she welcomed it.

"Ellen Jorth, I'm thinkin' yet . . . you lie!" he said, low and tense between his teeth.

"No! No!" she screamed wildly. Her nerve broke there. She could no longer meet those terrible black eyes. Her passionate denial was not only the last of her shameful deceit; it was the woman of her, repudiating herself and him, and all this sickening, miserable situation.

Isbel took her literally. She had convinced him. The instant held blank horror for Ellen.

"By God . . . then I'll have somethin' of you anyway," muttered Isbel thickly.

Ellen saw the blood bulge his powerful neck. She saw his dark, hard face, strange now, fearful to behold, come lower and lower, till it blurred and obstructed her gaze. She felt the swell and ripple and stretch—then the bind of his muscles, like huge coils of elastic rope. Then with savage rude force his mouth closed on hers. All Ellen's senses reeled, as if she were swooning. She was suffocating. The spasm passed, and a bursting spurt of blood revived her to acute and terrible consciousness. For the endless period of one moment he held her so that her breast seemed crushed. His kisses burned and bruised her lips. Then, shifting violently to her neck, they pressed so hard that she choked under them. It was as if a huge bat had fastened upon her throat.

Suddenly the remorseless, binding embraces—the hot and savage kisses—fell away from her. Isbel had let go. She saw him throw up his hands and stagger back a little, all the while with his piercing gaze on her. His face had been dark purple; now it was white.

"No . . . Ellen Jorth," he panted. "I don't . . . want any of you . . . that way." And suddenly he sank on the log and covered his face with his hands. "What I loved in you . . . was what I thought you were."

Like a wildcat Ellen sprang upon him, beating him with her fists, tearing out his hair, scratching his face in a blind fury. Isbel made no move to stop her, and her violence spent itself with her strength. She swayed back from him, shaking so that she could scarcely stand.

"You . . . damned . . . Isbel!" she gasped with hoarse passion. "You insulted me!"

"Insulted you?" Isbel laughed in bitter scorn. "It couldn't be done."

"Oh! I'll *kill* you!" she hissed.

Isbel stood up and wiped the red scratches on his face. "Go ahead. There's my gun," he said, pointing to his saddle sheath. "Somebody's got to begin this Jorth-Isbel feud. It'll be strictly business. I'm sick of it already. Kill me! First blood for Ellen Jorth!"

Suddenly the dark grim tide that had seemed to engulf Ellen's very soul cooled and receded, leaving her without its false strength. She began to sag. She stared at Isbel's gun. *Kill him,* whispered the retreating voice of her hate. But she was as powerless as if she were still held in Jean Isbel's giant embrace.

"I . . . I want to . . . kill you," she whispered, "but I can't. Leave me."

"You're no Jorth . . . the same as I'm no Isbel. We oughtn't be mixed in this deal," he said somberly. "I'm sorrier for you than I am for myself . . . you're a girl! You once had a good mother . . . a decent home. And this life you've led here . . . mean as it's been . . . is nothin' to what you'll face now. Damn the men that brought you to this! I'm goin' to kill some of them."

With that, he mounted and turned away. Ellen called out for him to take his horse. He did not stop or look back. She called again, but her voice was fainter, and Isbel was now leaving at a trot. Slowly she sagged against the tree, lower and lower. He headed into the trail leading up the cañon. How strange a relief Ellen felt! She watched him ride into the aspens and start up the slope, at last to disappear in the pines. It seemed at the moment that he took with him something that had been hers. A pain in her hand dulled the thoughts that wavered to and fro. After he had gone, she could not see so well. Her eyes were tired. What had happened to her? There was blood on her hands. Isbel's blood! She shuddered. Was it an omen? Lower she sank against the tree and closed her eyes.

Old John Sprague did not return. Hours dragged by—dark hours for Ellen Jorth, lying prostrate beside the tree, hiding the blue sky and golden sunlight from her eyes. At length the lethargy of despair, the black, dull misery wore away, and she gradually returned to a condition of coherent thought.

What had she learned? Sight of the black horse grazing near seemed to prompt the trenchant replies. Spades belonged to Jean Isbel. He had been stolen by her father or by

149

one of her father's accomplices. Isbel's vaunted cunning as a tracker had been no idle threat. Her father was a horse thief, a rustler, a sheepman only as a blind, a consort of Daggs, leader of the Hash Knife Gang. Ellen remembered the ill repute of that gang, away back in Texas years ago. Her father had gotten in with this famous band of rustlers to serve his own ends—the extermination of the Isbels. It was all very plain now to Ellen.

"Daughter of a horse thief an' rustler," she muttered.

Her thoughts sped back to the days of her girlhood. Only the very early stage at that time had been happy. In the light of Isbel's revelation the many changes of residence, the sudden moves to unsettled parts of Texas, the periods of poverty and sudden prosperity, all leading to the final journey to this god-forsaken Arizona—these were now seen in their true significance. As far back as she could remember, her father had been a crooked man. Her mother had known it. He had dragged her to her ruin. That degradation had killed her. Ellen realized that with poignant sorrow, with a sudden revolt against her father. Had Gaston Isbel truly and dishonestly started her father on his downhill road? Ellen wondered. She hated the Isbels with unutterable and growing hate, yet she had it in her to think, to ponder, to weigh judgments in their behalf. She owed it to something in herself to be fair. But what did it matter who was to blame for the Jorth-Isbel feud? Somehow Ellen was forced to confess that deep in her soul it mattered terribly. To be true to herself—the self that she alone knew—she must have right on her side. If the Jorths were guilty, and she clung to them and their creed, then she would be one of them.

"But I'm not," she mused aloud. "My name's Jorth, an' I reckon I have bad blood. But it never came out in me till today. I've been honest. I've been good . . . yes, *good*, as my mother taught me to be . . . in spite of all. Shore, my pride made me a fool . . . an' now have I any choice to make? I'm a Jorth. I must stick to my father."

All this summing up, however, did not wholly account for the pang in her breast. What had she done that day? The answer beat in her ears like a great, throbbing hammer stroke. In an agony of shame, in the throes of hate, she had perjured herself. She had sworn away her honor. She had basely made herself vile. She had struck ruthlessly at the great heart of a man who loved her. Ah! What thrust had rebounded to leave this dreadful pang in her breast. Loved her? Yes, the strange truth, the insupportable truth! She had to contend now, not with her father and her disgrace, not with the baffling presence of Jean Isbel, but with the mysteries of her own soul. Wonder of all wonders it was that such love had been born for her. Shame worse than all other shame it was that she should kill it by a poisoned lie. By what monstrous motive had she done that? To sting Isbel as he had stung her! But that had been base. Never could she have stooped so low except in a moment of tremendous tumult. If she had done sore injury to Isbel, what had she done to herself? How strange, how tenacious had been his faith in her honor! Could she ever forget? She must forget it. But she could never forget the way he had scorned those vile men in Greaves's store—the way he had beaten Bruce for defiling her name—the way he had stubbornly denied her own insinuations. She was a woman now. She had learned something of the complexity of a woman's heart. She could not change nature. All her passionate being thrilled to the manhood of her defender. But even while she thrilled, she acknowledged her hate. It was the contention between the two that caused the pang in her breast.

"An' now what's left for me?" murmured Ellen. She did not analyze the significance of what had prompted that query. The most incalculable of the days' disclosures was the wrong she had done herself. "Shore, I'm done for, one way or another. I must stick to Dad . . . or kill myself."

Ellen rode Spades back to the ranch. She rode like the wind. When she swung out of the trail into the open meadow in plain sight of the ranch, her appearance created a commotion among the loungers before the cabin. She rode Spades at a full run.

"Who's after you?" yelled her father, as she pulled the black to a halt. Jorth held a rifle. Daggs, Colter, the other Jorths were there, likewise armed, and watchful, strung with expectancy.

"Shore nobody's after me," replied Ellen. "Cain't I run a horse 'round heah without being chased?"

Jorth appeared both incensed and relieved.

"Hah! What you mean, girl, runnin' like a streak right down on us? You're actin' queer these days, an' you look queer. I'm not likin' it."

"Reckon these are queer times . . . for the Jorths," replied Ellen sarcastically.

"Daggs found strange hoss tracks crossin' the meadow," said her father. "An' that worried us. Someone's been snoopin' 'round the ranch. An' when we seen you runnin' so wild, we shore thought you was bein' chased."

"No. I was only trying out Spades to see how fast he could run," returned Ellen. "Reckon when we do get chased, it'll take some runnin' to catch me."

"Haw! Haw!" roared Daggs. "It shore will, Ellen."

"Girl, it's not only your runnin' an your looks that's queer," declared Jorth in dark perplexity. "You talk queer."

152

"Shore, Dad, you're not used to hearing Spades called Spades," said Ellen as she dismounted.

"*Humph!*" ejaculated her father, as if convinced of the uselessness of trying to understand a woman. "Say, did you see any strange horse tracks?"

"I reckon I did. And I know who made them."

Jorth stiffened. All the men behind him showed a sudden intensity of suspense.

"Who?" demanded Jorth.

"Shore it was Jean Isbel," replied Ellen coolly. "He came up heah, tracking his black horse."

"Jean . . . Isbel . . . trackin' . . . his . . . black . . . horse," repeated her father.

"Yes. He's not overrated as a tracker, that's shore."

Black silence reigned. Ellen cast a slow glance over her father, and the others, then she began to loosen the cinches of her saddle. Presently Jorth burst the silence with a curse, and Daggs followed with one of his sardonic laughs.

"Wal, boss, what did I tell you?" he drawled.

Jorth strode to Ellen, and, whirling her around with a strong hand, he held her facing him. "Did you see Isbel?"

"Yes," replied Ellen just as sharply as her father had asked.

"Did you talk to him?"

"Yes."

"What did he want up heah?"

"I told you. He was tracking the black horse you stole."

Jorth's hand and arm dropped limply. His sallow face turned a livid hue. Amazement merged into discomfiture and that gave place to rage. He raised a hand as if to strike Ellen. Suddenly Daggs's long arm shot up to clutch Jorth's wrist. Wrestling to free himself, Jorth cursed under his breath. "Let go, Daggs!" he shouted stridently.

"Am I drunk that you grab me?"

"Wal, you ain't drunk, I reckon," replied the other with sarcasm. "But there're shore some things I'll reserve for your private ear."

Jorth gained a semblance of composure, but it was evident that he labored under a shock.

"Ellen, did Jean Isbel see this black horse?"

"Yes. He asked me how I got Spades, an' I told him."

"Did he say Spades belonged to him?"

"Shore, I reckon he proved it. You can always tell a horse that loves its master."

"Did you offer to give Spades back?"

"Yes. But Isbel wouldn't take him."

"Hah! An' why not?"

"He said he'd rather I kept Spades. He was about to engage in a dirty, blood-spilling deal, an' he reckoned he'd not be able to care for a fine horse. I didn't want Spades. I tried to make Isbel take him. But he rode off . . . and that's all there is to that."

"Maybe it's not," replied Jorth, chewing his mustache and eyeing Ellen with a dark, intent gaze. "You've met this Isbel twice."

"It wasn't any fault of mine," retorted Ellen.

"I heah he's sweet on you. How aboot that?"

Ellen smarted under the blaze of blood that swept to neck and cheek and temple, but it was only memory that fired this shame. What her father and his crowd might think were matters of supreme indifference. Yet she met his suspicious gaze with truthful, blazing eyes.

"I heah talk from Bruce an' Lorenzo," went on her father. "An' Daggs heah. . . ."

"Daggs nothin'!" interrupted that worthy. "Don't fetch me in. I said nothin' an' I think nothin'."

"Yes, Jean Isbel *was* sweet on me, Dad . . . but he will never be again," returned Ellen in low tones. With that she pulled the saddle off Spades, and, throwing it over her shoulder, she walked off to her cabin.

Hardly had she gotten indoors when her father entered.

"Ellen, I didn't know that horse belonged to Isbel," he began in the swift, hoarse, persuasive voice so familiar to Ellen. "I swear I didn't. I bought him . . . traded with Slater for him. Honest to God I never had any idea he was stolen. Why, when you said 'that horse you stole', I felt as if you'd knifed me. . . ."

Ellen sat at the table and listened while her father paced to and fro, and by his restless action and passionate speech worked himself into a frenzy. He talked incessantly, as if her silence was condemnatory and as if eloquence alone could convince her of his honesty. It seemed that Ellen saw and heard with keener faculties than ever before. He had a terrible thirst for her respect. Not so much for her love, she divined, but rather that she would not see how he had fallen! She pitied him with all her heart. She was all he had, as he was all the world to her. And so, as she gave ear to his long, illogical rigmarole of argument and defense, she slowly found that her pity and her love were making vital decisions for her. As of old, in poignant moments, her father lapsed at last into a denunciation of the Isbels, and what they had brought him to. His sufferings were real, at least, in Ellen's presence. She was the only link that bound him to long-past happier times. She was her mother over again—the woman who had betrayed another man for him and gone with him to her ruin and death.

"Dad, don't go on so," said Ellen, breaking in upon her father's rant. "I will be true to you . . . as my mother was. I am a Jorth. Your place is my place . . . your fight is my fight

. . . never speak of the past to me again. If God spares us through this feud, we will go away and begin all over again, far off where no one ever heard of a Jorth. If we're not spared, we'll at least have had our whack at these damned Isbels."

Chapter Seven

During June Jean Isbel did not ride far away from Grass Valley. Another attempt had been made upon Gaston Isbel's life. Another cowardly shot had been fired from ambush, this time from a pine thicket bordering the trail that led to Blaisdell's ranch. Blaisdell heard this shot, so near his home was it fired. No trace of the hidden foe could be found. The ground all around that vicinity bore a carpet of pine needles that showed no trace of footprints. The supposition was that this cowardly attempt had been perpetrated, or certainly instigated, by the Jorths. But there was no proof. Gaston Isbel had other enemies in the Tonto Basin besides the sheep clan. The old man raged like a lion about this sneaking attack on him. His friend Blaisdell urged an immediate gathering of their kin and friends. "Let's quit ranchin' till this trouble settles," he declared. "Let's arm an' ride the trails an' meet these men halfway. It won't help our side any to wait till you're shot in the back." More than one of Isbel's supporters offered the same advice.

"No, we'll wait till we know for shore," was the stubborn cattleman's reply to all these promptings.

"Know! Wal, hell . . . didn't Jean find the black hoss up at Jorth's ranch?" demanded Blaisdell. "What more do we want?"

"Jean couldn't swear Jorth stole the black."

"Wal, by thunder, I can swear to it," growled Blaisdell. "An' we're losin' cattle all the time. Who's stealin' them?"

157

"We've always lost cattle ever since we started ranchin' heah."

"Gass, I reckon you want Jorth to start this fight in the open. But maybe he'll never do it."

"It'll start soon enough," was Isbel's gloomy reply.

Jean had not failed altogether in his tracking of lost or stolen cattle. It was just that circumstances had been against him, and there was something baffling about this rustling. The summer storms had set in early, and it had been his luck to have heavy rains wash out fresh tracks that he might have followed. The range was large and cattle were everywhere. Sometimes a loss was not discovered for weeks afterward. Gaston Isbel's sons were now the only men left to ride the range. Two of his riders had quit because of the threatened war, and Isbel had let another go, so that Jean did not often learn that cattle had been stolen until their tracks were old. Added to this was the fact that the Grass Valley country was covered with horse tracks and cattle tracks. The rustlers, whoever they were, had long been at the game, and, now that there was reason for them to show their cunning, they did it.

Early in July the hot weather came. Down in the red ridges of the Tonto it was hot desert. The nights were cool, the early mornings were pleasant, but the day was something to endure. When the white cumulus clouds rolled up out of the southwest, growing larger and thicker and darker, here and there coalescing into a black thunderhead, Jean welcomed them. He liked to see the gray streamers of rain hanging down low from a canopy of black, and the roar of rain on the trees as it approached like a trampling army was always welcome. The grassy flats, the red ridges, the rocky slopes, the thickets of manzanita and scrub oak and cactus were dusty, glaring, throat-parching places under the hot summer sun. Jean longed for the cool heights of the Tonto Rim, the shady pines, the dark, sweet verdure under the silver spruce, the tinkle and murmur of the clear rills. He often had another longing, too, which he bitterly stifled.

Jean's ally, the keen-nosed shepherd dog, had disappeared one day, and had never returned. Among the men at the ranch there was a difference of opinion as to what had happened to Shepp. The old rancher thought he had been poisoned or shot. Bill and Guy Isbel believed he had been stolen by sheepherders who were always stealing dogs. Jean inclined to the conviction that Shepp had gone off with the timber wolves. The fact was that Shepp did not return, and Jean missed him.

One morning at dawn Jean heard the cattle bellowing and trampling out in the valley, and, upon hurrying to a vantage point, he was amazed to see upwards of five hundred steers chasing a lone wolf. Jean's father had seen such a spectacle as this, but it was a new one for Jean. The wolf was a big gray-and-black fellow, rangy and powerful, and, until he got the steers all behind him, he was rather hard put to it to keep out of their way. Probably he had dogged the herd, trying to sneak in and pull down a yearling, and finally the steers had charged him. Jean kept along the edge of the valley in the hope they would chase him within range of a rifle, but the wary wolf saw Jean and sheared off, gradually drawing away from his pursuers.

Jean returned to the house for his breakfast, and then set off across the valley. His father owned one small flock of sheep that had not yet been driven up on the rim where all the sheep in that country were run during the hot dry summer down on the Tonto. Young Evarts and a Mexican boy named Bernardino had charge of this flock. The regular Mexican herder, a man of experience, had given up his job,

159

and these boys were not equal to the task of herding the sheep up in the enemies' stronghold.

This flock was known to be grazing in a side draw, well up from Grass Valley, where the brush afforded some protection from the sun and there was good water and a little feed. Before Jean reached his destination, he heard a shot. It was not a rifle shot, which fact caused Jean a little concern. Evarts and Bernardino had rifles, but to his keen eyes no small arms. Jean rode up in one of the black-brushed conical hills that rose on the south side of Grass Valley, and from there he took a sharp survey of the country. At first he made out only cattle and bare meadowland and the low, encircling ridges and hills. But presently, up toward the head of the valley, he descried a bunch of horsemen, riding toward the village. He could not tell their number. That dark moving mass seemed to Jean to be instinct with life, mystery, menace. Who were they? It was too far for him to recognize horses, let alone riders. They were moving fast, too.

Jean watched them out of sight, then turned his horse downhill again, and rode on his quest. A number of horsemen like that was a very unusual sight around Grass Valley at any time. What, then, did it portend now? Jean experienced a little shock of uneasy dread that was an unusual situation for him. Brooding over this, he proceeded on his way, at length to turn into the draw where the camp of the sheepherders was located. Upon coming in sight of it, he heard a hoarse shout. Young Evarts appeared running frantically out of the brush. Jean urged his horse into a run and soon covered the distance between them. Evarts appeared beside himself with terror.

"Boy, what's the matter?" queried Jean as he dismounted, rifle in hand, peering quickly from Evarts's white face to the camp, and all around.

"Ber-nardino! Ber-nardino!" gasped the boy, wringing his hands and pointing.

Jean ran the few remaining rods to the sheep camp. He saw the little teepee, a burned-out fire, a half-finished meal—and then the Mexican lad lying prone on the ground, dead, with a bullet hole in his ghastly face. Near him lay an old six-shooter.

"Whose gun is this?" demanded Jean as he picked it up.

"Ber-nardino's," replied Evarts huskily. "He . . . he jest got it . . . the other day."

"Did he shoot himself accidentally?"

"Oh, no! No! He didn't do it . . . a-tall."

"Who did then?"

"The men . . . they rode off . . . a gang . . . they did it," panted Evarts.

"Did you know who they were?"

"No. I couldn't tell. I saw them comin' an' I was skeered. Bernardino had gone fer water. I run an' hid in the brush. I wanted to yell, but they come too close. Then I heered them talkin'. Bernardino came back. They 'peared friendly-like. That made me raise up to look, an' I couldn't see good. I heered one of them ask Bernardino to let him see his gun. An' Bernardino handed it over. He was a big, tall man with shiny hair. He looked at the gun an' haw-hawed, an' flipped it up in the air, an', when it fell back in his hand, it . . . it went off bang! An' Bernardino dropped. I heered them talk some, but not what they said. Then they rode away. An' I hid there till I seen you comin'."

"Have you got a horse?" queried Jean sharply.

"No. But I can ride one of Bernardino's burros."

"Get one. Hurry over to Blaisdell. Tell him to send word to Blue and Gordon and Fredericks to ride like the devil to my father's ranch. Hurry now."

161

Young Evarts ran off without reply. Jean stood looking down at the limp and pathetic figure of the Mexican boy. "By heaven!" he exclaimed grimly. "The Jorth-Isbel war is on! Deliberate, cold-blooded murder! I'll gamble Daggs did this job. He's been given the leadership. He's started it. Bernardino, you were a faithful lad, and you won't go long unavenged."

Jean had no time to spare. Tearing the tarpaulin out of the teepee, he covered the lad with it, and then ran for his horse. Mounting, he galloped down the draw, over the little red ridges, out into the valley, where he put his horse to a run.

Action changed the sickening horror that sight of Bernardino had engendered. Jean even felt a strange, grim relief. The long, dragging days of waiting were over. Jorth's gang had taken the initiative. Blood had begun to flow, and it would continue to flow now till the last man of one faction stood over the dead body of the last man of the other. Would it be a Jorth or an Isbel? "My instinct was right," he muttered aloud. "That bunch of horses gave me a queer feelin'." Jean gazed all around the grassy cattle-dotted valley he was crossing so swiftly and toward the village, but he did not see any sign of the dark group of riders. They had gone in to Greaves's store, there no doubt to drink, and to add more enemies of the Isbels to their gang. Suddenly across Jean's mind flashed a thought of Ellen Jorth. *What'll become of her? What'll become of all the women? My sister? The little ones!*

No one was in sight around the ranch. Never had it appeared more peaceful and pastoral to Jean. The grazing cattle and horses in the foreground, the haystack half eaten away, the cows in the fenced pasture, the column of blue

GET
4 FREE BOOKS!

You can have the best Westerns delivered to your door for less than what you'd pay in a bookstore or online. Sign up for one of our book clubs today, and we'll send you 4 FREE* BOOKS, worth $23.96, just for trying it out...with no obligation to buy, ever!

❖

Authors include classic writers such as
LOUIS L'AMOUR, MAX BRAND, ZANE GREY
and more; PLUS new authors such as
COTTON SMITH, TIM CHAMPLIN, JOHNNY D. BOGGS
and others.

❖

As a book club member you also receive the following special benefits:

- 30% OFF all orders through our website & telecenter!
- Exclusive access to special discounts!
- Convenient home delivery and 10 days to return any books you don't want to keep.

There is no minimum number of books to buy,
and you may cancel membership at any time.
See back to sign up!

*Please include $2.00 for shipping and handling.

YES! ☐

Sign me up for the Leisure Western Book Club
and send my FOUR FREE BOOKS! If I choose to stay
in the club, I will pay only $14.00* each month,
a savings of $9.96!

NAME: _____

ADDRESS: _____

_____

TELEPHONE: _____

E-MAIL: _____

☐ **I WANT TO PAY BY CREDIT CARD.**

☐ VISA   ☐ MasterCard   ☐ DISCOVER

ACCOUNT #: _____

EXPIRATION DATE: _____

SIGNATURE: _____

Send this card along with $2.00 shipping & handling to:

**Leisure Western Book Club
20 Academy Street
Norwalk, CT 06850-4032**

Or fax (must include credit card information!) to: 610.995.9274.
You can also sign up online at www.dorchesterpub.com.

*Plus $2.00 for shipping. Offer open to residents of the U.S. and Canada only.
Canadian residents please call 1.800.481.9191 for pricing information.

If under 18, a parent or guardian must sign. Terms, prices and conditions subject to change. Subscription subject
to acceptance. Dorchester Publishing reserves the right to reject any order or cancel any subscription.

JOIN NOW!

smoke lazily ascending, the cackle of hens, the solid, well-built cabins—all these seemed to repudiate Jean's haste and his darkness of mind. This place was his father's ranch. There was not a cloud in the summer sky.

As Jean galloped up the lane, someone saw him from the door, and presently Bill and Guy, and then their gray-headed father, came out upon the porch. Jean saw how his father waved the womenfolk back, and then strode out into the lane. Bill and Guy reached his side first as Jean pulled his heaving horse to a halt. They all looked at Jean, swiftly and intently, with a little, hard, fiery gleam, strangely identical in the eyes of each. Probably before a word was spoken they knew what to expect.

"Wal, you shore was in a hurry," remarked Gaston Isbel.

"What the hell's up?" queried Bill grimly.

Guy Isbel remained silent and it was he who turned slightly pale. Jean leaped off his horse.

"Bernardino has just been killed . . . murdered with his own gun."

Gaston Isbel seemed to exhale a long-dammed bursting breath that let his chest sag. A terrible, deadly glint, pale and cold as sunlight on ice, grew slowly to dominate his clear eyes.

"A-huh!" ejaculated Bill Isbel hoarsely.

Not one of the three men asked who had done the killing. They were silent a moment, motionless, locked in the secret seclusion of their own minds. Then they listened absorbedly to Jean's brief story.

"Wal, that's the start," said his father. "I wish we'd had more time. Reckon I'd done better to listen to you boys an' have my men close at hand. Jacobs happened to ride over. That makes five of us besides the women."

163

"Aw, Dad, you don't reckon they'll attack us heah?" asked Guy Isbel.

"Boys, I always feared they might," replied the old man. "But I never really believed they'd have the nerve. Shore I might have figgered Daggs better. This heah secret bizness an' shootin' at us from ambush looked aboot Jorth's size to me. But I reckon now we'll have to fight without our friends."

"Let them come," said Jean. "I sent for Blaisdell, Blue, Gordon, and Fredericks. Maybe they'll get here in time. But if they don't, it needn't worry us much. We can hold out here longer than Jorth's gang can hang around. We'll want plenty of water, wood, and meat in the house."

"Wal, I'll see to that," rejoined his father. "Jean, you go out close by, where you can see all around, an' keep watch."

"Who's goin' to tell the women?" asked Guy Isbel.

The silence that momentarily ensued was an eloquent testimony to the hardest and saddest aspect of this strife between men. The inevitableness of it in no wise detracted from its sheer uselessness. Men from time immemorial have hated and killed each other, always to the misery and degradation of their women. Old Gaston Isbel showed this tragic realization in his lined face.

"Wal, boys, I'll tell the women," he said. "Shore you needn't worry none about them. They'll be game."

Jean rode away to an open knoll a short distance from the house, and here he stationed himself to watch all points. The cedared ridge back of the ranch was the one approach by which Jorth's gang might come close without being detected, but even so Jean could see them and ride to the house in time to prevent a surprise. The moments dragged by, and at the end of an hour Jean was in hope that Blaisdell would soon come. This hope was well founded. Presently he heard a clatter of hoofs on hard ground to the south, and, upon wheeling to look, he saw the friendly neighbor coming fast along the road, riding a big white horse. Blaisdell carried a rifle in his hand and the sight of him gave Jean a glow of warmth. He was one of the Texans who would stand by the Isbels to the last man. Jean watched him ride to the house—watched the meeting between him and his life-long friend. Then old Blaisdell's roar of rage floated out to Jean.

Out on the green of Grass Valley, where a long swelling plain swept away toward the village, there appeared a moving dark patch. A bunch of horses! Jean's body gave a slight start—the shock of sudden propulsion of blood through all his veins. Those horses bore riders. They were coming straight down the open valley, on the wagon road to Isbel's ranch. No subterfuge or secrecy or sneaking in that advance! A hot thrill ran over Jean.

"By Heaven, they mean business," he muttered. Up to the last moment he had unconsciously hoped Jorth's gang would not come boldly like that. The verifications of all a Texan's inherited instincts left no doubts, no hopes, no illusions—only a grim certainty that this was not conjecture or probability, but a physical fact. For a moment longer Jean watched the slowly moving dark patch of horsemen against the green background, then he hurried back to the ranch. His father saw him coming—strode out as before.

"Dad . . . Jorth is comin'," said Jean huskily. How he hated to be forced to tell his father that! The boyish love of old had flashed up.

"Whar?" demanded the old man, his eagle eyes sweeping the horizon.

"Down the road from Grass Valley. You can't see from here."

"Wal, come in an' let's get ready."

Isbel's house had been constructed with the idea of re-
pelling an attack from a band of Apaches. The large living
room of the main cabin was the one selected for defense
and protection. This room had two windows and a door
facing the lane and a door at each end, one of which opened
into the kitchen and the other into an adjoining cabin built
later. The logs of this main cabin were of large size and the
doors and window coverings were heavy, affording safer
protection from bullets than the other cabins. When Jean
went in, he seemed to see a host of white faces lifted to him.
His sister Ann, his two sisters-in-law, the children, all
mutely watched him with eyes that would haunt him.

"Wal, Blaisdell, Jean says Jorth an' his precious gang of
rustlers are on the way heah," announced the rancher.

"Damn me if it's not a bad day fer Lee Jorth!" declared
Blaisdell.

"Clear off that table," ordered Isbel, "an' fetch out all
the guns an' shells we got."

Once laid upon the table, these presented a formidable
arsenal that consisted of the three new .44 Winchesters that
Jean had brought with him from the Coast; the enormous
buffalo, or so-called needle, gun that Gaston Isbel had used
for years; a Henry rifle that Blaisdell had brought, and half
a dozen six-shooters. Piles and packages of ammunition littered the table.

"Sort out these heah shells," said Isbel. "Everybody
wants to get hold of his own."

Jacobs, the neighbor who was present, was a thick-set
bearded man, rather jovial among those lean-jawed Texans.
He carried a .44 rifle of an old pattern. "Wal, boys, if I'd
knowed we was in fer some fun, I'd hev' fetched more
shells. Only got me a magazine full. Mebbe them new

166

Forty-Fours will fit my gun."

It was discovered that the ammunition Jean had brought in quantity fitted Jacob's rifle, a fact that afforded peculiar satisfaction to all the men present.

"Wal, shore we're lucky," declared Gaston Isbel.

The women sat apart, in the corner toward the kitchen, and there seemed to be a strange fascination for them in the talk and action of the men. The wife of Jacobs was a little woman with a homely face and very bright eyes. Jean thought she would be a help in that household during the next doubtful hours.

Every moment Jean would go to the window and peer out down the road. His companions evidently relied upon him, for no one else looked out. Now that the suspense of days and weeks was over, these Texans faced the issue with talk and action not noticeably different from those of ordinary moments.

At last Jean espied the dark mass of horsemen out on the valley road. They were close together, walking their mounts, and evidently in earnest conversation. After several ineffectual attempts Jean counted eleven horses, every one of which he was sure bore a rider.

"Dad, look out!" called Jean.

Gaston Isbel strode to the door and stood looking without a word. The other men crowded to the window. Blaisdell cursed under his breath. Jacobs said: "By Golly! Come to pay us a call!" The women sat motionless with dark, strained eyes. The children ceased their play and looked fearfully to their mother.

When just out of rifle shot of the cabins, the band of horsemen halted and lined up in a half circle, all facing the ranch house. They were close enough for Jean to see their gestures, but he could not recognize any of their faces. It struck him singularly that not one of them wore a mask.

"Jean, do you know any of them?" asked his father.

"No, not yet. They're too far off."

"Dad, I'll get your old telescope," said Guy Isbel, and he ran out toward the adjoining cabin.

Blaisdell shook his big, hoary head and rumbled out of his bull-like neck: "Wal, now you're heah, you sheep fellers, what are you goin' to do aboot it?"

Guy Isbel returned with a yard-long telescope that he passed to his father. The old man took it with shaking hands and leveled it. Suddenly it was as if he had been transfixed. Then he lowered the glass, shaking violently, and his face grew gray with an exceedingly bitter wrath.

"Jorth!" he swore harshly.

Jean had only to look at his father to know that recognition had been like a mortal shock. It passed. Again the rancher leveled the glass.

"Wal, Blaisdell, there's our old Texas friend, Daggs," he drawled dryly. "An' Greaves, our honest storekeeper of Grass Valley. An' there's Stonewall Jackson Jorth. An' Tad Jorth with the same old red nose! An', say, damn if one of that gang isn't Queen, as bad a gunfighter as Texas ever bred. Shore I thought he'd been killed in the Big Bend country. So I heard. An' there's Craig, another respectable sheepman of Grass Valley. Haw! Haw! I don't recognize any more of them."

Jean forthwith took the glass and moved it slowly across the faces of that group of horsemen. "Simm Bruce," he said instantly. "I see Colter, and, yes, Greaves is there. I've seen the man next to him . . . face like a ham. . . ."

"Shore that is Craig," interrupted his father.

Jean knew the dark face of Lee Jorth by the resemblance

it bore to Ellen's, and the recognition brought a twinge. He thought, too, that he could tell the other Jorths. He asked his father to describe Daggs, and then Queen. It was not likely that Jean would fail to know these several men in the future. Then Blaisdell asked for the telescope, and, when he got through looking and cursing, he passed it on to others who, one by one, took a long look, until finally it came back to the old rancher.

"Wal, Daggs is wavin' his hand heah an' there, like a general aboot to send out scouts. Haw! Haw! An' 'pears to me he's not overlookin' our hosses. Wal, that's natural for a rustler. He'd have to steal a hoss or a steer before goin' into a fight or to dinner or to a funeral."

"It'll be his funeral if he goes to foolin' around them horses," declared Guy Isbel, peering anxiously out of the door.

"Wal, Son, shore it'll be somebody's funeral," replied his father.

Jean paid but little attention to the conversation. With sharp eyes fixed upon the horsemen, he tried to grasp their intention. Daggs pointed to the horses in the pasture lot that lay between them and the house. These horses were the best in the range and belonged mostly to Guy Isbel who was the horse fancier and trader of the family.

"Looks like they'd do some horse stealin'," said Jean.

"Lend me that glass," demanded Guy forcefully. He surveyed the band of men for a long moment, then he handed the glass back to Jean. "I'm goin' out there after my horses," he declared.

"No!" exclaimed his father.

"That gang came to steal an' not to fight. Can't you see that? If they meant to fight, they'd do it. They're out there arguin' about my horses." Guy picked up his rifle. He looked sullenly determined, and the gleam in his eyes was one of fearlessness.

"Son, I know Daggs," said his father. "An' I know Jorth. They've come to kill us. It'll be shore death for you to go out there."

"I'm goin' anyhow. They can't steal my horses out from under my eyes."

"Wal, Guy, you ain't goin' alone," spoke up Jacobs cheerily as he came forward.

The red-haired young wife of Guy Isbel showed no change on her grave face. She had been reared in a stern school. She knew men in times like these. But Jacobs's wife appealed to him: "Bill, don't risk your life for a horse or two."

Jacobs laughed and went out with Guy. To Jean their action seemed foolhardy, but it was thrillingly brave and defiant in the face of that gang. Jean kept a keen eye on them and saw instantly when the band became aware of Guy's and Jacobs's entrance to the pasture. It took only another second then to realize that Daggs and Jorth had deadly intent. Jean saw Daggs slip out of his saddle, rifle in hand. Others of the gang did likewise, until half of them were dismounted.

"Dad, they're goin' to shoot!" called out Jean sharply. "Yell to Guy and Jacobs. Make them come back."

The old man shouted; Bill Isbel yelled; Blaisdell lifted his stentorian voice.

Jean screamed piercingly: "Guy! Run! Run!"

But Guy Isbel and his companion strode on into the pasture, as if they had not heard, as if no menacing horse thieves were within miles. They had covered about a quarter of the distance across the pasture and were nearing the horses, when Jean saw red flashes and white puffs of

170

smoke burst out from the front of that dark band of rustlers. Then followed the sharp, rattling crack of rifles.

Guy Isbel stopped short, and, dropping his gun, he threw up his arms and fell headlong. Jacobs acted as if he had suddenly encountered an invisible blow. He had been hit. Turning, he began to run and ran fast for a few paces. There were more quick, sharp shots. He let go of his rifle. His running broke. Walking, reeling, staggering, he kept on. A hoarse cry came from him. Then a swift rifle shot pealed out. Jean heard the bullet strike. Jacobs fell to his knees, then forward on his face.

Jean Isbel felt himself turned to marble. The suddenness of this tragedy paralyzed him. His gaze remained riveted on those prostrate forms.

A hand clutched his arm—a shaking woman's hand, slim and hard and tense.

"Bill's killed," whispered a broken voice. "I was watchin'. They're dead . . . both dead!"

The wives of Jacobs and Guy Isbel had slipped up behind Jean and from behind him they had seen the tragedy.

"I asked Bill . . . not . . . to . . . go," faltered the Jacobs woman, and, covering her face with her hands, she groped back to the corner of the cabin where the other women, shaking and white, received her in their arms.

Guy Isbel's wife stood at the window, peering over Jean's shoulder. She had the nerve of a man. She had looked out upon death before. "Yes, they're dead," she said bitterly. "An' how are we goin' to get their bodies?"

At this, Gaston Isbel seemed to rouse from the cold spell that had transfixed him. "God, this is hell for our women," he cried out hoarsely. "My son . . . my son . . . murdered by the Jorths!" Then he swore a terrible oath.

Jean saw the remainder of the mounted rustlers get off,

and then, all of them leading their horses, they began to move around to the left.

"Dad, they're movin' 'round," said Jean.

"Up to some trick," declared Bill Isbel.

"Bill, you make a hole through the back wall, say aboot the fifth log up," ordered the father. "Shore we've got to look out."

The older son grasped a tool, and, scattering the children, who had been playing near the back corner, he began to work at the point designated. The little children backed away with fixed, wondering, glazed eyes. The women moved their chairs and huddled together as if waiting and listening.

Jean watched the rustlers until they passed out of his sight. They had moved toward the sloping brushy ground to the north end west of the cabins.

"Let me know when you get a hole in the back wall," said Jean, and he went through the kitchen and cautiously out another door to slip into a low-roofed shed-like end of the rambling cabin. This small space was used to store winter firewood. The chinks between the walls had not been filled with adobe clay and he could see out on three sides. The rustlers were going into the juniper brush. They moved out of sight, and presently reappeared without their horses. It looked to Jean as if they intended to attack the cabins. Then they halted at the edge of the brush and held a long consultation. Jean could see them distinctly, although they were too far distant for him to recognize any particular man. One of them, however, stood and moved apart from the closely massed group. Evidently, from his strides and gestures, he was exhorting his listeners. Jean concluded this was either Daggs or Jorth. Whoever it was had a loud, coarse voice and this and his actions impressed Jean with a suspicion that the man was under the influence of the bottle.

Presently Bill Isbel called Jean in a low voice. "Jean, I got the hole made, but we can't see anyone."

"I see them," Jean replied. "They're havin' a powwow. Looks to me like either Jorth or Daggs is drunk. He's arguin' to charge us, an' the rest of the gang are holdin' back. Tell Dad, an' all of you keep watchin'. I'll let you know when they make a move."

Jorth's gang appeared to be in no hurry to expose their plan of battle. Gradually the group disintegrated a little. Some of them sat down; others walked to and fro. Presently two of them went into the brush, probably back to the horses. In a few moments they reappeared, carrying a pack. When this was deposited on the ground, all the rustlers sat down around it. They had brought food and drink. Jean had to utter a grim laugh at their coolness, and he was reminded of many daredevil deeds known to have been perpetrated by the Hash Knife Gang. Jean was glad of a reprieve. The longer the rustlers put off an attack, the more time the allies of the Isbels would have to get here. However, it would be rather hazardous now for anyone to attempt to get to the Isbel cabins in the daytime. Night would be more favorable.

Twice Bill Isbel came through the kitchen to whisper to Jean. The strain in the large room, from which the rustlers could not be seen, must have been great. Jean told him all he had seen and what he thought about it. "Eatin' an' drinkin'!" ejaculated Bill. "Well, I'll be . . . ! That'll jar the old man. He wants to get the fight over."

"Tell him I said it'll be over too quick . . . for us . . . unless we are mighty careful," replied Jean sharply.

Bill went back, muttering to himself. There followed a long wait, fraught with suspense, during which Jean

173

watched the rustlers regale themselves. The day was hot and still, and the unnatural silence of the cabin was broken now and then by the gay laughter of the children. The sound shocked and haunted Jean. Playing children! Then another sound, so faint he had to strain to hear it, disturbed and saddened him—his father's slow tread up and down the cabin floor, to and fro, to and fro. What must be in his father's heart this day!

At length, the rustlers rose, and with rifles in hand they moved as one man down the slope. They came several hundred yards closer, until Jean, grimly cocking his rifle, muttered to himself that a few more rods closer would mean the end of several of that gang. They knew the range of a rifle well enough, and once more sheered off at right angles with the cabin. When they got even with the line of corrals, they stooped down and were lost to Jean's sight. This fact caused him alarm. They were, of course, crawling up on the cabins. At the end of that line of corrals ran a ditch, the bank of which was high enough to afford cover. Moreover, it ran along in front of the cabins, scarcely a hundred yards, and it was covered with grass and little clumps of brush, from behind which the rustlers could fire into the windows and through the clay chinks without any considerable risk to themselves. As they did not come into sight again, Jean concluded he had discovered their plan. Still he waited a while longer, until he saw faint little clouds of dust rising from behind the far end of the embankment. That discovery made him rush out and through the kitchen to the large cabin, where his sudden appearance startled the men.

"Get back out of sight!" he ordered sharply, and with swift steps he reached the door, and closed it. "They're behind the bank out there by the corrals. An' they're goin' to crawl down the ditch closer to us. It looks bad. They'll have grass an' brush to shoot from. We've got to be mighty careful how we peep out."

"A-huh! All right," replied his father. "You women keep the kids with you in that corner. An' you all better lay down flat."

Blaisdell, Bill Isbel, and the old man crouched at the large window, peeping through cracks in the rough edges of the logs. Jean took his post beside the small window with his keen eyes vibrating like a compass needle. The movement of a blade of grass, the flight of a grasshopper could not escape his trained sight.

"Look sharp now!" he called to the other men. "I see dust. They're workin' along, almost to that bare spot on the bank. I saw the tip of a rifle . . . a black hat . . . more dust. They're spreadin' along behind the bank."

Loud voices and thick clouds of yellow dust, coming from behind the highest and brushiest line of the embankment, attested to the truth of Jean's observations and also to a reckless disregard of danger.

Suddenly Jean caught a glint of moving color through the fringe of brush. Instantly he was strung like a whipcord. Then a tall hatless and coatless man stepped up in plain sight. The sun shone on his fair ruffled hair. Daggs!

"Hey you god-damned Isbels!" he bawled in magnificent derisive boldness. "Come out an' fight!"

Quick as lightning Jean threw up his rifle and fired. He saw tufts of fair hair fly from Daggs's head. He saw the squirt of red blood. Then three quick shots from Jean's comrades rang out. They all hit the swaying body of the rustler, but Jean knew with a terrible thrill that his bullet had killed Daggs before the other three struck. Daggs fell forward, his arms and half his body resting over the embankment. Then the rustlers dragged him back out of sight.

Hoarse shouts rose. A cloud of yellow dust drifted away from the spot.

"Daggs!" burst out Gaston Isbel. "Jean, you plucked off the top of his haid. I seen that when I was pullin' trigger. Shore we over heah wasted our shots."

"God, he must have been crazy or drunk . . . to pop up there . . . an' brace us that way," said Blaisdell, breathing hard.

"Arizona is bad for Texans," replied Isbel sardonically. "Shore it's been too peaceful heah. Rustlers have no practice at fightin'. An' I reckon Daggs forgot."

"Daggs made as crazy a move as that of Guy an' Jacobs," spoke up Jean. "They was overbold, an' he was drunk. Let them be a lesson to me."

Jean had smelled whisky upon his entrance to this cabin. Bill was a hard drinker, and his father was not immune. Blaisdell, too, drank heavily upon occasions. Jean made a mental note that he would not permit their chances to become impaired by liquor.

Rifles began to crack, and puffs of smoke rose all along the embankment for the space of a hundred feet. Bullets whistled through the windows to thud into the cabin wall behind. Other bullets splintered the rude window casing and spattered on the heavy doors, and one split the clay between the logs before Jean, narrowly missing him. Another volley followed, then another. The rustlers had repeating rifles and they were emptying their magazines. Jean changed his position. The other men profited by his wise move. The volleys had merged into one continuous rattling roar of rifle shots. Then came a sudden cessation of reports, with silence of relief. The cabin was full of dust, mingled with the smoke from the shots of Jean and his companions. Jean heard the stifled breaths of the children. Evidently they

176

were terror-stricken, but they did not cry out. The women uttered no sound.

A loud voice pealed from behind the embankment.

"Come out an' fight! Do you Isbels want to be killed like sheep?"

This sally gained no reply. Jean returned to his post by his window and his comrades followed his example. They exercised extreme caution when they peeped out.

"Boys, don't shoot till you see one," said Gaston Isbel. "Maybe after a while they'll get careless. But Jorth will never show himself."

The rustlers did not again resort to volleys. One by one, from different angles, they began to shoot, and they were not firing at random. A few bullets came straight in at the window to pat into the walls; a few others ticked and splintered the edges of the windows; most of them broke through the clay chinks between the logs. It dawned upon Jean that these dangerous shots were not accidental. They were well-aimed, and most of them hit low down. The cunning rustlers had some unerring riflemen and they were picking out the vulnerable places all along the front of the cabin. If Jean had not been lying flat, he would have been hit twice. Presently he conceived the idea of driving pegs between the logs, high up, and, kneeling on these, he managed to peep out from the upper edge of the window. But that position was awkward and difficult to hold for long.

He heard a bullet hit one of his comrades. Whoever had been struck never uttered a sound. Jean turned to look. Bill Isbel was holding his shoulder, where red splotches appeared on his shirt. He shook his head at Jean, evidently to make light of the wound. The women and children were lying face down and could not see what was happening. Plain it was that Bill did not want them to know. Blaisdell bound up the bloody shoulder with a scarf.

Steady firing from the rustlers went on, at the rate of one shot every few minutes. The Isbels did not return these. Jean did not fire again that afternoon. Toward sunset, when the besiegers appeared to grow restless or careless, Blaisdell fired at something moving behind the brush, and Gaston Isbel's huge buffalo gun boomed out.

"Wal, what're they goin' to do after dark, an' what're *we* goin' to do?" growled Blaisdell.

"Reckon they'll never charge us," said Gaston.

"They might set fire to the cabins," added Bill Isbel. He appeared to be the gloomiest of the Isbel faction. There was something on his mind.

"Wal, the Jorths are bad, but I reckon they'd not burn us alive," replied Blaisdell.

"Hah!" ejaculated Gaston Isbel. "Much you know about Lee Jorth. He would skin me alive an' throw red-hot coals on my raw flesh."

So they talked during the hour from sunset to dark. Jean Isbel had little to say. He was revolving possibilities in his mind. Darkness brought a change in the attack of the rustlers. They stationed men at four points around the cabins, and every few minutes one of these outposts would fire. These bullets embedded themselves in the logs, causing but little anxiety to the Isbels.

"Jean, what you make of it?" asked the old rancher.

"Looks to me this way," replied Jean. "They're set for a long fight. They're shootin' just to let us know they're on the watch."

"A-huh. Wal, what're you goin' to do aboot it?"

"I'm goin' out there presently."

Gaston Isbel grunted his satisfaction at this intention of Jean's.

178

All was pitch dark inside the cabin. The women had water and food at hand. Jean kept a sharp look-out from his window while he ate his supper of meat, bread, and milk. At last the children, worn out by the long day, fell asleep. The women whispered a little in their corner.

About nine o'clock Jean signified his intention of going out to reconnoiter. "Dad, they've got the best of us in the daytime," he said, "but not after dark."

"Jean, shore you'd want to be careful," admonished his father. "They'll be on the look-out for some Indian trick."

Jean buckled on a belt that carried shells, a Bowie knife, and revolver, and with rifle in hand he went out through the kitchen to the yard. The night was darker than usual, as some of the stars were hidden by clouds. He leaned against the log cabin waiting for his eyes to become perfectly adjusted to the darkness. Like an Indian, Jean could see well at night. He knew every point around cabins and sheds and corrals, every post, log, tree, rock, adjacent to the ranch. After perhaps a quarter of an hour of watching, during which time several shots were fired from behind the embankment and one each from the rustlers at the other locations, Jean slipped out on his quest.

He kept in the shadow of the cabin walls, then the line of orchard trees, then a row of orchard trees, then a row of currant bushes. Here, crouching low, he halted to look and listen. He was now at the edge of the open ground with the gently rising slope before him. He could see the dark patches of cedar and juniper trees. On the north side of the cabin a streak of fire flashed in the blackness, and a shot rang out. Jean heard the bullet hit the cabin. Then silence enfolded the lonely ranch and the darkness lay like a black blanket. A low hum of insects pervaded the air. Dull sheets of lightning illuminated the dark horizon to the south. Once

Jean heard voices, but could not tell from which direction they came. To the west of him there flared out another rifle shot. The bullet whistled down over Jean to thud into the cabin.

Jean made a careful study of the obscure gray-black open before him, and then the background to his rear. So long as he kept the dense shadows behind him he could not be seen. He slipped from behind his covert, and, gliding with absolutely noiseless footsteps, he gained the first clump of junipers. Here he waited patiently and motionlessly for another round of shots from the rustlers. After the second shot from the west side Jean sheered off to the right. Patches of brush, clumps of juniper, and isolated cedars covered this slope, affording Jean a perfect means for his purpose, which was to make a detour and come up behind the rustler who was firing from that side. Jean climbed to the top of the ridge, descended the opposite slope, made his turn to the left, and slowly worked up behind the point near where he expected to locate the rustler. Long habit in the open, by day and night, rendered his sense of direction almost as perfect as sight itself. The first flash of fire he saw from this side disclosed that he had come straight up toward his man. Jean's intention was to crawl up on this one of the Jorth gang and silently kill him with a knife. If the plan worked successfully, Jean meant to work around to the next rustler. Laying aside his rifle, he crawled forward on hands and knees, making no more sound than a cat. His approach was slow. He had to pick his way, be careful not to break twigs or rattle stones. His buckskin garments made no sound against the brush. Jean located the rustler, sitting on the top of the ridge at the center of an open space. He was alone. Jean saw the dull, red end of the cigarette he was smoking. The ground on the ridge top was rocky and not well adapted for Jean's purpose. He had to abandon the idea of crawling up to the rustler, whereupon he turned back, patiently and slowly, to get his rifle. Upon securing it, he began to retrace his course, this time more slowly than ever, hampered as he was by the rifle. But he did not make the slightest sound, and at length he reached the edge of the open ridge top, once more to espy the dark form of the rustler silhouetted against the sky. The distance was not more than fifty yards. As Jean rose to his knee and carefully lifted his rifle around to avoid the twigs of a juniper, he suddenly experienced another emotion besides the one of grim, hard wrath at the Jorths. It was an emotion that sickened him, made him weak internally, a cold, shaking, ungovernable sensation. Suppose this man was Ellen Jorth's father! Jean lowered the rifle. He felt it shake over his knee. He was trembling all over. The astounding discovery that he did not want to kill Ellen's father—that he could not do it— awakened Jean to the despairing nature of his love for her. In this grim moment of indecision, when he knew his Indian subtlety and ability gave him a great advantage on the Jorths, he fully realized his strange, hopeless, and irresistible love for the girl. He made no attempt to deny it any longer. Like the night and the lonely wilderness around him, like the inevitability of this Jorth-Isbel feud, this love of his was a thing, a fact. A reality. He breathed to his own inward ear, to his soul—he could not kill Ellen Jorth's father. Feud or no feud, Isbel or not, he could not deliberately do it. And why not? There was no answer. Was he not faithless to his father? He had no hope of ever winning Ellen Jorth. He did not want the love of a girl of her character. But he loved her. And his struggle must be against the insidious and mysterious growth of that passion. It swayed him already. It made him a coward. Through his mind and heart swept the memory of Ellen Jorth, her beauty and charm, her boldness and pathos, her shame and her degradation, and the sweetness of her outweighed the boldness, the mystery of her arrayed itself in unquenchable protest against her acknowledged shame. Jean lifted his face to the heavens, to the pitiless white stars, to the infinite depths of the dark blue sky. He could sense the fact of his being an atom in the universe of nature. What was he—what was his revengeful father—what were hate and passion and strife in comparison to the nameless something, immense and everlasting, that he sensed in this dark moment?

But the rustlers—Daggs—the Jorths—they had killed his brother Guy—murdered him brutally and ruthlessly. Guy had been a playmate of Jean's—a favorite brother. Bill had been secretive and selfish. Jean had not loved him as he had Guy. Guy lay dead down there on the meadow. This feud had begun to run its bloody course. Jean steeled his nerve. The hot blood crept back along his veins. The dark and masterful tide of revenge waved over him. The keen edge of his mind then cut out sharp and trenchant thoughts. He must kill when and where he could. This man could hardly be Ellen Jorth's father. Jorth would be with the main crowd, directing hostilities. Jean could shoot this rustler guard and his shot would be taken by the gang as the regular one from their comrade. Then swiftly Jean leveled his rifle, covered the dark form, grew cold and set, and pressed the trigger. After the report he rose and wheeled away. He did not look or listen for the result of his shot. A clammy sweat wet his face, the hollows of his hands, his breast. A horrible, leaden-thick sensation oppressed his heart. Nature had endowed him with Indian gifts, but the exercise of them to this end caused a revolt in his soul. Nevertheless, it was the Isbel blood that dominated him. The wind blew cool on his face. The burden upon his shoulders seemed to lift. The clamoring whispers grew fainter in his ears. By the time he had retraced his cautious steps back to the orchard, all his physical being was strung to the talk at hand. Something had come between his reflective self and this man of action.

Crossing the lane, he took to the west line of sheds and passed beyond them into the meadow. In the grass he crawled silently away to the right, using the same precaution that had actuated him on the slope, only here he did not pause so often, nor move so slowly. Jean aimed to go far enough to the right to pass the end of the embankment behind which the rustlers had found such efficient cover. This ditch had been made to keep water, during spring thaws and summer storms, from pouring off the slope to flood the corrals.

Jean miscalculated and found he had come upon the embankment somewhat to the left of the end, which fact however caused him no uneasiness. He lay there a while to listen. Again he heard voices. After a time a shot pealed out. He did not see the flash, but he calculated that it had come from the north side of the cabin.

In the next quarter of an hour Jean discovered that the nearest rustler guard was firing from the top of the embankment, perhaps a hundred yards distant, and a second one was performing the same office from a point apparently only a few yards farther on. Two rustlers close together! Jean had not calculated upon that. For a little while he pondered on what was best to do, and at length decided to crawl around behind them and as close as the situation made advisable.

He found the ditch behind the embankment a favorable path by which to stalk those enemies. It was dry and sandy, with borders of high weeds. The only drawback was that it was almost impossible for him to keep from brushing against the dry, invisible branches of the weeds. To offset this he wormed his way like a snail, inch by inch, taking a long time before he caught sight of the sitting figure of a man, black against the dark-blue sky. This rustler had fired his rifle three times during Jean's slow approach. Jean watched and listened a few moments, then wormed himself closer and closer, until the man was within twenty steps of him. Jean smelled tobacco smoke, but could see no light of pipe or cigarette, because the fellow's back was turned.

Chapter Eight

"Say, Ben," said one of the men to his companion, sitting hunched up a few yards distant, "shore it strikes me queer that Somers ain't shootin' any over thar."

Jean recognized the dry, drawling voice of Greaves and the shock of it seemed to contract the muscles of his whole thrilling body, like that of a panther about to spring.

"I was shore thinkin' thet same," said the other man. "An', say, didn't that last shot sound too sharp fer Somers's Forty-Five?"

"Come to think of it, I reckon it did," replied Greaves.

"Wal, I'll go around over thar an' see."

The dark form of the rustler slipped out of sight over the embankment.

"Better go slow an' careful," warned Greaves. "An' only go close enough to call Somers. Mebbe that damn' half-breed Isbel is comin' like some Injun on us."

Jean heard the soft swish of footsteps though wet grass. Then all was still. He lay flat, with his cheek on the sand, and he had to look ahead and upwards to make out the dark figure of Greaves on the bank. One way or another he meant to kill Greaves, and he had the willpower to resist the strongest gust of passion that had ever stormed his breast. If he arose and shot the rustler, that act would defeat his plan of slipping around on the other outposts who were firing at the cabins. Jean wanted to call softly to Greaves:—*You're right about the half-breed!*—and then, as he wheeled aghast, to kill him as he moved. But it suited Jean to risk leaping up on the man. Jean did not waste time in trying to understand the strange, deadly instinct that gripped him at the moment, but he realized he had chosen the most perilous plan to get rid of Greaves.

Jean drew a long, deep breath and held it. He let go of his rifle. He rose silently, as a lifting shadow. He drew the Bowie knife. Then, with light, swift bounds he glided up the bank. Greaves must have heard a rustling—a soft, quick pad of moccasin—for he turned with a start. At that instant Jean's left arm darted like a striking snake around Greaves's neck and closed, tight and hard. With his right hand free, holding the knife, Jean might have ended the deadly business in just one move, but when his bared arm felt the hot, bulging neck, something terrible burst out of the depths of him. To kill this enemy of his father's was not enough! Physical contact had unleashed the savage soul of the Indian. Yet there was more, and, as Jean gave the straining body a tremendous jerk backwards, he felt the same strange thrill, the dark joy that he had known when his fist had smacked the face of Simm Bruce. Greaves had leered—he had corroborated Bruce's vile insinuation about Ellen Jorth. So it was more than hate that actuated Jean Isbel.

Greaves was heavy and powerful. He wheeled himself feet first, over backwards, in a lunge like that of a lassoed steer. But Jean's hold held. They rolled down the bank into the sandy ditch, and Jean landed uppermost, with his body at right angles with that of his adversary.

"Greaves, your hunch was right," hissed Jean. "It's the half-breed. An' I'm goin' to cut you . . . first for Ellen Jorth . . . an' then for Gaston Isbel!"

Jean gazed down into the gleaming eyes. Then his right arm whipped the big blade. It flashed. It fell. Low down, as far as Jean could reach, it entered Greaves's body.

All the heavy muscular frame of Greaves seemed to contract and burst. His spring was that of an animal in its terror and agony. It was so tremendous that it broke Jean's hold. Greaves let out a strangled yell that cleared, swelling mildly, with a hideous mortal note. He wrestled free. The big knife came out. Supple and swift he got to his knees. He'd had his gun out when Jean reached him again. Like a bear Jean enveloped him. Greaves shot, but he could not raise the gun, or twist it far enough. Then Jean, letting go with his right arm, swung the Bowie. Greaves's strength went out in an awful, hoarse cry. His gun boomed again, then dropped from his hand. He swayed. Jean let go, and that enemy of the Isbels sank limply in the ditch. Jean's eyes roved for his rifle, caught the starlit gleam of it. Snatching it up, he leaped over the embankment and ran straight for the cabins. From all around yells of the Jorth faction attested to their excitement and fury.

A fence loomed up gray in the obscurity. Jean vaulted it, darted across the lane into the shadow of the corrals, and soon gained the first cabin. Here he leaned to regain his breath. His heart pounded hard and seemed too large for his breast. The hot blood beat and surged all through his body. Sweat poured off him. His teeth were clenched as tight as a vise, but it took effort on his part to open his mouth so he could breathe more freely and deeply. But those physical sensations were as nothing compared to the tumult of his mind. Then the instinct, the spell, let go its grip, and he could think. He had avenged Guy, he had depleted the ranks of the Jorths, he had made good the brag of his father, all of which afforded him satisfaction. But these thoughts were not accountable for all that he felt, especially for the bittersweet sting of the fact that death to the defiler of Ellen Jorth could not efface the doubt, the regret that seemed to grow with the hours.

Groping his way into the woodshed, he entered the kitchen, and, calling here, he went on into the main cabin.

"Jean! Jean!" came his father's shaking voice.

"Yes, I'm back," replied Jean.

"Are . . . you . . . all right?"

"Yes. I think I've got a bullet crease on my leg. I didn't know I had it till now. It's bleedin' a little. But it's nothin'."

Jean heard soft steps and someone reached shaking hands for him. They belonged to his sister Ann. She embraced him. Jean felt the heave and throb of her breast.

"Why, Ann, I'm not hurt," he said, and held her closely. "Now you lie down and try to sleep."

In the black starkness of the cabin Jean led her back to the corner, and his heart was full. Speech was difficult, because the very touch of Ann's hands had made him divine that the success of his venture in no wise changed the plight of the women.

"Wal, what happened out there?" demanded Blaisdell.

"I got two of them," replied Jean. "That fellow who was shootin' from the ridge west. An' the other was Greaves."

"Hah!" exclaimed his father.

"Shore, then, it was Greaves yellin'," declared Blaisdell. "By God, I never heard such yells! What'd you do, Jean?"

"I knifed him. You see, I'd planned to slip up on one after another. An' I didn't want to make noise. But I didn't get any farther than Greaves."

"Wal, I reckon that'll end their shootin in the dark," muttered Gaston Isbel. "We've got to be on the look-out for somethin' else. Fire, most likely."

The old rancher's surmise proved to be partially correct. Jorth's faction ceased the shooting. Nothing further was seen or heard from them. But this silence and apparent

188

break in the siege were harder to bear than deliberate hostility. The long, dark hours dragged by. The men took turns watching and resting, but none of them slept. At last the blackness paled, and gray dawn stole out of the east. The sky turned rose over the distant range, and daylight came.

The children awoke hungry and noisy, having slept away their fears. The women took advantage of the quiet morning hour to get a hot breakfast.

"Maybe they've gone away," suggested Guy Isbel's wife, peering out of the window. She had done that several times since daybreak. Jean saw her somber gaze search the pasture until it rested upon the dark, prone shape of her dead husband, lying face down in the open. Her look worried Jean.

"No, Esther, they've not gone yet," replied Jean. "I've seen some of them out there at the edge of the brush."

Blaisdell was optimistic. He said Jean's night work would have its effect and that the Jorth contingent would not renew the siege very determinedly. It turned out, however, that Blaisdell was wrong. Directly after sunrise they began to pour volleys from four sides and from closer range. During the night Jorth's gang had thrown up earth banks and constructed log breastworks from behind which they were now firing. Jean and his comrades could see the flashes of fire and streaks of smoke to such good advantage that they began to return the volleys.

In half an hour the cabin was so full of smoke that Jean could not see the womenfolk in their corner. The fierce attack then abated somewhat, and the firing became more intermittent, and therefore more carefully aimed. A glancing bullet cut a furrow in Blaisdell's hoary head, making a painful, although not serious, wound. It was Esther Isbel who stopped the flow of blood and bound Blaisdell's head, a task that she performed skillfully and without a tremor. The old Texan could not sit still during this operation. Sight of the blood in his hand, which he tried to rub off, appeared to inflame him to a great degree.

"Wal, we're goin' to go out thar," he kept repeating, "an' kill them all."

"No, we're goin' to stay heah," replied Gaston Isbel. "Shore I'm lookin' for Blue an' Fredericks an' Gordon to open up out there. They ought to be heah, an', if they are, you shore can bet they're got the fight sized up."

Isbel's hopes did not materialize. The shooting continued without any lull until about midday. Then the Jorth faction stopped.

"Wal, now what's up?" queried Isbel. "Boys, hold your fire an' let's wait."

Gradually the smoke wafted out of the windows and doors, until the room was once more clear. And at this juncture Esther Isbel came over to take another gaze out upon the meadow. Jean saw her suddenly start violently, then stiffen, with a trembling hand outstretched.

"Look!" she cried.

"Esther, get back," ordered the old rancher. "Keep away from that window."

"What the hell," muttered Blaisdell. "She sees somethin' or she's gone dotty."

Esther seemed turned to stone. "Look! The hogs have broken into the pasture! They'll eat Guy's body!"

Everyone was frozen with horror at Esther's statement. Jean took a swift survey of the pasture. A bunch of black hogs had, indeed, appeared on the scene and were rooting around in the grass not far from where lay the bodies of Guy Isbel and Jacobs. This herd of hogs belonged to the rancher and was allowed to run wild.

"Jane, those hogs . . . ," stammered Esther Isbel to the wife of Jacobs. "Come! Look! Do you know anythin' about hogs?"

The woman ran to the window and looked out. She stiffened as had Esther.

"Dad, will these hogs . . . eat human flesh?" queried Jean breathlessly.

The old man stared out of the window. Surprise seemed to hold him. The completely unexpected situation had staggered him.

"Jean . . . can you . . . can you shoot that far?" he asked huskily.

"At those hogs? No, they're out of range."

"Then, by God, we've got to stay trapped in heah an' watch an awful sight!" ejaculated the old man completely unnerved. "See that break in the fence? Jorth's done that . . . to let in the hogs!"

"Aw, Isbel, it's not so bad as all that," remonstrated Blaisdell, wagging his bloody head. "Jorth wouldn't do such a hell-bent trick."

"It's shore been done."

"Wal, mebbe the hogs won't find Guy an' Jacobs," returned Blaisdell weakly. Plain it was that he only hoped for such a contingency and certainly doubted it.

"Look!" cried Esther Isbel piercingly. "They're workin' straight up the pasture."

Indeed, to Jean it appeared to be the fatal truth. He looked blankly, feeling a little sick. Ann Isbel came to peer out of the window and she uttered a cry. Jacob's wife stood mute, as if dazed.

Blaisdell swore a mighty oath. "God damn it! Isbel, we cain't stand heah an' watch them hogs eat our people!"

"Wal, we'll have to. What else on earth can we do?"

Esther turned to the men. She was white and cold, except her eyes, which resembled gray flames.

"Somebody can run out there an' bury our dead men," she said.

"Why, child, it'd be shore death. You saw what happened to Guy an' Jacobs. We've jest got to bear it. Shore nobody need look out an' see."

Jean wondered if it would be possible to keep from watching. The thing had a horrible fascination. The big hogs were rooting and tearing in the grass, some of them lazy, others nimble, and all were gradually working closer and closer to the bodies. The leader, a huge, gaunt boar that had fared ill all his life in this barren country, was scarcely fifty feet away from where Guy Isbel lay.

"Ann, get me some of your clothes, an' a sunbonnet . . . quick," said Jean, forced out of his lethargy. "I'll run out there disguised. Maybe I can go through with it."

"No!" ordered his father positively and with dark face flaming. "Guy an' Jacobs are dead. We cain't help them now."

"But Dad . . . ," pleaded Jean. He had been wrought to a pitch by Esther's blaze of passion, by the agony in the face of Jane Jacobs.

"I tell you no!" thundered Gaston Isbel, flinging his arms wide.

"*I'll go!*" cried Esther, her voice ringing.

"You won't go alone!" the wife of Jacobs answered instantly, repeating unconsciously the words her husband had spoken.

"You stay right heah!" shouted Gaston Isbel hoarsely.

"I'm goin'," replied Esther. "You've no hold over me. My husband is dead. No one can stop me. I'm goin' out there to drive them hogs away an' bury him."

"Esther, for heaven's sake, listen," replied Isbel. "If you show yourself outside, Jorth an' his gang will kill you."

"They may be many, but no white men could be so low as that."

Then they pleaded with her to give up her purpose, but in vain. She pushed them back and ran out through the kitchen with Jacobs's wife following her. Jean turned to the window in time to see both women run out into the lane. Jean looked fearfully and listened for shots, but only a loud—"Haw, haw!"—came from the watcher outside. That coarse laugh relieved the tension in Jean's breast. Possibly the Jorths were not so black as his father had painted them. The two women entered an open shed and came forth with a shovel and spade.

"Shore they've got to hurry," burst out Gaston Isbel.

Shifting his gaze, Jean understood the import of his father's speech. The leader of the hogs had no doubt scented the bodies. Suddenly he broke into a trot.

"Run, Esther, run!" yelled Jean with all his might.

That urged the women to flight. Jean began to shoot. The hog reached the body of Guy and began snorting around. Jean's shot did not reach or frighten the beast. All the hogs now had caught a scent and went ambling toward their leader. Esther and her companion passed swiftly out of sight behind a corral. Loudly and piercingly, with some awful note, rang out their screams. The hogs appeared frightened. The leader lifted his long snout, looked, and turned away. The others had halted. Then they, too, wheeled and ran off.

All was silent then in the cabin and also outside wherever the Jorth faction lay concealed. All eyes manifestly were fixed upon the brave wives. They spaded up the sod and dug a grave for Guy Isbel. For a shroud Esther wrapped him in her shawl. Then they buried him. Next they hurried to the side of Jacobs, who lay some yards away. They dug a grave for him. Mrs. Jacobs took off her outer skirt to wrap around him. Then the two women labored hard to lift him and lower him. Jacobs was a heavy man. When he had been covered, his widow knelt beside his grave. Esther went back to the other who remained standing and did not look as if she were praying. Her aspect was tragic—that of a woman who had lost father, mother, sister, brother, and now her husband in this bloody Arizona land.

The deed and the demeanor of these wives of the murdered men surely must have shamed Jorth and his followers. They did not fire a shot during the ordeal, or give any sign of their presence.

Inside the cabin all was silent, too. Jean's eyes blurred so that he continually had to wipe them. Old Isbel made no effort to hide his tears. Blaisdell nodded his shaggy head and swallowed hard. The women sat, staring into space. The children in round-eyed dismay, gazed from one to the other of their elders.

"Wal, they're comin' back," declared Isbel in immense relief. "An' so help me . . . Jorth let them bury their daid!"

The fact seemed to have been monstrously strange to Gaston Isbel. When the women entered, the old man said brokenly: "I'm shore glad . . . an' I reckon I was wrong to oppose you . . . an' wrong to say what I did about Jorth."

No one had any chance to reply to Isbel, for the Jorth gang, as if to make up for lost time and surcharged feelings of shame, renewed the attack with such a persistent and furious volleying that the defenders did not risk a return shot. They all had to lie flat next to the lowest log in order to keep from being hit. Bullets rained in through the window. All the clay between the logs low down was shot away. This fusillade lasted for more than an hour, then gradually the fire diminished on one side, and then on the other, until it became desultory and finally ceased.

"A-huh! Shore they've shot their bolt," declared Gaston Isbel.

"Wal, I don't know aboot that," returned Blaisdell, "but they're short a hell of a lot of shells."

"Listen!" suddenly called Jean. "Somebody's yellin'.".

"Hey, Isbel," came a loud hoarse voice, "let your women fight for you!"

Gaston Isbel sat up with a start and his face turned livid. Jean needed no more to prove that the derisive voice from outside had belonged to Jorth. The old rancher lunged up to his full height and with reckless disregard of life he rushed to the window. "Jorth," he roared, "I dare you to meet me . . . man to man!"

This elicited no answer. Jean dragged his father away from the window. After that, a waiting silence ensued, gradually less fraught with suspense. Blaisdell started conversation by saying he believed the fight was over for that particular time. No one disputed him. Evidently Gaston Isbel was loath to believe it. Jean, however, watching at the back of the kitchen, eventually discovered that the Jorth gang had lifted the siege. Jean saw them congregate at the edge of the brush, somewhat lower down than they had been the day before. A team of mules, drawing a wagon, appeared on the road and turned toward the slope. Saddled horses were led down out of the junipers. Jean saw bodies, evidently of dead men, lifted into the wagon, to be hauled away toward the village. Seven mounted men, leading three riderless horses, rode out into the valley and followed the wagon.

"Dad, they're gone," declared Jean. "We had the best of

this fight . . . if only Guy an' Jacobs had listened!"

The old man nodded moodily. He had aged considerably during those two trying days. His hair was grayer. Now that the blaze and glow of the fight had passed, he showed a subtle change, a fixed and morbid sadness, a resignation to a fate he had accepted.

The ordinary routine of ranch life did not return for the Isbels. Blaisdell returned home to settle matters there, so that he could devote all his time to this feud. Gaston Isbel sat down to wait for the members of his clan.

The male members of the family kept guard in turn over the ranch that night. And another day dawned. It brought word from Blaisdell that Blue, Fredericks, Gordon, and Colmor were all at his house on the way to join the Isbels. This news appeared greatly to rejuvenate Gaston Isbel, but his enthusiasm did not last long. Impatient and moody by turns, he paced or moped around the cabin, always looking out, sometimes toward Blaisdell's ranch, but mostly toward Grass Valley.

It struck Jean as singular that neither Esther Isbel nor Mrs. Jacobs suggested a reburial of their husbands. The two bereaved women did not ask for assistance, but repaired to the pasture, and there spent several hours working over the graves. They raised mounds which they sodded, and then placed stones at the heads and feet. Lastly they fenced in the graves.

"I reckon I'll hitch up an' drive back home," said Mrs. Jacobs when she returned to the cabin. "I've much to do an' plan. Probably I'll go to my mother's home. She's old an' will be glad to have me."

"If I had any place to go to, I'd sure go," declared Esther Isbel bitterly.

Gaston Isbel heard this remark. He raised his face from his hands, evidently both nettled and hurt.

"Esther, shore that's not kind," he said.

The red-haired woman—for she did not appear to be a girl any more—halted before his chair and gazed down at him with a terrible flare of scorn in her gray eyes.

"Gaston Isbel, all I've got to say to you is this," she retorted, with the voice of a man. "Seein' that you an' Lee Jorth hated each other, why couldn't you act like men? . . . you damned Texans, with your bloody feuds, draggin' in every relation, every friend to murder each other! That's not the way of Arizona men. We've all got to suffer . . . an' our women be ruined for life . . . because *you* had differences with Jorth. If you were half a man, you'd go out an' kill him yourself, an' not leave a lot of widows an' orphaned children!"

Jean himself writhed under the lash of her scorn. Gaston Isbel turned a dead white. He could not answer her. He seemed stricken with merciless truth. Slowly dropping his head, he remained motionless, a pathetic and tragic figure, and he did not stir until the rapid beat of hoofs denoted the approach of horsemen. Blaisdell appeared on his white charger, leading a pack animal, and behind rode a group of men, all heavily armed and likewise with packs.

"Get down an' come in," was Isbel's greeting. "Bill . . . you look after their packs. Better leave the horses saddled."

The booted and spurred riders trooped in and their demeanor fitted their errand. Jean was acquainted with all of them. Fredericks was a lanky Texan, the color of dust, and he had yellow, clear eyes like those of a hawk. His mother had been an Isbel. Gordon, too, was related to Jean's family, although distantly. He resembled an industrious miner more than a prosperous cattleman. Blue was the most striking of the visitors, as he was the most noted. A little, shrunken, gray-eyed man with years of cowboy written all over him, he looked the quiet, easy, cool, and deadly Texan he was reputed to be. Blue's Texas record was shady and was seldom alluded to, as unfavorable comment had turned out to be hazardous. He was the only one of the group who did not carry a rifle. But he packed two guns, a habit often noted in Texans, and almost never in Arizonians.

Andrew Colmor, Ann Isbel's fiancé, was the youngest member of the clan, and the one closest in age to Jean. His meeting with Ann affected Jean powerfully and brought to a climax an idea that had been developing in Jean's mind. His sister devotedly loved this lean-faced, keen-eyed Arizonian, and it took no great insight to discover that Colmor reciprocated her affection. They were young. They had long life before them. It seemed to Jean a pity that Colmor should be drawn into this war. Jean watched them as they conversed apart, and he saw Ann's hands creep up to Colmor's breast, saw her dark eyes, eloquent, hungry, fearful, lifted with queries her lips did not speak. Jean stepped beside them and laid an arm over both their shoulders.

"Colmor, for Ann's sake you'd better back out of this Jorth-Isbel fight," he whispered.

Colmor looked insulted. "But Jean, it's Ann's father," he said. "I'm almost one of the family."

"You're Ann's sweetheart, an' by heaven I say you oughtn't to go with us," whispered Jean darkly.

"Go . . . with . . . you," faltered Ann.

"Yes. Dad is goin' straight after Jorth. Can't you tell that! An' there'll be one hell of a fight!"

Ann looked up into Colmor's face with all her soul in her eyes, but she did not speak. Her look was noble. She yearned to guide him right, yet her lips were sealed. Colmor betrayed the trouble of his soul. The code of men held him bound, and he could not break from it, although he divined in that moment how truly it was wrong.

"Jean, your dad started me in the cattle business," said Colmor earnestly. "An' I'm doin' well now. When I asked him for Ann, he said he'd be glad to have me in the family. Well, when this talk of fight come up, I asked your dad to let me go in on his side. He wouldn't hear of it. But after a while, as the time passed an' he made more enemies, he finally consented. I reckon he needs me now. An' I can't back out, not even for Ann."

"I would if I were you," replied Jean, and knew that he lied.

"Jean, I'm gamblin' to come out of the fight," said Colmor with a smile. He had no morbid fears or presentiments, such as troubled Jean.

"Why sure . . . you stand as good a chance as anyone," rejoined Jean. "It wasn't that I was worryin' about so much."

"What was it, then?" asked Ann steadily.

"If Andrew *does* come through alive, he'll have blood on his hands," returned Jean with passion. "He can't come through without it. I've begun to feel what it means to have killed my fellow man. An' I'd rather your husband an' the father of your children never felt that."

Colmor did not take Jean as subtly as Ann did. She shrank a little. Her dark eyes dilated. But Colmor showed nothing of her spiritual reaction. He was young. He had wild blood. He was loyal to the Isbels.

"Jean, never worry about my conscience," he said with a keen look. "Nothin' would tickle me any more than to get a shot at every damn' one of the Jorths."

That established Colmor's status in regard to the Jorth-

Isbel feud. Jean had no more to say. He respected Ann's friend and felt poignant sorrow for Ann.

Gaston Isbel called for meat and drink to be set on the table for his guests. When his wishes had been complied with, the women took the children into the adjoining cabin and shut the door.

"Hah! Wal, we can eat an' talk now."

First the newcomers wanted to hear particulars of what had happened. Blaisdell had told all he knew and had seen, but that was not sufficient. They plied Gaston Isbel with questions. Laboriously and ponderously, he rehearsed the experiences of the fight at the ranch, according to his impressions. Bill Isbel was exhorted to talk, but he had of late manifested a sullen and taciturn disposition. In spite of Jean's vigilance Bill had continued to imbibe red liquor. Then Jean was called upon to relate all he had seen and done. It had been Jean's intention to keep his mouth shut, just for his own sake, and secondly because he did not like to talk of his deeds. But when thus appealed to by these somber-faced, intent-eyed men, he divined that the more carefully he described the cruelty and baseness of their enemies and the more vividly he presented his participation in the first fight of the feud, the more strongly he would bind these friends to the Isbel cause. So he talked for an hour, beginning with his meeting with Colter on the Tonto Rim and ending with an account of his killing Greaves. His listeners sat through this long narrative with unabated interest, and at the close they were leaning forward, breathless and tense.

"Ah! So Greaves got his desserts at last!" exclaimed Gordon.

All the men around the table made comments, and the last, from Blue, was the one that struck Jean forcibly.

"Shore thet was a strange an' a hell of a way to kill Greaves. Why'd you do that, Jean?"

"I told you. I wanted to avoid noise an' I hoped to get more of them."

Blue nodded his lean, eagle-like head, and sat thoughtfully, as if not convinced of anything save Jean's prowess. After a moment Blue spoke again. "Then, goin' back to Jean's tellin' aboot trackin' rustled cattle, I've got this to say. I've long suspected that somebody livin' right heah in the valley has been drivin' off cattle an' dealin' with rustlers. An' now I'm shore of it."

This speech did not elicit the image from Gaston Isbel that Jean expected it would.

"You mean Greaves or some of his friends?"

"No. They wasn't none of them in the cattle business, like we was. Shore we all knowed Greaves was crooked. But what I'm figgerin' is that some so-called honest man in our settlement has been makin' crooked deals."

Blue was a man of deeds rather than words, and so much strong speech from him, who everybody knew to be remarkably reliable and keen, made a profound impression upon most of the Isbel faction. But to Jean's surprise his father did not rave. It was Blaisdell who supplied the rage and invective. Bill Isbel, also, was strangely indifferent to this new view on the situation of cattle stealing. Suddenly Jean caught a vague flash of thought of another's mind, and he wondered—could his brother Bill know anything about this crooked work alluded to by Blue? Dismissing the conjecture, Jean listened earnestly.

"An', if it's true, it shore makes this difference . . . we cain't blame all the rustlin' onto Jorth," concluded Blue.

"Wal, it's not true," declared Gaston Isbel roughly. "Jorth an' his Hash Knife Gang are at the bottom of all the

201

rustlin' in the valley, from years back. An' they've got to be wiped out!"

"Isbel, I reckon we'd all feel better if we talk straight," replied Blue coolly. "I'm heah to stand by the Isbels. An' you know what thet means. But I'm not heah to fight Jorth because he may be a rustler. The others may have their own reasons, but mine is this. You once stood by me in Texas when I was needin' friends. Wal, I'm standin' by you now. Jorth's your enemy, an' so he is mine."

Gaston Isbel bowed to this ultimatum, scarcely less agitated than when Esther Isbel had denounced him. His rabid and morbid hate of Jorth had eaten into his heart to take possession there, like the parasite that battened upon the life of its victim. Blue's steely voice, his cold, gray eyes, showed the unbiased truth of the man as well as his fidelity to his creed. Here again, but in a different manner, Gaston Isbel had the fact flung at him that other men must suffer, perhaps die, for his hate. The very soul of the old rancher apparently rose in passionate revolt against the blind, headlong, elemental strength of his nature. So it seemed to Jean who, in love and pity that hourly grew, saw through his father. Was it too late? Alas! Gaston Isbel could never be turned back! Yet something was altering his brooding, fixed mind.

"Wal," said Blaisdell gruffly, "let's get down to business. I'm for havin' Blue be foreman of this heah outfit, an' all of us to do as he says."

Gaston Isbel opposed this selection and, indeed, resented it. He intended to lead the Isbel faction.

"All right, then. Give us a hunch what we're goin' to do," replied Blaisdell.

"We're goin' to ride off on Jorth's trail . . . an' one way or another . . . kill him. . . . *kill him!* I reckon that would end the fight."

What did old Isbel have in his mind? His listeners shook their heads.

"No," asserted Blaisdell, "killin' Jorth might be the end of your desires, Isbel, but it'd never end *our* fight. We'll have gone too far. If we take Jorth's trail from heah, it means we've got to wipe out that rustler gang, or stay to the last man."

"Yes, by God!" exclaimed Fredericks.

"Let's drink to thet!" said Blue. Strangely they all turned to this Texas gunman, instinctively recognizing in him the brain and heart and the past deeds that fitted him for the leadership of such a clan. Blue had all in life to lose, and nothing to gain. Yet his spirit was such that he could not lean to all the possible gain for the future, and leave a debt unpaid. Then his voice, his look, his influence were those of a fighter. They all drank with him, even Jean, who hated liquor. And this act of drinking seemed the climax of the council. Preparations were at once begun for their departure on Jorth's trail.

Jean took but little time for his own needs. A horse, a blanket, a knapsack of meat and bread, a canteen, and his weapons with all the ammunition he could pack made up his outfit. He wore his buckskin suit, leggings, and moccasins. Very soon the cavalcade was ready to depart. Jean tried not to watch Bill Isbel say good bye to his children, but, of course, it was impossible not to. Whatever Bill was, as a man, he was father of those children, and he loved them. How strange that the little ones seemed to realize the meaning of this good bye! They were grave, somber-eyed, pale up to the last moment, then they broke down and wept. Did they sense that their father would never come back? Jean caught that dark, fatalistic presage. Bill Isbel's convulsed face showed that he, also, caught it. Jean did not see Bill say good bye to his wife. But he heard her. Old Gaston Isbel could not. He never looked at them. And his good bye to Ann was as if he were only riding to the village for a day. Jean saw woman's love, woman's intuition, woman's grief in her eyes. He could not escape her. "Oh, Jean, oh, Brother," she whispered as she enfolded him. "It's awful! It's wrong! Wrong! Wrong! Good bye! If killing *must* be . . . see that you kill the Jorths! Good bye!"

Even in Ann, gentle and mild, the Isbel blood spoke at the last. Jean gave Ann over to the pale-faced Colmor who took her in his arms. This cold-blooded devastation of a home was almost more than he could bear. There was love here. What would be left?

Colmor was the last one to come out to the horses. He did not walk erect, nor as one whose sight was clear. Then as the silent, grim men mounted their horses, Bill Isbel's eldest child, the boy, appeared in the door. His little form seemed instinct with a force vastly different from grief. His face was the face of an Isbel.

"Daddy . . . kill 'em all!" he shouted with a passion all the more fierce for its incongruity to the treble voice.

So the poison had spread from father to son.

Chapter Nine

Half a mile from the Isbel Ranch the cavalcade passed the log cabin of Evarts, father of the boy who had tended sheep with Bernardino. It suited Gaston Isbel to halt here. No need to call! Evarts and his son appeared so quickly as to convince observers that they had been watching.

"Howdy, Jake," said Isbel. "I'm wantin' a word with you alone."

"Shore, boss, get down an' come in," replied Evarts.

Isbel led him aside, and said something forcible that Jean divined from the very gesture that accompanied it. His father was telling Evarts that he was not to join in the Isbel-Jorth war. Evarts had worked for the Isbels a long time, and his faithfulness, along with something stronger and darker, showed in his rugged face as he stubbornly opposed Isbel. The old man raised his voice: "No, I tell you an' that settles it."

They returned to the horses, and, before mounting, Isbel, as if he remembered something, directed his somber gaze on young Evarts.

"Son, did you bury Bernardino?"

"Dad an' me went over yestiddy," replied the lad. "I shore was glad the coyotes hadn't been around."

"How aboot the sheep?"

"I left them there. I was goin' to stay, but bein' all alone . . . I got skeered. The sheep was doin' fine. Good water an' some grass. An' this ain't time for varmints to hang around."

"Jake, keep your eye on that flock," returned Isbel. "An', if I shouldn't happen to come back, you can call them sheep yours. I'd like your boy to ride up to the village. Not with us, or anybody would see him. But afterwards. We'll be at Abel Meeker's."

Again Jean was confronted with an uneasy premonition about some idea or plan his father had not shared with his followers. When the cavalcade started on again, Jean rode to his father's side and asked him why he had wanted the Evarts boy to come to Grass Valley. The old man replied that, if the boy could run to and fro in the village without danger, he might be useful in reporting what was going on at Greaves's store where undoubtedly the Jorth gang would hold forth. This appeared reasonable enough, so Jean smothered the objection he had meant to make.

The valley road was deserted. When a mile farther on the riders passed a group of cabins, just on the outskirts of the village, Jean's quick eye caught sight of curious and evidently frightened people trying to see while they avoided being seen. No doubt the whole settlement was in a state of suspense and terror. It was likely their dark, closely grouped band of horsemen appeared to them as Jorth's gang had looked to Jean. It was an orderly trotting march that manifested neither hurry nor excitement. But any Western eye could have caught the singular aspect of such a group, as if the intent of the riders was a visible thing.

Soon they reached the outskirts of the village. Here their approach had been watched for, or had been already reported. Jean saw men, women, children peeping from behind cabins and from half-opened doors. Farther on, Jean espied the dark figures of men, slipping out the back ways through orchards and gardens, and running north toward the center of the village. Could these be friends of the Jorth crowd, on the way with warnings of the approach of the Isbels? Jean felt convinced of it. He was learning that his father had not been absolutely correct in his estimation of the way Jorth and his followers were regarded by their neighbors. Not improbably there were really many villagers, who, being more interested in sheep raising than in cattle, had an honest leaning toward the Jorths. Some, too, no doubt had leanings that were dishonest in deed, if not in sincerity.

Gaston Isbel led his clan straight down the middle of the wide road of Grass Valley, until he reached a point opposite Abel Meeker's cabin. Jean espied the same curiosity from behind Meeker's doors and windows as had been shown all along the road. But presently, at Isbel's call, the door opened, and a short, swarthy man appeared. He carried a rifle.

"Howdy, Gass," he said. "What's the good word?"

"Wal, Abel, it's not good, but bad. An' it's shore started," replied Isbel. "I'm askin' you to let me have your cabin."

"You're welcome. I'll send the folks 'round to Jim's," returned Meeker. "An' if you want me, I'm with you, Isbel."

"Thanks, Abel, but I'm not leadin' any more kin an' friends into this heah deal."

"Wal, jest as you say. But I'd like damn' bad to jine with you. . . . my brother Ted was shot last night."

"Ted! Is he daid?" ejaculated Isbel blankly.

"We can't find out," replied Meeker. "Jim says that Jeff Campbell said thet Ted went into Greaves's place last night. Greaves allus was friendly to Ted, but Greaves wasn't thar. . . ."

"No, he shore wasn't," interrupted Isbel with a dark smile, "an' he never will be there again."

Meeker nodded with slow comprehension, and a shade crossed his face.

"Wal, Campbell claimed he'd heered of it from someone who was thar. Anyway, the Jorths were drinkin' hard an' they raised a row with Ted . . . same old sheep talk . . . an' somebody shot him. Campbell said Ted was thrown out back, an' he was shore he wasn't killed."

"A-huh! Wal, I'm sorry, Abel, your family had to lose in this. Maybe Ted's not bad hurt. I shore hope so. An' you an' Jim keep out of the fight, anyway."

"All right, Isbel. But I reckon I'll give you a hunch. If this heah fight lasts long, the whole damn' basin will be in it, on one side or t'other."

"Abe, you're talkin' sense," broke in Blaisdell. "An' that's why we're up heah for quick action."

"I heered you got Daggs," whispered Meeker, as he peered all around.

"Wal, you heered correct," drawled Blaisdell.

Meeker muttered strong words into his beard. "Say, was Daggs in that Jorth outfit?"

"He *was*. But he walked right into Jean's mark, which is a Forty-Four. An' I reckon his carcass would show some more."

"An' whar's Guy Isbel?" demanded Meeker.

"Daid an' buried, Abel," replied Gaston Isbel. "An' now I'd be obliged if you'll hurry your folks away, an' let us have your cabin an' corral. Have you got any hay for the horses?"

"Shore. The barn's half full," replied Meeker, as he turned away. "Come on in."

"No. We'll wait till you've gone."

When Meeker had gone, Isbel and his men sat their horses, and looked about them, and spoke low. Their advent had been expected, and the little town awoke to the imminence of the impending battle. Inside Meeker's house there was the sound of indistinct voices of women and the

208

bustle incident to a hurried vacating.

Across the wide road people were peering out on all sides, some hiding, others walking to and fro, from fence to fence, whispering in little groups. Down the wide road, at the point where it turned, stood Greaves's fort-like stone house. Low, flat, isolated, with its dark eye-like windows, it presented a forbidding and sinister aspect. Jean distinctly saw the forms of men, some dark, others in shirt sleeves, come to the wide door and look down the road.

"Wal, I reckon only aboot five hundred good hoss steps are separatin' us from that outfit," drawled Blaisdell.

No one replied to his jocularity. Gaston Isbel's eyes narrowed to a slit in his furrowed face and he kept them fastened upon Greaves's store. Blue likewise had a somber cast of countenance, not perhaps any darker or grimmer than those of his comrades, but more representative of intense preoccupation of mind. The look of him thrilled Jean, who could sense its deadliness yet could not grasp any more. Altogether the manner of the villagers, and the watchful pacing to and fro of the Jorth followers, and the silent boding front of Isbel and his men summed up for Jean the menace of the moment, that must very soon change to a terrible reality.

At a call from Meeker, who stood at the back of the cabin, Gaston Isbel rode into the yard, followed by the others of his party. "Somebody look after the horses," ordered Isbel, as he dismounted and took his rifle and pack. "Better leave the saddles on, leastways till we see what's comin' off."

Jean and Bill Isbel led the horses back to the corral. While watering and feeding them, Jean somehow received the impression that Bill was trying to speak, to confide in him, to unburden himself of some load. This peculiarity of

Bill's had become marked when he was perfectly sober, yet he had never spoken or even begun anything unusual. Upon the present occasion, however, Jean believed that his brother might have gotten rid of his emotion, or whatever it was, had they not been interrupted by Colmor.

"Boys, the old man's orders are for us to sneak 'round on three sides of Greaves's store, keepin' out of gunshot till we find good cover, an' then crawl closer an' pick off any of Jorth's gang who shows himself."

Bill Isbel strode off without a reply to Colmor.

"Well, I don't think so much of that," said Jean ponderingly. "Jorth has lots of friends here. Somebody might pick us off."

"I kicked, but the old man shut me up. He's not to be bucked ag'in now. Struck me as powerful queer. But no wonder."

"Maybe he knows best. Did he say anythin' about what he an' the rest of them are goin' to do?"

"Nope. Blue taxed him with that an' got the same as me. I reckon we'd better try it out for a while, anyway."

"Looks like he wants us to keep out of the fight," replied Jean thoughtfully. "Maybe though . . . Dad's no fool. Colmor, you wait here till I get out of sight. I'll go 'round an' come up as close as advisable behind Greaves's store. You take the right side. An' keep hid."

With that Jean strode off, going around the barn, straight out the orchard lane to the open flat, and then climbing a fence to the north of the village. Presently he reached a line of sheds and corrals to which he held until he arrived at the road. This point was about a quarter of a mile from Greaves's store and around the bend. Jean sighted no one. The road, the fields, the yards, the backs of the cabins all looked deserted. A blight had settled down upon the peaceful activities of Grass Valley. Crossing the road, Jean began to circle until he came close to several cabins, around which he made a wide detour. This took him to the edge of the slope, where brush and thickets afforded him a safe passage to a line directly back of Greaves's store. Then he turned toward it. Soon he was again approaching a cabin on that side and some of its inmates descried him. Their actions attested to their alarm. Jean half expected a shot from this quarter, such were his growing doubts, but he was mistaken. A man, unknown to Jean, closely watched his guarded movements, and then waved a hand, as if to signify to Jean that he had nothing to fear. After this he disappeared. Jean believed that he had been recognized by someone not antagonistic to the Isbels. Therefore, he passed the cabin, and, coming to a thick scrub-oak tree that offered shelter, he hid there to watch. From this spot he could see the back of Greaves's store, at a distance probably too far for a rifle bullet to reach. Before him, as far as the store, and on each side, extended the village common. In front of the store ran the road. Jean's position was such that he could not command sight of this road down toward Meeker's house, a fact that disturbed him. Not satisfied with this stand, he studied his surroundings in the hope of espying a better. He discerned what he thought would be a more favorable position, although he could not see much farther. Jean went back around the cabin, and, coming out into the open to the right, he got the corner of Greaves's barn between him and the window of the store. Then he boldly hurried into the open, and soon reached an old wagon, from behind which he proposed to watch. He could not see either window or door of the store, but if any of the Jorth contingent came out the back way, they would be within reach of his rifle. Jean took the risk of being shot at from either side.

So sharp and roving was his sight that he soon espied Colmor slipping along behind trees, some hundred yards to the left. All his efforts to catch a glimpse of Bill, however, were fruitless. And this appeared strange to Jean, for there were several good places on the right from which Bill could have commanded the front of Greaves's store and the whole west side.

Colmor disappeared among some shrubbery, and Jean seemed left alone to watch a deserted, silent village. Watching and listening, he felt that the time dragged, yet the shadows cast by the sun showed him that, no matter how tense he felt and how the moments seemed hours, they were really flying.

Suddenly Jean's ears rang with the vibrant shock of a rifle report. He jerked up, strung and thrilling. It came from in front of the store. It was followed by revolver shots, heavy, booming. Three he counted, and the rest were too close together to enumerate. A single hoarse yell pealed out, somehow trenchant and triumphant. Other yells, not so wild and strange, muffled the first one. Then silence clapped down on the store and the open square.

Jean was deadly certain that some of the Jorth clan would show themselves. He strained to still the trembling those sudden shots and that significant yell had caused him. No man appeared. No more sounds caught Jean's ears. The suspense, then, grew unbearable. It was not that he could not wait for an enemy to appear, but that he could not wait to learn what had happened. Every moment that he stayed there, with hands like steel on his rifle, with eyes of a falcon, only added to his dreadful dark certainty of disaster. A rifle shot swiftly followed by revolver shots! What could they mean? Revolver shots of different caliber, surely fired by different men. It was not these shots that accounted for

Jean's dread, but the yell which had followed. All his intelligence and all his nerve were not sufficient to fight down the feeling of calamity. At last, yielding to it, he left his post, and ran like a deer across the open, through the cabin yard, and around the edge of the slope to the road. Here his caution brought him to a halt. Not a living thing crossed his vision. Breaking into a run, he soon reached the back of Meeker's place and entered, to hurry forward to the cabin.

Colmor was there in the yard, breathing hard, his face working, and in front of him crouched several of the men with rifles ready. The road, to Jean's flashing glance, was apparently deserted. Blue sat on the doorstep, lighting a cigarette. Then on the moment Blaisdell strode to the door of the cabin. Jean had never seen him look like that.

"Jean . . . look . . . down the road," he said brokenly, and with big hand shaking he pointed down toward Greaves's store.

Like lightning Jean's glance shot down—down—down—until it stopped to fix upon the prostrate form of a man, lying in the middle of the road. A man of lengthy build, shirt-sleeved arms flung wide, white head in the dust—dead! Jean's recognition was as swift as his sight. His father! They had killed him. The Jorths! It was done. His father's premonition of death had not been false. Then, after these flashing thoughts, came a sense of blankness, momentarily almost oblivion, that gave place to a rending of the heart, that pain Jean had known only at the death of his mother. It passed, this agonizing pang, and its icy pressure yielded to a rushing gust of blood, fiery as hell.

"Who . . . did it?" whispered Jean.

"Jorth!" replied Blaisdell huskily. "Son, we couldn't hold him back . . . we couldn't. He was like a lion . . . an' he threw his life away! Oh, if it hadn't been for that, it'd not

213

be so awful. Shore, we come heah to shoot an' be shot. But not like that. By God, it was murder . . . murder!"

Jean's mute lips framed a query easily read.

"Tell him, Blue, I cain't," continued Blaisdell, and he tramped back into the cabin.

"Set down, Jean, an' take things easy," said Blue calmly. "You know we all reckoned we'd get plugged one way or another in this deal. An' shore it doesn't matter much how a fellar gits it. All that ought to bother us is to make shore the other outfit bites the dust . . . same as your old dad had to."

Under this man's tranquil presence, all the more quieting because it seemed to be so deadly sure and cool, Jean felt the uplift of his dark spirit, the acceptance of fatality, the mounting control of faculties that must wait. The little gunman seemed to have about his inert presence something that suggested a rattlesnake's inherent knowledge of its destructiveness. Jean sat down and wiped his clammy face.

"Jean, your dad reckoned to square accounts with Jorth, an' save us all," began Blue, puffing out a cloud of smoke. "But he reckoned too late. Mebbe years ago . . . or even not long ago . . . if he'd called Jorth out, man to man, there'd never been any Jorth-Isbel war. Gaston Isbel's conscience woke too late. Thet's how I figger it."

"Hurry. Tell me . . . how it . . . happened," panted Jean.

"Wal, a little while after you all left, I seen your dad writin' on a leaf he tore out of a book . . . Meeker's Bible, as you can see. I thought that was funny. An' Blaisdell gave me a hunch. Pretty soon along comes young Evarts. The old man calls him out of our hearin' an' talks to him. Then I seen him give the boy somethin', which I afterwards figgered was what he wrote on the leaf out of the Bible. Me an' Blaisdell both tried to git out of him what that meant.

But not a word. I kept watchin', an' after while I seen young Evarts slip out the back way. Mebbe half an hour I seen a bare-legged kid cross the road an' go into Greaves's store. Then shore I tumbled to your dad. He'd sent a note to Jorth to come out an' meet him face to face, man to man! Shore it was like readin' what your dad had wrote. But I didn't say nothin' to Blaisdell. I jest watched."

Blue drawled these last words, as if he enjoyed remembrance of his keen reasoning. A smile wreathed his thin lips. He drew twice on the cigarette and emitted another cloud of smoke. Quite suddenly, then, he changed. He made a rapid gesture—the whip of a hand, significant and passionate, and swift words followed.

"Colonel Lee Jorth stalked out of the store . . . out into the road . . . mebbe a hundred steps. Then he halted. He wore his long black coat an' his wide black hat, an' he stood like a stone.

" 'What the hell,' busted out Blaisdell, comin' out of his trance.

"The rest of us jest looked. I'd forgot your dad, for the minnit. So had all of us. But we remembered soon enough when we seen him stalk out. Everybody had a hunch then. I called him. Blaisdell begged him to come back. All the fellars had a say. No use! Then I shore cussed him an' told him it was plain as day thet Jorth didn't hit me like an honest man. I can sense such things. I knew Jorth had a trick up his sleeve. I've not been a gunfighter fer nothin'. Your dad had no rifle. He packed his gun at his hip. He jest stalked down that road like a giant, goin' faster an' faster, holdin' his head high. It shore was fine to see him. But I was sick. I heered Blaisdell groan, an' Fredericks thar cussed somethin' fierce. When your dad halted, I reckon aboot fifty steps from Jorth . . . then we all went numb. I heered your dad's voice . . . then Jorth's. They cut like knives. You could shore heah the hate they hed fer each other."

Blue had grown a little husky. His speech had grown gradually to denote his feeling. Underneath his serenity there was a different order of man.

"I reckon both your dad an' Jorth went fer their guns at the same time . . . an even break. But jest as they drew, someone shot a rifle from the store. Must hev' been a Forty-Five-Seventy. A big gun! The bullet must have hit your dad low down. Aboot the middle. He acted thet way, sinkin' to his knees. An' he was wild in shootin' . . . so wild that he must hev' missed. Then he wobbled . . . an' Jorth run in a dozen steps, shootin' fast, till your dad fell over. Jorth run closer, bent over him, an' then straightened up with an Apache yell, if I ever heered one. An' then Jorth backed slow . . . lookin' all the time . . . backed to the store, an' went in."

Blue's voice ceased. Jean seemed suddenly released from an impelling magnet that now dropped him to some numb, dizzy depth. Blue's lean face grew hazy. Then Jean bowed his head in his hands, and sat there, while a slight tremor shook all his muscles at once. He grew deathly cold and deathly sick. This paroxysm slowly wore away, and Jean grew conscious of a dull amazement at the apparent deadness of his spirit. Blaisdell placed a huge kindly hand on his shoulder.

"Brace up, son," he said, with voice now clear and resonant. "Shore it's what your dad expected . . . an' what we all must look for. If you was goin' to kill Jorth before . . . think how god-damned shore you're goin' to kill him now."

"Blaisdell's talkin'," put in Blue, and his voice had a cold ring. "Lee Jorth will never see the sun rise ag'in!"

216

Those calls to the primitive in Jean, to the Indian, were not in vain. But even so, when the dark tide rose in him, there was still a haunting consciousness of the cruelty of this singular doom imposed upon him. Strangely Ellen Jorth's face emerged back in the depths of his vision, pale, fading, like the face of a spirit floating by.

"Blue," said Blaisdell, "let's get Isbel's body soon as we dare, an' bury it. Reckon we can right after dark."

"Shore," replied Blue. "But you fellars figger thet out. I'm thinkin' hard. I've got somethin' on my mind."

Jean grew fascinated by the looks and speech and action of the little gunman. Blue, indeed, had something on his mind, and it boded ill to the men in that dark square stone house down the road. He paced to and fro in the yard, back and forth on the path to the gate, and then he entered the cabin to stalk up and down, faster and faster, until all at once he halted as if struck, flinging up his right arm in a singular fierce gesture.

"Jean, call the men in," he said tersely.

They all filed in, sinister and silent, with eager faces turned to the little Texan. His dominance showed markedly.

"Gordon, you stand in the door an' keep your eye peeled," went on Blue. "Now boys, listen . . . I've thought it all out. This game of manhuntin' is the same to me as cattle raisin' is to you. An' my life in Texas all comes back to me, I reckon, in good stead fer me now. I'm goin' to kill Lee Jorth! Him first, an' mebbe his brothers. I had to think of a good many ways before I hit on one I reckon will be shore. It's got to be *shore*. Jorth has got to die! Wal, heah's my plan. Thet Jorth outfit is drinkin' some, we can gamble on it. They're not goin' to leave that store. An' of course they'll be expectin' us to start a fight. I reckon they'll look

217

fer some such siege as they held 'round Isbel's ranch. But we shore ain't goin' to do thet. I'm goin' to surprise thet outfit. There's only one man among them who is dangerous, an' that's Queen. I know Queen. But he doesn't know me. An' I'm goin' to finish my job before he gets acquainted with me. After thet, all right."

Blue paused a moment, his eyes narrowing down, his whole face settling in hard cast of intense preoccupation as if he visualized a scene of extraordinary nature.

"Wal, what's your trick?" demanded Blaisdell.

"You all know Greaves's store," continued Blue. "How them windows have wooden shutters thet keep a light from showin' outside. Wal, I'm gamblin' thet, as soon as it's dark, Jorth's gang will be celebratin'! They'll be drinkin' an' they'll have a light, an' the windows will be shut. They're not goin' to worry none aboot us. Thet store is like a fort. It won't burn. An' shore they'd never think of us chargin' them in there. Wal, as soon as it's dark, we'll go 'round behind the lots an' come up jest acrost the road from Greaves's. I reckon we'd better leave Isbel where he lays till this fight's over. Mebbe you'll have more'n him to bury. We'll crawl behind them bushes in front of Coleman's yard. An' heah's where Jean comes in. He'll take an axe, an' his guns, of course, an' do some of his Injun sneakin' 'round to the back of Greaves's store. An' Jean, you must do a slick job of this. But I reckon it'll be easy for you. Back there it'll be dark as pitch fer anyone lookin' out of the store. An' I'm figgerin' you can take your time an' crawl right up. Now, if you don't remember how Greaves's back yard looks, I'll tell you."

Here Blue dropped on one knee on the floor, and with a finger he traced a map of Greaves's barn, and fence, the back door and window, and especially a break in the stone foundation that led into a kind of cellar where Greaves stored wood and other things that could be left outdoors.

"Jean, I take particular pains to show you where this hole is," said Blue, "because, if the gang runs out, you could duck in there an' hide. An' if they run out into the yard . . . wal, you'd make it a sorry run fer them. When you've crawled up close to Greaves's back door an' waited long enough to see an' listen . . . then you're to run fast an' swing your axe smash ag'in' the winder. Take a quick peep if ya want to. It might help. Then jump quick an' take a swing at the door. You'll be standin' to one side, so, if the gang shoots through the door, they won't hit you. Bang thet door good an' hard. Wal, now's where I come in. When you swing thet axe, I'll shore run fer the front of the store. Jorth an' his outfit will be some attentive to thet poundin' of yours on the back door. So I reckon. An' they'll be *lookin'* thet way. I'll run in . . . yell . . . an' throw my guns on Jorth."

"*Humph!* Is that all?" ejaculated Blaisdell.

"I reckon thet's all, an' I'm figgerin' it's a hell of a lot," responded Blue dryly. "Thet's what Jorth will think."

"Where do we come in?"

"Wal, you all can back me up," replied Blue dubiously. "You see my plan goes as far as killin' Jorth an' mebbe his brothers. Mebbe I'll get a crack at Queen. But I'll be shore of Jorth. After thet, all depends. Mebbe it'll be easy for me to get out. An' if I do, you fellars will know it an' can fill that storeroom full of bullets."

"Wal, Blue, with all due respect to you I shore don't like your plan," declared Blaisdell. "Success depends upon too many little things, any one of which might go wrong."

"Blaisdell, I reckon I know this heah game better than you," replied Blue. "A gunfighter goes by instinct. This trick will work."

"But suppose that front door of Greaves's store is barred," protested Blaisdell.

"It hasn't got any bar," said Blue.

"You're shore?"

"Yes, I reckon," replied Blue.

"Hell, man, aren't you takin' a terrible chance?" queried Blaisdell.

Blue's answer to that was a look that brought the blood to Blaisdell's face. Only then did the rancher really comprehend how the little gunman had taken such desperate chances before and meant to take them now, not with any hope or assurance of escaping with his life, but to live up to his peculiar code of honor.

"Blaisdell, did you ever heah of me in Texas?" he queried dryly.

"Wal, no, Blue, I can't swear I ever did," replied the rancher apologetically. "An' Isbel was always sort of mysterious aboot his acquaintance with you."

"My last name's not Blue."

"A-huh! Wal, what's it then, if I'm safe to ask?" returned Blaisdell gruffly.

"It's King Fisher," replied Blue.

The shock that stiffened Blaisdell must have been communicated to the others. Jean certainly felt amazement and saw the emotion not fully realized, when he found himself face to face with one of the most notorious characters ever known in Texas—an outlaw long supposed to be dead.

"Men, I reckon I'd've kept my secret if I'd any idee of comin' out of this Isbel-Jorth war alive," said Blue. "But I'm goin' to cash. I feel it heah. . . . Isbel was my friend. He saved me from bein' lynched in Texas. An' so I'm goin' to kill Jorth. Now I'll take it kind of you . . . if any of you come out of this alive . . . to tell who I was an' why I was on the

Isbel side. Because this sheep an' cattle war . . . this talk of Jorth an' the Hash Knife Gang . . . it makes me sick. I *know* there's been crooked work on Isbel's side, too. An' I never want it on record thet I killed Jorth because he was a rustler."

"By God, Blue! It's late in the day for such talk," burst out Blaisdell in rage and surprise. "But I reckon you know what you're talkin' aboot. Wal, I shore don't want to heah it."

At this juncture Bill Isbel quietly entered the cabin, too late to hear any of Blue's statement. Jean was positive of that for, as Blue was speaking those last revealing words, Bill's heavy boots had resounded on the gravel path outside. Yet something in Bill's look or in the way Blue averted his lean face or in the entrance of Bill at that particular moment, or all these together, seemed to Jean to add further mystery to the long-secret causes leading up to the Jorth-Isbel war. Did Bill know what Blue knew? Jean had an inkling that he did. At the moment, so perplexing and bitter, Jean gazed out the door down the deserted road to where his dead father lay, white-haired and ghastly in the sunlight.

"Blue, you could have kept that to yourself, as well as your real name," interposed Jean with bitterness. "It's too late now for either to do any good. But I appreciate your friendship for Dad, an' I'm ready to help carry out your plan."

That decision of Jean's appeared to put an end to protest or argument from Blaisdell or any of the others. Blue's fleeting, dark smile was one of satisfaction. Then upon most of this group of men seemed to settle a grim restraint. They went out and walked and watched; they came in again, restless and somber. Jean thought that he must have bent his gaze a thousand times down the road to the tragic figure of his father. That sight roused all emotions in his breast, and the one that stirred there most was pity. The pity of it! Gaston Isbel lying face down in the dust of the village street! Patches of blood showed on the back of his vest and on one white-sleeved shoulder. He had been shot through. Every time Jean saw this blood he had to stifle a gathering of wild, savage impulses.

Meanwhile, the afternoon hours dragged by, and the village remained as if its inhabitants had abandoned it. Not even a dog showed on the wide road. Jorth and some of his men came out in front of the store, and sat on the steps, in close conversing groups. Every move they made seemed significant of their confidence and importance. About sunset they went back into the store, closing the door and window shutters. Then Blaisdell called the Isbel faction to have food and drink. Jean felt no hunger. Blue, who had kept apart from the others, showed no desire to eat. Neither did he smoke, although early in the day he had never been without a cigarette between his lips.

Twilight fell. And darkness came. Not a light showed anywhere in the blackness.

"Wal, I reckon it's aboot time," said Blue, and he led the way out of the cabin to the back of the lot. Jean strode behind him, carrying his rifle and an axe. Silently the other men followed. Blue turned to the left and led through the field until he came within sight of a dark line of trees.

"Thet's where the road turns off," he said to Jean. "An' heah's the back of Coleman's place. Wal, Jean, good luck!"

Jean felt the grip of a steel-like hand and in the darkness he caught the gleam of Blue's eyes. Jean had no response in words for the laconic Blue, but he wrung the hard, thin hand, and hurried away in the darkness.

Once alone, his part of the business at hand rushed him

into eager, thrilling action. This was the sort of work he was fitted to do. In this instance it was important, but it seemed to him that Blue had coolly taken the perilous part—and this cowboy with gray in his thin hair was in reality the great King Fisher! Jean marveled at the fact, and he shivered all over for Jorth. In ten minutes—fifteen, more or less—Jorth would be gasping bloody froth and sinking down. Something in the dark, lonely, silent, oppressive summer night told Jean this. He strode on swiftly. Crossing the road at a run, he kept on over the ground he had traversed during the afternoon and in a few moments he stood, breathing hard, at the edge of the common behind Greaves's store.

A pinpoint of light penetrated the blackness. It made Jean's heart leap. The Jorth contingent was burning the big lamp that hung in the center of Greaves's store. Jean listened. Loud voices and coarse laughter sounded discord in the melancholy silence of the night. What Blue had called his instinct had surely guided him aright. Death of Gaston Isbel was being celebrated by revel.

In a few moments Jean had regained his breath. Then all his faculties set intensely to the action at hand. He seemed to magnify his hearing and his sight. His movements made no sound. He gained the wagon, where he crouched a moment.

The ground seemed a pale obscure medium, hardly more real than the gloom above it. Through this gloom of night, which looked thick like a cloud but was really clear, shone the thin bright point of light, accentuating the black square that was Greaves's store. Above this stood a gray line of tree foliage, and then the intensely dark blue sky studded with white, cold stars. A hound bayed lonesomely somewhere in the distance. Voices of men sounded more distinctly, some deep and low, others loud, unguarded, with

223

the vacant note of thoughtlessness.

Jean gathered all his forces, until sense of sight and hearing were in exquisite accord with the suppleness and lightness of his movements. He glided on about ten short swift steps before he halted. That was as far as his piercing eyes could penetrate. If there had been a guard stationed outside the store, Jean would have seen him before being seen. He saw the fence—reached it—entered the yard—glided in the dense shadow of the barn until the black square began to loom gray—the color of stone at night. Jean peered through the obscurity. No dark figure of a man showed against that gray wall—only a black patch, which must be the hole in the foundation mentioned by Blue. A ray of light now streaked out from the little back window. To the right showed the wide back door.

Farther in, Jean glided silently. Then he halted. There was no guard outside. Jean heard the *clink* of a cup, the lazy drawl of a Texan, and then a strong harsh voice—Jorth's. It strung Jean's whole being, tight and vibrating. Inside he was on fire while cold thrills rippled over his skin. It took tremendous effort of will to hold himself back another instant to listen, to look, to feel, to make sure. That instinct charged him with a mighty current of hot blood, straining, throbbing, damming.

When Jean leaped, this current burst. In a few swift bounds he gained his point halfway between door and window. He leaned his rifle against the stone wall. Then he swung the axe. *Crash!* The window shutter split and rattled to the floor inside. The silence then broke with a hoarse: "What's that?"

With all his might Jean swung the heavy axe at the door. *Smash!* The lower half caved in and banged to the floor. Bright light flared out the hole.

"Look out!" yelled a man in loud alarm. "They're batterin' the back door!"

Jean swung again, high on the splintered door. *Crash!* Pieces flew inside.

"They've got axes," hoarsely shouted another voice. "Shove the counter ag'in' the door."

"No!" thundered a voice of authority that denoted terror as well. "Let them come in. Pull your guns an' take to cover!"

"They ain't comin' in," was the hoarse reply. "They'll shoot in on us from the dark."

"Put out the lamp!" yelled another.

Jean's third heavy swing caved in part of the upper half of the door. Shouts and curses intermingled with the sliding of benches across the floor and the hard shuffle of boots. This confusion seemed to be split and silenced by a piercing yell, of different caliber, of terrible meaning. It stayed Jean's swing—caused him to drop the axe and snatch up his rifle.

"Don't anybody move!"

Like a steel whip this voice cut the silence. It belonged to Blue. Jean swiftly bent to put his eye to a crack in the hole of the door. Most of those visible seemed to have been frozen into unnatural positions. Jorth stood rather in front of his men, hatless and coatless, one arm outstretched, and his dark profile was set toward the little man just inside the door. This man was Blue. Jean needed only one flashing look at Blue's face, at his leveled, quivering guns, to understand why he had chosen this trick.

"Who're . . . you?" demanded Jorth in husky pants.

"Reckon I'm Isbel's right-hand man," came the biting reply. "Once tolerable well-known in Texas . . . King Fisher!"

The name must have been a guarantee of death. Jorth

recognized this outlaw and realized his own fate. In the lamplight his face turned a pale, greenish white. His outstretched hand began to quiver down.

Blue's left gun seemed to leap up and flash red and explode. Several heavy reports merged almost as one. Jorth's arm jerked limply, flinging his gun, and his body sagged in the middle. His hands fluttered like crippled wings and found their way to his abdomen. His death-pale face never changed its set look or position toward Blue, but his gasping utterance was one of horrible mortal fury and terror. Then he began to sway, still with that strange rigid set of his face toward his slayer until he fell.

His fall broke the spell. Even Blue, like the gunman he was, had paused to watch Jorth in his last mortal action. Jorth's followers began to draw and shoot. Jean saw Blue's return fire bring down a huge man who fell across Jorth's body. Then Jean, quick as the thought that actuated him, raised his rifle and shot at the big lamp. It burst in a flare. It crashed to the floor. Darkness followed—a black thick, enveloping mantle. Then red flashing of guns emphasized the blackness. Inside the store, there broke loose a pandemonium of shots, yells, curses, and thudding boots. Jean shoved his rifle barrel inside the door, and, holding it low down, he moved it to and fro while he worked lever and trigger until the magazine was empty. Then, drawing his six-shooter, he emptied that. A roar of rifles from the front of the store told Jean that his comrades had entered the fray. Bullets zipped through the door he had broken. Jean ran swiftly around the corner, taking care to sheer off a little to the left, and, when he got clear of the building, he saw a line of flashes in the middle of the road. Blaisdell and the others were firing into the door of the store. With nimble fingers Jean reloaded his rifle. Then swiftly he ran across the road, and down to get behind his comrades. Their shouting had slackened. Jean saw dark forms coming his way.

"Hello, Blaisdell!" he called warningly.

"That you, Jean?" returned the rancher, looming up. "Wal, we wasn't worried aboot you."

"Blue?" queried Jean sharply.

A little dark figure shuffled up to Jean. "Howdy, Jean," said Blue dryly. "You shore did your part. Reckon I'll need to be tied up, but I ain't hurt much."

"Colmor's hit!" called the voice of Gordon, a few yards distant. "Help me, somebody."

Jean ran to help Gordon hold up the swaying Colmor. "Are you hurt . . . bad?" asked Jean anxiously. The young man's head rolled and hung. He was breathing hard and did not reply. They had almost to carry him.

"Come on, men!" called Blaisdell, turning back toward the others who were still firing. "We'll let well enough alone. Fredericks, you an' Bill help me find the body of the old man. It's heah somewhere."

Farther on down the road the searchers stumbled over Gaston Isbel. They picked him up and followed Jean and Gordon, who were supporting the wounded Colmor. Jean looked back to see Blue dragging himself along in the rear. It was too dark to see distinctly, nevertheless Jean got the impression that Blue was more severely wounded than he had claimed to be. The distance to Meeker's cabin was not far, but it took what Jean felt to be a long and anxious time to get there. Colmor apparently rallied somewhat. When this procession entered Meeker's yard, Blue was lagging behind.

"Blue, how air you?" called Blaisdell with concern.

"Wal, I got . . . my boots . . . on . . . anyhow," replied Blue huskily.

227

He lurched into the yard and slid down on the grass and stretched out.

"Man! You're hurt bad!" exclaimed Blaisdell. The others halted in their slow march, and, as if by tacit unspoken word, lowered the body of Isbel to the ground. Then Blaisdell knelt beside Blue. Jean left Colmor to Gordon and hurried to peer down into Blue's thin face.

"No, I ain't hurt," said Blue in a much weaker voice. "I'm jest killed! It was Queen! You all heered me. Queen was . . . only badman in thet lot. I knowed it. I could . . . hev' killed him . . . but I was . . . after Lee Jorth . . . an' his brothers. . . ."

Blue's voice failed there.

"Wal," ejaculated Blaisdell.

"Shore was funny . . . Jorth's face . . . when I said . . . King Fisher," whispered Blue. "Funnier . . . when I bored . . . him through. . . . But it . . . was . . . Queen. . . ."

His whisper died away.

"Blue!" called Blaisdell sharply. Receiving no answer, he bent down in the starlight and placed a hand upon the man's breast.

"Wal, he's gone . . . I wonder if he was the old Texas King Fisher. No one would ever believe it. But if he killed the Jorths, I'll shore believe him."

Chapter Ten

Two weeks of lonely solitude in the forest had worked incalculable change in Ellen Jorth.

Late in June her father and her two uncles had packed and ridden off with Daggs, Colter, and six other men, all heavily armed, some somber with drink, others hard and grim with a foretaste of fight. Ellen had not been given any orders. Her father had forgotten to bid her good bye or had avoided it. Their dark mission was stamped on their faces.

They had gone, and keen as had been Ellen's pang, nevertheless their departure was a relief. She had heard their bluster and brag so often that she had her doubts of any great Jorth-Isbel war. Barking dogs did not bite. Somebody, perhaps on each side, would be badly wounded, possibly killed, and then the feud would go on as before, mostly talk. Many of her former impressions had faded. Development had been so rapid and continuous in her that she could look back to a day-by-day transformation. At night she would hate the sight of herself, but, when the dawn came, she would rise singing.

Jorth had left Ellen at home with the Mexican woman and Antonio. Ellen saw them only at meal times, and often not then, for she frequently visited old John Sprague or came home late to do her own cooking. It was but a short distance up to Sprague's cabin, and, since she had stopped riding the black horse Spades, she walked. Spades was accustomed to having grain and in the mornings he would come down to the ranch and whistle. Ellen had vowed she would never feed the horse and bade Antonio do it. But one morning Antonio was absent. She fed Spades herself. When she laid a hand on him and when he rubbed his nose against her shoulder, she was not quite so sure she hated him. "Why should I?" she queried. "A horse cain't help it if he belongs to . . . to. . . ." Ellen was not sure of anything except that more and more it felt good to be alone.

A whole day in the lonely forest passed swiftly, yet it left a feeling of being a long time. She lived by her thoughts. Always the morning was bright, sunny, sweet and fragrant and colorful, and her mood was pensive, wistful, dreamy. Always, just as much as the hours passed, thought intruded upon her happiness, and thought brought memory, and memory brought shame, and shame brought fight. Sunset after sunset she had dragged herself back to the ranch, sullen and sick and beaten. Yet she never ceased to struggle.

The July storms came, and the forest floor that had been so sere and brown and dry and dusty changed as if by magic. The green grass shot up, the flowers bloomed, and, along the cañon, beds of lacy ferns swayed in the wind and bent their graceful tips near the amber-colored water. Ellen haunted these cool dells, these pine-shaded, mossy-rocked ravines where the brooks tinkled and the deer came down to drink. She wandered alone. But there grew to be company in the rugged, fallen trees and the wind in the aspens and the music of the little waterfalls. If she could have lived in that solitude always, never returning to the ranch home that reminded her of her name, she could have forgotten and have been happy.

She loved the storms. It was a dry country and she had learned through years to welcome the creamy clouds that rolled from the southwest. They came sailing and clustering

230

and darkening, at last to form a great, purple, angry mass that appeared to lodge against the mountain's rim and burst into dazzling sheets of lightning and gray falls of rain. Lightning seldom struck near the ranch, but up on the Tonto Rim there was never a storm that did not splinter and crash some of the noble pines. During the storm season sheepherders and woodsmen generally did not camp under the pines. Fear of lightning was inborn in the natives, but for Ellen the dazzling white streaks, or the tremendous splitting, crackling shock, or the thunderous boom and rumble along the battlements of the rim held no terrors. A storm eased her breast. Deep in her heart was a hidden, gathering, imponderable storm and somehow, to be out when the elements were warring, when the earth trembled and the heavens seemed to burst asunder, afforded her strange relief.

The summer days became weeks, and further and further they carried Ellen on the wings of solitude and loneliness until she seemed to look back years at the self she had hated. And always, when the dark memory impinged upon peace, she fought and fought until she seemed to be fighting hatred itself. Scorn of scorn and hate of hate! Yet even her battles grew to be dreams. For when the inevitable retrospect brought back Jean Isbel and his love, and her cowardly falsehood, she would shudder a little, put an unconscious hand to her breast, and utterly fail in her fight, and drift off down to vague and wistful dreams. The clear and healing forest with its whispering wind and imperious solitude had come between Ellen and the meaning of the squalid sheep ranch, with its travesty of home, its tragic owner. It was coming between her two selves, the one that she had been proud to be, and the other that she did not know—the thinker, the dreamer, the romancer, the one who lived in fancy the life she loved.

The summer morning dawned that brought Ellen strange tidings. They must have been created in her sleep and now were realized in the glorious burst of golden sun, in the sweep of creamy clouds across the blue, in the solemn music of the wind in the pines, in the wild screech of the blue jays and the noble bugle of a stag. These heralded the day as no ordinary day. Something was going to happen to her. She divined it. She felt it. And she trembled. Nothing beautiful, hopeful, wonderful could ever happen to Ellen Jorth. She had been born to disaster, to suffer, to be forgotten, and die alone. Yet all nature about her seemed a magnificent rebuke to her morbidity. The same spirit that came out there with the thick amber light was in her. She lived, and something in her was stronger than wind.

Ellen went to the door of her cabin, where she flung out her arms, driven to embrace this nameless purport of the morning. A well-known voice broke in upon her rapture.

"Wal, lass, I like to see you happy an' I hate myself fer comin'. Because I've been to Grass Valley fer two days an' I've got news."

Old John Sprague stood there, with a smile that did not hide a troubled look.

"Oh! John! You startled me!" exclaimed Ellen, shocked back to reality. Slowly she added: "Grass Valley. News?"

She put out an appealing hand, which Sprague quickly took in his own, as if to reassure her.

"Yes, an' not bad so far as you Jorths are concerned," he replied. "The first Jorth-Isbel fight has come off. Reckon you remember makin' me promise to tell you if I heered anythin'? Wal, I didn't wait fer you to come up."

"So," Ellen heard her voice calmly saying. What was this lying calmly when there seemed to be a stone hammer at her heart? The first fight—not so bad for the Jorths! Then it had been bad for the Isbels. A sudden cold stillness fell upon her senses.

"Let's sit down outdoors," Sprague was saying. "Nice an' sunny this mornin'. I declare . . . I'm out of breath. Not used to walkin'. An' besides I left Grass Valley in the night . . . an' I'm tired. But excuse me from hangin' 'round thet village last night. There was shore. . . ."

"Who . . . who was killed?" interrupted Ellen, her voice breaking, low and deep.

"Guy Isbel an' Bill Jacobs on the Isbel side, an' Daggs, Craig, an' Greaves, on your father's side," stated Sprague with something of awed haste.

"Ah," breathed Ellen, and she relaxed to sink back against the cabin wall.

Sprague seated himself on the log beside her, turning to face her, and he seemed burdened with grave and important matters.

"I heered a good many conflictin' stories," he said earnestly. "The village folk is all skeered an' there's no believin' their gossip. But I got what happened straight from Jake Evarts. The fight come off day before yestiddy. Your father's gang rode down to Isbel's ranch. Daggs was seen to be wantin' some of the Isbel hosses . . . so Evarts says. An' Guy Isbel an' Jacobs run out in the pasture. Daggs an' some others shot them down. . . ."

"Killed them . . . that way?" put in Ellen sharply.

"So Evarts says. He was on the ridge an' swears he seen it all. They killed Guy an' Jacobs in cold blood. No chance fer their lives . . . not even to fight! Wal, then they surrounded the Isbel cabin. The fight lasted all that day an' all night an' the next day. Evarts says Guy an' Jacobs laid out thar all this time. An' a herd of hogs broke in the pasture

233

an' was eatin' the dead bodies. . . ."

"My God!" burst out Ellen. "Uncle John, you shore cain't mean my father wouldn't stop fightin' long enough to drive the hogs off an' bury those daid men?"

"Evarts says they stopped fightin', all right, but it was to watch the hogs," declared Sprague. "An' then, what d'ya think? The wimminfolks come out . . . the red-headed one, Guy's wife . . . an' Jacobs's wife . . . they drove the hogs away an' buried their husbands right there in the pasture. Evarts says he seen the graves."

"It is the women who can teach these bloody Texans a lesson," declared Ellen forcibly.

"Wal, Daggs was drunk, an' he got up from behind where the gang was hidin' an' dared the Isbels to come out. They shot him to pieces. An' that night some one of the Isbels shot Craig, who was alone on guard. An' last . . . this here's what I come to tell you . . . Jean Isbel slipped up in the dark on Greaves an' knifed him."

"Why did you want to tell me that particularly?" asked Ellen slowly.

"Because I reckon the facts in the case are queer . . . an' because Ellen, your name was mentioned," answered Sprague positively.

"My name . . . mentioned?" echoed Ellen. Her horror and disgust gave way to a quickening process of thought, a mounting astonishment. "By whom?"

"Jean Isbel," replied Sprague, as if the name and the fact were momentous.

Ellen sat still as a stone, her hands between her knees. Slowly she felt the blood recede from her face, prickling her skin down below her neck. That name locked her thought.

"Ellen, it's a mighty queer story . . . too queer to be a lie," went on Sprague. "Now, you listen. Evarts got this from Ted Meeker. An' Ted Meeker heard it from Greaves who didn't die till the next day after Jean Isbel knifed him. An' your dad shot Ted fer tellin' what he heered. No, Greaves wasn't killed outright. He was cut something turrible . . . in two places. They wrapped him all up an' next day packed him in a wagon back to Grass Valley. Evarts says Ted Meeker was friendly with Greaves an' went to see him as he was layin' in his room next to the store. Wal, accordin' to Meeker's story, Greaves came to an' talked. He said he was sittin' there in the dark, shootin' occasionally at Isbel's cabin when he heered a rustle behind him in the grass. He knowed someone was crawlin' up on him. But before he could get his gun around, he was jumped by what he thought was a grizzly bear. But it was a man. He shut off Greaves's wind an' dragged him back in the ditch. An' he said . . . 'Greaves, it's the half-breed. An' I'm goin' to cut you . . . *first for Ellen Jorth!* . . . an' then for Gaston Isbel!' Greaves said Jean ripped him with a Bowie knife. An' thet was all Greaves remembered. He died soon after tellin' this story. He must have fought awful hard. Thet second cut Isbel gave him went clear through him. Some of the gang was thar when Greaves talked, an' naturally they wondered why Jean Isbel had said . . . 'first for Ellen Jorth'. Somebody remembered thet Greaves had cast a slur on your good name, Ellen. An' then they had Jean Isbel's reason fer sayin' that to Greaves. It caused a lot of talk. An' when Simm Bruce busted in, some of the gang hawed-hawed him an' said as how he'd get the third cut from Jean Isbel's Bowie. Bruce was half drunk an' he began to cuss an' rave about Jean Isbel bein' in love with his girl. As bad luck would have it, a couple more fellars come in an' asked Meeker questions. He jist got to thet part . . . 'Greaves, it's the half-breed, an' I'm goin' to cut you . . .

first for Ellen Jorth . . .' when in walked your father! Then it all had to come out . . . what Jean Isbel had said an' done . . . an' why. How Greaves had backed Simm Bruce in slurrin' you!"

Sprague paused to look hard at Ellen.

"Oh . . . then . . . what did Dad do?" whispered Ellen.

"He said . . . 'By God, half-breed or not, there's one Isbel who's a man!' An' he killed Bruce on the spot, an' gave Meeker a nasty wound. Somebody grabbed him before he could shoot Meeker again. They threw Meeker out, an' he crawled to a neighbor's house where he was when Evarts seen him." Ellen felt Sprague's rough, but kindly, hand shaking her. "An' now, what do you think of Jean Isbel?" he queried.

A great insurmountable wall seemed to obstruct Ellen's thought. It seemed gray in color. It moved toward her. It was inside her brain.

"I tell you, Ellen Jorth," declared the old man, "thet Jean Isbel loves you . . . loves you turribly . . . an' he believes you're good."

"Oh . . . no . . . he doesn't," faltered Ellen.

"Wal, he jest does."

"Oh, Uncle John! He cain't . . . he cain't believe that!" she cried.

"Of course, he can. He does. You are good . . . good as gold, Ellen, an' he knows it. What a queer deal it all is! Poor devil! To love you thet turribly an' hev' to fight your people! Ellen, your dad had it correct. Isbel or not, he's a man. An' I say what a damn' shame you two are divided by hate. Hate thet you had nothin' to do with."

Sprague patted her hand, and rose to go. "Mebbe that fight will lick the trouble. I reckon it will. Don't cross bridges till you come to them, Ellen. I must hurry back now. I didn't take time to unpack my burros. Come up soon. An', say, Ellen, don't think hard any more of that Jean Isbel."

Sprague strode away, and Ellen neither heard nor saw him go. She sat perfectly motionless, yet had a strange sensation of being lifted by invisible and mighty power. It was like movement felt in a dream. She was being impelled upward when her body seemed immovable as stone. When her blood beat down this deadlock of all her physical being and rushed on and on through her veins, it gave her an irresistible impulse to fly, to sail through space, to run and run and run.

At that moment the black horse Spades, coming from the meadow, whinnied at sight of her. Ellen leaped up and ran swiftly, but her feet seemed to be stumbling. She hugged the horse and buried her hot face in his mane and clung to him. Then, just as violently, she rushed for her saddle and bridle and carried the heavy weight as easily as if it had been an empty sack. Throwing them upon him, she buckled and strapped with strong, eager hands. It never occurred to her that she was not dressed to ride. Up she flung herself. And the horse, sensing her spirit, plunged into strong, free gait down the cañon trail.

The ride, the action, the thrill, the sensations of violence were not all she needed. Solitude, the empty aisles of the forest, the far miles of lonely wilderness—were these the added all? Spades took a swinging, rhythmic lope up the winding trail. The wind fanned her hot face. The sting of whipping aspen branches was pleasant. A deep rumble of thunder shook the sultry air. Up beyond the green slope of the cañon massed the creamy clouds, shading darker and darker. Spades loped on the levels, leaped the washes, trotted over the rocky ground, and took to a walk up the long slope. Ellen dropped the reins over the pommel. Her hands could not stay set on anything. They pressed her breast, and flew out to caress the white aspens and to tear at the maple leaves, and gathered the lavender juniper berries, and came back again to her heart. Her heart that was going to burst or break! As it had swelled, so now it labored. It could not keep pace with her needs. All that was physical, all that was living in her had to be unleashed.

Spades gained the level forest. How the great brown-green pines seemed to bend their lofty branches over her, protectively, understandingly. Patches of azure blue sky flashed between the trees. The great white clouds sailed along with her, and shafts of golden sunlight, flecked with gleams of falling pine needles, shone down through the canopy overhead. Away in front of her, up the slow heave of forest land, loomed the heavy thunderbolts along the battlements of the Tonto Rim.

Was she riding to escape from herself? For no gait suited her until Spades was running hard and fast through the glades. Then the promise of dry wind, the thick odor of pine, the flashes of brown and green and gold and blue, the soft, rhythmic thuds of hoofs, the feel of the powerful horse under her, the whip of spruce branches on her bare knees, and the sense of her muscles contracting and expanding in hard action,—all those sensations seemed to quell for the time the mounting cataclysm in her heart.

The oak swales, the maple thickets, the aspen groves, the pine-shaded aisles and the miles of silver spruce all sped by her, as if she had ridden the wind, and through the forest ahead shone the vast open sky of the Tonto Basin, gloomed by purple and silver clouds, shadowed by gray storm, and in the west brightened by golden sky.

Straight to the rim she had ridden, and to the point

238

where she had watched Jean Isbel that unforgettable day. She rode to the promontory behind the pine thicket and beheld a scene that stayed her restless hands upon her heaving breast.

The world of sky and cloud and earthly abyss seemed one of storm-sundered grandeur. The air was sultry and still and smelled of the peculiar burnt-wood odor caused by lightning striking trees. A few heavy drops of rain were pattering down from the thin, gray edge of clouds overhead. To the east hung the storm—a black cloud lodged against the rim, from which long misty veils of rain streamed down into the gulf. The roar of rain sounded like the steady roar of the rapids of a river. Then a blue-white, piercingly bright, ragged sheet of lightning shot down out of the black cloud. It struck with a splitting report that shocked the very wall of rock under Ellen. Then the heavens seemed to burst open with thundering crash and close with mighty thundering boom. Long roar and longer rumble rolled away to the eastward. The rain poured down in roaring cataracts.

The south held a panorama of purple-shrouded range and cañon, cañon and range, on across the rolling leagues to the dim lofty peaks, all canopied over with angry, dusky, slow-drifting clouds, horizon-wide, smoky, and sulphurous. As Ellen watched, hands pressed to her breast, feeling incalculable relief in sight of this tempest and gulf that resembled her soul, the sun burst out from behind the long bank of purple cloud in the west and flooded the world there with golden lightning.

"It's for me!" said Ellen. "In my mind . . . my heart . . . my soul. . . . Oh, God! I know! I know now! I love him . . . love him . . . love him!" She cried it out to the elements. "Oh, I love Jean Isbel . . . an' my heart will burst or break!"

The might of her passion was like the blaze of the sun.

Before it all else retreated, diminished. The suddenness of the truth dimmed her sight. But she saw clearly enough to crawl into the pine thicket, through the clutching dry twigs, over the mats of fragrant needles to the cover where she had once spied upon Jean Isbel. And here she lay face down for a while, hands clutching the needles, breast pressed hard upon the ground, stricken and spent. But vitality was exceedingly strong in her. It passed, that weakness of realization, and she awakened to the consciousness of love.

In the beginning it was not consciousness of the man. It was new sensorial life, elemental, primitive, a liberation of a million inherited instincts, quivering and physical, over which Ellen had no more control than she had over the glory of the sun. If she thought at all, it was of her need to be hidden, like an animal, low down near the earth, covered by green thicket, lost in the wildness of nature. She went to nature, unconsciously seeking a mother. Love was a birth from the depths of her, like a rushing spring of pure water, long underground, and at last propelled to the surface by a convulsion.

Ellen gradually lost her tense rigidity and relaxed. Her body softened. She rolled over until her face caught the lacy golden shadows cast by sun and bough. Scattered drops of rain pattered around her. The air was hot, and its odor was that of dry pine and spruce fragrance, penetrated by brimstone from the lightning. The nest where she lay was warm and sweet. No eye save that of nature saw her in her abandonment. An ineffable and exquisite smile wreathed her lips, dreamy, sad, sensuous, the supremacy of unconscious happiness. Over her dark and eloquent eyes, as Ellen gazed upward, spread a luminous film, a veil. She was looking intensely, yet she did not see. The wilderness enveloped her with its secretive elemental sheaths of rock, of tree, of cloud, of sunlight. Through her thrilling skin poured the multiple and nameless sensations of the living organism stirred to supreme sensitiveness. She could not lie still, but all her movements were gentle, involuntary. The slow reaching out of her hand, to grasp at nothing visible, was similar to the lazy stretching of her legs, to the heave of her breast, to the ripple of muscles. Like a sleepy, indolent panther she rocked a little from side to side.

Ellen knew not what she felt. To her, that sublime hour was beyond thought. Such happiness was like the first dawn of the world to the sight of man. It had to do with bygone ages. Her heart, her blood, her flesh, her very bones were filled with instincts and emotions common to the race before intellect developed, when the savage lived only with his sensorial perceptions of all happiness, joy, bliss, rapture to which man was heir, in which intense and exquisite preoccupation of the senses, unhindered and unburdened by thought, was the greatest. Ellen felt that which life meant with its inscrutable design. Love was only the realization of her mission on the earth.

The dark storm cloud with its white, ragged ropes of lightning and down-streaming gray veils of rain, the purple gulf rolling like a colored sea to the dim mountains, the glorious, golden light of the sun,—these had enchanted her eyes with the beauty of the universe. They had burst the windows of her blindness. When she crawled into the green-brown covert, it was to escape too great perception. She needed to be encompassed by close, tangible things, and there her body paid the tribute to the realization of life. Shock, convulsion, pain, relaxation, and then unutterable and insupportable sensing of her environment and the heart! In one way she was a wild animal alone in the woods, forced into the mating that meant reproduction of its kind.

241

In another she was an infinitely higher being shot through and through with the most resistless and mysterious transplant that life could give to flesh. Her instinctive motions with her hands, always returning to her breast, betrayed the truth and the wonder of her state. It was her heart that was the birth and the center and the end of all this physical ecstasy. What had thought or character or custom or hate to do with Ellen Jorth then? She was bound by life to her sex. She was doomed to the bursting heart, the tingling veins, the thrilling nerves, the swelling breasts of a woman.

When that spell slackened its hold, there wedged into her mind a consciousness of the man she loved—Jean Isbel. Then emotion and thought strove for mastery over her. It was not herself or love that she loved but a living man. Suddenly he existed so clearly for her that she could see him, hear him, almost feel him. Her whole soul, her very life cried out to him for protection, for salvation, for love, for fulfillment. No denial, no doubt marred the white blaze of her realization. From the instant that she had looked up into Jean Isbel's dark face she had loved him. Only she had not known. She bowed now, and bent, and humbly quivered under the mastery of something beyond her ken. Thought clung to the beginnings of her romance—to the three times she had seen him. Every look, every word, every act of his returned to her now in the light of the truth. Love at first sight! He had sworn it, bitterly, eloquently, scornful of her doubts, and now a blind, sweet, shuddering ecstasy swayed her. How weak and frail seemed her body—too small, too slight for this monstrous and terrible enigma of fire and lightning and fury and glory—her heart! It must burst or break. Relentlessly memory pursued Ellen, and her thoughts whirled, and emotion conquered her. At last she quivered up to her knees as if lashed to action. It seemed

242

that first kiss of Isbel's, cool and gentle and timid, was on her lips, and her eyes closed and hot tears welled from under her lids. Her groping hands found only the dead twigs and the pine boughs of the trees. Had she reached out to clasp him? Then hard and violent on her mouth and cheek and neck burned those other kisses of Isbel's, and with the flashing, stinging memory came the truth that now she would have bartered her soul for them. Utterly she surrendered to the enormity of this love. Her loss of mother and friends, her wandering from one wild place to another, her lonely life among bold and rough men, had developed her for violent love. It overthrew all pride, it engendered humility, it killed hate. Ellen wiped the tears from her eyes, and, as she knelt there, she swept to her breast a fragrant spreading bough of pine needles. "I'll go to him," she whispered. "I'll tell him of . . . of my . . . my love. I'll beg him to take me away . . . away to the end of the world . . . away from heah . . . before it's too late."

It was a solemn, beautiful moment. But the last spoken words whispered hauntingly. "Too late?" she whispered. Suddenly it seemed that death itself shuddered in her soul. Too late! It was too late. She had killed his love. That Jorth blood in her—that poisonous hate—had chosen the only way to strike this noble Isbel to the heart. Basely, with an abandonment of womanhood, she had mockingly perjured her soul with a vile lie. She writhed, she shook under the whip of this inconceivable fact.

Lost! Lost! She wailed her misery. She might as well be what she had made Jean Isbel think she was. If she had been shamed before, she was now abased, degraded, lost in her own sight. If she would have given her soul for his kisses, she now would have killed herself to earn back his respect. Jean Isbel had given her at sight the deference that she had unconsciously craved, and the love that would have been her salvation. What a horrible mistake she had made of her life! Not her mother's blood, but her father's—the Jorth blood—had been her ruin.

Again Ellen fell upon the soft pine-needle mat, face down, and she groveled and burrowed there, in an agony that could not bear the sense of light. All she had suffered was as nothing to this. It had awakened to a splendid and uplifting love for a man who she had imagined she hated, who had fought for her name and had killed in revenge for the dishonor she had avowed—to have lost his love and what was infinitely more precious to her now in her ignominy—his faith in her purity—this broke her heart.

Chapter Eleven

When Ellen, utterly spent in body and mind, reached home that day, a melancholy, sultry twilight had fallen. Fitful flares of sheet lightning swept across the dark horizon to the east. The cabins were deserted. Antonio and the Mexican woman were gone. The circumstances made Ellen wonder, but she was too tired and too sunken in spirit to think long about it or to care. She fed and watered her horse, and left him in the corral. Then, supperless and without removing her clothes, she threw herself upon the bed, and at once sank into heavy slumber.

Sometime during the night she awoke. Coyotes were yelping, and from that sound she concluded it was near dawn. Her body ached; her mind seemed dull. Drowsily she was sinking into slumber again when she heard the rapid *clip-clop* of trotting horses. Startled, she raised her head to listen. The men were coming back. Relief and dread seemed to clear her stupor.

The trotting horses stopped across the lane from her cabin, evidently at the corral where she had left Spades. She heard him whistle. From the sound of hoofs she judged the number of horses to be six or eight. Low voices of men mingled with thuds, and cracking of straps, and flopping of saddles on the ground. After that, the heavy tread of boots sounded on the porch of the cabin opposite. A door creaked on its hinges. Next a slow footstep, accompanied by clinking of spurs, approached Ellen's door, and a heavy hand banged upon it. She knew this person could not be her father.

"Hullo, Ellen." She recognized the voice as belonging to Colter. Somehow its tone, or something about it, sent a little shiver down her spine. It acted like a revivifying current. Ellen lost her dragging lethargy.

"Hey, Ellen, are you there?" added Colter in louder voice.

"Yes, of course I'm heah," she replied. "What do you want?"

"Wal . . . I'm shore glad you're home," he replied. "Antonio's gone with his squaw. An' I was some worried about you."

"Who's with you, Colter?" queried Ellen, sitting up.

"Rock Wells an' Springer. Tad Jorth was with us, but we had to leave him over heah in a cabin."

"What's the matter with him?"

"Wal, he's hurt tolerable bad," was the slow reply. Ellen heard Colter's spurs jingle, as if he had uneasily shifted his feet.

"Whar's Dad an' Uncle Jackson?" asked Ellen.

A silence pregnant enough to augment Ellen's dread was finally broken by Colter's voice, somehow different. "Shore they're back on the trail. An' we're to meet them where we left Tad."

"Are you goin' away again?"

"I reckon. An' Ellen, you're goin' with us."

"I am not," she retorted.

"Wal, you are, if I have to pack you," he replied forcibly. "It's not safe heah, anyways. That damned half-breed Isbel with his gang are on our trail."

That name seemed like a red-hot blade at Ellen's leaden heart. She wanted to fling a hundred queries at Colter, but she could not utter one.

"Ellen, we've got to hit the trail an' hide," continued Colter anxiously. "You mustn't stay heah alone. Suppose them Isbels would trap you! They'd tear your clothes off an' rope you to a tree. Ellen, shore you're goin' . . . you heah me?"

"Yes . . . I'll . . . go," she replied, as if forced.

"Wal . . . that's good," he said quickly. "An' rustle tolerable lively. We've got to pack."

The slow jangle of Colter's spurs and his slow steps moved away out of Ellen's hearing. Throwing off the blankets, she put her feet to the floor and sat there a moment, staring at the blank nothingness of the cabin interior in the obscure gray of dawn. Cold, gray dawn, obscure—like her life, her future! And she was compelled to do what was hateful to her. As a Jorth she must take to the unfrequented trails and hide like a rabbit in the thickets. But the interest of the moment, a premonition of events to be, quickened her into action.

Ellen unbarred the door to let in the light. Day was breaking with an intense, clear, steely light in the east through which the morning star still shone white. A ruddy flare betokened the advent of the sun.

Ellen unbraided her tangled hair, and brushed and combed it. A queer, still pang came to her at sight of pine needles tangled in her brown locks. Then she washed her hands and face. Breakfast was a matter of considerable work and she was hungry.

The sun rose and changed the gray world of forest. For the first time in her life Ellen hated the golden brightness, the wonderful blue of sky, the scream of the eagle and the screech of the jay, and the squirrels she had always loved to feed were neglected that morning.

Colter came in. Either Ellen had never before looked attentively at him or else he had changed. Her scrutiny of his lean, hard features accorded him more Texan attributes than formerly. His gray eyes were as light, as clear, as fierce as those of an eagle. The sand-gray of his face, the long, drooping, fair mustache, hid the secrets of his mind, but not its strength. The instant Ellen met his gaze she sensed a power in him that she instinctively opposed. Colter had not been so bold or so rude as Daggs, but he was the same kind of man, perhaps the more dangerous for his secretiveness, his cool, waiting inscrutability.

" 'Mawnin', Ellen," he drawled. "You shore look good for sore eyes."

"Don't pay me compliments, Colter," replied Ellen. "An' your eyes are not sore."

"Wal, I'm shore sore from fightin' an' ridin' an' stayin' out," he said bluntly.

"Tell me . . . what's happened?" returned Ellen.

"Girl, it's a tolerable long story," replied Colter. "An' we've no time now. Wait till we get to camp."

"Am I to pack my belongin's or leave them heah?" asked Ellen.

"Reckon you'd better leave them heah."

"But if we do not come back. . . ."

"Wal, I reckon it's not likely we'll come . . . soon," he said rather evasively.

"Colter, I'll not go off into the woods with just the clothes I have on my back."

"Ellen, we shore got to pack all the grub we can. This shore ain't goin' to be a visit to neighbors. We've only pack hosses. But you make up a bundle of belongin's you care for an' the things you'll need bad. We'll throw it on some-where."

Colter stalked away across the lane, but Ellen found her-

248

self dubiously staring at his tall figure. Was it the situation that struck her with a foreboding perplexity, or was her intuition steeling her against this man? Ellen could not decide. But she had to go with him. Her prejudice was unreasonable at this portentous moment. She could not yet feel that she was solely responsible to herself.

When it came to making a small bundle of her belongings, she was in a quandary. She discarded this and put in that, and then reversed the order. Next in preciousness to her mother's things were the long-hidden gifts of Jean Isbel. She could part with neither.

While she was selecting and packing this bundle, Colter again entered and, without speaking, began to rummage in the corner where her father kept his possessions. This irritated Ellen.

"What do you want there?" she demanded.

"Wal, I reckon your dad wants his papers . . . an' the gold he left heah . . . an' a change of clothes. Now doesn't he?" returned Colter coolly.

"Of course. But I supposed you would have me pack them."

Colter vouchsafed no reply to this, but deliberately went on rummaging, with little regard for how he scattered things. Ellen turned her back on him. At length, when he left, she went to her father's corner and found that, as far as she was able to see, Colter had taken neither papers nor clothes, but only the gold. Perhaps, however, she had been mistaken, for she had not observed Colter's departure closely enough to know whether or not he carried a package. She missed only the gold. Her father's papers, old and musty, were scattered about, and these she gathered up to slip in her own bundle.

Colter, or one of the men, had saddled Spades, and he

was now tied to the corral fence, champing his bit and pounding the sand. Ellen wrapped bread and meat inside her coat, and, after tying this behind her saddle, she was ready to go. But evidently she would have to wait, and, preferring to remain outdoors, she stayed by her horse. Presently, while watching the men pack, she noticed that Springer wore a bandage around his head under the brim of his sombrero. His motions were slow and lacked energy. Shuddering at the sight, Ellen refused to conjecture. All too soon she would learn what had happened and all too soon, perhaps, she herself would be in the midst of another fight. She watched the men. They were making a hurried, slipshod job of packing food supplies from both cabins. More than once she caught Colter's gray gleam of gaze on her, and she did not like it.

"I'll ride up an' say good bye to Sprague," she said to Colter.

"Shore you won't do nothin' of the kind," he replied.

There was authority in his tone that angered Ellen and something else which inhibited her anger. What was there about Colter with which she must reckon? The other two Texans laughed aloud, to be suddenly silenced by Colter's harsh and lowered curses. Ellen walked out of hearing and sat upon a log where she remained until Colter hailed her.

"Get up an' ride!" he called.

Ellen complied with this order, and, riding up behind the three mounted men, she soon found herself leaving what for years had been her home. Not once did she look back. She hoped she would never see this squalid, bare pretension of a ranch again.

Colter and the other riders drove the pack horses across the meadow, off of the trails, and up the slope into the forest. Not very long did it take Ellen to see that Colter's object was to hide their tracks. He zigzagged through the forest, avoiding the bare spots of dust, the dry, sun-baked flats of clay where water lay in springs, and he chose the grassy open glades, the long pine-needle-matted aisles. Ellen rode at their heels, and it pleased her to watch for their tracks. Colter manifestly had been long practiced in this game of hiding his trail, and he showed the skill of a rustler. But Ellen was not convinced that he could ever elude a real woodsman. Not improbably, however, Colter was only aiming to leave a trail difficult to follow and which would allow him and his confederates ample time to forge ahead of pursuers. Ellen could not accept a certainty of pursuit. Yet Colter must have expected it, and Springer and Wells, also, for they had a dark, sinister, furtive demeanor that strangely contrasted with the cool, easy manner habitual to them.

They were not seeking the level routes of the forest land, that was sure. They rode straight across the thick-timbered ridge down into another cañon, up out of that and across rough rocky bluffs, and down again. These riders headed a little to the northwest and every mile brought them into wilder, more rugged country, until Ellen, losing count of cañons and ridges, had no idea where she was. No stop was made at noon to rest the laboring, sweating pack animals.

Under circumstances where pleasure might have been possible, Ellen would have reveled in this hard ride with a wonderful forest ever thickening and darkening. But the wild beauty of glade and the spruce slopes and the deep, bronze-walled cañons left her cold. She saw and felt, but had no thrill, except now and then a thrill of alarm when Spades slid to his haunches down some steep, damp, piney declivity. All the woodland, up and down, appeared to be richer, greener as they traveled farther west. Grass grew thick and heavy. Water ran in all ravines. The rocks were bronze and copper and russet, and some had green patches of lichen.

Ellen felt the sun now on her left cheek, knew that the day was waning and that Colter was swinging farther to the northwest. She had never before ridden through such heavy forest and down and up such wild cañons. Toward sunset the deepest and ruggedest cañon halted their advance. Colter rode to the right, searching for a place to get down. Not finding any, he led his followers to the left, and eventually headed down through a spruce thicket down a steep slope. Presently he dismounted and the others followed suit. Ellen found she could not lead Spades because he slid down upon her heels, so she looped the end of her reins over the pommel and left him free. She herself managed to descend by holding to branches and sliding all the way down that slope. She heard the horses cracking the brush, snorting, and heaving. One pack slipped and had to be removed from the horn and rolled down. At the bottom of this deep, green-walled notch roared a stream of water. Shadowed, cool, mossy, damp, this narrow gulch seemed the wildest place Ellen had ever seen. She could just see the sunset-flushed, gold-tipped spruce far above her. She even repacked the horse that had slipped his burden, and once more they resumed their progress ahead, now turning up this cañon. There was no horse trail, but deer and bear trails were numerous. The sun sank and the sky darkened, but still the men rode on, and the farther they traveled, the wilder grew the aspect of the cañon.

At length Colter broke a way through a heavy thicket of willows and entered a side cañon, the mouth of which Ellen had not even descried. It turned and widened, and at length opened out into a round pocket, apparently enclosed, and as lonely and isolated a place as even pursued rustlers could desire. Hidden by jutting wall and thicket of spruce were two old log cabins joined together by roof and attic floor, the same as the double cabin at the Jorth Ranch.

Ellen smelled wood smoke and presently, on going around the cabins, saw a bright fire. One man stood beside it, gazing at Colter's party, which evidently he had heard approaching.

"Hello, Queen," said Colter. "How's Tad?"

"He's holdin' on fine," replied Queen, bending over the fire where he turned pieces of meat.

"Where's Dad?" suddenly asked Ellen, addressing Colter. As if he had not heard her, he went on wearily loosening a pack.

"Queen, where's my father?" demanded Ellen sharply.

Queen looked at her. The light of the fire only partially shone on his face. Ellen could not see his expression, but from the fact that Queen did not answer her question, she got further intimation of an impending catastrophe. The long, wild ride had helped prepare her for the secrecy and taciturnity of men who had resorted to flight. Perhaps her father had been delayed or was still off on the deadly mission that had obsessed him, or there might be, and probably was, a darker reason for his absence. Ellen shut her teeth, and turned to the needs of her horse. Then, returning to the fire, she thought of her uncle.

"Queen, is my Uncle Tad heah?" she asked.

"Shore. He's in there," replied Queen, pointing at the nearest cabin.

Ellen hurried toward the dark doorway. She could see how the logs of the cabin had moved awry and what a big, dilapidated hovel it was. As she looked in, Colter loomed over her—placed a familiar and somehow masterful hand upon her. Ellen let it rest on her shoulder a moment. Must she forever be repulsing these rude men among whom her lot was cast? Did Colter mean what Daggs had always meant? Ellen felt herself weary, weak in body, and her spent spirit had not rallied. Yet, whatever Colter meant by his familiarity, she could not bear it. So she slipped out from under his hand.

"Uncle Tad, are you heah?" she called into the blackness. She heard the mice scamper and rustle and she smelled the musty old woody odor of a long unused cabin.

"Hello, Ellen," came a voice she recognized as her uncle's, yet it was strange. "Yes, I'm heah . . . bad luck to me! How're you buckin' up, girl?"

"I'm all right, Uncle Tad . . . only tired an' worried. I. . . ."

"Tad, how's your hurt?" interrupted Colter.

"Reckon I'm easier," replied Jorth wearily, "but shore I'm in bad shape. I'm spittin' blood. I keep tellin' Queen that bullet lodged in my lungs . . . but he says it went through."

"Wal, hang on Tad," replied Colter with a cheerfulness Ellen sensed was really indifferent.

"Oh, what the hell's the use?" exclaimed Jorth. "It's all . . . up with us . . . Colter."

"Wal, shut up, then," tersely returned Colter. "It ain't doin' you or us any good to holler."

Tad Jorth did not reply to this. Ellen heard his breathing and it did not seem natural. It rasped a little—and came hurriedly—then caught in his throat. Then he spat. Ellen shrunk back against the door. He was breathing through blood.

"Uncle, are you in pain?" she asked.

"Yes Ellen . . . it burns like hell," he said.

"Oh . . . I'm sorry. Isn't there something I can do?"

"I reckon not. Queen did all anybody could do for me . . . now . . . unless it's pray."

Colter laughed at this—the slow, easy, drawling laugh of a Texan. But Ellen felt pity for this wounded uncle. She had always hated him. He had been a drunkard, a gambler, a waster of her father's property, and now he was a rustler and a fugitive, lying in pain, perhaps mortally hurt.

"Yes, Uncle . . . I will pray for you," she said softly. The change in his voice held a note of sadness that she had been quick to catch.

"Ellen, you're the only good Jorth in the whole damned lot," he said. "God! I see it all now. . . . We've dragged you to hell!"

"Yes, Uncle Tad, I've shore been dragged some . . . but not yet . . . to hell," she responded with a break in her voice.

"You will be . . . Ellen . . . unless. . . ."

"Aw, shut up that kind of gab, will you," broke in Colter harshly.

It amazed Ellen that Colter should dominate her uncle, even though he was wounded. Tad Jorth had been the last man to take orders from anyone, much less a rustler of the Hash Knife Gang. This Colter began to loom up in Ellen's estimate as he loomed physically over her, a lofty figure, dark, motionless, somehow menacing.

"Ellen, has Colter told you yet . . . about . . . about Lee an' Jackson?" inquired the wounded man.

The pitch-black darkness of the cabin seemed to help fortify Ellen to bear further trouble.

"Colter told me Dad an' Uncle Jackson would meet us heah," she rejoined hurriedly.

Jorth could be heard breathing in difficulty, and he

coughed and spat again, and seemed to hiss. "Ellen, he lied to you. They'll never meet us . . . heah!"

"Why not?" whispered Ellen.

"Because . . . Ellen . . . ," he replied in husky pants, "your dad an' Uncle Jackson . . . are daid . . . an' buried!"

If Ellen suffered a terrible shock, it was a blankness, a deadness, and a slow, creeping failure of sense in her knees. They gave away under her and she sank on the grass against the cedar wall. She did not faint or grow dizzy or lose her sight, but in a while there was no process of thought in her mind. Suddenly then it was there—the quiet, spiritual rending of her heart—followed by a profound emotion of intimate and irretrievable loss—and after that grief and bitter realization.

An hour later Ellen found strength to go to the fire and partake of the food and drink her body sorely needed. Colter and the men waited on her solicitously and in silence, now and then stealing furtive glances at her from under the shadow of their black sombreros. The dark night settled down like a blanket. There were no stars. The wind moaned fitfully among the pines, and all about that lonely, hidden recess was in harmony with Ellen's thoughts.

"Girl, you're shore game," said Colter admiringly. "An' I reckon you never got it from the Jorths."

"Tad in there . . . he's game," said Queen in mild protest.

"Not to my notion," replied Colter. "Any man can be game when he's croakin' with somebody around, but Lee Jorth an' Jackson . . . they always was yellow clear to their gizzards. They was born in Louisiana . . . not Texas. Shore they're no more Texans than I am. Ellen, heah, she must have got another strain in her blood."

To Ellen these words had no meaning. She rose and asked: "Where can I sleep?"

"I'll fetch a light presently an' you can make your bed in there by Tad," replied Colter.

"Yes, I'd like that."

"Wal, if you reckon you can coax him to talk, you're shore wrong," declared Colter with that cold timbre of voice that struck like steel on Ellen's nerves. "I cussed but good an' told him to keep his mouth shut. Talkin' makes him cough an' that fetches up the blood. Besides, I reckon I'm the one to tell you how your dad an' uncle got killed. Tad didn't see it done, an' he was bad hurt when it happened. Shore all the fellers left have their idee about it. But I've got it straight."

"Colter . . . tell me now," insisted Ellen.

"Wal, all right, come over heah," he replied, and drew her away from the campfire, in the shadow away from the glow. "Poor kid! I shore felt bad about it." He put a long arm around her waist and drew her against him. Ellen felt it, yet did not offer any resistance. All her faculties seemed abandoned in a morbid and sad anticipation.

"Ellen, you shore know I always loved you . . . now, don't you?" he asked with suppressed breath.

"No, Colter. It's news to me . . . an' not what I want to heah."

"Wal, you may as well heah it right now," he said. "It's true. An' what's more . . . your dad gave you to me before he died."

"What? Colter, you must be a liar."

"Ellen, I swear to God I'm not lyin'," he returned in eager passion. "I was with your dad last an' heard him last. He shore knew I'd loved you for years. An' he said he'd rather you be left in my care than anybody's."

257

"My father gave me to you in marriage?" ejaculated Ellen in bewilderment.

Colter's ready assurance did not carry him over this point. It was evident that his words somewhat impressed and disconcerted him for the moment.

"To let me marry a rustler . . . one of the Hash Knife Gang!" exclaimed Ellen with weary incredulity.

"Wal, your dad belonged to Daggs's gang, same as I do," replied Colter, recovering his cool ardor.

"No!" cried Ellen.

"Yes, he shore did, for years," declared Colter positively. "Back in Texas. An' it was your dad that got Daggs to come to Arizona."

Ellen tried to fling herself away, but her strength and her spirit were ebbing, and Colter increased the pressure of his arm. All at once she sank limply. Could she escape her fate? Nothing seemed left to fight with or for.

"All right . . . don't hold me so . . . tight," she panted. "Now, tell me how Dad was killed . . . an' who . . . who. . . ."

Colter bent over so he could peer into her face. In the darkness, Ellen just caught the gleam of his eyes. She felt the virile force of the man in the strain of his body as he pressed her close. It all seemed unreal—a hideous dream—the gloom, the moan of the wind, the weird solitude, and this rustler with hand and will like cold steel.

"We'd come back to Greaves's store," Colter began. "An' as Greaves was daid, we all got free with his liquor. Shore some of us got drunk. Bruce was drunk, and Tad in there . . . he was drunk. Your dad put away more'n I ever seen him. But shore he wasn't exactly drunk. He got one of them weak an' shaky spells. He cried an' he wanted some of us to get the Isbels to call off the fightin'. He shore was

258

ready to call it quits. I reckon the killin' of Daggs . . . an' then the awful way Greaves was cut up by Jean Isbel . . . took all the fight out of your dad. He said to me . . . 'Colter, we'll take Ellen an' leave this heah country . . . an' begin life all over again . . . where no one knows us.' "

"Oh, did he really say that? Did he . . . really mean it?" murmured Ellen with a sob.

"I'll swear it by the memory of my daid mother," replied Colter. "Wal, when night come, the Isbels rode down on us in the dark an' began to shoot. They smashed in the door . . . tried to burn us out . . . an' hollered 'round for a while. Then they left an' we reckoned there'd be no more trouble that night. All the same we kept watch. I was the soberest one an' I bossed the gang. We had some quarrels about the drinkin'. Your dad said, if we kept it up, it'd be the end of the Jorths. An' he planned to send word to the Isbels next mawnin' that he was ready for a truce. An' I was to go fix it up with Gaston Isbel. Your dad went to bed in Greaves's room, an' a little while later your Uncle Jackson went in there, too. Some of the men laid down in the store an' went to sleep. I kept guard till aboot three in the mawnin'. An' I got so sleepy I couldn't hold my eyes open. So I waked up Wells an' Slater an' set them on guard, one at each end of the store. Then I laid down on the counter to take a nap."

Colter's low voice, the strain and breathlessness of him, the agitation with which he appeared to be laboring, and especially the simple matter-of-fact detail of his story, carried absolute conviction to Ellen Jorth. Her vague doubt of him had been created by his attitude toward her. Emotion dominated her intelligence. The images, the scenes called up by Colter's words, were as true as the gloom of the wild gulch and the loneliness of the night solitude—as true as the strange fact that she lay passively in the arm of a rustler.

"Wal, after a while I woke up," went on Colter, clearing his throat. "It was gray dawn. All was as still as death. An' somethin' shore was wrong. Bruce an' Slater had got to drinkin' again an' now laid daid drunk or asleep. Anyways, when I kicked them, they never moved. Then I heard a moan. It came from the room where your dad an' uncle was. I went in. It was just light enough to see. Your Uncle Jackson was layin' on the floor . . . cut half in two . . . daid as a doornail. Your dad lay on the bed. He was alive, breathin' his last. He says . . . 'That half-breed Isbel . . . knifed us . . . while we slept!' The winder shutter was open. I seen where Jean Isbel had come in an' gone out. I seen his moccasin tracks in the dirt outside an' I seen where he'd stepped in Jackson's blood, an' tracked it to the winder. You shore can see them bloody tracks yourself, if you go back to Greaves's store. Your dad was goin' fast. He said . . . 'Colter . . . take care of Ellen' . . . an' I reckon he meant a lot by that. He kept sayin' . . . 'My God, if I'd only seen Gaston Isbel before it was too late' . . . an' then he raved a little, whisperin' out of his haid . . . an' after that he died. I woke up the men, an' aboot sunup we carried your dad an' uncle out of town an' buried them. An' them Isbels shot at us while we were buryin' our daid! That's where Tad got his hurt. Then we hit the trail for Jorth's ranch. An', now, Ellen, that's all my story. Your dad was ready to bury the hatchet with his old enemy. An' that Nez Percé Jean Isbel, like the sneakin' savage he is, murdered your uncle an' then your dad . . . cut him horrible . . . made him suffer tortures of hell . . . all for Isbel revenge!"

When Colter's husky voice ceased, Ellen whispered through lips as cold and still as ice: "Let me go . . . leave me . . . heah . . . alone!"

"Why, shore. I reckon I understand," replied Colter. "I

hated to tell you. But you had to heah the truth aboot that half-breed. I'll carry your pack in the cabin an' unroll your blankets."

Releasing her, Colter strode off in the gloom. Like a dead weight Ellen began to slide until she slipped down full length beside the log, and then she lay in the cool, damp shadow, inert and lifeless so far as outward physical movement was concerned. She saw nothing and felt nothing of the night, the wind, the cold, the falling dew. For the moment she was crushed by despair and seemed to see herself sinking down and down into a black, bottomless pit, into an abyss where murky tides of blood and furious gusts of passion contended between her body and her soul. Into the stormy blast of hell! In her despair she longed, she ached for death. Born of infidelity, cursed by a taint of evil blood, further cursed by higher instinct for good and happy life, dragged from one lonely and wild and sordid spot to another, never knowing love or peace or joy or home, left to the companionship of violent and vile men, driven by a strange fate to love with unquenchable and insupportable love a half-breed, a savage, an Isbel, the hereditary enemy of her people, and at last the ruthless murderer of her father—what in the name of God had she left to live for? Revenge! An eye for an eye! A life for a life! But she could not kill Jean Isbel. Woman's love could turn to hate but not the love of Ellen Jorth. He could drag her by the hair in the dust, beat her, and make her a thing to loathe, and cut her mortally in his savage and implacable thirst for revenge—but with her last gasp she would whisper she loved him and that she had lied to him to kill his faith. It was that—his strange faith in her purity—which had won her love. Of all men, that he should be the one to recognize the truth of her, the womanhood yet unsullied—how strange, how terrible, how overpowering! False, indeed, was she to the Jorths! False as her mother had been to an Isbel! This agony and destruction of her soul was the bitter Dead Sea fruit— the sins of her parents visited upon her.

"I'll end it all," she whispered to the night shadows that hovered over her. No coward was she—no fear of pain or mangled flesh or death or the mysterious hereafter could ever stay her. It would be easy, it would be a last thrill, a transport of self-abasement and supreme self-proof of her love for Jean Isbel to kiss the rim rock where his feet had trod, and then fling herself down into the depths. She was the last Jorth. So the wronged Isbels would be revenged.

But he would never know . . . never know . . . I lied to him! she wailed mutely to the night wind. She was lost—lost on earth and to hope of heaven. She had neither right to live nor to die. She was nothing but a little weed along the trail of life, trampled upon, buried in the wind. She was nothing but a single rotten thread in a tangled web of love and hate and revenge, and she had broken.

Lower and lower she seemed to sink. Was there no end to the gulf of despair? If Colter had returned, he would have found her a rag and a toy—a creature degraded, fit for his vile embraces. To be thrust deeper into the mire, to be punished fittingly for her betrayal of a man's noble love and her own womanhood—to be made an end of, body, mind, and soul.

But Colter did not return.

The wind mourned, the owls hooted, the leaves rustled, the insects whispered their melancholy night song, the campfire flickered and faded. Then the wild forest land seemed to close imponderably over Ellen. All that she wailed in her despair, all that she confessed in her abasement was true, and hard as life could be—but she belonged to nature. If nature had not failed her, had God failed her? It was there—the lonely land of tree and fern and flower and brook, full of wild birds and beasts, where the mossy rocks could speak and the solitude had ears, where she had always felt herself unutterably a part of creation. Then a wavering spark of hope quivered through the blackness of her soul, and gathered light.

The gloom of the sky, the shifting clouds of dull shade, split asunder to show a glimpse of a radiant star, piercingly white, cold, pure, a steadfast eye of the universe, beyond all understanding and illimitable with its meaning of the past, and the present, and the future. Ellen watched it until the drifting clouds once more hid it from her strained sight.

What had that star to do with hell? She might be crushed and destroyed by life, but was there not something beyond? Just to be born, just to suffer, just to die—could that be all? Despair did not loose its hold on Ellen, the strife and pang of her breast did not subside. But with the long hours and the strange closing-in of the forest around her, and the fleeting glimpse of that wonderful star, with a subtle divination of the meaning of her beating heart and throbbing mind, and, lastly, with a voice thundering at her conscience that a man's faith in a woman must not be greater, nobler, than her faith in God and eternity—with them she checked the dark flight of her soul toward destruction.

Chapter Twelve

A chill, gray, somber dawn was breaking when Ellen dragged herself into the cabin and crept under her blankets, there to sleep the sleep of exhaustion.

When she awoke, the hour appeared to be late afternoon. Sun and sky shone through the sunken and decayed roof of the old cabin. Her uncle, Tad Jorth, lay on a blanket bed upheld by a crude couch of boughs. The light fell upon his face, pale, lined, cast in a still mold of suffering. He was not dead, for she heard his respiration.

The floor underneath Ellen's blankets was bare clay. She and Jorth were alone in this cabin. It contained nothing besides their beds and a rank growth of weeds along the decayed lower logs. Half of the cabin had a rude ceiling of rough-hewn boards that formed a kind of loft. This attic extended through to the adjoining cabin, forming the ceiling of the porch-like space between the two structures. There was no partition. A ladder of two aspen saplings, pegged to the logs and with braces between the steps, led up to the attic.

Ellen smelled wood smoke and odor of frying meat, and she heard the voices of men. She looked out to see that Slater and Somers had joined their party—an addition that might have strengthened it for defense, but did not lend her own situation anything favorable. Somers had always appeared the one best to avoid.

Colter espied her and called her to "come an' feed your pale face." His comrades laughed, not loudly, but guardedly, as if noise was something to avoid. Nevertheless, they awoke Tad Jorth, who began to toss and moan in the bed.

Ellen hurried to his side and at once ascertained that he had a high fever and was in a critical condition. Every time he tossed, he opened a wound in his right breast, rather high up. For all she could see nothing had been done for him except the binding of a scarf around his neck and under his arm. This scant bandage had worked loose. Going to the door, she called out: "Fetch me some water!"

When Colter brought it, Ellen was rummaging in her pack for some clothing or towel that she could use for bandages.

"Weren't any of you decent enough to look after my uncle?" she queried.

"Huh! Wal, what the hell," rejoined Colter. "We shore did all we could. I reckon you think it wasn't a tough job to pack him up the rim. He was done for then an' I said so."

"I'll do all I can for him," said Ellen.

"Shore, go ahaid. When I get plugged or knifed by that half-breed, I shore hope you'll be around to nurse me."

"You seem to be pretty shore of your fate, Colter."

"Shore as hell," he bit out darkly. "Somers saw Isbel an' his gang trailin' us to the Jorth Ranch."

"Are you goin' to stay heah . . . an' wait for them?"

"Shore, I've been quarrelin' with the fellars out there over that very question. I'm for leavin' the country. But Queen, the damn' gunfighter, is daid set to kill that cowman Blue who swore he was King Fisher, the old Texas outlaw. None but Queen is spoilin' for another fight. All the same they won't leave Tad Jorth heah alone." Then Colter leaned in at the door and whispered: "Ellen, I cain't boss this outfit. So let's you an' me shake them. I've got your dad's gold. Let's ride off tonight an' shake this country."

Ellen shook her head. "Neither would I leave my uncle heah alone."

Colter, muttering under his breath, left the door, and returned to his comrades. Ellen had received her first intimation of his cowardice, and his mention of her father's gold started a train of thought that persisted in spite of her efforts to put all her mind to attending her uncle. He grew conscious enough to recognize her and her working over him, and thanked her with a look that touched Ellen deeply. It changed the direction of her mind. This suffering and imminent death, which she was able to alleviate and retard somewhat, worked upon her pity and compassion so that she forgot her own plight. Half the night she was tending him, cooling his fever, holding him quiet. Well she realized that but for her ministrations he would have died. At length he went to sleep.

Ellen, sitting beside him in the lonely, silent darkness of that late hour, received again the intimations of nature, those vague and nameless stirrings of her innermost being, those whisperings out of the night and the forest and the sky. Something had a hold on her spirit. Something great would not let go of her soul. She pondered.

Attention to the wounded man occupied Ellen, and soon she redoubled her activities in this regard, finding in them something of protection against Colter. He had waylaid her as she went to a spring for water, and with a lunge like that of a bear he had tried to embrace her. But Ellen had been too quick.

"Wal, are you goin' away with me?" he demanded.

"No. I'll stick by my uncle," she replied.

That motive of hers seemed to obstruct his will. Ellen was keen to see that Colter and his comrades were at a last stand and disintegrating under a severe strain. Nerve and courage of the open and the wild they possessed, but only in a limited degree. Colter seemed obsessed by his passion for her, and, although Ellen did not yet fear him, in her stubborn pride she realized she ought to. After that incident she watched closely, never leaving her uncle's bedside except when Colter was absent. One or more of the men kept constant look-out somewhere down the cañon.

Day after day passed on the wings of suspense, of watching, of ministering to her uncle, of waiting for some hour that seemed fixed. Colter was like a hound upon her trail. At every turn he was there to importune her to run off with him, to frighten her with the menace of the Isbels, to beg her to give herself to him. It came to pass that the only relief she had was when she ate with the men, or barred the cabin door at night. Not much relief, however, was there to the shut and barred door. With one thrust of his powerful arm Colter could have caved it in. He knew this as well as Ellen. Still, she did not have the fear she should have had. There was her rifle beside her, and, although she did not allow her mind to run darkly on its possible use, still the fact of its being there at hand somehow strengthened her. Colter was a cat playing with a mouse, but not yet sure of his quarry.

Ellen came to know hours when she was weak—weak physically, mentally, spiritually, morally—when under the sheer weight of this frightful and growing burden of suspense she was not capable of fighting her misery, her abasement, her low ebb of vitality, and at the same time wholly withstanding Colter's advances. He would come into the cabin, and, utterly indifferent to Tad Jorth, he would try to make bold and unrestrained love to Ellen. When he caught her in one of her unresisting moments and was able to hold her in his arms and kiss her, he seemed to be beside himself with the wonder of her. At such moments, if he had any softness or gentleness in him, they expressed themselves in his sooner or later letting her go, when apparently she was about to faint. So it must have become fascinatingly fixed in Colter's mind that at times Ellen repulsed him with scorn and at other times could not resist him.

Ellen had escaped two crises in her relation with this man, and as a morbid doubt, like a poisonous fungus, began to strangle her mind, she instinctively divined that there was an approaching and final crisis. No uplift of her spirit came this time—no intimations—no whisperings. How horrible it all was! To long to be good and noble—to realize that she was neither—to sink lower day by day! Must she decay there like one of those rotting logs? Worst of all, there was the insinuating and ever-growing hopelessness. What was the use? What did it matter? Who would ever think of Ellen Jorth? "Oh God!" she whispered in her distraction, "is there nothin' left . . . nothing at all?"

A period of several days of less torment to Ellen followed. Her uncle apparently took a turn for the better and Colter let her alone. This last circumstance nonplussed Ellen. She was at a loss to understand it unless the Isbel menace now encroached upon Colter so formidably that he had forgotten her for the present.

Then one bright August morning, when she had just begun to relax her eternal vigilance and breathe without oppression, Colter encountered her, and, darkly silent and fierce, he grasped her and drew her off her feet. Ellen struggled violently, but the total surprise had deprived her of strength. That paralyzing weakness assailed her as never before. Without apparent effort Colter carried her, striding rapidly away from the cabins into the border of spruce trees at the foot of the cañon wall.

"Colter . . . where . . . oh, where are you takin' me?" she found voice to cry out.

"By God, I don't know," he replied with strong, vibrant passion. "I was a fool not to carry you off long ago. But I waited. I was hopin' you'd love me! An' now that Isbel gang has corralled us. Somers seen the half-breed up on the rocks. An' Springer seen the rest of them sneakin' around. I run back after my horse an' you!"

"But Uncle Tad! We mustn't leave him alone!" cried Ellen.

"We've got to," replied Colter grimly. "Tad shore won't worry you no more . . . soon as Jean Isbel gets to him."

"Oh, let me stay," implored Ellen. "I will save him!"

Colter laughed at the utter absurdity of her appeal and claim. Suddenly he set her down on her feet. "Stand still," he ordered. Ellen saw his big bay horse, saddled with pack and blanket, tied there in the shade of the spruce. With swift hands Colter untied and mounted him, scarcely moving his piercing gaze from Ellen. He reached to grasp her. "Up with you! Put your foot in the stirrup!" His will, like his powerful arm, were irresistible for Ellen at that moment. She found herself swung up in front of him. Then the horse plunged away. What with the hard motion and Colter's iron grasp Ellen was in a painful position. Her knees and feet came into violent contact with branches and snags. He galloped the horse, tearing through the dense thicket of willows that served to hide the entrance to the side cañon, and, when out in the larger and more open cañon, he urged him to a run. Presently when Colter put the horse to a slow rise of ground, thereby bringing him to a walk, it was just in time to save Ellen a serious bruising.

Again the sunlight appeared to shade over. They were in the pines. Suddenly with backward lunge Colter halted the horse. Ellen heard a yell.

"Turn back, Colter! Turn back!"

With an oath Colter wheeled his mount. "If I didn't run plumb into them," he ejaculated harshly. Scarcely had the goaded horse gotten a start when a shot rang out. Ellen felt a violent shock, as if her momentum had suddenly met with a check, and then she felt herself wrenched from Colter, from the saddle, and propelled into the air. She alighted on soft ground and thick grass, and was unhurt save for the violent wrench and shaking that had rendered her breathless. Before she could rise, Colter was pulling at her, lifting her to her feet. She saw the horse lying with bloody head. Tall pines loomed all around; another rifle cracked. "Run!" hissed Colter, and he bounded off, dragging her by the hand. Another yell pealed out. "Here we are, Colter!" That was Queen's shrill voice. Ellen ran with all her might, her heart in her throat, her sight failing to record more than a blur of passing pines and a blank green wall of spruce. Then she lost her balance, was falling yet could not fall because of that steel grip on her hand, and was dragged, and finally carried into a dense shade. She was blinded. The trees whirled and faded. Voices and shots sounded far away. Then something black seemed to be wiped across her feeling.

It turned to gray, to moving blankness, to dim, hazy objects, spectral and tall, like blanketed trees, and, as Ellen fully recovered consciousness, she was being carried through the forest.

"Wal, little one, that was a close shave for you," said Colter's hard voice, growing clearer. "Reckon you keelin' over was natural enough."

He held her lightly in both arms, her head resting above his left elbow. Ellen saw his face as a gray blur, then taking sharper outline, until it stood out distinctly, pale and clammy, with eyes cold and masterful in their intense flare. As she gazed upward, Colter turned his head to look back through the woods, and his motion betrayed a keen, wild vigilance. The veins of his lean brown neck stood out like whipcords. Two comrades were stalking beside him. Ellen heard their stealthy steps and she felt Colter sheer from one side or the other. They were proceeding cautiously, fearful of the rear, but not wholly trusting to the fore.

"Reckon we'd better go slow an' look before we leap," said one whose voice Ellen recognized as Springer's.

"Shore. That open slope ain't to my likin' with our Nez Percé friend prowlin' 'round," drawled Colter as he set Ellen down on her feet.

Another of the rustlers laughed. "Say, can't he twinkle through the forest? I had four shots at him. Harder to hit than a turkey runnin' crossways."

This facetious speaker was the evil-visaged, sardonic Somers. He carried two rifles and wore two belts of cartridges.

"Ellen, shore you ain't so daid white as you was," observed Colter, and he chucked her under the chin with familiar hand. "Set down heah. I don't want you stoppin' any bullets. An' there's no tellin'."

Ellen was glad to comply with his wish. She had begun to recover wits and strength, yet she still felt shaky. She observed that their position then was on the edge of a well-wooded slope from which she could see the grassy cañon floor below. They were on a level bench, projecting out from the main cañon wall that loomed gray and rugged and pine-fringed. Somers and Colter and Springer gave careful attention to all points of the compass, especially in the direction from which they had come. They anticipated being trailed or circled or headed off, but did not manifest much concern. Somers lit a cigarette; Springer wiped his face with a grimy hand, and counted the shells in his belt, which appeared to be half empty. Colter stretched his long neck like a vulture and peered down the slope, and through the aisles of the forest up toward the cañon rim.

"Listen," he said tersely, and bent his head a little to one side, ear to the slight breeze. They all listened. Ellen heard the beating of her heart, the rustle of leaves, the tapping of a woodpecker, and faint, remote sounds that she could not name.

"Deer, I reckon," spoke up Somers.

"A-huh! Wal, I reckon they ain't trailin' us yet," replied Colter. "We gave them a shade better'n they sent us."

"Short 'n' sweet!" ejaculated Springer, and he removed his black sombrero to poke a dirty forefinger through a bullet hole in the crown. "Thet's how close I come to cashin'. I was lyin' behind a log listenin' an' watchin', an', when I stuck my head up a little . . . *zam!* Somebody made my bonnet leak."

"Where's Queen?" asked Colter.

"He was with me first off," replied Somers. "An' then, when the shootin' slacked . . . after I'd plugged that big, red-faced, white-haired pal of Isbel's. . . ."

"Reckon that was Blaisdell," interrupted Springer.

"Queen . . . he got tired layin' low," went on Somers. "He wanted action. I heered him chewin' to himself, an', when I asked him what was eatin' him, he up an' growled he was goin' to quit this Injun fightin'. An' he slipped off in the woods."

"Wal, that's the gunfighter of it," declared Colter, wagging his head. "Ever since that cowman, Blue, braced us an' said he was King Fisher, why Queen has been sulkier and sulkier. He cain't help it. He'll do the same trick as Blue tried. An' shore he'll get his everlastin'. But he's the Texas breed, all right."

"Say, do you reckon Blue really was King Fisher?" queried Somers.

"Naw!" ejaculated Colter with a downward sweep of his hand. "Many a would-be gunslinger has borrowed Fisher's name. But Fisher is daid these many years."

"A-huh! Wal, mebbe, but don't you fergit it . . . thet Blue was no would-be," declared Somers. "He was the genuine article."

"I should think," affirmed Springer.

The subject irritated Colter, and he dismissed it with another forcible gesture and a counter question. "How many left in that Isbel outfit?"

"No tellin'. There shore was enough of them," replied Somers. "Anyhow, the woods was full of flyin' bullets. Springer, did you account for any of them?"

"Nope . . . not thet I noticed," responded Springer dryly. "I had my chance at the half-breed. Reckon I was nervous."

"Was Slater near you when he yelled out?"

"No. He was lyin' beside Somers."

"Wasn't that a queer way fer a man to act?" broke in Somers. "A bullet hit Slater, cut him down the back as he was lyin' flat. Reckon it wasn't bad. But it hurt him so that he jumped right up an' staggered around. He made a target big as a tree. An' mebbe them Isbels didn't riddle him!"

"That was when I got my crack at Bill Isbel," declared Colter with grim satisfaction. "When they shot my horse out from under me, I had Ellen to think of an' couldn't get my rifle. Shore had to run, as you seen. Wal, as I only had my six-shooter, there was nothin' for me to do but lay low an' listen to the sping of lead. Wells was standin' up behind a tree aboot thirty yards off. He got plugged, an', fallin' over me, he begin to crawl my way, still holdin' onto his rifle. I crawled along the log to meet him. But he dropped aboot halfway. I went on an' took his rifle an' belt. When I peeped out from behind a spruce bush, then I seen Bill Isbel. He was shootin' fast, an' all of them was shootin' fast. That was when they had the open shot at Slater. Wal, I bored Bill Isbel right through his middle. He dropped his rifle, an', all bent double, he fooled around in a circle till he flopped over the rim. I reckon he's layin' right up there somewhere below that daid spruce. I'd shore like to see him."

"Wal, you'd be as crazy as Queen if you tried that," declared Somers. "We're not out of the woods yet."

"I reckon not," replied Colter. "An' I've lost my horse. Where'd you leave yours?"

"They're down the cañon, below thet willow break. An' saddled an' none of them tied. Reckon we'll have to look them up before dark."

"Colter, what're we goin' to do?" demanded Springer.

"Wait heah a while . . . then cross the cañon an' work 'round up under the bluff, back to the cabin."

"An' then what?" queried Somers, doubtfully eying Colter.

"We've got to eat . . . we've got to have blankets," rejoined Colter testily. "An' I reckon we can hide there an' stand a better show in a fight than runnin' for it in the woods."

"Wal, I'm givin' you a hunch that it looked like you was runnin' fer it," retorted Somers.

274

"Yes, an' packin' the girl," added Springer. "Looks funny to me."

Both rustlers eyed Colter with dark and distrustful glances. What he might have replied never transpired, for the reason that his gaze, always shifting around, had suddenly fixed on something.

"Is that a wolf?" he asked, pointing up to the rim. Both his comrades moved to get in line with his finger. Ellen could not see from her position.

"Shore, thet's a big loafer," declared Somers. "Reckon he scented us."

"There he goes along the rim," observed Colter. "He doesn't act leery. Looks like a good sign to me. Mebbe the Isbels have gone the other way."

"Looks bad to me," rejoined Springer gloomily.

"An' why?" demanded Colter.

"I seen thet animal. First time I reckoned it was a loafer. Second time it was right near them Isbels. An' I'm damned now if I don't believe it's that half-loafer sheep dog of Gass Isbel's."

"Wal, what if it is?"

"Ha! Shore we needn't worry about hidin' out," replied Springer sententiously. "With thet dog Jean Isbel could trail a grasshopper."

"The hell you say," muttered Colter. Manifestly such a possibility put a different light upon the present situation. The men grew silent and watchful, occupied by brooding thought and vigilant surveillance of all points. Somers slipped off into the brush, soon to return, with intent look of importance.

"I heered somethin'," he whispered, jerking his thumb backwards. "Rollin' gravel . . . crackin' of twigs. No deer! Reckon it'd be a good idee for us to step 'round acrost this bench."

"Wal, you fellers go, an' I'll watch heah," returned Colter.

"Not much," said Somers, while Springer leered knowingly.

Colter became incensed, but he did not give away to it. Pondering a moment he finally turned to Ellen. "You wait heah till I come back. An' if I don't come in reasonable time, you slip across the cañon an' through the willows to the cabins. Wait till about dark." With that he possessed himself of one of the extra rifles and belts and silently joined his comrades. Together they noiselessly stole into the brush.

Ellen had no other thought than to comply with Colter's wishes. There was her wounded uncle who had been left unattended and she was anxious to get back to him. Besides, if she had wanted to run off from Colter, where could she go? Alone in the woods she would get lost and die of starvation. Her lot must be cast with the Jorth faction until the end. That did not seem far away.

Her strained attention and suspense made the moments fly. By and by several shots pealed out far across the side cañon on her right, and they were answered by reports sounding closer to her. The fight was on again. But these shots were not repeated. The flies buzzed, the hot sun beat down and sloped to the west, the soft warm breeze stirred the aspens, the ravens croaked, the red squirrels and blue jays chattered.

Suddenly a quick short yelp electrified Ellen, brought her upright with sharp, listening rigidity. Surely it was not a wolf and hardly could it be a coyote. Again she heard it. The yelp of a sheep dog! She had heard that often enough to know. She rose to change her position so she could command a view of the rocky bluff above. Presently she espied what really appeared to be a big timber wolf. But now the yelp satisfied her that it really was a dog. She watched him. Soon it became evident that he wanted to get down over the bluff. He ran to and fro, and then out of sight. In a few moments his yelp sounded from lower down, at the base of the bluff, and it was now the cry of an intelligent dog that was trying to call someone to his aid. Ellen grew convinced that the dog was near where Colter had said Bill Isbel had plunged over the declivity. Would the dog yelp that way if the man was dead? Ellen thought not.

No one came, and the continuous yelping of the dog got on Ellen's nerves. It was a call for help. Finally she surrendered to it. Since her natural terror when Colter's horse was shot from under her and she had been dragged away, she had not recovered from fear of the Isbels. But calm consideration now convinced her that she could hardly be in a worse plight in their hands than if she remained in Colter's. So she started out to find the dog.

The wooded bench was level for a few hundred yards, and then it began to have rugged, rocky ledges up toward the rim. It did not appear far to where the dog was barking, but the latter part of the distance proved to be a hard climb over jumbled rocks and through thick brush. Panting and hot, she at length reached the top of the bluff, to find that it was not very high.

The dog espied her before she saw him, for he was coming toward her when she discovered him. Big, shaggy, grayish-white and black, with wild, keen face and eyes, he assuredly looked the reputation Springer had accorded him. But sagacious, guarded as was his approach, he appeared friendly.

"Hello, doggie," panted Ellen. "What's wrong . . . up heah?"

He yelped, his ears lost their stiffness, his body sank a little, and his bushy tail wagged to and fro. What a gray, clear intelligent look he gave her! Then he trotted back.

Ellen followed him around a corner of bluff to see the body of a man lying on his back. Fresh earth and gravel lay about him, attesting to his fall from above. He had neither coat nor hat, and the position of his body and limbs suggested broken bones. As Ellen hurried to his side, she saw that the front of his shirt, low down, was a bloody blotch. But she could lift his head; his eyes were open; he was perfectly conscious. Ellen did not recognize the dusty-skinned face, yet the mold of features, the look of the eyes, seemed strangely familiar.

"You're . . . Jorth's . . . girl," he said, a faint voice of surprise.

"Yes, I'm Ellen Jorth," she replied. "An' are you Bill Isbel?"

"All thet's left of me. But I'm thankin' God that somebody come . . . even a Jorth."

Ellen knelt beside him and examined the wound in his abdomen. A heavy bullet had, indeed, as Colter had avowed, torn clear through his middle. Even if he had not sustained other serious injury from the fall over the cliff, that terrible bullet wound meant death very shortly. Ellen shuddered. How inexplicable her men! How cruel, bloody, mindless!

"Isbel, I'm sorry . . . there's no hope," she said, low-voiced. "You've not long to live. I cain't help you. God knows I'd do so if I could."

"All over," he sighed, with his eyes looking beyond her. "I reckon . . . I'm damn' glad. But you can . . . do somethin' for me . . . will you?"

"Indeed, yes. Tell me," she replied, lifting his dusty head

278

on her knee. Her hands trembled as she brushed his wet hair back from his clammy brow.

"I've somethin' . . . on my conscience," he whispered.

The woman, the sensitive in Ellen, understood and pitied him then.

"Yes," she encouraged him.

"I stole cattle . . . my dad's an' Blaisdell's . . . an' made deals . . . with Daggs. All the crookedness . . . wasn't on . . . Jorth's side. I want . . . my brother Jean . . . to know."

"I'll try . . . to tell him," whispered Ellen, out of her great amazement.

"We were all . . . a bad lot . . . except Jean," went on Isbel. "Dad wasn't fair. God, how he hated Jorth! Jorth, yes, who was . . . your father. Wal, they're even now."

"How so?" faltered Ellen.

"Your father killed Dad. At the last . . . Dad wanted to . . . save us. He sent word . . . he'd meet him . . . face to face . . . an' let that end the feud. They met out in the road. But someone shot Dad down . . . with a rifle . . . an' then your father finished him."

"An' then, Isbel," added Ellen with unconscious, mocking bitterness, "your brother murdered my dad!"

"What?" whispered Bill Isbel. "Shore you've got . . . it wrong. I reckon Jean . . . could have killed . . . your father. But he didn't. Queer, we all thought."

"Ah! Who did . . . kill my father?" burst out Ellen, and her voice rang like great hammers at her ears.

"It was Blue. He went in the store . . . alone . . . faced the whole gang. Bluffed them . . . taunted them . . . told them he was King Fisher. Then he killed . . . your dad . . . an' Jackson Jorth. Jean was out . . . back of the store. We were out . . . front. There was shootin'. Colmor was hit. Then Blue run out . . . bad hurt. Both of them . . . died in

Meeker's yard. My sister's a widow before she married."

"An' so Jean Isbel has not killed a Jorth!" said Ellen in strange, deep voice.

"No," replied Isbel earnestly. "I reckon this feud . . . was hardest on Jean. He never lived heah. An' my sister Ann said . . . he got sweet on you. Now did he?"

Slow, stinging tears filled Ellen's eyes, and her head sank low and lower. "Yes . . . he did," she murmured tremulously.

"A-huh! Wal, that accounts," replied Isbel wonderingly. "Too bad! It might have been. A man always sees . . . different when . . . he's dyin'. If I had . . . my life . . . to live over again! My poor kids . . . deserted in their babyhood . . . ruined for life! All for nothin'. May God forgive. . . ."

Then he choked and whispered for water.

Ellen laid his head back, and, rising, she took his sombrero and started hurriedly down the slope, making dust fly and rocks roll. Her mind was a seething ferment. Leaping, bounding, sliding down the weathered slope, she gained the bench, to run across that, and so on down into the open cañon to the willow-bordered brook. Here she filled the sombrero with water and started back, forced now to walk slowly and carefully. It was then, with the violence and fury of intense muscular activity denied her, that the tremendous import of Bill Isbel's revelation burst upon her, transporting her, transforming her very flesh and blood, and transfiguring the very world of golden light and azure sky and speaking forest land that encompassed her.

Not a drop of the precious water did she spill. Not a misstep did she make. Yet so great was the spell upon her that she was not aware she had climbed the steep slope until the dog yelped his welcome. Then, with all the flood of her emotion surging and resurging, she knelt to allay the parching thirst of this dying enemy whose words had changed finality to strength, hate to love, and the gloomy hell of despair to something unutterable. But she had returned too late. Bill Isbel was dead.

Chapter Thirteen

Jean Isbel, holding the wolf-dog Shepp in leash, was on the trail of the most dangerous of Jorth's gang, the gunman Queen. Dark drops of blood on the stones and plain tracks of a rider's sharp-heeled boots behind coverts indicated the trail of a wounded, slow-traveling fugitive. Therefore, Jean Isbel held in the dog and proceeded with the wary eye and watchful caution of an Indian.

Queen, true to his colors and emulating Blue with the same magnificent effrontery and with the same paralyzing suddenness of surprise, had appeared as if by magic last night at the camp of the Isbel faction. Jean had seen him first, in time to leap like a panther into the shadow. But he carried in his shoulder Queen's first bullet of that terrible encounter. Upon Gordon and Fredericks fell the brunt of Queen's fusillade, and they, shot to pieces, staggering and falling, held passionate grip on life long enough to draw and still Queen's guns and send him reeling off into the darkness of the forest.

Unarmed, and hindered by a painful wound, Jean had kept a vigil near camp all that silent and menacing night. Morning disclosed Gordon and Fredericks stark and ghastly beside the burned-out campfire, their guns clutched immovably in stiffened hands. Jean buried them as best he could, and, when they were under ground with flat stones on their graves, he knew himself to be, indeed, the last of the Isbel clan. All that was wild and savage in his blood and desperate in his spirit rose to make him more than man and less than human. Then, for the third time during these tragic last days, the wolf-dog Shepp came to him.

Jean washed the wound Queen had given him, and bound it tightly. The keen pang and burn of the lead was a constant and all-powerful reminder of the grim work left for him to do. The whole world was no longer large enough for him and whoever was left of the Jorths. The heritage of blood his father had bequeathed him, the unshakable love for a worthless girl who had so dwarfed and obstructed his will and so bitterly defeated and reviled his poor romantic boyish faith, the killing of hostile men, so strange in its after-effects, the pursuits and fights, and loss one by one of his confederates—these had finally engendered in Jean Isbel a wild, unshakable thirst, these had been the cause of his retrogression, these had unalterably and ruthlessly fixed in his darkened mind one fierce passion—to live and die the last man of the Jorth-Isbel feud.

At sunrise, Jean left this camp, taking with him only a small knapsack of meat and bread, and with the eager, wild Shepp in leash he set out on Queen's bloody trail. Black drops of blood on the stones and an irregular trail of footprints proved to Jean that the gunman was hard hit. Here he had fallen, or kneeled, or sat down evidently to bind his wounds. Jean found strips of scarf, red and discarded, and the blood drops failed to show on more rocks. In a deep forest of spruce, under silver-tipped spreading branches, Queen had rested, perhaps slept. Then, laboring with dragging steps, not improbably with a lame leg, he had gone on, up out of the dark green ravine to the open, dry, pine-tipped ridge. Here he had rested, perhaps waited to see if he was pursued. From that point his trail spoke an easy language for Jean's keen eye. The gunman knew he was pursued. He had seen his enemy. Therefore, Jean proceeded with a slow caution, never getting within revolver range of ambush, using all his woodcraft to trail this man and yet save himself. Queen traveled slowly, either because he was wounded or else because he tried to ambush his pursuer, and Jean accommodated his pace to that of Queen. From noon of that day they were never far apart, never out of hearing of a rifle shot.

The contrast of the beauty and peace and loneliness of the surroundings to the nature of Queen's flight often obtruded its strange truth into the somber turbulence of Jean's mind, into that fixed columnar idea around which fleeting thoughts hovered and gathered like shadows. Early autumn had touched the heights with its magic wand, and the forest seemed a temple in which man might worship nature and life rather than steal through the dells and under the arched aisles like a beast of prey. Aspens quivered on the green and gold leaves of the glades; maples in the ravine fluttered their red and purple leaves. The needle-matted carpet under the pines vied with the long lanes of silvery grass, alike enticing to the eye of man and beast. Sunny rays of light, flecked with dust and flying insects, slanted down from the overhanging, brown-limbed, green-massed foliage. Roar of wind in the distant forest alternated with soft breeze close at hand. Small, dove-gray squirrels ran all over the woodland, very curious about Jean and his dog, rustling the twigs, scratching the bark of trees, chattering and barking, frisky, saucy, and bright-eyed. A plaintive twitter of wild canaries came from the region above the tree tops—first voices of birds in their pilgrimage toward the south. Pine cones dropped with soft thuds. The blue jays followed these intruders in the forest, screeching their displeasure. The dropping seeds from the spruces pattered like rain. A woody, earthy, leafy fragrance, damp with the current of life, mingled with a cool, dry, sweet smell of withered grass and rotting pines.

Solitude and lonesomeness, peace and rest, wild life and nature reigned here. It was a golden-green region enchanting to the gaze of man. An Indian would have walked there with his spirits, and, even as Jean felt all this elevating beauty and inscrutable spirit, his keen eye once more fastened upon the blood-red drops Queen had again left on the gray moss and rock. His wound had reopened. Jean felt the thrill of the scenting panther.

The sun set, twilight gathered, night fell. Jean crawled under a dense, low, spreading spruce, ate some bread and meat, fed the dog, and lay down to rest and sleep. His thoughts burdened him, heavy and black as the mantle of night. A wolf mourned a hungry cry for a mate. Shepp quivered under Jean's hand. That was the call that had lured him from the ranch. The wolf blood in him yearned for the wild. Jean tied the cowhide leash to his waist. When this dark business was at an end, Shepp could be free to join the lonely mate mourning out there in the forest. Then Jean slept.

Dawn broke cold, clear, frosty, with silvered grass sparkling with a soft, faint rustling of falling aspen leaves. When the sun rose red, Jean was again on the trail of Queen. By a frosty-ferned brook, where water tinkled and ran clear as air and cold as ice, Jean quenched his thirst, leaning on a stone that showed drops of blood. Queen, too, had to quench his thirst. What good, what help, Jean wondered, could the cold, sweet, granite water, so clear to woodsmen and wild creatures, do this wounded, hunted rustler? Why did he not wait in the open to fight and face the death he had meted? Where was that splendid and terrible daring of the gunman? Queen's love of life dragged him on and on, hour by hour, through the pine groves and spruce woods, through the oak swales and aspen glades, up and down the rocky gorges, around the windfalls and over the rotting logs.

The time came when Queen made no attempt at ambush. He gave up trying to trap his pursuer by lying in wait. He gave up trying to conceal his tracks. He grew stronger, or in desperation increased his energy, so that he redoubled his progress through the wilderness. That, at best, would count only a few miles a day, and he began to circle to the northwest, back toward the deep cañon where Blaisdell and Bill Isbel had reached the end of their trails. Queen had evidently left his comrades, had lone-handed it in his last fight, but was now trying to get back to them. Somewhere in these wild, deep forest brakes the rest of the Jorth faction had found a hiding place. Jean let Queen lead him there.

Ellen Jorth would be with them. Jean had seen her. It had been his shot that killed Colter's horse, and he had withheld further fire because Colter had dragged the girl behind him, protecting his body with hers. Sooner or later Jean would come upon their camp. She would be there. The thought of her dark beauty wasted in wantonness upon these rustlers added a deadly rage to the blood-lust and righteous wrath of his vengeance. Let her again flaunt her degradation in his face—and by the God she had forsaken, he would kill her and so end the race of Jorths!

Another night fell, dark and cold, without starlight. The wind moaned in the forest. Shepp was restless. He sniffed the air. There was a step on the trail. Again a mournful, eager, wild, and hungry wolf cry broke the silence. It was deep and low, like that of a baying hound, but infinitely wilder. Shepp strained to get away. During the night, while Jean slept, he managed to chew the cowhide leash apart and run off.

Next day no dog was needed to trail Queen. Fog and low-drifting clouds in the forest and a misty rain had put the rustler off his bearings. He was lost and showed that he realized it. Strange how a matured man, fighter of a hundred battles, steeped in bloodshed, and on his last stand, should grow panic-stricken upon being lost! So Jean Isbel read the signs of the trail.

Queen rushed to and fro, and circled and wandered through the foggy, dripping forest, until he headed down into a cañon. It was one that notched the Tonto Rim and led down and down, mile after mile into the Tonto Basin. Not soon had Queen discovered his mistake. When he did do so, night overtook him.

The weather cleared before morning. Red and bright the sun burst out of the east to flood that low basin land with light. Jean found that Queen had traveled on and on, hoping no doubt to regain what he had lost, but in the darkness he had climbed to the manzanita slopes instead of back up the cañon. Here he had fought the hold of that strange brush of Spanish name until he fell exhausted.

Surely Queen would make his stand and wait somewhere in this devilish thicket for Jean to catch up with him. Many and many a place Jean would have chosen had he been in Queen's stead. Many a rock and dense thicket Jean circled or approached with extreme care. Manzanita grew in patches that were impenetrable except for a small animal. The brush was a few feet high, seldom so high that Jean could not look over it, and of a beautiful appearance, having glossy, small leaves, a golden berry, and branches of dark red color. These branches were tough and unbendable, every bush, hard as steel, sharp as thorns, as clutching as cactus. Progress was possible through there only by endless detours to find the half-closed aisles between patches, or else by crashing through with main strength, or walking right over the tops. Jean preferred this last method, not because it was the easiest, but for the reason that he could see ahead so much farther. So he literally walked across the tips of the manzanita brush. Often he fell through, and had to step up again; many a branch broke with him, letting him down, but for the most part he stepped from fork to fork, or branch after branch, with the balance of an Indian and the patience of a man whose purpose was sustaining and immutable.

On that south slope under the rim the hot sun beat down. There was no breeze to temper the dry air. Before midday Jean was laboring, wet with sweat, parching with thirst, dusty and hot and tiring. It amazed him, the doggedness and tenacity of life shown by this wounded rustler. The time came when under the burning raze of the sun he was compelled to abandon the walk across the tips of the manzanita bushes and take to the winding, open thresh that ran between. It would have been poor sight, indeed, that could not have followed Queen's labyrinthine and broken passage through the brush. Then the time came when Jean espied Queen, far ahead and above, crashing like a black bug along the bright green slope. Sight then acted upon Jean as upon a hound in the chase. But he governed his actions, if he could not govern his instincts. Slowly but surely he followed the dusty, hot trail, and never a patch of blood failed to send a thrill along his veins.

Queen headed up toward the rim, finally vanished from sight. Had he fallen? Was he hiding? But the hour disclosed that he was crawling. Jean's keen eye caught the slow moving of the brush, and enabled him to keep just so close to the rustler, out of the range of the six-shooters he carried. All the interminable hours of the hot afternoon that snail-pace flight and pursuit kept on.

Halfway up to the rim the growth of manzanita gave place to open, yellow, rocky slope dotted with cedars. Queen took to a slow-ascending ridge and left his bloody tracks all the way to the top, where in the gathering darkness the weary pursuer lost them.

Another night passed. Daylight was relentless to the rustler. He could not hide his trail. But somehow in a desperate last rally of strength he reached a point on the heavily timbered ridge that Jean recognized as being near the scene of the fight in the cañon. Queen was nearing the rendezvous of the rustlers. Jean crossed tracks of horses and then more tracks that he was certain had been made days past by his own party. To the left of this ridge must be the deep cañon that had frustrated his effort to catch up with the rustlers on the day Blaisdell lost his life and Bill Isbel disappeared. Something warned Jean that he was nearing the end of the trail, and an unaccountable sense of imminent catastrophe seemed foreshadowed by vague dreads and doubts in his gloomy mind. Jean felt the need of rest, of food, of ease from the strain of the last weeks, but his spirit drove him implacably.

Queen's rally of strength ended at the edge of an open, bald ridge that was bare of brush or grass and was surrounded by a line of forest on three sides and on the fourth by a low bluff that raised its gray head above the pines. Across this dusty open Queen had crawled, leaving unmistakable signs of his condition. Jean took long survey of the circle of trees and of the low, rocky eminence, neither of which he liked. It might be easier to keep to cover, Jean thought, and work around to where Queen's trail entered the forest again, but he was tired, gloomy, and his eternal vigilance was failing. Nevertheless, he stilled for the thousandth time that bold prompting of his vengeance, and, taking to the edge of the forest, he went to considerable pains to circle the open ground. Suddenly sight of a man, sitting back against a tree, halted Jean.

He stared to make sure his eyes did not deceive him. Many times stumps and snags and rock had taken on strange resemblance to a standing or crouching man. This was only another suggestive blunder of the mind behind his eyes—what he wanted to see he imagined he saw. Jean glided in from tree to tree, until he made sure that this sitting image, indeed, was that of a man. He sat bold-upright, facing back across the open, hands resting on his knees— and closer scrutiny showed Jean that he held a gun in each hand.

Queen! At the last his nerve had revived. He could not crawl any farther, he could never escape, so with the courage of fatality he chose the open, to face his foe and die. Jean had a thrill of admiration for the rustler. Then he stalked out from under the pines and strode forward with his rifle ready.

A watching man could not have failed to espy Jean. But Queen never made the slightest move. Moreover, his stiff, unnatural position struck Jean so singularly that he halted with a muttered exclamation. He was now about fifty paces from Queen, within range of those small guns. Jean called sharply: "Queen!" Still the figure never relaxed in the slightest.

Jean advanced a few more paces, rifle up, ready to fire the instant Queen lifted a gun. The man's immobility brought the cold sweat to Jean's brow. He stopped to bend the full, intense power of his gaze upon this inert figure. Suddenly over Jean flashed its meaning. Queen was dead! He had backed up against the pine, ready to face his foe, and he had died there. Not a shadow of a doubt entered Jean's mind as he started forward again. He knew. After all, Queen's blood would not be on his hands. Gordon and Fredericks in their death throes had given the rustler mortal wounds. Jean kept on, marveling the while. How ghastly thin and hard those four days of flight had been for Queen.

Jean reached him—looked down with staring eyes. The guns were tied to his hands. Jean started violently as the whole direction of his mind shifted. A lightning glance showed that Queen had been propped against the tree—another showed boot tracks in the dust.

"By heaven, they've fooled me," hissed Jean, and quickly as he leaped behind the pine he was not quick enough to escape the cunning rustlers who had waylaid him thus. He felt the shock, the bite and burn of lead before he heard a rifle crack. A bullet had ripped through his left forearm. From behind the tree he saw a puff of white smoke along the face of the bluff—the very spot his keen and gloomy vigilance had descried as one of menace. Then several puffs of white smoke and ringing reports betrayed the ambush of the tricksters. Bullets barked the pine and whistled by. Jean saw a man dart from behind a rock and, leaning over, run for another. Jean's swift shot stopped him midway. He fell, got up, and floundered behind a bush, scarcely large enough to conceal him. Into that bush Jean shot again and again. He had felt pain in his wounded arm, but the sense of that shock clung in his consciousness, and this, with the tremendous surprise of the deceit and sudden release of long-dammed incriminating passion, caused him to empty the magazine of his Winchester in a terrible haste to kill the man he had hit.

These were all the loads he had for his rifle. Blood passion had made him blunder. Jean cursed himself, and his hand moved to his belt. His six-shooter was gone. The sheath had been loose. He had tied the gun fast, but the strings had been torn apart. The rustlers were shooting again. Bullets thudded into the pine and whistled by. Bending carefully, Jean reached one of Queen's guns and jerked it from his hand. The firearm was empty. Both of his guns were empty. Jean peeped out again to get the line in which the bullets were coming, and, marking a course from his position to the cover of the forest, he ran with all his might. He gained the shelter. Shrill yells behind him warned him that he had been seen, that his reason for flight had been guessed. Looking back, he saw two or three men scrambling down the bluff. Then the loud neigh of a frightened horse pealed out.

Jean discarded his useless rifle and headed down the ridge slope, keeping to the thickest line of pines and sheering around the clumps of spruce. As he ran, his mind whirled with grim thought of escape, of his necessity to find the camp where Gordon and Fredericks were buried, there to procure another rifle and ammunition. He felt the wet blood dripping down his arm, yet no pain. The forest was too open for good cover. He dared not run uphill. His only course was ahead, and that soon ended in an abrupt declivity too precipitous to descend. As he halted, panting for breath, he heard the ring of hoofs on stone, then the thudding beat of running horses on soft ground. The rustlers had sighted the direction he had taken. Jean did not waste time to look. Indeed, there was no need, for as he bounded along the cliff to the right a rifle cracked and a bullet whizzed over his head. It lent wings to his feet. Like a deer he sped along, leaping cracks and logs and rocks, his ears filled by the rush of wind, until his quick eye caught sight of thick-growing spruce foliage close to the precipice. He sprang down into the green mass. His weight precipitated him through the upper branches. But lower down his spread arms broke his fall, then retarded it until he caught. A long, swaying limb let him down and down, where he grasped another and a stiffer one that held his weight. Hand on hand he worked toward the trunk of this spruce, and, gaining it, he found other branches close together down which he hastened hold by hold and step by step, until all above him was black, dense foliage and beneath him the brown, shady slope. Sure of being unseen from above, he glided noiselessly down inside the trees, slowly regaining freedom from that constriction of his breast.

Passing on to a gray-lichened cliff, overhanging and gloomy, he paused there to rest and to listen. A faint ring of hoof on stone came to him from above, apparently farther on to the right. Eventually his pursuers would discover that he had taken to the cañon. But for the moment he felt safe. The wound in his arm drew his attention. The bullet had gone clear through without breaking either bone. His shirt sleeve was soaked with blood. Jean rolled it back, and tightly wrapped his scarf around the wound, yet still the dark-red blood oozed out and dripped down into his hand. He became aware of a dull, throbbing pain.

Not much time did Jean waste in arriving at what was best to do. For the time being he had escaped, and whatever had been his peril it was past. In dense, rugged country like this he could not be caught by rustlers. But he had only a knife left for a weapon, and there was very little meat in the pocket of his coat. Salt and matches he possessed. Therefore, the imperative need was for him to find the last camp where he could get the rifle and ammunition, bake bread, and rest up before taking again the trail of the rustlers. He had reason to believe that this cañon was the one where the fight on the rim and later on in a bench of wood-land below had taken place.

Thereupon he arose and glided down under the spruces toward the level, grassy open he could see between the trees. As he proceeded, with the slow step and wary eye of an Indian, his mind was busy. Queen had in his flight un-erringly worked in the direction of this cañon until he became lost in the fog, and, upon regaining his bearings, he had made a wonderful and heroic effort to surmount the manzanita slope and the rim and find the rendezvous of his comrades. But he had failed up there on the ridge. In thinking it over, Jean arrived at a conclusion that Queen, finding he could go no farther, had waited, guns in hands, for his pursuer, and he had died in this position. Then by strange coincidence his comrades had happened to come across him, and, recognizing the situation, they had taken the shells from his guns and propped him up with the idea of luring Jean on. They had arranged a cunning trick and ambush, which had all but snuffed out the last of the Isbels. Colter probably had been at the bottom of this crafty plan. Since the fight at the Isbel Ranch, now seemingly far back in the past, this man Colter had loomed up more and more as a stronger and more dangerous antagonist than either Jorth or Daggs. Before that he had been little known to any of the Isbel faction, but it was Colter now who controlled the remnant of the gang and who had Ellen Jorth in his pos-session.

The cañon wall above Jean, on the right, grew more rugged and loftier, and the one on the left began to show wooded slopes and brakes, and at last a wide expanse with a winding willow border on the west and a long, low, pine-dotted brush on the east. It took several moments of study for Jean to recognize the rugged bluff above this bench. On up that cañon several miles was the site where Queen had surprised Jean and his comrades at their campfire. Somewhere in this vicinity was the hiding place of the rustlers.

Jean proceeded with the utmost stealth, absolutely certain that he would miss no sound, movement, sign, or anything unnatural to the wild peace of the cañon. His first sense to register something was his keen smell. Sheep! He was amazed to smell sheep. There must be a flock not far away. Then from where he glided along under the trees, he saw down to open places in the willow brake and noticed sheep tracks on the dark, muddy bank of the brook. Next he heard faint tinkle of bells, and at length, when he could see farther into the open enlargement of the cañon, his surprised gaze fell upon an immense gray, woolly patch that blotted out acres and acres of grass. Thousands of sheep were grazing there. Jean knew there were several flocks of Jorth's sheep on the mountain in the care of herders, but he had never thought of them being so far west, more than twenty miles from Chevelon Cañon. His roving eyes could not descry any herders or dogs. But he knew there must be dogs close to that immense flock. Whatever his cunning, he could not hope to elude the scent and sight of shepherd dogs. It would be best to go back down the way he had come, wait for darkness, then cross the cañon and climb out, and work around to his objective point. Turning at once, he started to glide back, but almost immediately he was brought, stockstill and thrilling, by the sound of hoofs.

Horses were coming in the direction he wished to take. They were close. His swift conclusion was that the riding men who had pursued him up on the rim had worked down into the cañon. One circling glance showed him that he had no sure covert near at hand. It would not do to risk their passing him there. The border of woodland was narrow and not dense enough for close inspection. He was forced to turn back up the cañon, in the hope of soon finding a hiding place or a break in the wall where he could climb up.

Hugging the base of the wall, he slipped on, passing the point where he had espied the sheep, and gliding on until he was stopped by a bend in the dense line of willows. It sheered to the west there and ran close to the high wall. Jean kept on until he was stooping under a curling border of willow thicket, with branches slim and yellow, and masses of green foliage that brushed against the wall. Suddenly he encountered an abrupt corner of rock. He rounded it, to discover that it ran at a right angle with the one he had just passed. Peering up through the willows, he ascertained that there was a narrow crack in the main wall of the cañon. It had been concealed by willows low down and leaning spruces above—a wild, hidden retreat! Along the base of the wall there were tracks of small animals. The place was odorous, like all dense thickets, but it was not dry. Water ran through here somewhere. Jean drew easier breath. All sounds except the rustling of birds or mice in the willows had ceased. The brake was pervaded by a dreary emptiness. Jean decided to steal on a little farther, then wait till he felt he might safely dare go back.

The golden-green gloom suddenly brightened. Light showed ahead. Parting the willows, he looked into a narrow, winding cañon with an open, grassy, willow-streaked lane in the center, and on each side a thin strip of woodland. His surprise was short-lived. A crashing of horses back of him in the willows gave him a shock. He ran out of the willows, along the base of the wall, back of the trees. Like the strip of woodland in the main cañon, this one was scant and had but little underbrush. There were young spruces growing with thick branches clear to the grass, and under them he could have concealed himself. But with a certainty of sheep dogs in the vicinity he could not think of hiding except as a last reserve. Those horsemen, whoever they were, were as likely to be sheepherders as not. Jean slackened his pace to look back. He could not see any moving objects, but he still heard horses, although not so close now. Ahead of him this narrow gorge opened out like the neck of a bottle. He would run on to the head of it and find a place to climb to the top.

Hurried and anxious as Jean was, he yet received an impression of the singular wild nature of this side gorge. It was a hidden, pine-fringed crack in the rock-ribbed and cañon-cut tableland. Above him, the sky seemed a winding stream of blue. The walls were red and bulged out in spruce-greened shelves. From wall to wall was scarcely a distance of a hundred feet. Jumbles of rock obstructed his close holding to the wall. He had to walk at the edge of the timber. As he progressed, the gorge widened into wilder, ruggeder aspect. Through the trees ahead he saw where the wall circled to meet the cliff to the left, forming an oval depression, the nature of which he could not ascertain. But it appeared to be a small opening surrounded by dense thicket and the overhanging walls. Anxiety increased to alarm. He might not be able to find a place to scale those rough cliffs. Breathing hard, Jean halted again. The situation was growing critical again. His physical condition was growing worse. Loss of sleep and rest, lack of food, the long pursuit of Queen, the wound in his arm, and the desperate run for his life—these had awakened him to the extent that, if he undertook any strenuous effort, he would fail. His cunning weighed all chances.

The shade of wall and foliage above, and another jumble of ruined cliff, hindered his survey of the ground ahead, and he almost stumbled upon a cabin hidden on three sides, with a small, bare clearing in front. It was an old, ramshackle structure like others he had run across in the cañons. Cautiously he approached and peeped around the corner. At first swift glance it had all the appearance of long disuse. But Jean had no time for another look. A *clip-clop* of trotting horses on hard ground brought the same pell-mell rush of sensations that had driven him to wild flight scarcely an hour past. His body jerked with its instinctive impulse—then quivered with his restraint. To turn back would be risky, to run ahead would be fatal, to hide was his one hope. No covert behind! And the *clip-clop* of hoofs sounded closer. One moment longer Jean held mastery over his instincts of self-preservation. To keep from running was almost impossible. It was the sheer primitive animal sense to escape. He drove it back, and glided along the front of the cabin.

Here he saw that the cabin adjoined another. Reaching the door, he was about to peep in when the thud of hoofs and voices close at hand transfixed him with a grim certainty that he had not an instant to lose. Through the thin, black-streaked line of trees he saw moving red objects. Horses! He must run. Passing the door, his keen nose caught a musty woody odor and the tail of his eye saw bare dirt floor. This cabin was unused. He halted—gave a quick look back. The first thing his eye fell upon was a ladder, right beside the door, against the wall. He looked up. It led to a loft that, dark and gloomy, stretched halfway across the cabin. An irresistible impulse drove Jean. Slipping inside, he climbed up the ladder to the loft. It was like night up there. But he crawled on the rough-hewn rafters, and, turning with his head toward the opening, he stretched out and lay still.

What seemed an interminable moment ended with a

trample of hoofs outside the cabin. It ceased. Jean's vibrating ears caught the jingle of spurs and a thud of boots striking the ground.

"Wal, sweetheart, heah we are home again," drawled a slow and mocking Texas voice.

"Home! I wonder, Colter . . . did you ever have a home . . . a mother . . . a sister . . . much less a sweetheart?" was the reply, bitter and caustic.

Jean's palpitating, hot body suddenly stretched, still and cold, with the intensity of shock. His very bones seemed to quiver and stiffen with ice. During the instant of realization his heart stopped, and a slow, contracting pressure enveloped his breast and moved up to constrict his throat. That woman's voice belonged to Ellen Jorth. The sound of it had lingered in his dreams. He had stumbled upon the rendezvous of the Jorth faction. Hard, indeed, had been the fates meted out to those individuals of the Isbels and Jorths who had passed to their deaths. But no ordeal, not even Queen's, could compare with this desperate one Jean must endure. He had loved Ellen Jorth strangely, wonderfully, and he had scorned evil repute to believe her good. He had spared her father and her uncle. He had weakened or lost the cause of the Isbels. He loved her now, desperately, deathlessly, knowing from her own lips that she was worthless—loved her the more because he had felt her terrible shame. And to him—the last of the Isbels—had come the cruelest of dooms—to be caught like a crippled rat in a trap, to be compelled to lie helpless, wounded, without a gun, to listen, and perhaps to see Ellen Jorth at the very truth of her mocking insinuation. His will, his promise, his creed, his blood must hold him to the stern decree that he should be the last man of the Jorth-Isbel war. But could he lie there to hear—to see—when he had a knife and an arm?

Chapter Fourteen

Then followed the leathery flop of saddles to the soft turf, and the stamp of loosened horses. Jean heard a noise at the cabin door, a rustle, and then a knock of something hard against wood. Silently he moved his head to look down through a crack between the rafters. He saw the glint of a rifle leaning against the sill. Then the doorstep was darkened. Ellen Jorth sat down with a long, tired sigh. She took off her sombrero and the light shone on the rippling, dark-brown hair, hanging in a tangled braid. The curved nape of her neck showed a warm tint of golden tan. She wore a gray blouse, soiled and torn, that clung to her lissome shoulders.

"Colter, what are you goin' to do?" she asked suddenly. Her voice carried something Jean did not remember. It thrilled into the icy fixity of his senses.

"We'll stay heah," was the response, and it was followed by a clinking step of spurred boot.

"Shore I won't stay heah," declared Ellen. "It makes me sick when I think of how Uncle Tad died in there alone, helpless . . . sufferin'. The place seems haunted."

"Wal, I'll agree that it's tough on you, but what the hell *can* we do?"

A long silence ensued that Ellen did not break.

"Somethin' has come off 'round heah since early mawnin'," declared Colter. "Somers an' Springer haven't got back. An' Antonio's gone. Now, honest, Ellen, didn't you heah rifle shots off somewhere?"

"I reckon I did," she responded gloomily.

"An' which way?"

"Sounded to me up on the bluff, back pretty far."

"Wal, shore that's my idee. An' it makes me think hard. You known Somers come across the last camp of the Isbels. An' he dug into a grave to find the bodies of Jim Gordon an' another man he didn't know. Queen kept good his brag. He braced that Isbel gang an' killed those fellars. But either him or Jean Isbel went off, leavin' bloody tracks. If it was Queen, you can bet Isbel was after him. An' if it was Isbel's tracks, why shore Queen would stick to them. Somers an' Springer couldn't follow the trail. They're shore not much good at trackin', though for days they've been ridin' the woods, hopin' to run across Queen. Wal, now, mebbe they run across Isbel, instead. An' if they did an' got away from him, they'll be heah sooner or later. If Isbel was too many for them, he'd hunt for my trail. I'm gamblin' that either Queen or Jean Isbel is daid. I'm hopin' it's Isbel. Because if he ain't daid, he's the last of the Isbels, an' mebbe I'm the last of Jorth's gang. Shore I'm not hankerin' to meet the half-breed . . . that's why I say we'll stay heah. This is as good a hidin' place as there is in the country. We've grub. There's water an' grass."

"Me . . . stay heah with you . . . alone!"

The tone seemed a contradiction to the apparently accepted sense of her words. Jean held his breath, but he could not still the slowly mounting and accelerating faculties within that were involuntarily rising to meet some strange, nameless import. He felt it. He imagined it would be the catastrophe of Ellen Jorth's calm acceptance of Colter's proposition. Yet down in Jean's perishable heart lived something that would not die. No mere words could kill it. How poignant that moment of her silence! How terribly he realized that, if his intelligence and his emotion had believed her betraying words, his soul had not!

Ellen Jorth did not speak. Her brown head hung thoughtfully. Her supple shoulders sagged a little.

"Ellen, what's happened to you?" asked Colter.

"All the misery possible to a woman," she replied dejectedly.

"Shore, I don't mean that way," he continued persuasively. "I ain't gainsayin' the hard facts of your life. It's been bad. Your dad was no good. But I mean I cain't figger the change in you."

"No, I reckon you cain't," she said. "Whoever was responsible for your make-up left out a mind . . . not to say feelin'."

Colter drawled a low laugh. "Wal, have that your own way. But how much longer are you goin' to be like this heah?"

"Like what?" she rejoined sharply.

"Wal, this stand-offishness of yours?"

"Colter, I told you to let me alone," she said sullenly.

"Shore, an' you did that before. But this time you're different. An', wal, I'm gettin' damn' tired of it."

Here the cool, slow voice of the Texan sounded an inflexibility before absent, a timbre that hinted of illimitable power.

Ellen Jorth shrugged her lithe shoulders, and, slowly rising, she picked up the little rifle and turned to step into the cabin.

"Colter," she said, "fetch my pack an' my blankets in heah."

"Shore," he returned with good nature.

Jean saw Ellen Jorth lay the rifle lengthwise in a chink between two logs, and then slowly turn, back to the wall.

302

Jean knew her then, yet did not know her. The brown flash of her face seemed that of an older, graver woman. His strained gaze, like his waiting mind, had expected something, he knew not what—a hardened face, a ghost of beauty, a recklessness, a distorted, bitter, lost expression in keeping with her fortunes. But he had reckoned falsely. She did not look like that. There was incalculable change. The beauty remained but somehow different. Her red lips were parted. Her brooding eyes, looking out straight from under the level, dark brows, seemed sloe-black and wonderful with their steady, passionate light.

Jean in his eager, hungry devouring of that beloved face did not at the first instant grasp the significance of its expression. He was seeing the features that had haunted him. But quickly he interpreted her expression as the somber, hunted look of a woman who would bear no more. Under the torn blouse her full breast heaved. She held her hands clenched at her sides. She was listening, waiting for that jangling, slow step. It came, and with the sound she subtly changed. She was a woman hiding her true feelings. She relaxed, and that strong, dark look of fury seemed to fade back into her eyes.

Colter appeared at the door, carrying a roll of blankets and a pack.

"Throw them heah," she said. "I reckon you needn't bother coming in."

This angered the man. With one long stride he stepped over the doorsill, down into the cabin, and flung the blankets at her feet, and then the pack after it. Whereupon he deliberately sat down in the door, facing her. With one hand he slid off his sombrero, which fell outside, and with the other he reached in his upper vest pocket for the little bag of tobacco that showed there. All the time he looked at her. By light now unobstructed, Jean descried Colter's face and sight of it sounded the roll and drum of his passions.

"Wal, Ellen, I reckon we'll have it out right now an' heah," he said, and with tobacco in one hand, paper in the other, he began the operation of making a cigarette. However, he scarcely removed his glance from her.

"Yes?" queried Ellen Jorth.

"I'm goin' to have things the way they were before . . . an' more," he declared. The cigarette paper shook in his fingers.

"What do you mean?" she demanded.

"You know what I mean," he retorted. Voice and action were subtly unhinging this man's control of himself.

"Maybe I don't. I reckon you'd better talk plain."

The rustler had clear, gray-yellow eyes, flawless, like crystal, and suddenly they danced with little, fiery flecks.

"The last time I laid my hand on you I got bit for my pains. An' shore that's been ranklin'."

"Colter, you'll get bit again if you put your hands on me," she said, dark, straight glance on him. A frown wrinkled the level brows.

"You mean that?" he asked thickly.

"I shore do."

Manifestly he accepted her assertion. Something of incredulity and bewilderment, that had vied with his resentment, utterly disappeared from his face. "Heah I've been waitin' for you to love me," he declared with a gesture not without dignified emotion. "You givin' in without that wasn't so much to me."

At these words of the rustler's, Jean Isbel felt an icy, sickening shudder creep into his soul. He shut his eyes. The end of his dream had been long in coming, but at last it had arrived. A mocking voice, like a hollow wind, echoed through that region—that lovely and ghost-like ball of his heart that had harbored faith.

She burst into speech, louder and sharper, the first words of which Jean's strangely throbbing ears did not distinguish.

"God damn you! I never gave in to you, an' I never will."

"But girl . . . I kissed you . . . hugged you . . . handled you . . . ," he expostulated, and the making of the cigarette ceased.

"Yes, you did . . . you brute . . . when I was so down-hearted and weak and couldn't lift my hand," she flashed.

"A-huh! You mean I couldn't do that now?"

"I should smile I do, Jim Colter," she replied.

"Wal, mebbe . . . I'll see . . . presently," he went on, straining with words. "But I'm shore curious. Daggs, then . . . he was nothin' to you?"

"No more than you," she said morbidly. "He used to run after me . . . long ago it seems. I was only a girl then . . . innocent . . . an' I'd not known any but rough men. I couldn't all the time . . . every day . . . every hour . . . keep him at arm's length. Sometimes before I knew . . . I didn't care. I was a child. A kiss meant nothing to me. But after I knew. . . ."

Ellen dropped her head in brooding silence.

"Say, do you expect me to believe that?" he queried with a derisive leer.

"Bah! What do I care what you believe?" she cried with lifting head.

"How about Simm Bruce?"

"That coyote! He lied about me, Jim Colter . . . and any man half a man would have known he lied."

"Wal, Simm always bragged aboot you bein' his girl," asserted Colter. "An' he wasn't over-particular aboot details of your love-makin'!"

Ellen gazed out of the door, over Colter's head, as if the forest out there was a refuge. She evidently sensed more about the man than appeared in his slow talk, in his slouching position. Her lips shut in a firm line, as if to hide their trembling and to still her passionate tongue. Jean, in his absorption, magnified his perceptions. Not yet was Ellen Jorth afraid of this man, but she feared the situation. Jean's heart was at bursting pitch. All within him seemed chaos—a wreck of beliefs and convictions. Nothing was true. He would wake presently out of a nightmare. Yet, as surely as he quivered there, he felt the imminence of a great moment—a lightning flash—a thunderbolt—a balance struck.

Colter attended to the forgotten cigarette. He rolled it, lighted it, all the time with lowered, pondering head, and, when he had puffed a cloud of smoke, he suddenly looked up with face as hard as flint, eyes as fiery as molten steel. "Wal, Ellen . . . how about Jean Isbel . . . our half-breed Nez Percé friend . . . who was shore seen handlin' you familiar?" he drawled.

Ellen Jorth quivered as under a lash, and her brown face turned a dusky scarlet, that, slowly receding, left her pale. "Damn you, Jim Colter!" she burst out furiously. "I wish Jean Isbel would jump in that door . . . or down out of that loft! He killed Greaves for defiling my name! He'd kill you for your dirty insult. And I'd like to watch him do it. You cold-blooded liar! You lied about my father's death. And I know why. You stole my father's gold. An' now you want me . . . you expect me to fall into your arms. My heavens, cain't you tell a decent woman? Was your mother decent? Was your sister decent? Bah! I'm appealing to deaf ears. But, you'll *heah* this, Jim Colter. I'm not what you think I am. I'm not the . . . the damned hussy you liars have made me out. I'm a Jorth, alas! I've no home . . . no relations . . .

no friends! I've been forced to live my life with rustlers . . . vile men like you an' Daggs an' the rest of your ilk. But I've been *good!* Do you heah that? I *am* good . . . an' so help me God, you an' all your rottenness cain't make me bad!"

Colter straightened to his tall height and the laxity of the man had vanished.

Vanished also was Jean Isbel's suspended, icy dread, the cold clogging of his fevered mind—vanished in a white, living, leaping flame. Silently he drew his knife and lay there, watching with the eyes of a wildcat. The instant Colter stepped far enough over toward the edge of the loft, Jean meant to bound erect and plunge down upon him. But Jean could wait now. Colter had a gun at his hip. He must never have a chance to draw it.

"A-huh! So you wish Jean Isbel would hop in heah, do you?" queried Colter. "Wal, if I had any pity on you, that's done for it."

A sweep of his long arm, so swift Ellen had no time to move, brought his hand in clutching contact with her. The force of it flung her half across the cabin room, leaving the sleeve of her blouse in his grasp. Pantingly she put out that bared arm and her other to ward him off as he took long, slow strides toward her.

Jean rose half to his feet, dragged by almost ungovernable passion to risk all on one leap, but this distance was too great. Colter, blind as he was to all outward things, would hear, would see in time to make Jean's effort futile. Shaking like a leaf, Jean sank back, eye again to the crack between the rafters.

Ellen did not retreat, or scream, or move. Every line of her body was instinct with fight, and the magnificent blaze of her eyes would have checked a less callous brute.

Colter's big hand darted between Ellen's arms and fastened on the front of her blouse. He did not try to hold or draw her close. The unleashed passion of the man required violence. In one savage pull he tore off her blouse, exposing her white rounded shoulders and heaving bosom, where instantly a wave of red burned upward.

Overcome by the tremendous violence and spirit of the rustler, Ellen sank to her knees, with blanched face and dilating eyes, trying with folded arms and trembling hands to hide her nudity.

At that moment the rapid beat of hoofs on the hard trail outside halted Colter in his tracks.

"Hell!" he exclaimed. "An' who's that?" With a fierce action he flung the remnants of Ellen's blouse in her face, and turned to leap out the door.

Jean saw Ellen catch the blouse and try to wrap it around her, while she sagged against the wall and stared at the door. The hoof beats pounded to a solid thumping halt just outside.

"Jim . . . thar's hell . . . to pay!" rasped out a panting voice.

"Wal, Springer, I reckon I wished you'd paid it without spoilin' my deals," retorted Colter, cool and sharp.

"Deals? Ha! You'll be forgettin' . . . your lady love . . . in a minnit," replied Springer. "When I catch . . . my breath."

"Where's Somers?" demanded Colter.

"I reckon he's all shot up . . . if my eyes didn't fool me."

"Where is he?" yelled Colter.

"Jim . . . he's layin' up in the bushes 'round that bluff. I didn't wait to see how he was hurt. But he shore stopped some lead. An' he flopped like a chicken with its head cut off."

"Where's Antonio?"

"He run like the greaser he is," declared Springer disgustedly.

"A-huh! An' where's Queen?" queried Colter, after a significant pause.

"Dead!"

The silence ensuing was fraught with a suspense that held Jean in cold bonds. He saw the girl below rise from her knees, one hand holding the blouse to her breast, the other extended, and with strange, repressed, almost frantic look she swayed toward the door.

"Wal, talk," ordered Colter harshly.

"Jim, there ain't a hell of a lot," replied Springer, drawing a deep breath, "but what there is shore is interestin'. Me an' Somers took Antonio with us. He left his woman with the sheep. An' we packed up the cañon, clumb out on top, an' made a circle back on the ridge. That's the way we've been huntin' fer tracks. Up thar in a bare spot we ran plumb into Queen, sittin' against a tree, right out in the open. Queerest sight you ever seen! The damn' gunfighter had set down to wait for Isbel who was trailin' him, as we suspected . . . an' he died thar. He wasn't cold when we found him. Somers was quick to see a trick. So he propped Queen up an' tied the guns to his hands . . . an', Jim, the queerest thing about that deal was this . . . Queen's guns was empty! Not a shell left! It beat us holler. We left him thar an' hid up high on the bluff, mebbe a hundred yards off. The hosses we left back of a thicket. An' we waited thar a long time. But shore enough the half-breed come. He was too smart. Too much Injun! He would not cross the open, but went around. An' then he seen Queen. It was great to watch him. After a little he shoved his rifle an' went right for Queen. This is when I wanted to shoot. I could have plugged him. But Somers says wait an' make it sure. When

309

Isbel got up to Queen, he was sort of half hid by the tree. An' I couldn't wait no longer, so I shot. I hit him, too. We all begun to shoot. Somers showed himself an' that's when Isbel opened up. He used up a whole magazine on Somers, an' then sudden-like he quit. It didn't take me long to figger mebbe he was out of shells. When I seen him run, I was certain of it. Then we run for the hosses, an' rode after Isbel. Pretty soon I seen him, runnin' like a deer down the ridge. I yelled an' spurred after him. There is where Antonio quit me. But I kept on. An' I got a shot at Isbel. He ran out of sight. I follered him by spots of blood on the stones an' grass, until I couldn't trail him no more. He must have gone down over the cliffs. He couldn't have done nothin' else without me seein' him. I found his rifle, an' here it is to prove what I say. I had to go back to climb down off the rim, an' I rode fast down the cañon. He's somewhere along that west wall, hidin' in the brush, hard hit, if I know anythin' about the color of blood."

"Wal, that beats me holler, too," ejaculated Colter.

"Jim, what's to be done?" inquired Springer eagerly. "If we're sharp, we can corral that half-breed. He's the last of the Isbels."

"More, pard. He's the last of the Isbels' outfit," declared Colter. "If you can show me blood in his tracks, I'll trail him."

"You can bet I'll show you," rejoined the other rustler. "But, listen, wouldn't it be better for us first to see if he crossed the cañon? I reckon he didn't. But let's make sure. An', if he didn't, we'll have him somewhar along that west cañon wall. He's not got no gun. He'd never run that way if he had. Jim, he's our meat!"

"Shore, he'll have that knife," pondered Colter.

"We needn't worry about that," said the other positively.

"He's hard hit, I tell you. All we got to do is find that bloody trail again, an' stick to it . . . goin' careful. He's layin' low like a crippled wolf."

"Springer, I want the job of finishin' that half-breed," hissed Colter. "I'd give ten years of my life to stick a gun down his throat an' shoot it off."

"All right. Let's rustle. Mebbe you'll not have to give much more'n ten minnits. Because I tell you I can find him. It'd been easy . . . but, Jim, I reckon I was afraid."

"Leave your hoss for me an' go ahaid," the rustler then said brusquely. "I've a job in the cabin heah."

"Haw! Haw! Wal, Jim, I'll rustle a bit down the trail an' wait. No huntin' Jean Isbel alone . . . not fer me. I've had a queer feelin' about thet knife he used on Greaves. An' I reckon you'd oughta let thet Jorth hussy alone long enough to. . . ."

"Springer, I reckon I've got to hawg-tie her before. . . ." His voice became indistinguishable, and footfalls attested to a slow moving away of the men.

Jean had listened with ears acutely strung to catch every syllable while his gaze rested upon Ellen who stood beside the door. Every line of her body denoted a listening intensity. Her back was toward Jean, so that he could not see her face. And he did not want to see, but could not help seeing her naked shoulders. She put her head out of the door. Suddenly she drew it in quickly and half turned her face, slowly raising her white arm. This was the left one and bore the mark of Colter's hard fingers.

She gave a little gasp. Her eyes became large and staring. They were bent on the hand that she had removed from a step of the ladder. On hand and wrist showed a bright, red smear of blood.

Jean, with a convulsive leap of his heart, realized that he

had left his bloody tracks on the ladder as he had climbed. That moment seemed the supremely terrible one of his life.

Ellen Jorth's face blanched and her eyes darkened and dilated with exceeding amazement, and flashing thought, to become fixed with horror. That instant was the one in which her reason connected the blood on the ladder with the escape of Jean Isbel. One moment she leaned there, still as a stone except for her heaving breast, and then her fixed gaze changed to a swift, dark blaze, comprehending yet inscrutable, as she flashed it up the ladder to the loft. She could see nothing, yet she knew, and Jean knew that she knew he was there. A marvelous transformation passed over her features and even over her form. Jean choked with the ache in his throat. Slowly she put the bloody hand behind her while with the other she still held the torn blouse to her breast.

Colter's slouching musical step sounded outside, and it might have been a strange breath of infinitely vitalizing and passionate life blown into the wellsprings of Ellen Jorth's being. Isbel had no name for her then. The spirit of a woman had been to him a thing unknown. She swayed back from the door against the wall in singular, softened poise, as if all the steel had melted out of her body. As Colter's tall shadow fell across the threshold, Jean Isbel felt himself staring with eyeballs that ached—straining, incredulous sight at this woman who in a few seconds had bewildered his senses with her transfiguration. He saw but could not comprehend.

"Jim . . . I heard . . . all Springer told you," she said.

The look of her dumbfounded Colter and her voice seemed to shake him visibly. "Suppose you did. What then?" he demanded harshly, as he halted with one booted foot over the threshold. Malignant and forceful, he eyed her darkly, doubtfully.

"I'm afraid," she whispered.

"What of? Me?"

"No. Of . . . of Jean Isbel. He might kill you an' . . . then where would I be?"

"Wal, I'm damned!" ejaculated the rustler. "What's got into you?" He moved to enter, but a sort of fascinated inaction bound him.

"Jim, I hated you a moment ago," she burst out. "But now . . . with that Jean Isbel somewhere near . . . hidin' . . . watchin' to kill you . . . an' maybe me, too . . . I . . . I don't hate you any more. Take me away."

"Girl, have you lost your nerve?" he demanded.

"My God, Colter, cain't you see?" she implored. "Won't you take me away?"

"I shore will . . . presently," he replied grimly. "But you'll wait till I've shot the lights out of this Isbel."

"No!" she cried. "Take me away now. An' I'll . . . I'll give in. I'll be what you want. You can do with me . . . as you like."

Colter's lofty frame leaped as if at the release of bursting blood. With a lunge he cleared the threshold to loom over her.

"Am I out of my haid, or are you?" he asked in low, hoarse voice. His darkly corded face expressed most extreme amazement.

"Jim, I mean it," she whispered, edging an inch nearer him, her white face uplifted, her dark eyes unreadable in their eloquence and mystery. "I've no friend but you. I'll be . . . yours. I'm lost. What does it matter? If you want me . . . take me now . . . before I kill myself."

"Ellen Jorth, there's somethin' wrong about you," he responded. "Did you tell the truth . . . when you denied ever bein' a sweetheart of Simm Bruce?"

313

"Yes, I told you the truth."

"A-huh! An' how do you account for layin' me out with every dirty name you could give tongue to?"

"Oh, it was temper. I wanted to be let alone."

"Temper! Wal, I reckon you've got one," he retorted grimly. "An' I'm not shore you're not crazy or lyin'. An hour ago I couldn't touch you."

"You may now . . . if you promise to take me away . . . at once. This place has got on my nerves. I couldn't sleep heah with that Isbel hidin' around. Could you?"

"Wal, I reckon I'd not sleep very deep."

"Then let us go."

He shook his lean, eagle-like head in slow, doubtful vehemence, and his piercing gaze studied her distrustfully. Yet all the while there was manifest in his strung frame an almost irrepressible violence, held in abeyance to his will. "What about your bein' so good?" he inquired with a return of the mocking drawl.

"Never mind what's past," she flashed with passion dark as his. "I've made my offer."

"Shore there's a lie aboot you somewhere," he muttered thickly.

"Man, could I do more?" she demanded in scorn.

"No. But it's a lie," he returned. "You'll get me to take you away an' then fool me . . . run off . . . God knows what. Women are all liars."

Manifestly he could not believe in her strange transformation. Memory of her wild and passionate denunciation of him and his kind must have scared even his calloused soul and the ruthless nature of him had not weakened or softened in the least as to his intentions. This weathervane veering of hers bewildered him, obsessed him with its possibilities. He had the look of a man who was divided between

314

love of her and hate, whose love demanded a return, but whose hate required a proof of her abasement. Not proof of surrender, but proof of her shame! The ignominy of him thirsted for its like. He could grind her beauty under his heel, but he could not soften to this feminine inscrutability. Whatever was the truth of Ellen Jorth in this moment, beyond Colter's gloomy and stunted intelligence, beyond even the love of Jean Isbel, it was something that held the balance of mastery. She read Colter's mind. She dropped the torn blouse from her hand and stood there, unashamed, with the curve of her white breast pulsing, eyes black as night and full of hell, her face white, tragic, terrible, yet strangely lovely.

"Take me away," she whispered, stretching one white arm toward him, then the other.

Colter, even as she moved, had leaped with inarticulate cry and radiant face to meet her embrace. But it seemed, just as her left arm flashed up toward his neck, that he saw her bloody hand and wrist. Strange how that checked his ardor—threw up his lean head like that of a striking bird of prey.

"Blood! What the hell!" he ejaculated, and in one sweep he grasped her. "How'd you do that? Are you cut? Hold still."

Ellen could not release her hand.

"I scratched myself," she said.

"Where? All that blood!" Suddenly he flung her hand back with fierce gesture, and the gleams of his yellow eyes were like the points of leaping flames. They pierced her— read the secret falsity of her. Slowly he stepped backward guardedly, his hand moved to his gun and his glance caught the interior of the cabin. As if he had the nose of a hound, and sight to follow scent, his eyes bent to the dust of the ground before the door. He quivered—grew rigid as stone—and then moved his head with exceeding slowness—as if searching through a microscope in the dust—farther to the left—to the foot of the ladder—and up one step—another—a third—all the way up to the loft. Then he whipped out his gun and wheeled to face the girl.

"Ellen, you've got your half-breed *heah!*" he said with a terrible smile.

She neither moved nor spoke. There was a suggestion of collapse, but it was only a change where the alluring softness of her hardened into a strange, rapt glow and in it seemed the same mastery that had characterized her former aspect! Herein the treachery of hers was revealed. She had known what she meant to do in any case.

Colter, standing at the door, reached a long arm toward the ladder, where he laid his hand on a rung. Taking it away, he held it palm outward for her to see the dark splotch of blood.

"See?"

"Yes, I see," she said ringingly.

Passion wrenched him, transformed him. "All that . . . about leavin' heah . . . with me . . . aboot givin' in . . . was a lie!"

"No, Colter. It was the truth. I'll go . . . yet . . . now . . . if you'll spare . . . *him.*" She whispered the last word and made a slight movement of her hand toward the loft.

"Girl," he exploded incredulously, "you love this half-breed . . . this Isbel? You *love* him!"

"With all my heart! Thank God! It has been my glory. It might have been my salvation. But now I'll go to hell with you . . . if you'll spare him."

"Damn my soul!" rasped out the rustler, as if something of respect was wrung from that sordid depth of him. "You

. . . you woman! Jorth will turn over in his grave. He'd rise out of his grave if this Isbel got you."

"Hurry! Hurry!" implored Ellen. "Springer may come back. I think I heard a call."

"Wal, Ellen Jorth, I'll not spare Isbel . . . nor you," he returned with dark and meaning leer, as he turned to ascend the ladder.

Jean Isbel, too, had reached the climax of his suspense. Gathering all his muscles in a knot, he prepared to leap upon Colter as he mounted the ladder. But Ellen Jorth screamed piercingly and snatched her rifle from its resting place, and, cocking it, she held it forward and low.

"Colter!"

Her scream and his uttered name stiffened him.

"You will spare Jean Isbel!" she rang out. "Drop that gun . . . drop it!"

"Shore, Ellen . . . easy now. Remember your temper. I'll let Isbel off." He sank quiveringly to a crouch.

"Drop your gun! Don't turn 'round. Colter! *I'll kill you!*"

But even then he failed to divine the meaning and the spirit of her.

"Aw, now, Ellen," he entreated in louder, huskier tones, and, as if dragged by fatal doubt of her still, he began to turn.

Crash! The rifle emptied its contents in Colter's breast. All his body sprang up. He dropped the gun. Both hands fluttered toward her. An awful surprise flashed over his face.

"So . . . help . . . me . . . God!" he whispered with blood thick in his voice. Then darkly, as one groping, he reached for her with shaking hands. "You . . . you white-throated hussy! I'll. . . ."

He grasped the quivering rifle barrel. *Crash!* She shot

317

him again. As he swayed over her and fell, she had to leap aside, and his clutching hands tore the rifle from her grasp. Then in convulsion he writhed, to heave on his back and stretch out—a ghastly spectacle. Ellen backed away from it, her white arms wide, a slow horror blotting out the passion of her face.

Then from without came a shrill call and the sound of rapid footsteps. Ellen leaned against the wall, still staring at Colter.

"Hey, Jim . . . what's the shootin'?" called Springer breathlessly.

As his form darkened the doorway, Jean once again gathered all his muscular force for a tremendous spring.

Springer saw the girl first and he appeared thunderstruck. His jaw dropped. It needed not the white gleam of her person to transfix him. Her eyes did that and they were riveted in unutterable horror upon something on the ground. Thus, instinctively directed, Springer espied Colter.

"You . . . you shot him!" he shrieked. "What for . . . you hussy! Ellen Jorth, if you've killed him, I'll. . . ."

He strode toward where Colter lay.

Then Jean, rising silently, took a step, and like a tiger he launched himself into the air, down upon the rustler. Even as he leaped, Springer gave a quick upward look and he cried out. Jean's moccasined feet struck him squarely and sent him staggering into the wall where his head hit hard. Jean fell, but bounded up as the half-stunned Springer drew his gun. Then Jean lunged forward with a single sweep of his arm—and looked no more.

Ellen ran, swaying, out of the door, and once clear of the threshold she tottered out in the grass, to sink to her knees. The bright, golden sunlight gleamed upon her white shoulders and arms. Jean had one foot out of the door when he saw her and he wheeled back to get her blouse. But Springer had fallen upon it. Snatching up a blanket, Jean ran out.

"Ellen! Ellen! Ellen!" he cried. "It's over!" And reaching her, he bent to wrap her in the blanket.

She wildly clutched his knees. Jean was conscious only of her white, agonized face and the dark eyes with their look of terrible strain.

"Did you . . . did you . . . ?" she whispered.

"Yes . . . it's over," he said gravely. "Ellen, the Isbel-Jorth feud is ended."

"Oh, thank God!" she cried in breaking voice. "Jean . . . you are wounded. The blood on the step!"

"My arm. See. It's not bad. Ellen, let me wrap this 'round you." Folding the blanket around her shoulders, he held it there and entreated her to get up. But she only clung the closer. She hid her face on his knees. Long shadows rippled over her, shaking the blanket, shaking Jean's hands. Distraught, he did not know what to do, and his own heart was bursting.

"Ellen, you must not kneel . . . there . . . that way," he implored.

"Jean! Jean!" she moaned, and clung the tighter.

He tried to lift her up, but she was a dead weight, and with that hold on him seemed anchored at his feet.

"I killed Colter," she gasped. "I *had* to . . . kill him! I offered . . . to fling myself away. . . ."

"For me!" he cried poignantly. "Oh Ellen! Ellen! The world has come to an end! Hush! Don't keep sayin' that. Of course, you killed him. You saved my life. For I'd never have let you go off with him. Yes, you killed him! You're a Jorth an' I'm an Isbel. We've blood on our hands . . . both

319

of us . . . I for you an' you for me!"

His voice of entreaty and sadness strengthened her and she raised her white face, loosening her clasp to lean back and look up. Tragic, sweet, despairing, the loveliness of her, the significance of her there on her knees, thrilled him to his soul.

"Blood on my hands," she whispered. "Yes. It was awful . . . killing him. But it's past. Jean, all I care for in this world is for your forgiveness . . . and your faith that saved my soul!"

"Child, there's nothin' to forgive," he responded. "Nothin'. Please, Ellen. . . ."

"I lied to you!" she cried. "I lied to you!"

"Ellen, listen . . . darlin'." And the tender epithet brought her head and arms back. "I know . . . now," he faltered on. "I found out today what I believed. An' I swear to God . . . by the memory of my dead mother . . . down in my heart I never, never, never believed what they . . . what you tried to make me believe. *Never!*"

"Jean . . . I love you . . . love you . . . love you," she breathed with exquisite, passionate sweetness. Her dark eyes burned up into his.

"Ellen, I can't lift you up," he said in trembling eagerness, "but I can kneel with you . . . to you!"

Her white arms flashed from under the blanket and wound around his neck and she buried her wet face in his breast.

"Jean, I did not deserve . . . so much . . . all I thought . . . hoped for now . . . was to have you believe me good. Good as you thought me . . . as you made me!"

"Ellen, will you . . . marry me?" he whispered.

"Oh, Jean . . . dare we live for one another? Dare we be happy?"

320

"Child, it's our only hope. Let us make our love atone for the hate of our fathers. We have been doomed by their sins. Not that . . . nor anythin' can keep us apart. I am a slayer of men, but I think God spoke to me today."

"Jean, I had less faith in God than you had in me. But I repent. Come, kiss me . . . love, master, husband . . . as you did that day on the rim. All the agony I have suffered is not too much to pay for this . . . your faith an' love."